THE STONE EATER

BOOK 3 OF THE MAGIC EATERS TRILOGY

CAROL BETH ANDERSON

The Stone Eater by Carol Beth Anderson

Published by
Eliana Press
P.O. Box 2452
Cedar Park, TX 78630

www.carolbethanderson.com

Copyright © 2021 by Carol Beth Anderson

Cover Design:
Mariah Sinclair (thecovervault.com)

Map: BMR Williams

Paperback ISBN: 978-1-949384-07-9
Hardcover ISBN: 978-1-949384-18-5

First Edition

To my kids' teachers . . . and to every teacher. The year 2020 brought challenges none of us anticipated. You've continued to help your students learn to read better and write creatively, to master algebra and biology and computer programming. You've juggled technical difficulties, social distancing, and contact tracing . . . all with aplomb, wearing an annoying mask.

You're a true hero.

CHARACTERS AND PLACES

Characters

Ulmin (ULL-min) Abrios, King of Cellerin
Dani (DANN-ee), Nora's aunt and Ulmin's sister-in-law
Chef Pryn (PRINN), Ulmin's chef
Nora Abrios (AH-bree-ose), Princess of Cellerin
Krey (KRAY) West
Ovrun Kensin (OV-run KENN-sin)
Zeisha Dennivan (ZAY-shuh DEN-ni-van), the Anya
(AHN-yuh)
Kebi (KEB-ee), trog
Sarza (SAHR-zuh) Phip, seer
Osmius (OZ-me-us), dragon
Eira (EYE-ruh), trog
Prime Minister Osk, leader of Cruine
General Etal (ee-TALL), Cellerinian Army General
Ambrel Kaulder (AM-brel CALL-der), Nora's mother
Hatlin (HAT-lin), New Therroan activist
Joli (JOE-lee)

Varia (VAH-ree-uh), Joli's mother
Tiam (TEE-um), Joli's father
Sharai (shuh-RYE), Cellerin's former Minister of Lysting
Emissary Loryn (LO-rin)
Lott, former royal guard
Kevlin (KEV-lin), Lott's friend
Gild, dragon
Vin, dragon
Kadin (KAY-din), master feather lyster
Wallis (WALL-iss), New Therroan activist
T, New Therroan activist
Mayor Ashler, Mayor of Tirra
Min, Krey's aunt
Evie, Krey's aunt

Places

Anyari (ann-YAHR-ee), a planet settled by human colonists
Cellerin (SELL-err-in), kingdom around Cellerin Mountain
Deroga (der-OH-guh), large, preday city
Cruine (croo-EEN), nation east of Cellerin
Cellerin City, capital of Cellerin, east of Cellerin Mountain
New Therro (THAIR-oh), province north of Cellerin City
Tirra (TEE-ruh), town southwest of Cellerin Mountain

Immerse yourself in the story by listening to the audiobook of *The Stone Eater*. Get it on Amazon or Audible.

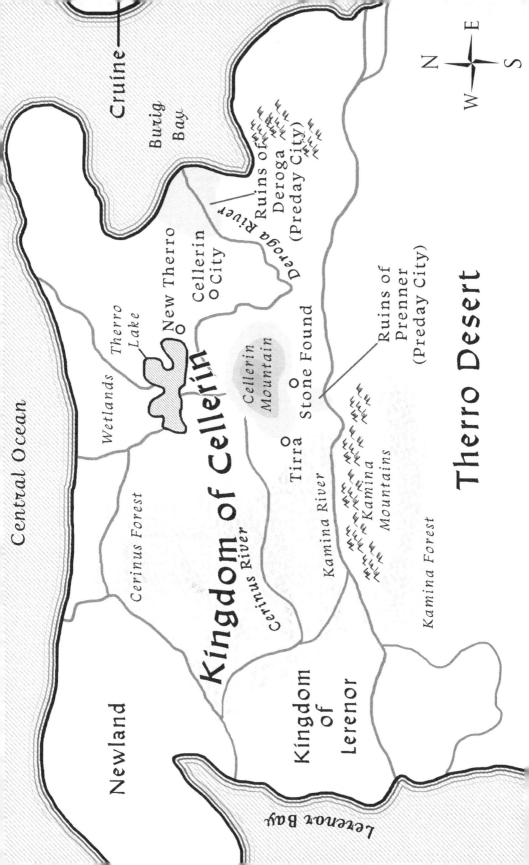

THE STONE EATER: 1

First things first.

King Ulmin Abrios never felt truly awake until he fueled up. Blinking into the deep darkness of his room, he reached for the insulated canister on his bedside table. It had two compartments, separated by a perforated ceramic disc. Every night, Chef Pryn filled the bottom chamber with ice and the top with fuel.

As Ulmin removed the lid, his heart began to race. That made him laugh. He was like a little boy when it came to his first fuel of the day.

His fingers brushed across the canister's contents, and his throat compressed with fury. After a massive dragon in Deroga had burned his hands last month, the army's blood lysters had done their best to heal their king. But his palms and fingers had still scarred, compromising his sense of touch.

A deep breath diluted his anger. He knew what he was touching, even if he couldn't feel the texture. The canister was full of soft, delicately thin layers of animal brain matter, cut into strips. The ice would be melted by now, but it had kept them fresh. He delighted in

1

how cool they felt against his warm, scarred skin. From the odor wafting up—sweet with a hint of bitter earthiness—Ulmin knew the fuel came from a cervid.

He pinched several pieces of fuel and put them in his mouth, resisting the instinct to lick his fingers. A few minutes later, when he'd eaten it all, he sighed, tapping his damp fingers together. *Oh, what the hell; life's pleasures are meant to be enjoyed!* Ulmin licked his fingers with relish.

Before getting out of bed, he lit a candle, then dipped his fingers in the cool water in the canister's bottom chamber. He rubbed it on his neck, sighing in relief. The palace complex was terribly hot. As the day went on, it would only get worse.

Ulmin walked to his sitting room, his flickering candle lighting the way. He took a deep breath, relishing the lingering scent of paint. Over three months ago, when Nora and her allies had sneaked into the palace, dragon fire had destroyed a portion of the residence. Thanks to the building's fire-suppression system—an underground cistern, pumps, hoses, and royal guards trained in using it all—the flames hadn't reached any of the bedrooms. The smoke damage, however, had been extensive, leading to a remodel of the king's quarters.

Ulmin reached the door to the hallway. He stopped and flipped the light switch. The electricity had been out for a week, but he kept trying, just in case. When the room brightened, his mouth broke into a smile. He blew out his candle, murmuring, "Back in business."

When he'd started creating a stone dome over his palace, Ulmin hadn't considered the fact that it would block sunlight from reaching the solar panels. His was the only building in Cellerin with solar power. The day the large batteries had lost the last of their power, he'd been furious.

He'd instructed a staff member to find workers to move the panels to the top of the dome. They'd also expanded the system with additional panels and batteries. To help the workers climb the stone outside, Ulmin had used his magical faculty to create handholds, footholds, and anchor points for ropes. Only one person had fallen to their death. Not too bad, considering how high the dome was. Once the work was done, the king had smoothed the stone, making it impossible to climb.

Ulmin flipped the light switch on and off several times, grinning as the room came in and out of focus. Then he froze, eyes fixed on his hand. When had his skin become so wrinkled and thin? He seemed to be aging more quickly of late. It probably didn't help that his appetite for food had been waning, even as his need for his dark fuel increased. Yet he didn't feel old or weak. He was spry, energetic . . . and when he did start to feel weary, a little magic renewed him right away.

He dropped his hand, refusing to worry about the appearance of his skin. He was the most powerful man in the kingdom, possibly in the world. Why should a liver spot or two bother him?

Exiting his quarters, he greeted the two stoic guards outside his door. He strolled through the living room, which had been completely rebuilt after the fire destroyed it.

From afar, he saw electric light coming from the kitchen. Excellent, Pryn was awake—and, judging by the smell, he was cooking sausage. These days, Ulmin seemed to wake earlier and earlier. He'd even made it to the kitchen before his chef a few times, leading Pryn to adjust the breakfast schedule. Ulmin took several more steps.

Hearing a low voice emanating from the kitchen, Ulmin slowed. He identified his sister-in-law, Dani. His whole body tensing, he quietly advanced until he could make out her words.

"You know he's controlling everyone in this place!" Dani's voice was barely above a whisper, but it was full of shrill passion. "You're his friend and his . . . his . . . supplier. He rarely controls you. If anyone's going to stop him—"

3

"He's my king!" Pryn said, his quiet voice matching Dani's intensity. "I can't stop him; I don't even want to!"

"Just talk to him! It's not too late for him. He could still choose people over power if he wanted to. He just needs to hear from someone he trusts, and—"

Pryn cut her off again. "Dani! I don't have the expertise to judge my king's leadership methods!"

"You can be honest with me, Pryn. I'm not testing you; I—"

Ulmin stepped into the kitchen. Dani stiffened, snapping her mouth closed.

"We can all be honest." The king's voice rang through the small space. "At least I thought we could."

His eyes locked on Dani's. Hers were wide. Scared. He shook his head sadly and captured her mind. Her features slackened. "Everything is fine," he said, his voice soothing and soft. "You're safe and happy here." With a nudge of his mind, her mouth widened into a smile. He pulled her into a hug.

Why was Dani so different from Ulmin's staff? They didn't need constant control. He roamed around the property at all hours of the day and sometimes even at night, conducting short, gentle, mind-controlled interrogations. They didn't dare betray him, knowing he'd discover disloyalty and punish it by imprisonment or death.

Dani, on the other hand, had begun questioning his decisions. Disrespecting his authority. After years of only occasionally using his brain-lysting faculty on her, he'd been forced to change his tactic, controlling her throughout the day. He made a mental note: starting tomorrow, he'd capture her mind as soon as he woke in the morning, and he wouldn't let it go until he went to bed.

It was all for her good. Ulmin could sense her serene joy as he held her. So much more pleasant than the rebellion he'd heard in her voice moments before.

He released her and gave her a wide smile. "Shall we eat?"

"If that's what you'd like."

Ulmin's gaze rose to find Pryn watching the exchange. The chef's face broke into a grin. "Chepple sausage, anyone?"

"And maybe a little something on the side for me?" Ulmin asked, giving Pryn a wink.

Pryn chuckled. "Always."

1

Dear Dani,

As promised, I'm writing you within an hour of my arrival. Uncle Quin welcomed me to his home, one of the nicest in Cellerin City. He has a ballroom that could fit hundreds of dancers. My guest quarters are almost as big as my suite back home!

I'm trying to pretend this is a normal vacation, a celebration of my eighteenth birthday. But every time I start to relax, I remember the truth.

I'm here to meet Prince Ulmin and possibly marry him. Whether I want to or not.

Dani, if he's dreadful, will you abduct me in the middle of the night and find a ship to carry us across the ocean? Please?

-Letter from Ambrel Kaulder to Dani Kaulder
Dated Centa 12, 180 PD

"BY THE STONE," Nora breathed.

She stood in the doorway of the trogs' new Interclan Center. Deroga was home to nearly two thousand trogs, and the center was more than large enough to accommodate all of them. Only a couple hundred, however, had arrived. The party would officially start at dark, and the sky was still painted twilight gray.

Innumerable flickering candles and glowing lanterns lent an air of luminous mystery to the luxurious old building. The floor was made of some preday material that looked like glossy marble, threaded with meandering, metallic veins. Throughout the room, wide columns extended up to the soaring ceiling. Murals, painted in the bright style trogs preferred, adorned the walls. Round, wooden tables covered much of the floor, but a sizeable space in the middle was clear for dancers, a few of whom were already moving to a fast-paced song.

Nora's eyes traveled up a wide, curved staircase, settling on a landing where a band of at least fifteen trogs was playing. The music featured intricate harmonies floating over throbbing drums. She drew in a happy breath, smiling even bigger when the scent of bread and roasted meat filled her nose.

Krey's voice broke the spell. "Are you going in, or should we stand here for the rest of the night?"

Nora swiveled her head to arch an eyebrow at him. He could've walked past her through the wide doorway if Ovrun and Zeisha hadn't stopped alongside her, both as frozen by the beauty as she was. "You hate not being in the lead, don't you?" Nora tried to keep a chiding tone, but she felt her lip twitch.

Krey smirked. "I wouldn't mind if I could see anything past this guy." He gave Ovrun's broad back a shove that didn't budge him a simmet.

Zeisha's trog friend Kebi approached, already holding a drink, her short curls turned into a halo by the candlelight. "The food is delicious! Come in! I save a table for us."

Behind Nora, Sarza said, "Food? Why are we still standing here?"

They entered and followed Kebi through the room. Ovrun drew Nora's hand into his, weaving their fingers together. "Still wish you were with Hatlin tonight?" His breath tickled her ear.

She smiled. She'd complained earlier that she'd had to cancel her standing Friday-night meeting with their New Therroan contact. "No way. Hatlin can wait a week. I'm ready for a good party."

He squeezed her hand. "Me too."

A stack of plates awaited them at a table. They each took one and made their way to a large buffet. After filling her plate and getting a drink, Nora settled herself between Ovrun and Sarza. Kebi and Zeisha sat next to them, and Krey arrived last.

An uncomfortable silence fell on the table. Nora raised a confused eyebrow, before realizing the only seat available to Krey was next to Zeisha. It had been five weeks since their breakup, and the awkwardness between them still made Nora cringe.

Zeisha stood. "I think I'll look around—"

Krey set his plate down, his shaggy, thick hair falling into his eyes. "It's okay, Zei. Let's all enjoy dinner."

Zeisha lowered herself back to her seat. Conversation resumed.

Krey wasn't over Zeisha; anyone could see that. Nora frequently caught him watching his ex with longing in his eyes. Once, he'd reached out as if to touch her glossy curls, before he caught himself and pulled his hand back.

Beneath the table, Ovrun squeezed Nora's knee. When she lifted her eyes to him, his full lips widened into a big smile. She returned it, though she almost felt guilty being so happy when two of her friends were struggling.

The room got louder as more people entered. By the time everyone at Nora's table had cleaned their plates, they were shouting to be heard over the trogs and the band, which had doubled in size.

This was Deroga's first-ever interclan party. Last month's fight against King Ulmin and his invading soldiers had forged an unprecedented alliance between the trog clans. While this party was meant to celebrate the victory over the king, Nora sensed they were celebrating their relative unity more than anything.

"Would anyone like to dance?" Kebi asked.

"Yes!" Nora and Zeisha said, standing in unison. Ovrun rose too, while Sarza and Krey stayed seated.

"Not tonight," Krey said.

Nora's eyes fell on Sarza, who drew back, her chair seeming to swallow her thin frame. She shook her head emphatically. "I don't dance."

"We'll change that by the end of the night."

"You're underestimating how much of a fool I'd make of myself out there."

"You're underestimating how determined I am." Without waiting for a response, Nora took Ovrun's hand and headed for the dance floor.

Summer had officially arrived eight days earlier. The weather outside was beautiful, but sticky, sweaty people crowded the dance floor, the heat of their moving bodies pervading the space.

Nora couldn't get enough of it. She needed the distraction. Lately, countless questions about the future had jostled for attention in her brain. Her father had lost his mind and his ability to make rational decisions. Nora had to take his crown . . . but how? She couldn't figure it out on her own, and nobody was prepared to guide her. Not Hatlin, who was busy trying to get the army out of his hometown. Not Sarza, the seer, whose visions since the battle hadn't been useful at all. Not Zeisha, the new Anya, who had no idea what was next for Cellerin.

Such uncertainty didn't bother Zeisha, who seemed content where she was, free of worries about the future. Nora was determined to follow in her footsteps, if only for one night. Tomorrow's problems could wait. During fast songs, she danced until her heart threatened to gallop across the room. The band's music slowed, and Nora pressed closer to Ovrun, resting her head on his upper chest. His fingers trailed lightly across her back. The touch made her shiver, despite the heat. She felt his chest vibrate with a laugh.

When the song ended and a faster one began, Nora shouted over the noise, "I need a drink!"

Ovrun nodded and led her back to their table, where their mugs waited. Someone had brought over a pitcher of water. Nora sat, filled her cup, and greedily drank.

A couple of former militia members passed their table. "Come dance!" one of them called.

Nora smiled at Krey and Sarza. "It's great dancing music. You two should join us."

Krey's eyes were locked on the dance floor. "I'm not . . . ready for that."

She followed his gaze. Zeisha was swaying to the music along with Kebi and other trogs. "Maybe it's time to make some new memories."

He pulled his gaze back to Nora. "Not yet. But next time there's a chance to dance, I'll do it."

"Promise?"

"I promise."

Satisfied, she turned to Sarza, ready to use her most persuasive arguments to get the girl on the dance floor. But Sarza was slumped in her chair, chin resting on her chest, clearly having a vision.

Several seconds later, her head righted itself, her torso straightened, and her arms flailed like someone had woken her from a nightmare. Her hand caught the clay water pitcher, sending it tumbling off the table, spilling its contents along the way. When it struck the hard floor, it shattered.

"Damn it!" Sarza blurted, rushing to pick up the broken pieces.

Ovrun, Krey, and Nora all stood to help her. "I got it," Nora said, gesturing for Ovrun and Krey to sit. She joined Sarza on the floor. As they retrieved the sharp clay shards, Nora kept her voice light, saying, "Must've been some vision."

Sarza shrugged, her gaze still on the floor. "I saw that we'll have a rainstorm soon. Sometimes I do weird things at the end of a vision, even if I didn't see anything disturbing." She let out a harsh chuckle. "Every once in a while my visions look like seizures. I'm sure you can imagine how that went over in the middle of a chapel service one time." When Nora didn't respond, Sarza looked up, the muscles around her mouth tightening. "Just laugh; I know it's funny."

Nora blinked. She'd had over a month to get to know Sarza, who sat with Nora and her friends at meals and sometimes even hung out with them at night around bonfires or in rooftop gardens. But she didn't often join in their conversations and rarely opened up about her life as a seer. Nora kept her voice low. "It sounds painful. Not funny." Planning to reach out and touch Sarza's shoulder, she set the clay pieces on the table. When she saw the seer's dark eyes, full of challenge, she kept her hands to herself. "I'm not gonna laugh at you."

The other girl's narrow shoulders loosened a bit.

With a small smile, Nora said, "I should rephrase that. You're my friend now, so I will laugh when you're being funny. But not when you're in pain."

She didn't realize Krey had squatted next to them until he spoke. "Don't listen to her, Sarza. She cracked up when I broke my ankle during the battle."

"That was because I was injured too, and I was hysterical." Nora pushed Krey's arm. His balance wavered, and he fell on his backside. A giggle erupted from her mouth. "That's the kind of thing we all laugh at," she told Sarza. "Not real pain."

Sarza stared at her, blinking rapidly. By the sky, was she going to cry? Again, Nora almost reached out, but Sarza jumped up, tossing her clay shards on an empty plate. She added Nora's to the mix and rushed off with it.

Nora raised her eyebrows. Krey shrugged. They both resumed their seats at the table with Ovrun.

When Sarza returned with another pitcher of water, her hard expression was back in place. She pulled out her chair and plopped down, not looking at anyone. The table's occupants were silent, though music and chatter saturated the air around them. Eyes locked on the table's surface, Sarza finally spoke. Nora had to lean forward to be sure she heard the girl's words.

"I don't expect you to call me a friend. Any of you. I've been different since the day I had my first vision. I've made peace with it. You don't have to coddle me or try not to laugh or pretend you care about me. You don't have to drag me to parties like this. You don't owe me anything for the visions I had during the battle." Her gaze met Nora's. "Being alone is part of being different. I'm good at being alone."

Nora was about to respond, but Ovrun spoke first. "To be honest, Sarza, I don't fit in either. I'm no magic eater, but for months, I've been living in a bunkhouse with a magical militia. Hell, I've been hanging out with royalty"—he gestured at Nora—"even though I'm a poor kid who never dreamed of anything bigger than owning a farm."

Ovrun's words clawed at Nora's heart. He was right, the two of them had deep differences. She didn't care that he hadn't grown up privileged. It wasn't his past that concerned her. It was his future.

As her feelings for him grew dangerously close to something she'd call *love*, Nora found herself more and more fixated on whether Ovrun could truly be happy with her. Surely there were trog women who'd jump at the chance to leave Deroga and farm the land with a gorgeous Cellerinian. Or maybe he should take a look at Zeisha. They'd be the most good-natured couple on the planet. He could even go back to that girl Joli he'd dated before meeting Nora, or to any of the other girls in Cellerin City who were probably still nursing crushes on him.

Sensing that she was spiraling into the type of anxious contemplation that could ruin a party, Nora made a resolution. For the rest of the night, she wouldn't think about anything deeper than the absolute beauty of Ovrun's cream-colored trog shirt stretching across his shoulders. Tonight was all about having fun. All that other stuff could wait.

Ovrun was still talking to Sarza. "Being different doesn't mean you have to be alone. Nobody should have to be alone." His voice wasn't loud, but its firmness made it carry across the table. The words sat there, waiting for a challenge.

Sarza pressed her lips together, arms folded across her narrow ribcage.

"We're pretty nice people," Nora said. "Most of the time."

Krey laughed at that, but Sarza's stance didn't soften.

This girl needed friends, something Nora certainly understood. There had to be a way to break through the seer's hard exterior. "Dance with us," she blurted. "Everyone's too hot and sweaty to care if you know how."

"I've—" Sarza unfolded her arms and ran her fingers through her short, shaggy hair. "I don't know how to dance. I've never tried."

Nora's jaw dropped.

"Never?" Krey asked.

Sarza's shrug was full of defensive pain.

"I've seen you drill with a knife," Nora said. "You're rhythmic and graceful. Just bring that skill onto the dance floor." She gestured to the landing where over fifty musicians were now playing. "This song's slow. You've got this."

Several seconds passed before Sarza said, "Fine." She stood, walking toward the dance floor by herself.

Nora let out an exasperated sigh. "You're supposed to dance with us, not alone!" She and Ovrun rushed to catch up with the seer.

When they reached the dance floor, Sarza stopped at the edge of the slowly moving mass of bodies, a tree beside swaying grasses.

"Just move," Nora said, demonstrating. "Think of your knife drills. Close your eyes if that makes it easier."

Sarza squeezed her eyes shut. Then she took Nora's advice literally, moving her arms in a series of thrusts and parries, shifting her weight from one foot to the other. She spun and ducked, reached her arms wide then crossed them, completing drills she'd done countless times.

As the song continued, something changed. Sarza found the rhythm of the music. She slowed, each shift of her arms and legs smoother than the last. Her moves lost their harsh violence, transitioning into graceful, curving sweeps, as if she were slicing the air rather than stabbing it. She'd begun with her right hand fisted, holding an imaginary knife, but soon, she released her fingers, letting them glide through the air like the feathers of a bird. Her straight hair, which had grown into a shaggy bob, seemed to float around her head as she moved.

Sarza was no longer drilling. She was dancing.

And she was *good.*

Nora and Ovrun stood frozen, mouths gaping. A few trogs had stopped too, drawn away from their own dances by the closed-eyed seer's nimble moves.

If Sarza opened her eyes to find an audience, she might never dance again. Nora waved her arms at the people around her, mouthing, *"Dance!"* She put her own arms around Ovrun's neck, and everyone started moving just as the song came to a sweet, slow close.

Sarza's eyes shot open, and her limbs stiffened again as she looked around her, as if expecting a public critique. When nothing of the sort happened, she relaxed a bit.

Nora pulled away from Ovrun and approached the seer with a smile she hoped wasn't too enthusiastic. "That was amazing." She gave Sarza an impulsive hug and rejoiced to feel the young woman's skinny arms squeezing her back.

When they separated, Sarza said, "It wasn't so bad." Her surprised smile revealed how much she'd enjoyed it.

"This song is a fast one," Nora said. "Should we join the mob?" She gestured to the undulating crowd.

"Okay."

Sarza let loose in a way Nora wouldn't have thought her capable of. Zeisha and Kebi found them, and Kebi taught them all some trog moves. Ovrun never seemed to tire as he danced with Nora, spinning her wildly during some songs, holding her close during others.

At last, the party wound down. Nora, Zeisha, Krey, Ovrun, and Sarza walked through Deroga's dark streets, letting the breeze cool their sweaty bodies. Sarza chatted easily with the others, only acting uncomfortable when they complimented her dancing.

As Nora listened to the conversation, something strange squeezed at her heart. She was trying to identify it when Ovrun murmured quietly, "Seems like our seer is really fitting in."

"She is." Nora smiled, though she felt a little sick. *What's wrong with me?*

Then it struck her. Tomorrow, Sarza would be exactly who she was tonight: the seer who was at last finding her place in this group.

Nora, on the other hand, would again be Cellerin's princess and heir, expected to steal her father's crown.

A break from reality was a good thing. She'd needed this party. But it changed nothing. Sure, she had friends. She could depend on them for support and laughter, and, in Ovrun's case, a little heat to keep things interesting.

But none of that's what I need these days, is it? She needed direction, assurance, someone to take her hand and tell her how to bring her father down so she could save her country. Nobody here could provide that for her. Nobody anywhere could. Sure, they'd brainstorm with her and support her and fight alongside her. But she was the one who'd eventually lead her country. The responsibility for getting this right fell on her shoulders alone.

She chewed on that bitter word—*alone*—as they walked through the dark streets.

2

I met a neighbor girl today. Reymi is seventeen, and we became fast friends. Her family drove me in their carriage to Cellerin Mountain. We hiked for over an hour until we reached a lookout—nowhere near the top, of course, but high enough to see a lot of the land between the mountain and the capital.

I stood there for a few minutes, quietly enjoying the view, before it hit me that everything I was looking at might one day be mine to rule.

I'm not sure if that thought is terrible or wonderful.

-Letter from Ambrel Kaulder to Dani Kaulder
Dated Centa 13, 180 PD

NORA SQUINTED into the pale-orange sky, which held no sign of the flying reptid she was seeking.

"Do you think he'll come?" Ovrun asked. His voice echoed off the buildings on either side of the deserted Derogan street.

"Yeah. I'm sure his timing is just off. I told him to come halfway between dawn and noon. That's kind of vague."

But she wasn't as sure as she wanted to be. These days, Osmius didn't always answer when she called him. He'd faithfully taken her to see Hatlin last night and on other Fridays before that. But when she'd canceled last week's meeting so she could attend the party, she'd sensed the great dragon's relief.

Osmius wanted to lie in his cave and mourn his mate over the coming months . . . or years . . . or forever. He'd agreed to take Nora and Ovrun on an aerial tour of Cellerin, but he'd have to drag himself out of the darkness and into the sunlight. Could he manage it?

Nora slipped her arm around Ovrun's waist. When he tugged her into his side, her floppy, fabric hat smashed against his chest. All the trogs wore these hats to protect against the summer sun. She let out a short giggle and pulled away, trying to straighten the brim.

Ovrun grinned. "That's the least fashionable thing I've ever seen you wear."

"I carry it off way better than you do."

When he laughed, his identical hat quivered.

Less than a minute later, Nora pointed into the distance. When it became clear that the approaching creature was a dragon, not a bird, she and Ovrun tightened their chin straps while they waited for Osmius.

As the dragon landed, he pulled in his broad, golden wings, creating a gust of wind that blew Nora's thin shirt against her. This, too, was part of the trogs' summer uniform: a loose, woven shirt with long sleeves, paired with drawstring pants. Her outfit was light tan, while Ovrun had an off-white shirt and brown pants. As comfortable as her new wardrobe was, Nora missed her tailored clothes.

Hello, Osmius.

Nora-human.

She climbed up his iridescent-gray, basket-weave scales, in front of his left wing, then scooted forward to hang onto the dragon's neck. Ovrun mounted behind her.

You wish to show your mate the land? Osmius asked, curving his neck to gaze at her through his golden, faceted eyes.

Nora didn't bother to correct him. He knew Ovrun wasn't her mate in any sense of the word, but he insisted on teasing her with the term. It struck her that it was the first time he'd done so since Taima had died six weeks ago. Holding back an influx of emotion, she replied, *I want him to know more about Cellerin. And I need to see how things are going.*

He responded by lifting into the air. Nora held onto his scales with her fingers and the toes of her boots as they gently rose into the sky over Deroga.

What do you wish to see? The dragon's voice sounded tired.

As much as you can show us. We brought food and water in our packs, so if you're up for an all-day tour, we are too. Maybe we could start with your mountains?

Osmius veered south, toward the range where he lived. After a long, silent trip over Deroga and many clommets of open land, they at last reached the mountains. Osmius flew over some of the shorter peaks. Ice and snow still covered the tallest ones. Yesterday, the dragon had brought Nora some of that ice to renew the fuel stash for her and other ice lysters in Deroga.

"It's beautiful!" Ovrun shouted over the brisk wind.

Nora smiled. "Just you wait; there's so much more to see!" She reached out to Osmius. *We could go to the desert after this.*

If you wish. However, we cannot visit the pond.

Nora's heart dropped. She'd hoped to take Ovrun to the places Osmius had shown her nearly four months ago, where planet magic—the force she now knew as the Well—was active. She'd drunk water from a pond that had given her incredible energy and enhanced her senses. *Why not?*

I call him your mate because I like to see your cheeks redden,

Osmius said, his serious tone contrasting with his words. *Yet you have not committed your life to him. You know how closely the Well's truths are guarded. If you choose Ovrun as the next king of this land, we shall show him its wonders.*

Nora nodded. When she'd met the man known as the Anya in the nation of Cruine, she'd immediately pegged him as the secretive sort. He'd lived in a cabin as a hermit, for the sky's sake. He could activate the power of the Well anywhere on the planet, yet he'd rarely done so.

When he and Zeisha had used the Well to defeat Nora's father in Deroga, they'd done their best to shroud their actions in secrecy. But nobody who'd been there would ever forget the great spouts of lava that had shot into the air. Rumors were running rampant around Deroga, and doubtless throughout Cellerin, since the king's army had seen the same magic.

Few people knew Zeisha was the Anya. While Ovrun was aware of Zeisha's new abilities, he wasn't aware there were areas in Cellerin where the magic of the Well was still active.

Osmius had shown Nora those sights because he believed the future queen should know the kingdom she was fighting for. Of course he wouldn't want her to share that knowledge with anyone but the nation's future king.

She'd invited Ovrun today because she was seriously considering making such a commitment to him. He needed to see more of the nation that might one day call him king. They'd agreed that if such a thing ever happened, he'd leave the actual ruling to her . . . but he would still have the title, and he'd support her every step of the way. It was the most generous thing anyone had ever offered her. But was it truly what he wanted?

Nora-human.

Osmius's voice in her head made her flinch. He was so much quieter these days; she'd gotten used to flights with little conversation. *Yes?*

You shall make the right choice.

The dragon couldn't hear her thoughts unless she shared them with him. When he came up with some astonishingly relevant comment like that, she always wondered if she'd inadvertently let their minds connect. *I, um . . . don't know what you mean,* she said.

He laughed, and if there was a more perfect, soothing sound in the whole world, she couldn't imagine it. She squeezed his neck tighter.

They flew over the northeastern portion of the Therro Desert, not going anywhere near the pond. When they'd been over sandy dunes for several minutes, Ovrun spoke up.

"Can we land for a few minutes?"

Osmius spiraled down and alighted atop a dune. Nora looked up at the sky as she dismounted. The sun was directly overhead. "Ready for lunch?" she asked Ovrun.

He climbed down after her. "Maybe in a few minutes. I have an idea first." He took off his pack and hat, then pulled Nora's off too, setting the items atop the dune. "Ready?"

"For what?"

He gave her a big smile, then lay on the fine sand and pushed himself off, rolling sideways down the dune. It was a fairly steep slope, and he picked up speed quickly.

Nora didn't hesitate. She threw herself after him, laughing with glee the whole way. At the bottom, she bumped into Ovrun just as he was sitting up.

She looked down at her clothes. They'd already been sand-colored, but now they were covered in a layer of fine grit. It had forced itself down her neckline and into the waistband of her pants, where her shirt was now untucked. "I don't even want to think about all the places I have sand stuck to me," she said.

Ovrun lifted a playful eyebrow. "I do."

She threw a handful of sand at his chest, then stood, wiggling to shake the stuff off. She removed the leather band holding back her straight, shoulder-length hair. When she shook her head, more sand flew out. "That was the most fun I've had in a long time." She stopped moving and cocked her head at Ovrun. "I'm usually the one to think of outlandish ideas like that."

He stood, brushing himself off. "You've been quieter lately. I thought you needed a little fun."

That broadened her smile. "Again?"

"Race you to the top!" He was running before he finished speaking.

There was no way she'd beat him. She was tall, but his legs were even longer than hers. Still, she tried, her muscles protesting with every step through the sand.

Ovrun reached the top, winning handily. He lifted his eyes and arms to the sky, grains of sand still falling from his shirt and his dark hair. "King of the desert!" he bellowed.

Nora slowed, admiring the taut abdominal muscles she glimpsed under the hem of his shirt. *He makes a great-looking king.* She shared the thought with Osmius.

He is strong, Osmius replied. But there was grief in his words, and Nora knew he was thinking of Taima, whose strength had far surpassed her mate's.

After a few more rolls down the dune and a quick picnic lunch, they flew along a route only Osmius knew, passing over communities of various sizes, including the capitals of a couple of Cellerinian provinces. Nora had visited some of these places in the past, and they seemed just as vibrant and free as ever. Maybe the king's madness hadn't touched these people yet.

At last, they arrived at a destination Nora had been anticipating visiting: New Therro. She'd visited the city with her parents when she was young, but she didn't remember much about it. As Osmius had done over other inhabited areas, he flew too high to be identified as a dragon. Then he shared his keen vision with Nora.

Crisp images filled her mind. The streets were nearly empty, and over half of those who were visible wore the black-and-blue uniforms of the Cellerinian Army. Every week, Hatlin told Nora how the king was cracking down on the province. When soldiers from the occupying army caught New Therroans speaking against the king, they threw the supposed traitors into makeshift prisons or executed them.

The king was ruling by fear. Even this far above the city, Nora could feel it. Then she saw one place where the street was far from empty. *Do you see all those people?* she asked Osmius, pointing.

He turned his head, bringing the street into better focus. A line of people perhaps a clommet long waited to enter a building. Someone exited the building, carrying a crate of food.

At least he's feeding them, Nora thought.

A soldier stepped out of the building and spoke to those at the front of the line, shooing them away. The crowd dispersed.

Nora's pulse quickened with fury. *There are productive farms around the city; there should be enough food for the entire population!*

Then she remembered something else Hatlin had told her. The king had recently raised taxes on New Therro, including taking a good portion of their produce and livestock.

Shall we move on? Osmius asked.

Nora was about to answer when the scene below erupted into chaos.

Six people rushed up the stairs of the food-distribution building. They didn't even make it to the top step when the soldiers guarding the door attacked with swords, bows, and guns.

A bullet struck a male citizen. He fell, blood spreading across his chest. A woman took a sword in her belly. When she looked down to see the blade protruding from her, her eyes went wide with shock. Her knees crumpled. For a moment, she stared at the soldier holding the weapon. Her mouth moved, and Nora could tell the single word she'd spoken: "Why?" Then her gaze went blank. The soldier withdrew his sword, letting her body fall.

Nora squeezed her eyes shut. She didn't want to see this horror. The picture, however, remained, traveling from Osmius's mind to hers. She considered disconnecting from his sight, but a sudden sense of piercing responsibility prevented her. If all went well, she'd soon be queen over this province. She needed to see the truth.

The soldiers pushed two people down the stairs. Four additional soldiers surrounded them, beating them viciously with boots and fists. The two citizens soon stilled, but the attack didn't stop.

One woman remained. She'd been at the back of the group and had retreated to the middle of the street. Seeing the violence, she turned and fled. An arrow to the leg took her down. A bullet to the head ensured she didn't get up again.

At last, the beating at the bottom of the stairs ended. The victims lay in pools of blood, not moving. Nora swallowed bile that pressed against the back of her throat. Her breaths came faster. *We have to stop my father,* she told Osmius, *but I don't know how!*

You will know the next step when it is time, Osmius said.

Nora bit back a snarky comment about needing answers, not pointless platitudes.

After a brief silence, Osmius asked, *Shall we go?*

Not yet. Those people are Cellerinians. My father doesn't respect them, but I do. Even in death.

They continued to watch as the soldiers dragged all six bodies into the middle of the street and set them on fire. Nora gripped Osmius's scales so hard that her fingertips ached. *Let's go.*

After another long flight, they were over Cellerin City. To Nora's relief, it looked as it always had. Rather than flying over the palace grounds, Osmius turned southwest, avoiding the area entirely. Even when he was this high, he rarely flew directly above the palace. Ulmin had controlled Osmius in the past and would do so again if he saw him.

Next, they went to Cellerin Mountain, the largest freestanding peak in the world, and soared over the communities along parts of its periphery. Seven months ago, Nora had traveled through this area on dirt roads, spending some of the journey in a steamcar and the rest of it in a wagon. She and her father had been on a royal tour, celebrating the two-hundredth anniversary of The Day.

Nora recognized the area where the stone had been found. Ground zero of the apocalypse. A small museum drew visitors year round. She'd been there. It was a strange place, filled with eerie memories of a terrible tragedy, but colored with hope because of the magic that had entered the world that day.

Faster than she would've predicted, they reached Tirra, Krey's hometown. Nora couldn't help laughing a bit as she remembered her first glimpse of Krey, flying over the square where she and her father were trying to hold a meaningful celebration. Ovrun had been one of the guards to usher Nora off the stage, lest the erratic feather lyster attack her. Who'd have guessed that less than two months later, she'd end up fleeing the capital city with both those boys, in the hopes of finding and freeing Zeisha?

She turned to tell Ovrun where they were.

"Too bad Krey's not here!" he replied.

"Trust me, he wouldn't want to be riding with us!" They both laughed. Krey hated flying on dragons.

It was early dusk when Osmius landed on a flat shelf on the side of the mountain, not too far from Cellerin City.

Ovrun sat up. "I don't have the best memories of this place."

"None of us do," Nora said softly. She dismounted and looked around, stretching. Behind them was a dark cave. Taima had been chained in that space for months before Osmius sent Nora, Ovrun, and Krey to save her. They were successful, but Ovrun had been shot in the arm. Nora swallowed and shuddered. *Why did we come here?*

You wanted to see your land, Osmius replied. *The view from here is excellent.*

He again shared his vision with her. He was right; it was an incredible view once she saw all the details his sight provided. But she'd already seen all this from the air. Osmius hadn't come because this was a great lookout point. He'd come here to feel close to Taima.

She reached a hand toward his head. He bent his neck and

brought his warm cheek into her palm. *I love you, you know,* she said, sending gentleness and kindness to him along with the words.

A smoky sigh exited his nostrils. *And I love you, Nora-human.*

"You're quiet again," Ovrun said a few minutes later, "and I can't exactly roll down this slope to cheer you up this time." He pointed to the sharp drop-off several mets away.

Nora took her hand off Osmius and turned to Ovrun. "I can't get it out of my head. What we saw in New Therro."

"What did you see?"

That's when it hit her. He hadn't seen anything. He'd been flying peacefully above a city that looked normal from that height, and he hadn't had the privilege of sharing Osmius's sight. At the time, she'd been so consumed with what she saw that it hadn't occurred to her Ovrun was unaware of it.

That ache she'd felt after the party the previous weekend returned. She could describe the travesty in New Therro, and he'd share her concern. But it would remain her problem to solve.

She shook off the thought. Ovrun was here to support her. Maybe he couldn't fix the nation of Cellerin, but he'd let her lean on him while she attempted it.

"Can we sit?" she asked softly.

He nodded, lowering himself into the dirt.

Nora cuddled up to him, taking her hat off and resting her head on his heart. Quietly, she told him the nightmare she'd witnessed. He pulled her closer as she spoke.

When she stopped talking, he whispered just the right words to her—about how strong she was and how much faith he had in her. Then they both fell silent.

Ovrun's arms gave her a little relief from the weight she was carrying—the stifling mixture of doubt and fear for the unknown future. She wanted this type of security every day for the rest of her life.

But could she ask that of him? Would he be content holding her up for the next sixty years? Or would she end up pulling him down?

"Ovrun?" Nora murmured into his chest.

"Hmm?"

She pulled away and gestured to the scene before them. Even without dragon sight, she could make out countless clommets of blurry land in shades of brown and green. A few wispy clouds cast dancing shadows on the terrain. "What do you think of ruling this land?"

He smiled down at her. "I don't care about that. I just want to be by your side."

The words were sweet and earnest, but her stomach twisted tighter than before. Unwilling to let him see the emotional storm on her face, she pulled him into a tight hug. "You know," she said, keeping her voice light, "whoever gets me, gets the land and people and responsibilities too. It's like committing yourself to someone who's got a third leg. It's gonna get in the way sometimes, and you can't just cut it off."

Ovrun laughed. "You keep trying to scare me away. It's not working."

He didn't get it though; she was sure of that. Even if he left the ruling to her, he'd still be king. He'd spend his days stuck within the walls of a palace. He'd have to dress up, cultivate a public image, and attend long, boring state dinners. They'd talked about all that, and he'd insisted he was fine with it. But he couldn't truly understand it until he experienced it. And he couldn't experience it without marrying her. By then, he'd be stuck.

Would he *feel* stuck? Something deep inside—fear or instinct, she wasn't sure—told her he would, eventually.

And what would happen when she inevitably found herself turning to Ovrun to discuss tough leadership decisions? She feared part of her would always expect him to play a traditional, monarchial role—and he had no desire to take on such a responsibility. If she constantly had to go elsewhere for support, would she feel stuck too?

Maybe I should end things with him.

It was a thought that entered her mind far too often lately, sometimes keeping her up at night. But right now . . . right now, his arms were tight around her, lending her warmth and security. That was exactly what she needed.

She rested a hand on Ovrun's heart, letting its steadiness bring her comfort. Allowing it to distract her from her persistent questions.

3

This morning, I put on a robe and stumbled into the dining room, assuming Uncle Quin and I would be the only ones eating breakfast.

A very well-dressed woman was at the table, deep in conversation with our uncle. I turned and dashed up the stairs, where I got dressed, threw my hair into a bun, and put on a quick coat of lipstick.

When I got back to the dining room, the woman stood and said, "Your robe looked more comfortable." Then she introduced herself. As Queen Onna.

Yes, you read that correctly. The queen, my possible future husband's grandmother, saw me in my robe!

We chatted awkwardly through breakfast. I guess I did okay, because she invited me for dinner at the palace to meet Prince Ulmin in two days.

The prince is the stone lyster, not me . . . but my stomach feels like I swallowed a bucket of rocks.

-*Letter from Ambrel Kaulder to Dani Kaulder*
Dated Centa 14, 180 PD

ZEISHA AND KEBI sat on the bank of the Deroga River, far enough from trog territory that no one was likely to find them. They were on their midday break from their assignment on one of the Star Clan's rooftop gardens. A blanket of heat covered the city, and they'd agreed to visit the river before eating.

Zeisha dipped her fingers in the delightfully cool water. She closed her eyes, listening. After a few minutes, she looked up and grinned.

Kebi, who was soaking her bare feet in the water, asked, "What is it?"

Zeisha didn't answer. Instead, she called on the Well—the magic of the planet Anyari—within the water.

She knew the moment it awakened. The rushing water felt *alive*. Laughter bubbled from Zeisha's chest. "The Well wants to have some fun."

Connecting with the Well was entirely different from vine eating, Zeisha's other talent. There was intelligence in the magic of Anyari. Zeisha attributed it to God, though she knew some Anyas of the past had seen it differently. The more she experimented with the Well, the more she was convinced it had a personality.

She'd sensed its justice and love when she worked with it on the day of the battle for Deroga. After that, she assumed she'd only connect with the Well occasionally. The Anya who'd given her his power told her he rarely used his magic.

But his skill with the Well had far surpassed Zeisha's. He'd carried on a conversation while creating a fence made of spurting lava. Zeisha couldn't imagine such multitasking. Maybe he'd somehow inherited such strength. He'd come from a family of Anyas, one per generation.

Zeisha longed to ask him how he'd gotten so strong. He'd died before she'd gotten the chance.

All Zeisha knew was that the Well kept calling to her. The morning after the battle, she'd known she wasn't supposed to sit there and wait for the perfect time to connect to Anyari. The Well wanted her to experiment—safely and secretly—until she truly understood its capacity and hers.

Zeisha had no idea why. In fact, the Anya she'd met might not approve of her kneeling next to this river, preparing to play with the magic in the water. But he'd told her to listen to the voice that guided her. Right now, that voice was telling her to be silly—a quality that had never described her. Her heart whispered to the eager magic within the water. And it responded.

From myriad spots in the river, narrow streams of water arced far up in the air, then started falling on Zeisha and Kebi like a sudden rain shower. Kebi's mouth dropped open in shock. Laughing, she stood and raised her arms.

Zeisha removed her hands from the river and came to her feet, exulting in the cool relief from the day's heat. Her wide-brimmed hat got soggy and heavy, and she threw it to the ground.

After dropping her own hat, Kebi stepped closer to Zeisha, facing her. Zeisha lifted her gaze to her friend's warm, brown eyes, then found her focus drifting to details of Kebi's face she'd never noticed before. The angle of her narrow nose. A pale, crescent-shaped scar next to her left eye. The slight indentation at the center of her bottom lip, now host to a tiny drop of water. Zeisha fought off a sudden, inexplicable urge to rest her thumb in that little divot on Kebi's lip.

Kebi extended both hands. Zeisha's eyes dropped, fixing on those smooth, pale palms. Something—an emotion, almost tangible and not quite identifiable—flickered between them. A soft smile stole over Zeisha's lips as she placed her hands in Kebi's.

30

Kebi's mouth widened into a sudden, mischievous grin. She tightened her hands on Zeisha's, then leaned back and began spinning. Zeisha followed suit, shrieking with laughter as they spun faster. Her curls flung water into the air, and dizziness sent delicious lightness into her head. Apparently she wasn't the only one feeling silly today.

Kebi's feet slipped on the slick grass. They both fell, laughing. Zeisha dipped a hand into the water and asked the Well to reduce its shower to a drizzle. Both women lay back on the wet grass. When Zeisha shifted, her fingers brushed against Kebi's. Warmth filled her chest, and she was suddenly extra aware of herself and her surroundings. Cool clean river water on her tongue. The scent of wet grass. Heat from the sun in the pale-orange sky. The tingle of her finger where it had just touched Kebi's.

They lay in comfortable silence. Zeisha found herself musing about the recent changes in her life, each one an emotional landmark on her journey. She'd sensed a shift in her soul the moment she'd met the Anya in Cruine six weeks ago, then again two days later, when she'd sat with Krey on a bench and realized they needed to break up.

And just now, when Kebi had extended her hands, Zeisha had felt it once more—the sense that her life was drifting suddenly and unexpectedly from the path she'd been on. She welcomed the shift and was willing to dwell peacefully in it . . . whatever it was. But she wasn't quite ready to analyze it.

A few minutes later, Zeisha returned to the river and again dipped her fingers in. She sent the Well her gratitude and asked it to go dormant. A rush of love and acceptance filled her, and the streams of water stopped.

She sat next to Kebi, who'd risen to her knees and was wringing out the hem of her shirt. "Thanks for coming with me," Zeisha said. "I've been spending time almost every day experimenting with the Well, and . . . it's nice sharing that with someone. With you."

Kebi smiled. "I should thank you. I do not laugh so hard since before my wife dies a year ago."

Zeisha sobered. "Really? You haven't been this happy in a whole year?"

"Not until today. And Dera is happy when I am happy. I know she is."

A smile spread over Zeisha's mouth again. She'd never dreamed she'd become close to a trog, but Kebi had welcomed her to Deroga from the first day they'd met. Because of her, the city had begun feeling like home.

Kebi had begun feeling like home.

When had that happened?

At last, Zeisha spoke. "We need to go change. What'll we say if someone asks what happened to us? Should we tell them we fell in the river?"

Kebi stood and extended a hand to help Zeisha up. "The truth is, the river falls on us."

Zeisha took her hand and stood, laughing.

Zeisha had just finished putting on dry clothes when someone knocked on the bunkhouse door. "Come in!" she called.

The door opened, revealing a trog woman who assisted Eira, the Star Clan's unofficial leader. Normally well groomed, she was currently red faced and sweaty. "There you are. I look for you on your rooftop, but it is empty."

"I'm sorry," Zeisha said, wincing on the assistant's behalf. Climbing to that rooftop was always difficult, and it was pure misery in the summer. "Kebi and I took our lunch break." Her stomach growled, reminding her she still hadn't eaten.

"Eira sends me to fetch you," the woman said. "Go to her office while I return home to change clothes. Hurry, an important guest waits for you."

Before Zeisha could ask any questions, the assistant rushed off.

Zeisha stepped onto the street to find Kebi approaching the building. She gave her friend a quick explanation and promised to meet her on the roof afterward. Kebi offered to bring lunch for both of them, and Zeisha gratefully agreed.

A couple of minutes later, Zeisha knocked on Eira's office door, calling out a greeting. The door opened, revealing a short, bald man.

Zeisha's eyes widened. "Prime Minister Osk!"

"Our Anya." The leader of the nation of Cruine lowered his head.

"Please don't bow to me," Zeisha said quietly.

Osk met her gaze with a nod and stepped aside so she could enter. Eira was sitting at her desk, face flushed with heat despite the open shutters at every window.

As Zeisha and Osk sat in front of the desk, she tried to hide her curiosity over his arrival. She hadn't planned to tell him she was the new Anya. But when Eira had sent a Cruinite trade ship back home with news of the old Anya's death, Osk had dispatched a messenger to ask if the Anya had perhaps passed his gift to Zeisha.

When Zeisha read the letter, it boggled her mind. What had Osk seen in her during their brief time together that led him to guess she was the new Anya? Whatever it was, there was no sense hiding the truth. She'd given Eira permission to tell him he was right. Based on the timing of this visit, Zeisha was pretty sure Osk had hopped on a boat as soon as his messenger returned with the news.

Osk turned to Zeisha. "I've come to invite you to Cruine."

"You want me to visit?"

One of his brows rose. "I want you to live there as my honored guest. You may settle wherever you like, whether in a city or in solitude. I am the only one in Cruine who knows of your gift, and I will protect that knowledge. A portion of the prime minister's budget has always been used to support the Anya. You will live in comfort, with all your needs met."

Letting the silence stretch, Zeisha listened to the voice within her. At last, she responded, "Thank you, but Cruine isn't my home."

"The Anya has always lived in Cruine." Osk's Cruinite accent was refined, but a current of command ran through his words. This was a man who was used to being obeyed.

Zeisha met Osk's gaze without fear. "I know if I moved to Cruine, I'd be welcome there."

He nodded earnestly. "Indeed."

In the past, he would've intimidated Zeisha, but now, the peace that filled her was too thick to allow fear to enter. "Maybe someday I'll realize I'm meant to move there. Right now, I'm where I'm supposed to be."

"I don't think you understand." He leaned toward her. "The Anya is part of Cruine's heritage. When I was sworn into office, I learned that one of my most important duties is to protect the Anya and the knowledge of the Well. I can't do that if you're in Cellerin."

"I don't think *you* understand," Zeisha replied gently. "The Well doesn't belong to one nation. Neither do I." From the corner of her eye, she saw Eira smile.

Osk pressed his lips together and sat back in his seat, watching Zeisha with what looked like grief. At last, he said, "You do realize the damage Anyas of the past did, do you not? You know how harmful the Well is when it's misused? And when the power is given to those who shouldn't have it?"

"I do. The Anya told me to pass my gift to one person—my own child, or someone who's like my child. That's what I'll do, and not until I know in my heart that it's time." Seeing the uncertainty in his gaze, she continued, "He also told me to listen. Prime Minister, I've heard a voice in my heart since I was a child. These days, I hear it clearer than ever. I know you don't have any reason to trust me, but I—"

He interrupted, "I have trusted you since I met you, Zeisha."

Her eyes widened. "Then trust me when I tell you, I'm not supposed to leave Deroga today."

Osk looked out one of the open windows. Zeisha waited, giving him a smile when he met her gaze again. He returned the smile, but his was resigned. "The leaders of Cruine have always respected the decisions of your predecessors. I must honor your choice to stay here, though it grieves me to lose our Anya."

Her smile brightened, though her voice was soft. "You haven't lost me, Prime Minister. Like I said, the Well belongs to all of us. I'm pretty sure the one who speaks to me doesn't care much about national borders. If I'm meant to be in your area, I'll be there."

"I'm glad to hear that. If I need to contact you, where will I find you?"

Zeisha hadn't anticipated the question, but the answer came easily. "For now, Deroga is my home." She stood, and Osk did the same. "It was good to see you again."

He drew in a deep breath. "Eira tells me you were with our Anya in his final moments. Thank you."

"He was a good man."

Osk took both her hands and locked his gaze with hers. "He chose a good heir."

THE STONE EATER: 2

"Come in," Ulmin said.

The tall army captain in charge of New Therro held both hands out and bowed his head, then entered. Ulmin tried to recall the man's name, then decided it didn't matter. He gestured to the other man in the room, who stood near the window. "You know General Etal."

The captain brought his fists together over his heart in a salute. "Yes, sir." Slick sweat covered his face.

"Take your jacket off," Ulmin said. When the soldier had complied, Ulmin held out his hand. "Pleasure to meet you."

The captain shook the king's hand, and Ulmin took control of his mind. The muscles in the man's face and shoulders slackened. Ulmin looked over his shoulder at General Etal. "Much better, wouldn't you say?"

"Yes, sir."

"Let's sit." Ulmin gestured to an arrangement of several chairs across the room near a fireplace he couldn't imagine needing anytime soon. When they were all settled, he asked the captain, "What do you think of my dome?"

"It makes it hot in here. I'm not sure why you had to cover the whole place." The captain's blank expression didn't change as he spoke the words.

Fury flared in Ulmin's chest, but he forced a laugh past it. "Well, don't hold back." Of course, the man wouldn't. That was the beauty and the drawback of mind control: total honesty. "Give me an update on New Therro."

In a clear monotone, the captain replied, "The people are hungry but mostly docile. We punish crimes harshly, and the number of incidents decreases almost every week."

"What kinds of crimes?"

"Stealing. Violence. Disobedience. Disloyalty in word or action."

Ulmin nodded. These were the same issues Etal had been telling him about. "How many did you arrest last week?"

"Seven."

"Ages?"

"Fourteen to sixty-two."

"How many were killed, rather than arrested? Ages too."

"Five. Sixteen to forty-seven."

"Troop deaths?"

"None, Your Majesty."

"Much better than the week before," General Etal said.

"Agreed." Ulmin sat back, threading his fingers together behind his head and crossing his right ankle over his left knee. "Tell them when they have a week with no arrests or executions, we'll increase the food supply by twenty-five percent."

The captain acknowledged the order, but General Etal sat up straighter. "Sir, if we do so, we may not have enough food for the troops."

Ulmin's right eye twitched in annoyance. He rarely controlled the general; the man was smart and performed better when his mind was free. But he had a nasty habit of questioning his monarch. Removing his hands from behind his head, Ulmin said, "We have plenty of food in Cellerin City."

"You want us to send it up to New Therro?"

"No." A slight smile made the corners of Ulmin's mouth twitch. "I want all the peacekeepers who are currently living inside New Therro to stay there. Bring the rest of the army—those camped outside the city—to the capital."

The general tapped his fingers against the arm of his chair. "We had five thousand troops prior to the Derogan battle. We lost four hundred in the fighting. You then released our eighteen hundred New Therroan soldiers. Five hundred troops are currently peacekeepers." His brows drew together. "That leaves twenty-three hundred."

"I can do math," Ulmin spat, though he hadn't bothered to calculate the numbers. That wasn't his job. "Bring them to the city."

"Why?"

That smile tugged at the king's lips again. This time, he let it form. "New Therro is experiencing greater peace than ever before. Their loyalty to the crown is at last returning. Imagine how strong my kingdom will be when we bring the same unity to our capital."

General Etal's jaw dropped. "Cellerin City is already unified. You have many supporters—"

"And just as many who whisper their complaints to each other," Ulmin said. "The path from murmurs to sedition is a short one." He couldn't be more sure of anything. If his own daughter could turn against him, citizens who didn't know him personally would certainly do the same. A flash of dark, straight hair and laughing eyes filled his mind. *Oh, Nora.*

The general wet his lips. "So you'll . . . invade the capital?"

"Not invade." A chuckle escaped Ulmin's chest. "Occupy. Inhabit, if you prefer that term. Our soldiers will bring peace. Many of them have families here. They will be welcomed."

The sweltering air seemed to amplify the sound of the general's swallow. He stood and brought his fists to his heart. "It will be done, Your Majesty."

"Of course it will." Finding he couldn't tolerate these men any longer, Ulmin stood. Both officers quickly came to their feet. "Get him out of here," Ulmin told General Etal. "On your way out, tell my receptionist I need a large glass of ice water. Have her send someone to fan me as well."

The general held his hands out in yet another bow. "Yes, Your Majes—"

"Just go."

They did. Ulmin sank into the seat behind his desk and reached into the clay pot next to his pen. As soon as his stiff, scarred fingers touched the fuel within, his anxiety lessened. When he took a bite, all was well again.

4

I woke this morning, out of my mind with nerves. Tomorrow, I'll meet the prince. To distract myself, I spent most of the day with my new friend Reymi, practicing magic.

I softened the soil around some bushes Uncle Quin wants to pull out of his garden. Reymi let me loosen the ground under her until she fell in and was buried up to her waist. We both got a good laugh out of that.

Then I watched Reymi fly. Yes—she's a feather lyster, the first one I've seen in at least a year. All I could think was that flying must be so much more freeing than playing with dirt.

I ended the day as nervous as I'd begun it. Tomorrow, I'll meet Ulmin, and I'm afraid I'll melt into a puddle of anxiety as soon as I lay eyes on him.

-Letter from Ambrel Kaulder to Dani Kaulder
Dated Centa 15, 180 PD

Nora sat on the warm, dusty ground and leaned back against Osmius, who'd been resting comfortably for some time. She settled into the crook of his neck, feeling his body swell and compress with each breath.

Maybe he's not coming, Nora said.

Shall we return to Deroga?

Not yet. She'd been waiting for Hatlin for at least an hour. It wasn't like him to not show up. She fixed her eyes on the flickering flame of the candle she'd stuck in the dirt. The wax was half gone. If it melted all the way to the ground, she'd mount Osmius and go home.

Such a thought infuriated her. It had been nearly two weeks since the aerial tour of Cellerin. She still had no idea what their next step was in defeating her father. Last week, Hatlin had told her he had an idea, but he needed to look into it before he shared it with her. She'd been looking forward to this meeting, hoping he'd give her some direction.

A sound reached her ears, barely audible, like someone was shouting from far away.

Hatlin is calling your name, Osmius said.

Are you sure?

More than a bit of dragon ego infused his next words. *Need you ask?*

He was right. Dragon hearing was as acute as dragon sight. Nora heard the shout again, a smidge louder. This time, Hatlin said a lot more than just her name, though she couldn't decipher any of it.

Get on my back! Osmius's voice resonated urgently in Nora's mind.

She leapt to her feet and started climbing up without question. Halfway up, she said, *I left the candle!*

Leave it!

Nora draped her leg over Osmius's back. He lifted into the air.

She cried out; her hands and feet weren't yet secure. She grasped his scales tightly, and he turned toward the voice they'd heard.

When we reach Hatlin, tell him to mount! Osmius commanded.

He hates riding on—

Her protest ended when a gunshot sounded. Just as they reached the big, flying man, a second shot rang through the dark air.

"Get on the dragon's back!" Nora shouted, pushing herself farther forward.

To her utter surprise, Hatlin flew above Osmius and grasped onto the great dragon's gray scales. "Go!" he shouted.

Another shot. An uncomfortably close voice, clearly another feather lyster, screamed, "Stop! I'll shoot again!"

They took a terrifyingly sharp turn, and Osmius breathed a wide stream of fire toward the voice. Someone cried out, though it sounded more like fear than pain. Osmius flew backward, continuing to breathe fire for several seconds. It worked; the gunshots ceased. He turned and flew with his head facing toward Deroga again.

Nora's heart felt like it would leave her chest. When she was certain they'd escaped the other feather lyster, a giddy, relieved grin stretched over her mouth. She turned to shout over her shoulder, "Who was shooting at us?"

Hatlin responded with loud, panicked breaths. Poor guy. He'd just been shot at, and now he was riding a creature he was deathly afraid of.

"You can fly on your own," Nora called back to him. "I know you prefer it."

"Too . . . tired," he gasped. Then he puked.

Nora screwed up her mouth and tried to hold back her own gorge.

"Can you . . . fly me to Deroga?" Hatlin's voice was weak.

"Just tell me what's going on!" Nora insisted. When her fellow passenger gagged again, she let out a harsh sigh. "Never mind. We'll talk once we get there."

Osmius continued cutting a sleek path through the night sky.

As soon as Osmius landed in the dark Derogan street and folded his wings, Hatlin clambered off his back, jostling Nora as he did so.

She smirked. "I take it you enjoyed the flight?"

He didn't seem to hear her. He was kneeling in the street, taking long breaths, when her feet hit the dirt.

Nora told Osmius good night, and he lifted into the air. She turned to Hatlin. "As soon as you've recovered, we'll go to the others." As they'd flown, Hatlin had gathered his wits enough to suggest she bring her friends to hear whatever it was he needed to share.

Before long, he stood, his broad shoulders slumped with exhaustion. "Let's go."

Nora led him through the Star Clan's streets to the bunkhouses where she, her friends, and the former militia members stayed. She woke Ovrun, Krey, Zeisha, and Sarza, and they all gathered in the dusty street. Ovrun and Sarza both had lanterns.

"Listen," Hatlin said. "I got a lot to tell you. But I'm beat after all that flying. Do you have any food? Maybe some water? I drank all mine."

Krey nodded. "We'll take you to our dining room. It's just a few minutes' walk from here."

When they reached their destination, Zeisha found some fruit and water for Hatlin. They all sat at a table.

"First, can you tell us why a feather lyster was pursuing you?" Nora asked.

Hatlin took a long drink of water. "I snuck into New Therro a few days ago, just to find out how everything's going. They told me the army brought in a feather eater to watch the city. While I was there, they got a second one. One of them saw me when I was trying to fly out tonight. They both ended up following me. I thought I lost them, but one caught up when I stopped for a rest. Now that they know about me, they'll be looking for me."

43

"What does that mean for your part in the rebellion?" Krey asked.

"I don't know." Hatlin ate a few bites of fruit, then wiped his mouth with the back of his hand. "Things are bad in New Therro. Not that I have to tell you that. The princess here saw it for herself recently. My people aren't giving up. But some of them are now seeing that we'll never get our independence while Ulmin's king."

"Does that mean you'll help me take him down?" Nora asked.

"We'll get to that. First, I gotta tell you about Cellerin City."

Dread bloomed in Nora's chest. "What about it?"

"Most of the army marched back there about a week ago."

Her forehead wrinkled in confusion. "You just said they're still occupying New Therro."

"They are. Five hundred of them. But the rest of them used to be camped outside New Therro, doing training exercises. They're the ones who moved."

"Why?" Nora asked, but Hatlin was taking another drink. His eyes were red with weariness. "What's going on in the capital?" she pressed.

He swallowed the water. "They're occupying it. Just like they're doing to New Therro."

"WHAT?" The bellow belonged to Ovrun, who punctuated it with a fist to the table. "My mother and sister live there! Is the army killing and starving people, like they are in New Therro?"

Nora's eyes widened. Ovrun rarely got angry. She placed a hand on his back. His muscles were hard as stone.

"They're not killing or starving people," Hatlin said.

"What are they doing?" Krey asked in a low, controlled voice.

"They're entering houses without permission," Sarza said flatly. When everyone looked her way, she said, "I had a short vision about a week ago. I figured it was in New Therro, but . . . well, now I think it was Cellerin City. That's what they're doing, right?"

Hatlin sighed. "Yeah. Some of the officers are with their families, but others have demanded to live with people around the city. If a soldier asks you for a bedroom, you give it to them. Unless you want them to arrest you."

"They're not protection officers, they're soldiers!" Nora spat. "They should be defending our citizens, not arresting them!"

Hatlin's voice got lower, but a certain intense brightness entered his eyes. "They've been doing a lot worse to the New Therroans, and we're citizens too."

Nora let out her breath and looked down at her hands. "You're right." But she'd half forgotten that, hadn't she? New Therro had always retained its own culture, and as furious as she was about her father's treatment of the people there, they felt less like *her* people than those in the capital did.

Her mind raced back to last year, when the two-hundredth anniversary of The Day was coming up. Nora had chatted with her father about several potential routes for their royal tour. New Therro hadn't been on any of them. *No wonder they want to be independent. We've always treated them like outsiders.*

She turned her attention back to Hatlin, who was finishing up his fruit. "What else can you tell us?"

"There's a curfew in the capital now, ten 'til dawn. And the soldiers are doing a lot of . . . watching. Every chapel in the city had officers standing at the back during services on Sunday. They sit in pubs and by water pumps, listening to conversations. If they hear anything negative about the king, they give that person a warning."

A harsh laugh exited Krey's mouth. "How much you wanna bet those warnings turn into arrests by next week?"

"I'd never bet against you on that. Not after what I've seen."

Nora couldn't stop shaking her head. "We have to stop this. We have to stop *him*."

"That's the other reason I came." Hatlin shoved his empty plate out of the way and propped his elbows on the table, eyes locked on Nora. "You can't fight your daddy if you're in trogtown. It's time for you to go back to Cellerin City."

Nora's pulse picked up its pace. "I agree. But where are we

supposed to stay? The minute I leave this place and my father finds out where I am, he'll take me home."

Hatlin spread his hands wide. "I don't know. But I do have a contact in the city who might be able to help you get to your father."

"Who?"

Hatlin crossed his arms and leaned back, a proud smile on his face. "Bet you didn't know one of his former ministers has New Therroan heritage."

Krey leapt from his seat and shouted, "We are *not* working with Minister Sharai!"

Hatlin's mouth dropped open. "Guess you did know."

"Yeah, she was the Minister of Lysting!" Krey looked at Hatlin like that should explain it all. When Hatlin's face remained blank, Krey said, "She's the one who organized the magic-eater militia! It's her fault Zeisha was kidnapped!"

Hatlin blinked. "Oh."

"Krey, have a seat," Nora said.

His only response was a glare.

"Please?" she snapped. "Like an adult?"

He plopped back into his chair, fiery eyes fixed on her. "Don't tell me you want to work with that woman."

"All I want is to hear what Hatlin has to say, considering he risked his life to say it."

Krey's jaw visibly clenched, but he stayed quiet.

"Well." Hatlin took a long drink of water. "I thought this was good news, but maybe not. Here goes. Sharai's heard rumors about how bad things are in New Therro. She started asking around, wondering if anyone was trying to stop it. She and me, we've got mutual friends. So I met with her, the day after the army came to town. I . . . may have mentioned I know some people who are planning to take down the king."

Krey's anger boiled over again. "You told her about us?"

"Nothing specific!" Hatlin insisted. "I didn't tell her your names. But she's all in, I'm telling you. Whatever she did in the past, she knows now that the king is ruining his country. She wants to meet you all."

"That's *not* gonna happen," Krey spat.

"Krey!" Nora's insistent tone drew his eyes back to her. "I don't trust Sharai any farther than I could throw her. But it's not like we have a lot of resources. Let's hear him out!"

"Thank you, Princess," Hatlin said. "Listen, I don't like the lady. New Therroans who work for the monarchy aren't exactly popular. But I believe her when she says she wants to take Ulmin down."

"I think we should hear what she has to say." Nora kept her voice low and her eyes on Krey.

Lips pressed into a tight line, he drew in a sharp breath through his nose, then released it. When he spoke, anger simmered in his voice. "How do you expect me to work with her? And what about Zeisha, you think she wants to meet this lady? For that matter, how could you ever trust her, Nora?"

"I specifically said I *don't* trust her. But we should talk to her." She leaned forward. "Krey, she did horrible things. I don't deny that. But she knows my father in a way I don't. She worked with him at least fifteen years. She understands palace politics. We can't say no to a resource like that."

Krey stared at her for several long seconds, before finally turning to Zeisha. His voice turned gentle. "Your opinion should be the most important one at this table. Do you want to meet this woman?"

All eyes found Zeisha. She returned their gazes with a confident, serene one of her own. By the stone, she'd changed from the broken girl they'd rescued.

"I agree that going to Cellerin City is necessary," Zeisha said. "I even agree that this former minister is worth listening to." She drew in a deep breath, fixing her gaze on Krey. "But you don't need my permission to talk to her. I'm staying in Deroga."

Stillness fell over the room.

Krey broke it. "If you come with us, we won't expect you to fight, not with your vines, and not with . . ." He trailed off, his gaze briefly flickering to Hatlin, who didn't know Zeisha was the Anya. "Not with any of your skills," he said.

"Deroga is my home," Zeisha said. "For now, at least. I know that for sure. I also know if I'm needed, I'll be ready to serve."

Krey's head drooped, his shaggy, black hair falling in his eyes. Nora's heart ached for him. He'd found it awkward to see his ex every day, but he clearly wasn't ready to be separated from her.

"What about you, Sarza?" Nora asked. "And Ovrun? Do you want to go to the capital?"

She'd known Ovrun would agree, but it was still a relief when he said, "Absolutely."

"Me too," Sarza said, "Unless I have a vision showing me otherwise."

"Well, then—"

The door opened, and Eira entered. "A member of the night watch sees lantern light," the white-haired trog said as she approached. "When she looks through the window and sees a man who does not have permission to enter trog territory, she wakes me." She closed her mouth, brows raised expectantly.

Nora introduced Hatlin, then concluded with, "I'm afraid all of us but Zeisha will be leaving Deroga soon. My father is mistreating his people, and we have to go to the capital to stop him."

Eira nodded, like she'd expected that. "Will you take the militia with you?"

Nora blinked. "We haven't gotten that far yet." She looked at Hatlin. "I'd like you to stay here with us and help us figure out a plan, if you're willing to."

He nodded slowly. "It's probably the safest place for me right now." He shifted his gaze to Eira. "If you allow it."

"He's trustworthy," Nora said. "I promise."

Eira examined him for a long moment, then asked, "Are you willing to work?"

"Of course."

"You may stay until the others leave." She addressed the whole group. "When will that be?"

Nora sighed. "I don't know. We have to figure out where we're going first. And how I'm supposed to dethrone a king." She let out a short laugh. "Minor details."

Eira tapped two fingers on her chin, a thoughtful expression on her face. "I wonder if we may help," she said. "The king's fallen soldiers give us the gift of guns and ammunition. We trogs must keep most of them for defense, but I will send some with you."

"That would be amazing," Nora said.

"I have one other resource in mind. First, I must ask: do any of you like to read?"

For the second time that night, Krey fairly jumped from his chair. "I do!"

"These are very old books."

Krey grinned. "Even better."

5

I met Prince Ulmin Abrios tonight.

Maybe before I tell you about him, I should go into detail about every dish the chef served us, or the beautiful palace, or the well-trained pack of caynins that roam the property.

I'm laughing now, because even with all the clommets separating us, I can hear you screaming at me to get on with it! So I'll skip ahead to the only details either of us care about. The prince is tall, with broad shoulders. He's nice looking, though nothing in his face made my heart beat faster than it was already beating.

Dinner went smoothly. I ate with the prince, his father, and the queen. They asked me questions about my life back home.

Then the prince took me to the garden, where we talked about whatever we wanted. We sat there for hours, covering topics from lysting to history to preday technology.

The longer we talked, the more attractive the prince became. Because, Dani . . . he's brilliant. I'm not sure if my heart's enraptured yet, but my mind is. No question.

We'll see each other again tomorrow. I've only got half a day to wait, but it feels like too long.

-Letter from Ambrel Kaulder to Dani Kaulder
Dated Centa 16, 180 PD

KREY HAD NEVER SEEN A MORE beautiful room.

Not the structure itself. That was unimpressive, with a low ceiling, white walls, and floors made of an ugly, gray preday material.

It was the room's contents that had Krey's heart thumping wildly. From his position at the bottom of the basement stairs, he took it in: a whole room of bookshelves, stocked full of preday books.

Four shelves faced him, with more disappearing into the basement's dark depths. He took slow, reverent steps down the center aisle. Later, he'd count the shelves, but now, he wanted to lose himself in the scents of the room. He drew in long, heady breaths of leather and other binding materials. Of millions of paper pages. He almost believed if he breathed in deeply enough, he'd hear the hushed voices of ancient people who'd huddled over these tomes.

Every book in here had been printed before The Day. That meant the vast majority were at least 250 years old. Very few paper books were printed in the final generations before the apocalypse, when nearly everything was digital.

Krey's aunts, Min and Evie, had spent decades curating the largest library of preday books in Cellerin. As Krey finally reached the room's far wall, he let out a low laugh. What would they think if they knew there was a collection several times that size in the basement of a nondescript trog building?

For that matter, what would book traders think if they knew? A stash of books like this could make a savvy trader incredibly wealthy. They'd probably end up selling a lot of the books to other rich people who wanted to show them off, not read them. Thank the stone the trogs had protected these treasures from such a fate.

Nora's hushed voice reached his ears. "This might be the most magical place I've ever seen."

Krey felt a grin take over his mouth as he turned slowly to face her—slowly because Eira had warned them that if they somehow dropped one of their lanterns and burned down the Star Clan's library, they should burn themselves up too, rather than face her fury.

At first, he'd wanted to come alone. He could think of few indulgences as tempting as solitary hours in a library. But the night before, when Eira had invited them to peruse the trogs' old books on warfare and politics, Nora had been nearly as excited as Krey. Now, seeing her wide, awe-filled eyes and gaping mouth, he was glad she'd come.

She pulled her eyes away from the books, meeting his gaze. "You're giving me a weird look."

"Oh . . . I'm just surprised, I guess. I didn't know you were this into books."

"I've always loved books. I just never liked my tutors. I'd check out big stacks of books from the palace library, and my tutors would tell me they weren't the *right* books. Then they'd force me to read their books, which were always boring. It was like they wanted me to hate reading."

"So why don't you?"

She grinned. "I found ways to read what I wanted to. I always had a novel in the bathroom. I spent so much time in there, all my tutors were convinced I had a digestive disorder."

Krey laughed, the sound bouncing off dusty pages and leather bindings. He almost told Nora about the night he'd set his blanket aflame reading by candlelight, but he forced himself to focus on why they were here. "Let's find the books Eira was telling us about."

"Which side did she say was nonfiction?" Nora asked.

"Left." He turned that direction. "She said we should look at the third and fourth shelves from the back."

Perhaps half an hour later, they'd set aside two tall stacks of books. "We need to find a place to read," Krey said.

Nora turned. "Why not stay here? It's cooler underground than it is outside. Besides, I'm not ready to go back to the real world yet."

"I'd stay here for the next month if I could, but do you really want to sit on this hard floor?"

"I saw a table in the back." Nora led him to a tiny table wedged into the corner of the room, with two stools tucked underneath.

"This'll work," Krey said.

"Perfect." Nora set her lantern on the table. "Let's figure out what we're reading first."

Krey carried his lantern back to their stacks of books. He and Nora each chose one, then returned to the table. When they were settled, he opened his book carefully, the feel of the ancient paper bringing immediate stillness to his heart.

Time always passed differently when he was reading. Minutes and hours lost meaning, replaced by the more pertinent measure of increased knowledge. As he read of ancient battles and machinations, Krey realized he was made to research this stuff. He'd always loved trying to figure out the *how* and *why* of magic. War and politics fed the same part of his mind.

Nora was just as engrossed as he was. Every once in a while, one of them stopped the other to share a particularly helpful passage. Krey focused on the big picture—how troops moved and governments formed. Nora picked up on the human side of things, like why people followed some leaders yet despised others and how war affected the civilian population.

Twice, they got in drawn-out debates about what they'd read, their raised voices devouring the library's hush. Each time, the argument peaked, then waned as they adjusted their views and met in the middle. They both seemed to realize they didn't have time for their usual stubbornness.

Krey finished his book—reading certain passages in depth and skimming others—and returned to the shelves. He stretched as he walked, working out the kinks he'd gotten from sitting in the same position for so long.

As he knelt next to the stacks of books they'd chosen, using the lantern light to peruse the titles on their spines, he found himself shaking his head. Nora was obviously smart, but he'd never seen her dive into learning like this. They'd been too busy fleeing and fighting. He'd had to leave his own passion for books behind temporarily. Now here he was, picking up that passion again—and finding that one of his new friends shared it. *That's pretty damn cool.*

He chose a book and returned to the table.

"About time," Nora said. She didn't look up, but Krey saw a smile playing on her lips.

"I was gone for maybe two minutes!"

"Hey, I'm not complaining. I can't expect you to be as devoted to this quest for knowledge as I am."

He smiled as he sat, not letting her rile him. "I like this side of you," he heard himself say.

She finally lifted her eyes from the page she was reading. "What, my sarcastic side?"

"No, I'm all too familiar with that." He laughed when she made a face at him. "I mean you diving into these books. I didn't know you were like that. It's—"

He halted, because the word that had been about to come out of his mouth was totally inappropriate. He'd been about to say, *It's hot.*

What the hell? Where did that come from?

"It's what?"

He recovered quickly. "It's a good quality for a future queen to have."

A soft smile stole over her mouth. "Thank you."

"Yeah, well, let's get back to it."

They returned to the old books, breaking occasionally to discuss topics such as weapons and taxes. Nora read aloud a chapter about advisors, and they got in a heated argument about whether Sharai was worth listening to. Realizing they were too far apart on that topic to compromise, they dropped it.

Krey was reading about the nuclear weapons in Anyari's distant past when Nora said, "I need to grab another book."

He looked up. "You've got sixty seconds. Since you're so devoted to this *quest for knowledge*."

"I'll be back in thirty."

True to her word, she returned to the table almost immediately. "Check out this cover. Have you ever seen anything like it?" She ran the tips of her long fingers over the embossed border of the book she'd chosen.

"That's beautiful," Krey said, admiring the intricate scrollwork.

"Feel it." She took his hand.

Krey froze.

Nora looked up, a questioning smile on her lips. "Feel it, Krey. The texture—after all these years, it's still so soft."

He nodded, letting her guide his hand onto the book. As soon as she'd put it in the right place, she let go.

He ran his fingers on the embossed area, but all he could think about was what her hand had felt like. It was warm and strong, her skin rougher than he would've expected—the result of months of bow hunting and shimshim cleaning, he supposed. Her fingers on his had felt good. Too good. What was wrong with him? Maybe the fumes from all the books were affecting his brain.

"It's great, right?" Nora said.

He cleared his throat. "Yeah."

Nora opened her book, and Krey forced his attention to the words in front of him. Before long, he was engrossed again.

At last, Nora closed the first book she'd picked up. "My eyes need a break."

Krey finished the paragraph he was reading, suddenly realizing how weary his own eyes were. He rubbed them, noted the page he was on, and closed the book. "I can't believe Eira showed us this place."

"It's a mark of trust," Nora said. "And, despite herself, I think she likes us."

Krey smirked. "I wouldn't go that far."

"Speaking of liking people . . ." Nora gave him a hesitant smile. "How are you doing? With Zeisha?"

"That," Krey said, "was the worst conversational segue I've ever heard."

Nora laughed. "I've been meaning to ask you, but there are always too many people around. So . . . any chance you two will get back together? You made a great couple."

His heart ached as he considered the question. He missed so much about Zeisha. Her unconditional love. The way she felt in his arms. Their history together—no one else knew him like she did.

All at once, his unsettling thoughts about Nora made sense. He wasn't interested in her; that would be ridiculous. He just missed Zeisha. He missed being loved.

"You're thinking pretty hard about my question," Nora said.

He shrugged. "I don't know. I hope there's still a chance." Needing to escape from her sympathetic gaze, he asked, "What about you and Ovrun? Everything going okay?"

The question did the trick; she swiveled her head to look at the wall, drawing her bottom lip between her teeth. After a long moment, she murmured, "I might be falling in love with him."

"That's great!" Krey said, unsure why he suddenly felt like he'd eaten something rancid. "Have you told him?"

"I said I might be. I'm not sure yet. And . . ." She swallowed, bringing her gaze back to Krey. "I don't know if I'm good for him."

"What do you mean? The guy idolizes you."

"Yeah." Another swallow. "That's the problem. I don't think he sees me or his future clearly. We've been happy in Deroga. But it's not like we're gonna stay here. And be honest, can you really see him living in a palace for the rest of his life?"

Still anxious to banish the strange effect Nora was having on him today, Krey nearly blurted that of course Ovrun would be happy living in the palace. But the words stuck in his throat. Ovrun had stood on a rooftop, telling Krey about his dream of living a peaceful, rural life. He couldn't experience that if he married a princess. With no idea how to answer her, Krey said, "You've known about Ovrun's dreams for a long time. Why is it bothering you now?"

Nora shook her head slowly. "You don't have a corner on being an ass, you know."

He raised an eyebrow. "What do you mean?"

"For the longest time, I didn't want to think about my future with Ovrun. I was too busy enjoying the present."

"Why does that make you an ass?"

"Because he kept trying to talk to me about the future, and I didn't want to listen. I didn't really care what he needed; I just wanted to have fun. And then . . ." She let out a long breath. "I started caring for him more, and his future started mattering to me. He's willing to give up his dreams, but I don't know if I can let him." Groaning, she rested an elbow on the table and propped her chin on one hand. "I don't know what to do, Krey."

He certainly didn't have any answers for her. "You're smart. You'll figure it out."

"That's not even sort of helpful."

He chuckled. "I know."

"I guess we should get back to reading." When he nodded, she dropped her gaze to her book.

Krey did the same. But the words were gibberish; he was too distracted. Why did his imagination keep fixating on Nora—on her passion for these books and the feel of her fingers on his hand? Was he really that desperate to fill the void Zeisha had left behind?

Zeisha. The woman I still love deeply. Just like Ovrun loves Nora.

By the orange sky above, what was wrong with him? One of his closest friends was madly in love with Nora. She was the definition of *unavailable*. And even if that weren't the case, Krey was certain of one thing. She deserved better than a brain eater who carried his addiction like a pack full of live explosives, ready to blow up his life again at any moment.

Zeisha, too, deserved better than him. But for some reason he'd never understand, when he'd eaten shimshim brains four months ago, she'd loved him through it all. Through his detox and the following difficult days. And while he'd never even tried to measure up to her absolute goodness, he knew one thing for sure: he'd made her happy.

Yes, she'd stepped back to consider her new role as the Anya. He'd tried to accept that. But now they'd both had almost two months to think things through. In that time, Krey had become sure of one thing: No one would ever love him the way Zeisha had.

An odd yearning filled his heart, and all at once, he knew what he had to do. He closed his book. "It's gotta be lunchtime by now." As if on cue, his stomach let out a growl that seemed to bounce off every book in the basement library.

Nora laughed. "Can we come back after we eat?"

Krey lifted his eyes to her, relieved to see her casual, friendly grin. Nothing had changed between them. "I'm gonna see if I can find Zeisha. Then I'll meet you back here."

Her smile softened, and she squeezed his shoulder, like a sister might do. "Good luck, Krey."

Zeisha was hard at work in a rooftop garden with Kebi, baking under the mid-afternoon sun.

"Hey," a voice called from above.

Her head snapped up. "Krey! You almost gave me a heart attack!"

He alighted between two rows of chinnin, an Anyarian grain the trogs used for most of their baking. "Sorry. I wanted to see if we could have lunch together, but I didn't realize how late it was until Nora and I left the library. I brought juice and bread, if you'd like a snack."

His eyes drifted to Kebi, who was kneeling, pulling weeds. Quietly, he said, "I was hoping you and I could talk alone."

Zeisha felt her mouth open, but sound didn't come out. She couldn't imagine what Krey might want to discuss. No, that wasn't true. She *could* imagine, and the intense look on his face supported her hunch. This was a conversation she didn't want to have.

But it was one she needed to have.

"Kebi, do you mind if I take a little break?" she asked.

"Of course not," Kebi said with a smile.

Zeisha led Krey across the big roof, past a line of bollaberry bushes. They sat facing each other in a patch of deep-brown soil. Krey pulled a small loaf of bread from his pack and split it between the two of them, then poured juice into two small cups.

Zeisha took a drink of the juice but merely picked at the bread's crust. "What did you want to discuss?"

He wasn't eating either. "Us."

"Our . . . friendship?"

He gave her a sad, helpless smile. "Zei. We're good together. And I'm not talking about friendship."

"We're better apart." The frankness of her words surprised her, but she didn't want to take them back.

"You really think that? Still?" He didn't give her time to respond. "You know what I think? I think we're both lonely, because we're meant to be together. I think deep down, we still love each other. And I *know* if we tried this thing again, you'd see that I'm different. I'll let you be whoever you need to be now. I'll support you, and I won't push you—"

"Are you really lonely?" Her quiet voice drove his words to a halt. "Or are you just afraid to move on?"

His blinking eyes and open mouth told her she'd hit on something true.

"Krey, I haven't given you any indication . . ." She didn't finish the thought, seeing the pain it elicited in his eyes. "Why are you bringing this up now?"

59

He crushed and twisted the bread in his hands, sending crumbs cascading to the soil. "You knew I was a brain eater from the beginning. And you never held it against me. Even when I went back to it. Maybe I'm just now realizing what a gift that was. You're a gift, and I'll never meet anyone else like you. I just . . . it seemed like a good time to tell you that."

There was something he wasn't saying, but it was no longer Zeisha's job to scrutinize his heart. He was right; she did still love him, but not in the same way she once had. If she pressed him to open up further, he might read too much into her concern.

At a loss for words, she found her gaze drifting over the berry bushes and settling on Kebi. As if the trog sensed it, her eyes lifted to meet Zeisha's. Her soft smile anchored Zeisha in the moment, taking the edge off her discomfort. Turning back to Krey, Zeisha said gently, "I don't know what's really going on with you, but you need to talk to someone about it. Maybe Ovrun."

Krey let out a sudden, harsh laugh. "I can't talk to him about this."

Zeisha narrowed her eyes but didn't press. She took a deep breath. "Krey, we're not getting back together."

He stiffened, a tinge of defensive anger entering his words. "You can't know that."

"I can, because I know myself." Her heart ached as she saw the pain on his face. "I'm sorry."

He crossed his arms and looked away again, sipping his juice.

"Whatever you're dealing with," Zeisha said, "I'm not the answer." She gave him a friendly smile. "But you're surrounded by supportive people. Maybe you could talk to Nora."

Again, a humorless laugh. "That won't work either."

She drained her small cup of juice, considering what she should say. At last, she spoke. "I know this isn't what you want to hear, but you'll find someone else."

"Why would someone else put up with my crap the way you did?" A strained smile stretched his lips, but she got the feeling it wasn't a joke.

"Because you're a good guy."

"How can you say that? After I went back to an addiction I'd promised to leave behind? I broke your trust!"

"You also left home to find me. You risked your life to save the militia, then Deroga. When you messed up, you worked hard to rebuild trust. You're a true friend—to me and Ovrun and Nora."

He blinked. "Thanks."

"I meant it. Every word."

"If that's the case . . ." His expression was all helpless desire. "Zeisha, please."

"It's time for both of us to figure out our lives. Separately."

"Okay," he said, though it clearly wasn't. "I . . . had to ask."

"I know." She handed him her cup.

With efficient hands, he put his bread, the jug of juice, and both cups back in his pack. "I should go."

Zeisha wanted to say something to make the moment less awkward, but what was she supposed to do? Give him false hope? When he stood, she did the same. "I'm glad you came."

Krey nodded and, without a word, ran toward the stair access at the center of the roof.

"Aren't you going to fly?" Zeisha asked.

"I need a good run."

Shaking her head, Zeisha watched him go. *What was that really all about?*

6

This morning, I went to an early chapel service with Uncle Quin. I have no idea what the clergywoman said. I was too excited to see the prince.

He picked me up mid-morning for a drive through some farms outside the city. To stay anonymous, we kept the carriage curtains closed. We had only one guard, who pulled double duty as our driver.

Ulmin—he told me to call him that—pointed out details through a gap in the curtains: an orchard where an elderly woman creates new hybrid fruit every year, fields that aren't producing as much as they should, an efficient new water pump design the monarchy funded.

He isn't just a prince; he's a twenty-year-old man who's preparing to be king. When his mother died six years ago, he became the heir. Queen Onna seems healthy, but nothing in life is certain. He has to be ready to rule at any moment.

I'm still not sure whether I want to be a queen. But after riding through the country with Ulmin today, I can tell you one thing: I'd trust my nation to his hands. He's a good, capable man. Whether or not I marry him, I'm glad to have met him.

-Letter from Ambrel Kaulder to Dani Kaulder
Dated Centa 17, 180 PD

———

SARZA CLIPPED the last wet garment to the clothesline. She returned the empty laundry basket to the workers rinsing clothes nearby and left without a word.

For over two months, ever since the battle for Deroga, she'd worked at the Star Clan's laundry house. She'd gladly taken on the job of hanging clothes out to dry. It was a solitary position, unlike washing or rinsing. Those workers kept up an annoying chatter all day.

Hanging clothes was boring, but it sure beat sitting in a high-rise building, watching the mundane lives of trogs below. That was what Sarza had done as a Cellerinian Army spy. Her superiors had left her in Deroga to gather information, never guessing she'd switch sides and defend the trogs.

Sarza had always been the solitary sort, but being truly alone, not speaking to another human for months, had nearly driven her mad. Working quietly all day, then joining others for dinner and conversation, was the perfect balance.

The problem was, her new routine was keeping her visions away. Her gift—or curse, or whatever it was—tended to be most active when life was unpredictable or stressful. Nora and the others needed Sarza's visions to resume. It had been nearly two weeks since Hatlin announced they should move to Cellerin City. They still had no idea how to safely relocate to a city that was occupied by the king's army.

For the last few days, Sarza had limited her sleep, hoping exhaustion would bring on some visions. It hadn't worked. She was in a prophetic drought.

Yawning, Sarza entered the small dining room used by those the trogs called *new-city folk*: Nora and her friends, the former magical militia, and now, Sarza and Hatlin. He and Zeisha were already sitting at a table. Sarza picked up a plate of food from the small kitchen and joined them.

"It's our resident seer!" Hatlin said with a wide smile.

Sarza flushed. Hatlin had a knack for making her feel like the whole world was looking at her.

Zeisha patted a paper-wrapped parcel she'd set on the table. "I got birthday bread for Nora. Ovrun's picking up some juice. You're staying to celebrate, right?"

"Sure," Sarza mumbled as she dug into her food. She still wasn't used to being treated like she was part of a group.

"Good. Wait 'til you see the bread. It's not a normal loaf."

Sarza swallowed, then cleared her throat. "I've seen it before, just not close up. I was here during your birthday party." She pointed at a stack of furniture in the corner of the room. "I was hiding back there. Spying on you." Her even voice didn't reflect the anxious twist in her gut. She hated reminding these people she'd watched their private moments. But she refused to lie about it. Let them reject her; she'd survive like she always had.

Zeisha let out a rueful laugh. "That was a very emotional day for me. I'm sorry you had to witness it."

Sarza stared at her. "Doesn't it piss you off? Knowing I spied on you?"

Zeisha's smile faded. "We've all done things we regret. All that matters is who we are now."

Zeisha was probably thinking about her time in the magical militia. Unable to form a response, Sarza focused on her food.

Hatlin stood. "Happy eighteenth birthday, Nora Abrios!" he boomed.

Every militia member in the room cheered as Nora, Krey, and Ovrun sat at the table, carrying full plates. Ovrun placed a jug of juice next to the birthday bread.

"Thanks so very much for announcing it to all of Deroga, Hatlin," Nora said, but she was smiling.

He spoke past a big bite of food. "Any time, Your Highness."

"Sorry we're late," Ovrun said. "I had to pick up these two intellectuals from the library. They lose all sense of time down there." He gave Nora an adoring look, which she returned.

When Hatlin finished eating, he propped his elbows on the table and addressed Krey and Nora. "You've been spending a lot of time in that library. You learning anything useful?"

Krey's eyes flicked briefly to Ovrun and Nora, then dropped to his food. "We haven't spent that much time there."

"Twenty-plus hours a week reading sounds like a lot of time to me!" Hatlin said. Eira had given Nora and Krey permission to work part time in their normal trog positions so they could research the rest of the week. "I'd be bored after the first fifteen minutes!"

Nora sighed. "I love being down there, but it's getting frustrating. Most of the information isn't applicable. The books were all written when Anyari's population was large and technologically advanced. The Cellerinian Army is nothing like the forces they had in the past. And then there's us." She gestured around the room. "Even if the militia members help us take down my father, we can't exactly call ourselves an army. Not to mention how different weapons were back then."

Krey looked up from his food. "We need to get to the capital. Then at least we can assess what's happening and come up with a plan." He turned to Sarza.

She spoke before he could. "No, I haven't had any visions today. I'm too . . . happy." She spoke the word with a sneer. "I'm pretty sure the best seers are tortured ones. Having the same routine every day doesn't help either."

"You need to shake things up," Ovrun said. "Why don't you

switch jobs each day? You can hunt with me one day, then work in the butcher shop or the bakery, then work with Zeisha in a garden or take a lookout shift with Krey."

Sarza nodded slowly. "That's a good idea. Well, all but the bakery. I can't work around stoves; I might fall into one if I have a vision." She let out a little laugh.

"That would be tragic," Nora said. "You might smash all the bread."

The table lit up with laughter, and Sarza even heard herself chuckle.

When they'd eaten, Zeisha unwrapped the birthday bread, and Nora's party began. Sarza ate her fair share and downed a cup of the weak wine trogs called *juice*.

They were the only ones left in the room when a crash of thunder interrupted their conversation. Seconds later, rain began hammering the roof. They all rushed to close the shutters.

"Guess we'll have to extend the party until we can walk back to our dorms," Krey said when they were back at the table. "We might be here all night."

Ovrun snorted. "You'd stay stuck inside because of a storm? C'mon, man, a little rain, a little mud . . . it's good for us! Connects us to nature."

Hatlin laughed loudly. "I'm guessing the princess disagrees."

Nora took Ovrun's hand and pulled his arm around her shoulders. "You can take Ovrun out of the outdoors, but you can't take the outdoors out of Ovrun." She grinned, though it looked a little strained. "As for me, I'd rather not have soggy shoes for the next two days, thank you very much."

"Better get used to being stuck inside, Ovrun!" Hatlin said, still chuckling. "One of these days, you might find yourself spending all your time in the palace, doing whatever kings do."

Silence fell over the table. Sarza's gaze found Ovrun, whose face had taken on a reddish tinge. Next to him, Nora was looking off to the side, her bottom lip clamped between her teeth.

"Uh . . . sorry," Hatlin said. "I thought you two . . . seems I spoke too soon."

"It's okay. Anyone want more juice?" Eyes fixed on the pitcher, Nora poured the rest of the juice. Conversation resumed. Before long, the group's laughter drowned out the rain.

Sarza sat back, again sensing she wasn't truly part of this group. They knew each other too well. Even Hatlin, a newcomer who was way older than the others, seemed to jump right back into things after a blunder that would've made Sarza want to crawl into a hole and die.

When they all drank a toast to Nora's official adulthood, Ovrun pulled the princess in for a kiss. Sarza's cheeks warmed. Her eyes found Krey, who was watching Zeisha with sad eyes.

The romantic drama was yet another way she didn't fit in. She didn't want any of that in her life. Not now, not ever.

Sarza stood and excused herself, muttering that she needed to pee. The others warned her she'd get wet outside, but she waved them off and walked into the storm.

In seconds, she was soaked. A block down the street, she stopped, raising her face to the pelting rain, hoping it would wash away her confusion. She would never have anything in common with the people in there. Why did they keep including her?

Because I have visions. The answer was obvious, and Sarza didn't know why she hadn't thought of it before. They were probably just putting up with her. What they needed was her gift, not her company. They'd keep her around as long as she was useful.

She squared her shoulders. At least they valued something about her. That was more than she'd gotten from anyone else. It would have to be enough.

Tomorrow, she'd talk to Eira about switching up her work schedule. And every night at dinner, she'd do her best to sit with her new group of peers and try not to consider them friends.

Flickering, amber light illuminated a few dozen faces of trogs and new-city folk. Despite the warm night, they were sitting around a campfire on a deserted Derogan street. *Not a bad way to spend an evening*, Sarza thought.

Conversations filled the air, but she wasn't listening to any of them. She was too busy thinking about how she'd spent her day. She'd hopped from job to job for a week. Today, she'd worked with one of the Star Clan's tailors, an old man who used few words to guide her as she assisted him.

And she'd loved it.

Sarza had done plenty of sewing, having grown up in an over-flowing household where no one ever had enough clothes, and the ones they did have constantly needed mending. She'd always been on the lookout for better ways to cut a sleeve or sew a button.

When the trog tailor had seen her expert mending skills, he'd handed her a bolt of woven fabric and asked if she could create a shirt. She'd spent most of the day on the project, needle flying. Tomorrow, she'd finish it. Staring into the fire, Sarza pondered how she might improve on the trogs' basic clothing patterns.

All at once, pressure filled her brain. She barely had time to announce, "I'm about to—" before her head flopped forward, and a vision began.

She saw herself in Deroga, working with the tailor, a stack of completed pieces on a table behind her. The scene faded gradually into another. She, Nora, Ovrun, and Krey walked down a snowy Derogan street.

That scene ended abruptly. Another began, just as suddenly. In the new vision, it was still summer. Sarza, Nora, Ovrun, Krey, and Hatlin stood atop a stark, stony hill, dawn light casting a peach haze over the land. A river, crossed by a bridge, flowed at the bottom of the hill. Straight irrigation canals fed water from the river to many clommets of farms, their fields covering the land as far as she could see.

The image faded, and Sarza jolted back to reality. Everyone from the last vision, plus Zeisha, had gathered around her.

"What did you see?" Nora asked eagerly.

"I saw two options," Sarza said slowly. "We can stay in Deroga, living peacefully for months on end."

"Or?" Krey pressed.

"Or . . . we can travel to an area of farmland outside Cellerin City." Sarza let her gaze wander to the flames again, drawing in a deep breath. Sometimes visions didn't tell her everything, but she usually got an urge afterward to help her make sense of it all.

"Farmland?" Nora asked.

"Don't say anything," Sarza said curtly, holding her hand up and closing her eyes. She rubbed her sore temples. A minute or two passed before she again looked at the group. "I believe we can safely stay at one of the farms."

Krey's mouth widened in a big smile. "That gets us a whole lot closer to the palace than we are now. It'll be much easier to act from there. When should we go?"

"In the vision, we all had hair about the same length as it is now, and it was still summer. So I'd say we should leave soon."

"You saw all of us?" Krey asked, leaning forward.

"All but Zeisha."

Zeisha nodded, like she'd known that would be the answer. Krey sat back, his expression indecipherable.

"Where exactly is this farm you're talking about?" Nora asked.

Sarza shrugged. "Somewhere near Cellerin City . . . but I'm not sure where. We'll need to travel at night. I saw us standing on a hill at dawn, overlooking more farms than I could count. Once we leave, I'm sure my urges can get us there. Hopefully I'll know more once we're on the hill."

Hatlin spoke for the first time since Sarza had pulled out of her vision. "I got one question."

"Yeah?"

"Do I have to ride a dragon there?"

Nora laughed aloud.

Sarza smirked. "A dragon would get us there faster . . . but I don't think we can all fit. I suppose you and Krey could fly on your own power."

"Thank the stone," Krey and Hatlin said in unison.

THE STONE EATER: 3

ULMIN LEANED back in the cushioned seat of the open-top steamcar, letting the morning breeze cool his skin. Sky above, it felt good to get out of the constant heat of the stone dome. His hair, which had grown shaggy, blew into his mouth. He spit it out and laughed aloud, turning to the guard who sat on the back seat next to him. "Feels great, doesn't it?"

The guard's expression was serene. Controlled. "Yes, Your Majesty."

The car sputtered a bit as it drove into Cellerin City. Ulmin made a mental note to bring in a mechanic to get it running smoothly again. He kept the car stored for months on end; perhaps he should take it out more often.

Sitting up straighter, Ulmin tapped the driver's shoulder. "Stop the car."

The driver obeyed. The royal guards surrounding the car brought their orsas to a halt.

Ulmin turned to the ranking guard. "I see soldiers on the street, but no people. Why is that? It's mid-morning; the city should be alive!"

The guard had the same peaceful, vacant expression as his colleague. "I don't know, Your Majesty."

"Bring a soldier here to talk to me."

The guard trotted off, returning quickly with a foot soldier. The woman bowed. Ulmin briefly considered controlling her, but he'd regretted doing so with the captain who visited his office. His palace staff had a healthy respect for him; they'd never disclose his mind magic. He couldn't trust a random soldier to have the same sense of loyalty.

"Thank you for your service," he told the woman.

"Of course, Your Majesty."

He gave her a friendly smile. "I'd expect to see citizens in the streets at this time of day. Where are they?"

She opened her mouth, closed it, and swallowed before croaking, "They—uh—they're afraid. Of the soldiers. We—we're not violent without cause, Your Majesty, we—"

He interrupted with a laugh. "A bit of fear is a healthy thing, don't you think? However, it's a glorious day! We're going to the Fern Street Chapel for this morning's service. Gather your fellow soldiers. Knock on doors. Bring the citizens of Cellerin City into the streets along our route. I want to see my people!"

The soldier saluted again, then ran off down the street.

Ulmin instructed his driver to wait. He took a moment to refuel, eating a tiny brain he'd stashed in his pocket. Several minutes later, citizens lined the street ahead. The steamcar rumbled forward, more slowly than before. As it approached the small crowd, cheers erupted. Ulmin stood, holding the seat in front of him, and waved at his people.

The rest of the drive was full of cheers and goodwill. By the time they reached the chapel, Ulmin's heart was lighter than it had been in months. The car came to a halt. Ulmin waited for his guards to dismount their orsas before stepping out. Surrounded by mind-controlled men and women who would die for him without a second thought, he confidently strode up the steps and into the chapel.

Three Cellerinian soldiers standing at the back came to attention as soon as they saw him.

The clergyman at the front was reading a passage from the Sacrex, the Rimorian book of scripture. When he raised his eyes and saw the small group at the back of the chapel, he stopped talking mid-sentence.

Ulmin laid a hand on the back of one of the guards in front of him. "Announce me, then let me see my people."

"His Majesty Ulmin Abrios, King of Cellerin!" the guard called. He stepped to the side, allowing the beaming king to view the attendees.

Ulmin's smile almost faltered when he counted only four families scattered through the large space. Shaking off his disappointment, he spoke. "I cannot tell you how happy I am to greet Cellerin City's most faithful. Please, continue the service."

The clergyman wrapped up in two minutes. Ulmin invited the service's attendees to come speak with him.

All was well until a man with three children, the smallest perhaps four years old, approached. The little boy looked up at his father through wide, thick-lashed eyes. "Daddy, will these soldiers hurt us?"

The father, who was lowering his hands after bowing, stiffened. "No, son, these are royal guards. The man in the middle is King Ulmin."

The boy met Ulmin's eyes, then turned back to his father and spoke in an audible whisper. "He looks like a bad man."

Had the words come from an adult or even an older child, Ulmin's vengeance would have been swift. More than ever these days, he understood the importance of enforcing unity in his land. But this was a little boy who knew no better. He simply needed to be taught.

Ulmin knelt. The boy drew back, bumping into his father's leg. "It's all right, son," Ulmin said, gently taking the boy's hand and his mind. He had to hold back a delighted laugh at the simple beauty he sensed in the child. "I'm a good man, and I'm here to protect my people. You'll be one of my most loyal citizens, won't you?"

"Yes." The boy nodded, his brown curls bouncing.

"I knew it." Ulmin squeezed the boy's hand and sent him a strong sense of loyalty, praying some of it penetrated deep enough to remain in that precious mind forever. After several lovely moments, he broke the connection.

The boy's little forehead wrinkled in confusion. "What happened?"

"You showed me what a delightful, loyal young man you are." Ulmin turned his attention to the father. "I know you'll continue to teach him to love God and serve his king."

"I will." The words sounded strained as they left the man's tight lips. "Thank you, Your Majesty. Thank you."

7

Yesterday, Ulmin told me he'd leave today for a week-long trip to New Therro. He surprised me by interrupting my breakfast to say goodbye. (*I wasn't in a robe—I learned my lesson the first time!*) We chatted in the living room for almost an hour before a royal guard told him it was time to go.

Ulmin wanted to kiss me; I know he did. I wanted it too. But the guard and Uncle Quin were watching, so he kissed one of my hands instead.

He'll only be gone a week, but I miss him already. Is that weird, Dani? Or pathetic?

Don't answer that.

-Letter from Ambrel Kaulder to Dani Kaulder
Dated Centa 18, 180 PD

"Want to dance?" Nora asked.

"Sure," Ovrun said.

"I was asking Zeisha."

Laughter flowed over their little table. Zeisha stood and joined Nora on the makeshift dance floor.

Nora figured it must be nearly midnight. Before long, it would be time to leave for whatever farmland Sarza had seen in her vision. Nora, Ovrun, Krey, and Zeisha were celebrating their last night together. They'd invited Sarza and Hatlin to join them, but both had declined. With just the four of them relaxing and laughing, it felt like the early days in Deroga, after the militia was freed.

Eira had heard of the plan and sent two musicians to play for them. The current song was a fast one. Nora and Zeisha made up their own dance moves, kicking and whirling until they were out of breath.

The two of them had grown fairly close as the weeks passed in Deroga. On the nights Nora didn't stay up too late in the library with Krey, she and Zeisha often spent hours whispering and laughing from their neighboring beds in the bunkhouse. She kept hoping her friend's joy would rub off on her.

The next song was slow. Nora took Zeisha's hands, and they swayed to the music, catching their breath. "I wanted a minute alone with you," Nora said, "to tell you how glad I am we became friends." She gestured with her chin toward Krey and Ovrun. "The guys are great, but . . . well, they're not the same. I'll miss you."

Zeisha dropped Nora's hands and drew her into a tight hug. "I'll miss you too."

Nora pulled back and gripped Zeisha's shoulders. "Will you be happy here?"

Zeisha smiled. "I will. It's my home."

"Good." Nora froze when she heard Osmius in her mind. A few seconds later, she said, "We have to leave soon. Osmius is on his way. Have you said goodbye to Krey?"

"No."

"Do you want to?"

Zeisha nodded.

"I'll send him over." Nora returned to the table. "Krey, Osmius will be here soon. You'd better fuel up if you haven't. And Zeisha wants to talk to you."

Krey nodded, pulling open his pack and retrieving a full bag of feathers.

"I'll get Hatlin and Sarza," Ovrun said, standing.

Krey walked to Zeisha, who was sitting at a table across the room. Nora knew she shouldn't watch them, but she couldn't help herself. She tried not to be too obvious about it.

Krey sat across from Zeisha, eating feathers as they spoke softly, their words drowned out by the continued music. When they both smiled, then laughed, Nora felt a relieved grin steal over her own face. The conversation ended with a long, tight hug. When they returned to Nora, they were laughing again.

"It's good to see the two of you . . . you know," Nora said.

Krey's brows drew together. "*Good to see us* what?"

Nora felt the skin on her cheeks grow warmer. "Being, uh . . ." She fumbled for the right words.

"He's messing with you, Nora," Zeisha said.

Krey smirked, a feather protruding from his lips.

"You're an ass," Nora said with a laugh.

They thanked the musicians, then went outside, where Hatlin and Sarza waited, along with Eira. The trog gathered them into a circle, then said, "You will always be members of the Star Clan."

Nora had expected a longer speech from the woman they'd worked with for months, but the simple statement turned out to be just what she needed to hear.

Eira lifted her hand. In the trog way, she touched fingertips with the five of them who'd soon depart.

They walked to the wide, deserted street where Osmius was waiting. After giving Zeisha another hug, Nora mounted the dragon, along with Sarza and Ovrun. It would be a leisurely trip, with Krey and Hatlin flying alongside Osmius and setting the pace.

"Fly toward Cellerin City," Sarza said. "I'll tell you any time I have an urge to change direction."

They lifted into the starry sky.

Hours later, they passed south of Cellerin City. Nora was chatting silently with Osmius when Sarza said, "We'll land on a hill, just ahead."

"How do you know?" Nora asked over her shoulder. "Can you see it?" In the bare light of predawn, details of the landscape below were impossible to make out.

"I just know. We need to descend now."

Sarza continued to shout directions until Osmius alighted atop a particular hill. Krey and Hatlin landed behind him. Nora, Sarza, and Ovrun dismounted onto the broad, rocky hilltop. The sound of a rushing river floated up to them.

"This is it," Sarza said. "Now, we wait until I get another urge or vision."

"How long do you think that'll take?" Krey asked.

"No idea. We'll be here at least until there's enough light for us to look at all the farms. That's what I saw us doing in my vision."

Hatlin passed out bread and fruit he'd carried in his pack, and they all began to eat.

Nora-human, Osmius said, *I must go. Once dawn arrives, people may see me.*

She handed her food to Ovrun and made her way back to Osmius's shadowy form, holding her arms in the air. He lowered his neck, and she wrapped her arms as far as she could around it.

I'll let you know where we end up, Nora said. *You do the same.*

Osmius had agreed to find a new den. His home in the mountains south of Deroga was too far away for telepathic communication. *You know where I will stay.*

He'd told her he planned to return to the cave where Taima had been held prisoner, but Nora had discouraged him from it. He was grieving enough already. *Osmius, are you sure—*

I am strong enough to face my memories.

Nora squeezed his neck tighter. *I know you are.* She released him, and he rose into the air.

Ovrun took Nora's hand and led her several dozen mets away from the others before sitting with her in a small patch of wiry grass. In comfortable silence, they ate the rest of their breakfast.

When they were done, Nora asked, "How do you feel about leaving Deroga?"

"The trogs were good to us, but you know I love getting away from all those tall buildings. Flying felt great." He pulled her tight into his side and kissed the top of her head. "This feels great too."

She lifted her chin and pressed her lips to his.

They sat silently for several minutes before she spoke again. "The palace is somewhere in that direction." She pointed north and slightly east. Right now, all they could see were patches of shadows that would turn into buildings, trees, and fields as the sun rose. "I've been think-ing," she said lazily, cuddling closer to Ovrun, "we'll have to build a new palace after we take down my father. I can't imagine dismantling that stone dome, and I'm certainly not planning to live inside it."

His chest vibrated with soft laughter. "That would pretty much be my definition of hell, being trapped under a stone ceiling all the time."

Nora pulled away. Ovrun's arm slid off her shoulder and down her back. She tried to see his features in the dim, gray light. "Some-times a palace does feel like a trap, Ovrun. Even with sunlight overhead."

His hand found her cheek and rested there, warm and solid. "You'll be there. It'll never feel like a trap."

They'd had similar conversations countless times since Ovrun had first told her he was willing to wear a crown. The offer was incredibly selfless. He'd always dreamed of living in the country, surrounded by nature—not living in a palace, surrounded by syco-phants. He claimed it was what he genuinely wanted to do. Why was it that the more he assured her, the less she believed him?

Nora snuggled into Ovrun's side again and shut her eyes. She'd dozed off when he murmured, "Look."

She followed his pointing finger, turning to the east. The sun was barely visible over the horizon. Nora stood and faced it. The sky was cloudless, which didn't make for a particularly beautiful sunrise. But the warmth and brightness brought calm to her spirit. She drew in deep breaths, imagining the light filling her up.

She didn't turn back to Ovrun until the sun was completely over the horizon. He was standing too, his gaze fixed on the land below. Past the river at the base of the hill sat countless farms with fields both lush and fallow, barns, and homes. Not all of the land was cleared. There were groupings of trees and even a few orchards. In the distance, she could barely make out a small vineyard.

Nora's eyes found Ovrun again. He was gazing at the rural land-scape with an expression she'd only ever seen directed at her.

Desire.

He wasn't looking at crops and buildings. He was looking at his dream.

As Nora watched him—the shoulders that could support a moun-tain; the eyes whose adoration she so often basked in; the tilt of his chin, which spoke of his longing for the open land—she came to two simultaneous realizations.

She loved Ovrun.

And he would never be happy at the palace.

She gaped at him, unable to breathe. Her body was frozen, but her mind sprinted ahead. *Why is this happening now? Maybe I'm just freaked out because we're moving. Maybe I'm just scared. Maybe—*

But the *maybes* were lies. She'd been avoiding the truth for months, and now it spread across her mind, as clear as the sunlit farms spreading across the landscape. *He's offering me a gift, but I can't accept it if it'll make him miserable. Especially not when I love him. I can't. I can't.*

Emotion built in her chest, bubbling like a boiling pot. All at once, her lungs drew in the air she'd been denying them. Her loud gasp broke the silence.

Nora's hand came to her mouth just as Ovrun spun to look at her, eyes wide. "What's wrong?"

She held her mouth tight as tears filled her eyes. Ovrun closed the distance between them and pulled her to his chest.

Nora refused to cry. They weren't alone, and by the sky, this was supposed to be a good day. They were looking for a farm to settle on, a home base from which they could bring down her father. She should be focused on strategizing, not relational insecurities.

But that look she'd seen in Ovrun's eyes had branded itself on her mind. *I can't do this right now!* she silently insisted. Quick, panicked breaths expanded and contracted her chest. With every inhale, she smelled Ovrun's distinct scent. With every exhale, she tried to expel her unwelcome emotions.

"Hey," Ovrun said softly. "Sit down. It's okay. Come on, let's sit." He guided her to the ground, not letting go of her.

Nora tried to slow her breaths, spitting out curses when she couldn't.

"Deep breaths," Ovrun said. "It's okay."

Footsteps approached. Nora buried her head deeper into Ovrun's shirt.

"She'll be okay," Ovrun said.

"What happened?" It was Krey's voice, soft and concerned.

"I don't know."

"Let me know if I can do anything." Krey's footsteps departed.

When Nora finally caught her breath, she sat up, eyes on the farms below.

Ovrun shifted to face her and took her hands, looking miserable. "What happened? What's wrong?"

Nora shook her head hard. "This is really not the time to talk about it."

"Seems like a good time to me. We're stuck here until Sarza tells us something."

"I—" Nora's throat tightened, but again, she refused to cry. "I don't want to talk with them here." She pulled one hand from Ovrun's and used her thumb to point over her shoulder.

"They can't hear us. They're way over there, and besides, the river is loud."

"I don't even know what to say!" Her breaths were coming too fast again. By the stone, there was never a good time to have a complete emotional breakdown, but this had to rank as the worst timing ever.

Ovrun chuckled softly. "I think we're past having to come up with perfect words, don't you? Just tell me what's going on." When she remained silent, his forehead wrinkled up. "Come on, Nora. You know I'm gonna worry about you until I know what's wrong."

That plea convinced her. She couldn't keep this inside. Bad timing or not, she couldn't suddenly lose her mind in front of Ovrun, then claim everything was fine.

"I saw you looking at the farms." She kept her voice quiet, though she knew the others couldn't hear a word she said.

He tilted his head, a confused smile pulling up one corner of his lips. "That made you panic?"

"Ovrun"—she ran her free hand through her hair—"I saw *how* you looked at them. It was the same way you look at me. That down there—that's the life you want to live. It always has been."

He laughed again, but it sounded awkward. "If you're saying I want a farm in the same way I want you . . . that's ridiculous, Nora."

She huffed. "Not in the same way. But you do want it. You wanted it for years before you met me." She let go of his hand, suddenly annoyed, though she wasn't sure why. Pulling her knees into her chest, she said, "Living at a palace would crush your dream. Don't you see that?"

"No!" A hint of anger hardened his face. "All I see is the girl I love. We've gone over this so many times! I don't need all that." His hand gestured emphatically toward the farms, but his eyes didn't leave her. "You're what I want more than anything."

Nora pulled her legs in tighter, drawing in deep breaths. Ovrun scooted closer and leaned his forehead against hers. He brought up one hand and cupped the back of her neck.

"You're what I want," he said again.

Her chest tightened. "I can't be the one to take your dream away."

"You're not. I'm just swapping one dream for a better one. That's my choice. I'll never regret it, I swear to you."

"I think you will," she whispered.

"Believe me." He pulled back far enough to meet her gaze. "I won't."

She pushed herself to her feet, welcoming the pounding of her heart and accompanying wave of anger. She shouldn't be forced to convince him of something he knew was true. At least, he'd know it if he were honest with himself. They'd gotten closer and closer on the premise that he could live happily as a king. And it had all been a lie —one he'd convinced himself of, then convinced her of. *We should've ended this thing months ago, the minute our feelings deepened.*

Ovrun's hand found her shoulder, and when she didn't turn toward him, he stepped around to face her. His muscular arms were crossed over his broad chest. Did he know how stupidly distracting he was when he stood like that? She was trying to think here. With her brain, not her hormones.

"I love you, Nora," he said, his voice low and tight. "I think you love me too. I think that scares you, and you're sabotaging this because you don't know what to do with those feelings."

"Seriously?" Nora flung her hands wide as she shouted the word.

Suddenly remembering where she was, she looked across the hill. Sure enough, Krey, Hatlin, and Sarza were all watching them.

She stomped off, descending the gradual slope until she couldn't see the others. Ovrun followed. They faced off, both breathing hard, crossed arms creating a double barrier between them.

"I do love you." Nora spat the words, regretting them as soon as she saw Ovrun's expression soften. When he unfolded his arms and reached for her, Nora held out both hands. "Please don't touch me—just listen."

Ovrun froze, eyeing her warily.

Nora gave up on keeping her voice quiet. "It's because I love you that I can't let you lose part of yourself! I've always known your dream to live in the country was important to you. I've spent a lot of time lately doubting whether you could actually be happy giving that up. And when I saw you over there, I realized—you can't. You think you can, but . . . that dream's too deep in you! It's not just going away!"

"So you're asking me to give you up instead of giving up my dream of living on a farm?" Now he'd raised his voice too.

"Ovrun, the palace will never meet your need to live peacefully in nature! But you can fall in love with another woman! Someone else can meet that need!"

He stepped closer and took her shoulders. Despite the fire in his eyes, his grip was gentle. "Why would I want another woman when I can have you?"

"And why would I want a man who isn't strong enough to stand up for what he really needs?"

Immediately, she knew she'd crossed a line, from anger to cruelty. He watched her, eyes wide. Then he turned away, but not fast enough to hide the pain twisting his mouth.

"Damn it," she muttered. She hadn't even meant what she'd said. At least she didn't think she had. But whether or not the attack was true, it had hit him like a bullet to the heart. Nothing else she'd said today had convinced him . . . but maybe those impulsive words would.

She almost ran after him and apologized, but she needed him to be angry. Otherwise, she might end up changing her mind. And staying with Ovrun would be even more cruel than the words she'd just spoken.

He walked halfway down the hill, then turned and trudged back toward her. Standing just out of reach, he studied her eyes. He must not have found what he wanted there, because his shoulders fell. "So that's it?"

Nora squeezed her eyes and lips shut, a wave of sorrow nearly knocking her down. She drew a harsh breath in through her nose, held it, and forced herself to look at him. "Yes."

His chin trembled, and tears filled his eyes.

It might've been the worst possible thing to do, but Nora couldn't help herself. She pulled him into her arms.

After several seconds, he returned the embrace.

Ovrun realized he was holding Nora so tightly, she was probably finding it hard to breathe. He loosened his grip a bit but didn't let go.

How had this happened? Their day had begun with so much promise, riding a dragon to find their next home. As the sun had risen, he'd found himself mesmerized by the beautiful fields and charming farmhouses. And yes, he'd briefly given in to the dream that tugged at his heart, imagining himself and Nora living in one of those homes, caring for the land and for each other.

She was part of his silly farm fantasy. Maybe he should've told her that. Except he knew it wouldn't make a difference. Because that particular dream couldn't come true. That was her whole point.

He understood what she was saying, but she didn't get it. A perfect little farm wouldn't truly be perfect without her there. He'd made his choice: she was more important than his other dreams. Why couldn't she believe that?

Tears ran down his cheeks, dampening Nora's hair. He drew in a deep breath, trying to contain his emotion.

Nora's arms loosened. He forced himself to let her go, then wiped his cheeks. She stepped away and turned her back to him. He watched the small movements of her shoulders as she breathed in and out. Without meaning to, he timed his breaths to hers.

"Are you two okay?" It was Krey, standing on the slope above them.

"Any word from Sarza?" Nora asked without looking up.

"Yeah," Krey said. "She knows which farm we're supposed to walk to."

Nora and Ovrun joined the others, avoiding Krey's and Hatlin's curious looks. Sarza, thank the sky, only had eyes for the landscape below.

"It's pretty far," the seer said, "so I'll point out some landmarks. See the farm with the white roof? Look to the west toward that orchard. Now look north . . ." She continued guiding them, finally saying, "You might have to squint, but there's a black roof and a red one next to it. See them?"

Ovrun's pulse sped up. Dread pooled in his gut. He blinked, trying to convince himself he was imagining things. Every moment, his certainty grew.

"That's where we're going?" Krey asked.

"Yeah. I don't know why they'll welcome us, but I think they will."

Not peeling his eyes away from the farm, Ovrun said, "Tell me this is a joke."

"I don't make many jokes," Sarza said.

"What's wrong?" Krey asked.

"I know that farm." Ovrun shook his head with a humorless laugh. "My ex lives there."

8

Happy Panyar Day! It'll take a couple of weeks for you to get this letter, but here, we're still celebrating the holiday. For the next fifteen minutes, anyway.

I hoped to experience Panyar Day in the capital, but last night, Uncle Quin informed me we were going to his cousin's farm. He saw my disappointment, but he just chuckled and said he was sure I'd have a good time.

I'll give credit to his cousin; he knows how to throw a party. The food was great, and the games were fun. After dark, a band played.

After dancing for a while, I walked to the drink table. I felt a tap on my shoulder and turned to see the broad shoulders and grinning mouth of the prince of Cellerin.

He held a finger to his lips and beckoned me to follow him behind the house. In a whisper, he told me he'd arranged with Uncle Quin to surprise me. We danced with no audience, pressed close together and swaying to our own rhythm, until someone finally came and found us. Then we danced with the others until the band went home.

-*Letter from Ambrel Kaulder to Dani Kaulder*
Dated Centa 25, 180 PD

"YOUR EX?" Krey stared at Ovrun, who was gritting his teeth, glaring into the distance.

Ovrun cursed.

Nora was watching Ovrun too, breathing quickly, her lips pressed together. "Is something going on?" Krey asked. "I mean, besides the obvious awkwardness of—"

"What's going on is," Ovrun interrupted, "we're walking to my ex's farm and asking her parents if we can stay there." Without looking at any of them, he started down the hill.

Sarza followed, muttering, "You're all way too emotional."

Hatlin went next, seeming unaffected by whatever was happening with the teenagers he'd been stuck with for three weeks.

Nora didn't move. Her eyes were locked on Ovrun.

Krey approached but stood far enough away to give her the space she seemed to need. "What the hell happened?" he asked softly.

She blinked, and the morning sun shone off a film of moisture in her eyes. "I told him I loved him."

"That's great!" Krey said, though his twisting gut disagreed. Their hours in the library had given him way too many opportunities to dwell on everything he liked about Nora. *I'm such an ass. SUCH an ass.*

She interrupted his self-flagellation. "I also broke up with him."

Krey's feet moved of their own accord, bringing him right up to her. Her words had sent a terrible lightness into his chest, a sense of hope he refused to embrace. *Ass. Ass. Ass.* "Why?"

"You know why." She turned her gaze to him. "I care too much about him to let him give up his dreams for me."

True sympathy squeezed his heart. *Better late than never.* Krey's feelings about Nora were all over the place, but he didn't want to see her and Ovrun in pain. "Damn it, Nora. I'm sorry."

She wrapped both arms around his waist, laying her head on his shoulder. Krey responded by instinct, returning her embrace, his arms firm around her shoulders.

She felt soft and warm and . . . *Oh by the ever-loving stone, this was a bad idea, but it's not like I can push her away.* He turned his mind to the most boring thing he could think of, calculating how many diced feathers he might still have in the pouch in his sleeve and in his backpack. *I've got at least twenty pieces left in my sleeve, and the pack is half full. I've never counted how many fit in there; that would be a good thing to know. I could calculate how many I use every quarter-hour on average. Then I could—*

Nora pulled away, wiping her eyes. "Thanks. I needed that."

I didn't, his flummoxed mind protested. He laid an awkward hand on her shoulder. "I really am sorry. It sucks."

She sniffled and pointed at Ovrun, Hatlin, and Sarza, who were at the bottom of the hill, approaching a bridge. "We better catch up."

Dreary exhaustion weighed down Nora's legs. Her eyes kept turning to Ovrun. He hadn't looked at her once as they walked from one farm to the next, staying far away from barns and homes. His shoulders were square, his steps sure. Did his heart ache with the same deep, sharp pain that was consuming her? Or had he somehow closed himself off from it?

Hatlin, Krey, and Sarza chatted a bit, but Nora didn't join in. It took all her energy just to keep moving. Every so often, she caught Krey watching her, concern compressing his brow. She tried to smile, but she knew it looked as fake as it was.

There were maybe twenty steps between her and Ovrun, but it might as well have been a thousand clommets. Nora couldn't stop thinking about what she'd said to him: *Why would I want a man who isn't strong enough to stand up for what he really needs?* The words sat in her belly, sharp and heavy. They'd fulfilled their purpose, pushing him away. She'd be lucky if he ever talked to her again. Would she take it back if she could?

She wasn't sure. And that made her feel even worse.

She fell behind the rest of the group. When Krey and Hatlin looked back to check on her, she waved them on. Walking with them would be nice. They'd distract her. Krey knew what was going on and would do his best to support her.

But drawing close to her friends would set her up for future disappointment. If there was one positive element of this eminently crappy morning, it was this: breaking up with Ovrun put everything in perspective. It erased her natural optimism, bringing stark clarity to all her relationships.

Ovrun wasn't the only person whose dreams didn't line up with hers. Once Nora was queen, everyone would leave. Krey would do something big, making his mark on the world. Hatlin would return to his New Therroan friends. Maybe Sarza would find work as a tailor.

Ovrun was the only one of them Nora had been depending on to stay at her side. And now she'd sent him away too. It had been a massively idiotic act . . . yet it was right. She was terribly certain of that.

She'd be alone once she was queen, so she'd better get used to it now.

After perhaps an hour of brisk walking, Ovrun pointed at the next farm and called, "It's that one." He turned to walk along the banks of a canal that bordered a green field. Ten minutes later, they stopped at a white fence surrounding an expansive, bright-yellow, single-story house.

Ovrun turned to face them, his eyes still avoiding Nora. "Wait here." He opened the gate, strode to the front door, and knocked.

A round-faced woman of medium height, with long, straight, brown hair pulled into a low ponytail, opened the door. "Ovrun!" she said, pulling him into a hug.

After a short conversation, he turned and beckoned his fellow travelers. There was a small smile on his lips, and Nora's shoulders relaxed a bit to see it.

The woman led them into the house, to a huge living room. "Come and sit, please."

A hint of unexpected peace stole over Nora's anxious mind when she entered the room. There were several couches and chairs, all made of dark-stained wood with cushions in a variety of bright colors. The white walls featured paintings of farms and animals. Dark beams ran across the ceiling between large skylights that covered the room in brightness. The floor's wooden planks matched the furniture and ceiling beams.

"Now this is a house!" Hatlin said, his voice bouncing off the walls and floor.

They all sat. Sarza looked around her with wide eyes, like she'd never been in a home this nice. Krey's gaze found a small, well-stocked bookshelf in the corner. Ovrun sat stiffly, watching the hallway the woman had walked down.

She soon returned, stopping at the room's entrance, her smile making the space even brighter. Someone was behind her, hidden in shadows. "I'm sorry, I forgot to introduce myself in the excitement. We haven't seen Ovrun in so long! I'm Varia. This is Joli." She looked over her shoulder, beckoning the other person closer.

The first time Ovrun had mentioned his ex to Nora was in Deroga's suburbs, at a warehouse he'd visited with Joli. Since then, they'd occasionally talked about her. *She's just part of his past*, Nora told herself. Then the truth punched her in the gut: *I'm part of his past now too.*

Joli stepped into the room. She was of average height, like her mom. Her wavy, medium-brown hair came to her shoulders. She looked like a farm girl in all the best ways. The sun had darkened her skin to a deep brown and painted her hair with lighter streaks of brown tinged with copper. Her sleeveless shirt and pants cut off at the knees showed off toned arms and legs. Joli was pretty, but more than that, she was remarkably cute, with a small nose and a nervous smile that highlighted the little gap between her front teeth.

"Ovrun," Joli said in a melodious voice, "it's good to see you."

Ovrun nodded at Joli, then returned his gaze to Varia. "Sorry to drop in like this. We, uh"—his eyes flitted to Sarza briefly—"didn't know we were coming here until this morning."

Varia's brow creased, but she didn't ask for clarification. "I'll get Tiam. Joli, make them feel welcome." She exited.

"I'll get water for everyone," Joli said. "I'm sure you're hot." Her eyes flitted to Ovrun, a blush darkening her cheeks. "From walking here, I mean." She hurried out of the room.

A few minutes later, she returned, holding a tray of mugs and a pitcher. At the same time, Varia entered with a man at her side. He was slightly shorter than his wife, with broad shoulders and hips and a full head of gray hair. His skin looked like leather, despite the wide-brimmed hat he carried that should've protected him from the sun.

Joli handed out the cups of water. She and her parents sat on an unoccupied sofa, her father settling with his thick arms crossed over his chest. His gray brows drew together over eyes that glared at Ovrun.

Just when I was thinking we were welcome here, Nora thought.

"This is my husband, Tiam," Varia said. "Ovrun, we'd love for you to introduce your friends."

"And tell us why you're here," Tiam said in a smooth tone that didn't match his rough exterior.

"Of course." Ovrun sat up straighter. "This is Hatlin, Sarza, Krey, and—" He gestured to Nora. "Uh . . ."

"You forgot her name?" Tiam asked, one of his thick brows rising.

Nora never knew if strangers would recognize her. Most people had never seen her in person, and the drawings of her in the newspaper weren't always the best quality. Through her teenage years, everyone had known her for her chin-length hair. It had been months since she'd gotten it cut, and it now hit her shoulders.

She wasn't sure why Ovrun was hesitant to introduce her, but someone needed to do it. Nora pasted on a professional smile and said, "My name is Nora Abrios."

She had to hold back a laugh when she saw the family's varied reactions. Varia went still, her only movement the rapid blinking of her eyes. Joli tensed, her mouth forming an O. And Tiam's eyebrows furrowed further, creating a single, bushy line.

"You brought royalty here?" Tiam said it like he was accusing Ovrun of bringing a fire-breathing dragon. Which Nora supposed was an option if this went badly enough.

"We heard the princess was missing," Varia said.

Nora's eyes didn't leave Tiam. Animosity covered him like a noxious cloud. If she told him the truth, he might turn her in, just because he hated her.

Or he might join her quest because he hated the king.

No one else seemed inclined to speak, so she took another chance. "I've been in hiding, but I'm returning to Cellerin City because my father has lost his mind, and I intend to take his crown. Our nation needs a new ruler."

Over the course of the next few seconds, Tiam transformed. He uncrossed his arms, and the sun-hardened skin of his face creased with a broad smile. "Well, why didn't you say so?" He stood and crossed to Nora, holding out his hand.

She rose and took it. His fingers crushed hers as he pumped her arm up and down. "Any enemy of that bastard is a friend of mine." He winked, slapping a hand on her shoulder. "No offense."

Nora didn't particularly like hearing her father called a bastard, but she couldn't entirely disagree with it either. "It's good to meet you."

Tiam returned to his seat and leaned forward, propping his elbows on his knees. "Tell us how we can help."

Sarza chewed a big bite of the casserole Varia had made for dinner. A sense of satisfaction—not an emotion she was used to—warmed her chest. They were here, with people who'd welcomed them and would help them, all because of her vision.

I guess there's something to be said for sharing my prophecies with others. Half a year ago, she'd never have thought that. Of course, half a year ago, she'd never have guessed she'd be staying in this big, fancy house, eating an amazing, home-cooked meal.

They hadn't even had to ask to stay here; Tiam and Varia had insisted. Joli still seemed a little nervous, probably because of her history with Ovrun. But once she'd gotten away from her ex, she'd loosened up. She'd been happy to show Sarza and Nora to the room they'd be sharing.

Sarza's jaw had dropped when they entered the bedroom. It was huge, big enough for at least six beds, though it only held two. When she'd taken a nap, it had been like resting on a cloud.

"Sarza, you should probably explain that part," Ovrun said.

Sarza looked up, eyes wide and mouth full. Every person at the table was watching her. She chewed quickly, scrambling to figure out what they were discussing. It was no use; the last thing she'd heard was Varia telling them all to dig in.

Krey rescued her. "Varia asked how we decided to come to their house."

Sarza swallowed, heat filling her cheeks. "Uh . . ." Her eyes found Nora, who nodded encouragingly. Okay, apparently they trusted these people. "I'm a seer."

"You can see the future?" Joli asked, her eyes bright. "That's incredible!"

A sarcastic laugh escaped Sarza's mouth. At this very table were two flyers and a girl who could talk to dragons. Getting headaches from annoying visions wasn't all that impressive. "I had a vision of a bunch of farms," she explained, "so we traveled here. Once we got to that big hill past the river, I got another vision where I saw your farm. I knew you'd help us."

"That must be so cool, seeing things in advance!" Joli said.

Sarza scowled. "Sometimes I pass out or have seizures during my visions. Afterwards, I usually feel sick. It's not all that great."

"Oh." Sympathy filled Joli's eyes. "I had no idea. Was it like that for seers in the past too?"

"I'd ask them if I could, but they're all dead."

"You haven't read any preday books on seers?" Nora asked.

"I've never even held a preday book."

Nora closed her eyes briefly. "Oh—right. Sorry."

Sarza returned her attention to her food, once again way too aware of how different she was from all these people. They had no idea what it was like, growing up as the weirdest child in a big, poor family. Nora was nice enough, but she was still a princess. Of course she'd forget that plenty of people didn't have access to preday books.

And Sarza wasn't about to tell them she could barely read. Her visions had distracted her from school, and she'd always been behind her peers. That was one of the reasons she'd been excited to join the army. They didn't care if it took her half a minute to sound out a long word; they were just glad she could use a knife and ride an orsa.

Tiam's voice broke the awkward silence. "We're glad your gift brought you here." He turned to the others. "What's our first step?"

Nora put down her fork. "Hatlin knows one of my father's former ministers. He wants us to meet with her. He thinks she'll help us."

Tiam frowned. "Because royal ministers are known for being so helpful?"

"Exactly!" Krey exclaimed. "I don't trust any of them, and I trust this one less than the rest."

"I wouldn't bring her here if I wasn't convinced her loyalties had changed," Hatlin said.

"Well, if she double-crosses us, I've got a nice, deep well we can drop her in," Tiam said with a feral grin. His words earned him laughter from most of the table and a gentle slap on the arm from his wife.

Sarza found herself laughing too. *I think I like this guy.*

9

Ulmin wants to see me every day. We agreed we should know each other well if we're considering marriage. (I hope if I keep writing that word, it'll start feeling natural. It's not working yet.)

We met for a private lunch today at the palace, between his meetings. We laughed so much during that short meal. About halfway through, I started noticing things: the muscles of Ulmin's arms beneath his rolled-up sleeves. A dimple in his cheek. And his dark eyes—I think I could look in their depths forever.

It's like he's a different person than he was when I first met him. But that was just ten days ago, so I suppose I'm the one that changed.

-Letter from Ambrel Kaulder to Dani Kaulder
Dated Centa 26, 180 PD

Krey woke to the smell of sausage cooking. The night before, they'd all agreed to work at the farm to pay for their room, board, and other necessities. Based on last night's dinner and the scent of breakfast, he thought they'd gotten the better end of the deal.

Before long, most of their group sat down to eat. Hatlin was gone, having ridden one of the family's orsas to Cellerin City well before sunrise. He hoped to connect with Sharai. When the meal ended, Tiam asked Joli to show the newcomers around the farm so they could choose where to work.

She led them toward a red barn, next to a black-roofed stable—the buildings Sarza had pointed out from afar. It was a gorgeous, mid-summer morning, sunny and warm.

"Who are the workers in the fields?" Sarza asked.

"They're from Cellerin City," Joli replied. "A few of them ride in on orsas every day, but most live in our bunkhouse." She pointed across their land to a long, single-story building.

"It looks like they're all dressed the same," Sarza said.

Krey squinted. Sure enough, they were all in gray pants and white shirts.

"Their jobs can get messy," Joli replied, "so we provide them with work clothes."

Sarza's brows rose, and she sounded almost eager. "Do you need a tailor? For sewing and mending the workers' clothes?"

Joli stopped, as did the others. "We hire it out to someone in the city. Do you sew?"

Sarza nodded.

"I'm sure you could take that job while you're here! Do you want to head back now and ask my mom? She usually has a stack of things that need to be mended."

Without a word, Sarza turned and strode back toward the house. The rest of them kept walking.

Joli showed them through the barn, where grains and grasses were stored for the animals. The stable next door held several orsas. Nora's expression had been tight with pain since her breakup the day before. She didn't look like she'd slept a bit. But when she saw the beasts, a grin overtook her face. She quickly got permission to enter a stall. Once inside, she hugged a dark-gray orsa's broad neck, burrowing her face into the soft, long hair at its chin. She spoke to the beast in a soothing, high-pitched tone, like she was talking to a baby.

Krey remembered her having a similar moment with her own orsa, Blue, when Krey had first arrived at the palace. He'd laughed then and nearly did the same now when he heard her croon, "My full name is Ulminora, but you can call me Nora."

His chuckle stuck in his chest, stopped by a certain tight warmth. Nora had never lacked passion—whether for bollaberry juice or Ovrun or her nation—but there was something incredibly sweet about her fervor for the animals she loved. She pulled her face out of the orsa's beard and let go of its neck. Her enthusiastic eyes and smile brightened the dim stable. "May I care for the orsas?"

Krey didn't hear Joli's reply. His entire attention was captured by Nora. Her eager smile. The grace of her tall form as she reached up, gently scratching the short fur between the orsa's ears. Her round hips that somehow lent a tempting shape to her simple drawstring pants. Her full lips, parted with a smile. Her dark eyes and soft skin. Even the scar on her cheek drew his gaze—a thin, pale line that would forever mark her as brave. Unstoppable.

By the sky, she was beautiful.

No. Krey almost said the word aloud. He pulled his eyes away, his mind racing. What was wrong with him? Nora wasn't beautiful; he would've noticed that before now.

Or would he have? When he'd first met her, all he'd seen was the arrogant princess he was determined to hate. She could've been the prettiest girl on Anyari, and he wouldn't have realized it. Anyway, Zeisha had been at the forefront of his mind. Krey hadn't had any attraction to spare. Eventually, Nora became a friend. A partner in crime. Not *Princess Nora* but *just plain Nora.*

Except she wasn't *plain.* She never had been; he realized that now.

His gaze drifted back to her. As she talked to Joli, Nora gathered her hair off her face, which shone with a thin layer of sweat. With quick hands, she tied it into a bun using a leather loop made of blue shimshim skin. The movement pulled her shirt up, and the smooth, narrow band of skin at her waist drew Krey's gaze like a magnet.

Stop it, he chided himself. He turned his entire body away to look at the orsas on the other side of the stable. . . then swiveled his head to find her again.

"Sounds good," Nora said. "Let's get going so we can see the rest of the farm." Her gaze shifted to Krey. "What?" she asked.

"What do you mean, what?" His mouth was suddenly dry.

"You looked like you wanted to say something."

"Oh no, I was just—you know how sometimes you look places, and you don't realize you're looking . . ." Heat rushed into his face, and he cursed inwardly, hoping the dimness in the stable covered his embarrassment. He couldn't remember the last time he'd blushed.

"Okay." Nora's eyes narrowed. Krey would give his left arm to know what she was thinking. But she just turned back toward the stall and murmured her goodbyes to the orsa.

As they exited, Krey's entire body filled with an odd buzz. He couldn't deny the truth.

She's gorgeous.

His shoulders fell as the immensity of the realization hit him. *What the hell am I supposed to do with that?*

The answer, clearly, was to ignore it. Yes, Nora was intelligent and funny and kind and driven and, it turned out, really, horrifyingly *pretty* . . . but she was still Ulminora Abrios, Cellerin's future queen. Who'd just gone through a breakup.

And I'm a brain lyster who can't be trusted to stay away from my dark fuel. We've all seen what happens when that type of person wears a crown. It was one thing for Zeisha to risk her future by trusting me. I'd never ask Nora to risk her nation.

Krey pushed away any further thoughts of Nora, forcing his

attention to their tour. His heartbeat gradually slowed as Joli led them through the grounds, telling them the farm's history.

They arrived at a wellhouse. A sizable pump covered the hole in the ground. There was no way to drop Minister Sharai down there if she betrayed them. *Damn it*, Krey thought, a grin playing with his lips.

When they'd seen the whole place, he offered to help a hired hand who cared for various grazing animals. Ovrun asked to join the field workers. His face lit up when Joli agreed.

How could Ovrun be so enthusiastic? Caring for animals all day wouldn't be the most exciting work, but Krey figured it would beat hoeing and harvesting. At least he could interact with animals. Crops were inexorably dull.

They returned to the house to report back to Joli's parents and put on work clothes, which they'd picked up from the dorms. Krey and Ovrun quickly changed and were about to go outside again when someone knocked on the front door. Varia opened it to reveal Hatlin.

"I'm surprised you rode back during the day," Krey said. Hatlin was a known member of the New Therroan resistance, and if he was recognized, he could be arrested.

"I was in a closed carriage."

"Who drove?" Krey asked.

Hatlin stepped aside to reveal someone standing behind him.

Krey had never stood this close to the woman, but he recognized her in an instant. The former Minister Sharai.

She was thin and tall, and everything about her spoke of expensive practicality. Her short, straight hair was cut well, her clothes perfectly tailored and free of unnecessary adornments. Painstakingly shaped eyebrows rose a smidge as her light-brown eyes examined Krey. She spoke to him through lips colored with a boring shade of mauve lipstick. "I believe you broke into my office."

Krey's voice was low, but he didn't try to hide his disgust. "I believe you enslaved my girlfriend."

Varia blinked, then managed a smile. "Please, come in."

Krey was so tense, he was surprised he could walk normally. He glared at Sharai the whole way to the living room. She'd sat in her comfortable palace office, organizing the magic-eater militia. Should he sit across the room from her to make his distaste abundantly clear, or should he take a spot next to her, letting her know she wouldn't get away with anything?

What kind of a question is that? He joined Sharai on the couch, mere simmets between them.

"I'll get Nora," Ovrun said.

"Sarza should be here too." Krey didn't take his eyes off Sharai. "She has good instincts. About people."

"I'll fetch her," Varia said.

Krey's aggressive stare didn't phase Sharai a bit. She returned it and spoke in a voice as cultured and practical as her garb. "You have good reason not to trust me. However, I saw what the king was becoming before he sent me away. I want him out of the palace as much as you and the princess do."

"I doubt that," Nora said dryly as she and Ovrun entered. Varia and Sarza were behind them.

Sharai stood. "Good morning, Your Highness." She performed the royal bow.

"None of that," Nora said. She fixed tired eyes on Sharai. "Let's all sit. I'd love to hear why I should believe anything you say."

As the others got settled, Krey propped an elbow on the arm of the sofa. "I'm looking forward to this."

Sharai didn't take her eyes off Nora. "Your Highness, I've been—"

"It's Nora," Nora interrupted.

"I've been looking forward to explaining my role in the militia to you. I knew you would want to know why I supported such a horrific experiment."

Krey released a loud sigh, rolling his eyes.

"My niece was one of the militia members," Sharai said.

Krey sat up straighter. "What?"

Attention still on Nora, Sharai said, "At first, I thought lysters were joining the militia willingly. When I learned differently, I spoke to the king, insisting he return the lysters to their homes. He assured me he would. The next day, he told me my niece had been transported to the training grounds in Deroga, and if I didn't keep my head down and my mouth shut, her family would never see her again."

"What's her name?" Krey asked, his voice hard.

"Vistmer."

"I remember her," Ovrun said.

"There aren't many New Therroan lysters," Nora said. "I find it hard to believe your niece happens to be one."

Sharai remained calm. "Her family lives in Cellerin City. Her mother isn't New Therroan, and she's a lyster."

"If that's true," Krey shot back, "it only gives her daughter a five percent chance of being a magic eater."

"Out of nine children, she's the only lyster."

Hatlin spoke up. "I asked around and confirmed as much of this story as I could. I wouldn't've brought her here otherwise. Sharai does have a brother with nine kids. One of them's named Vistmer. She's an ash eater, and she's been gone from home for about a year. Just up and left one day. Her parents heard she was in some apprenticeship program, but she hasn't contacted them in ten months."

"You didn't tell your brother the truth?" Nora asked, aghast.

Sharai expelled a short sigh, the first sign of her impatience with all the questioning. "If a group of angry New Therroans traveled to Deroga to pick up my niece, don't you think the king would find out? I'm not about to put her in danger like that. I told my brother that his daughter was safe."

Krey turned to Hatlin. "Why didn't you tell us this story?"

Hatlin opened his mouth, but Sharai was the one to speak. "I insisted on telling you myself. I knew the princess would want to see my face to determine if she believed me." She drew in a deep breath. "When I joined the king's staff nearly twenty years ago, I hoped to advocate for New Therroans. I worked my way up to the Minister of Lysting position, despite the fact that I am not a lyster. The king seemed to listen to me. He began negotiating with New Therro. Then his wife died, and he grew hard. He stopped negotiating. Eventually, he started this militia, and for the first time, I saw a truly cruel side of him. When he fired me and the rest of the ministers, I knew he'd lost his mind."

Nora's brows furrowed. "Didn't you suspect he was losing his mind when he started controlling the lysters in the militia?"

"He didn't control them directly. It was two other people, a general and The Overseer. I don't know who they were or how they did it."

Krey's jaw dropped for a moment, before he forced it closed. *She doesn't know Ulmin was the general.*

Nora's eyes briefly flitted to Krey. He could see the wheels of her brain turning as she considered Sharai's words. He shook his head, a plea for her to stay quiet.

She crossed her legs and turned to Sarza. "Any thoughts on whether we should work with Sharai?"

"I got nothing," Sarza said.

Nora addressed Sharai again. "We'd like to work with you, but there's a whole lot you don't know. And I'm not ready to share all of it with you. I need to spend more time with you first."

"Understandable," Sharai said.

"If it's okay with our hosts, I'd like you to live here with us." Nora glanced over at Varia, who nodded with a friendly smile.

"You want me to stay on a farm?" Sharai blurted.

Krey shot a broad grin her way. "You'll have to work too. Earn your keep."

"I have a home in Cellerin City—a life there!"

Nora stood. "Do you want to take my father down or not?"

Sharai came to her feet. "Of course I do."

"Well, if I can live with trogs for months on end, I'm pretty sure you can spend some time around orsas and crops."

Sharai's jaw muscles flexed, and she pressed her lips together.

"Very well. I have some things I need to retrieve from my house in the city—"

"I'm sure Hatlin would be happy to take your carriage and bring back anything you need," Nora said.

Krey almost laughed aloud when Sharai's lips twisted. Sure, she and Hatlin both had New Therroan heritage, but she clearly felt he was beneath her.

Sharai quickly recovered her professional demeanor. "If possible, I'd like to meet with you alone, Nora."

Krey fully expected her to refuse. She'd want him, Ovrun, and Sarza there for any discussions, right? They were all a team.

But Nora gave a brisk nod. "Very well. We can go to my bedroom." She led Sharai out of the room.

Krey shook off the unexpected sense of betrayal and returned his attention to the others in the room. Joli was sitting with her mother, as silent as they'd been during the conversation.

Hatlin smiled. "Not a likable woman, but I think she'll help us!"

Ovrun sat with his arms crossed, like he just wanted to leave—but that seemed to be his default position when he was around Joli or Nora. *No wonder he's so excited to spend all day in the fields.*

Krey stood. "I guess Ovrun and I should get to work."

"Hatlin," Joli said, "I can show you around since you weren't here earlier."

The four of them headed out. Joli and Hatlin went one direction, Krey and Ovrun the other. As soon as Joli was gone, Ovrun released a sigh, his body shedding its tension.

"Tell me about Joli," Krey said.

Ovrun held up his hands and shrugged. "What do you want to know?"

"Whatever you want to share."

"We met when I helped with their harvest one year. She liked me; I liked her; our parents approved. It was my first real relationship. Lasted a couple of years. I ended up working for them full time when I was done with school." A smile took over his mouth. "Sometimes we'd take the orsas out on a Sunday, telling our parents we were going to explore around Cellerin Mountain. Instead, we'd go to the Derogan suburbs."

Krey laughed. "Yeah, I remember the blankets you left behind. I'm sure Nora remembers that too."

Ovrun groaned. "What did I do to deserve being locked up in a house with my old ex and my new ex?"

Krey gestured at the fields they were walking through. "You're not exactly locked up."

"You know what I mean."

"Why did you and Joli break up?"

"I have no idea." Ovrun took a deep breath and let it out in a *whoosh*. "That's why things are still so weird between us. She just ended things one day. Told me she never wanted to see me again. At least Nora gave me a reason, even if it was a bad one."

Krey shook his head. "Sorry, man."

They soon separated, Krey heading toward a group of grazing animals and their keeper, Ovrun toward the field workers. His broad shoulders drooped, even as he walked through the fields he loved.

Nora settled in a chair next to the unlit fireplace in her room, staring at Sharai, who sat opposite her. The grief of yesterday's breakup had kept her up most of the night. Today, she was sleepy and achy, sadness and uncertainty weighing her down.

"You seem to have done well leading this little group," Sharai said, "but you're not a child anymore. It's time to act like an adult and a royal."

Ironically, Sharai's words and tone made Nora feel like a little kid. She shifted in her seat. "What do you mean?"

"First of all, when someone bows and calls you *Your Highness*, accept it."

Nora didn't respond.

Sharai continued, "You want to take the crown. Yet you've allied with a small-town boy, some girl whose opinion you seem to care about far too much, and a royal guard. How are they supposed to support you? Within your little group, Hatlin's your only useful ally. He's not very smart, but he has life experience, and between him and me, we may be able to bring the rest of the New Therroans onto your team. As for the others . . . if they can fight, great. If they can't, why are they your allies?"

Nora wasn't ready to disclose Sarza's ability, but she could certainly tell Sharai about Krey's head for strategy and Ovrun's strength and loyalty. Apparently her subconscious had a different idea, because she heard herself say, "They're my friends."

One of Sharai's brows lifted. "Rulers don't have friends. They have subjects."

The words were harsh. They also confirmed everything Nora had been thinking.

"I know it's not what you want to hear," Sharai said, "but the farther I moved up the ladder of power, the more I realized I was the only person I could depend on. Your father learned that a long time ago."

Nora shook her head. "I used to watch him interact with his staff and ministers, including you. He treated you as friends."

"On the surface, yes. But did he ever hesitate to fire someone if there was a mere whiff of disloyalty?"

Nora didn't answer, but she recalled staff who'd been there one day and gone the next, often with no explanation.

"Until recently," Sharai said, "he was skilled at making tough choices. That's because he kept his relationships with his subjects shallow. Becoming attached to those beneath him would've made it too difficult to do what was right for his kingdom."

Nora's mind was so terribly fuzzy after the day and night she'd suffered through. Staring at a knot on the wood floor, she tried to untangle the flurry of thoughts Sharai's words had brought to her mind. She'd always thought her father was simply hiding the toll that difficult decisions took on him. But had there ever truly been a toll? Maybe his friendliness had been nothing more than a way to engender loyalty.

And if his relationships with underlings had been fake, how had he truly seen his family? Nora was too weary to mull over her own fraught relationship with him, but his devotion to one person had been unquestionable. She met Sharai's gaze again and stated, "He loved my mother."

Sharai nodded slowly. "Perhaps. But that's not why he married her. Onna chose Ambrel as the future queen because she had money and magic. It's possible that your father and mother fell in love eventually. If so, they were lucky. Whatever their feelings for one another, however, he was always the heir. While your mother held the title of queen, she was his subordinate. I'm certain they were both constantly aware of that fact."

Nora's stomach twisted as she remembered public events at which her mother had bowed to her own husband. How must that have felt, bowing to the person she'd pledged her heart to?

"Nora." A smile that was genuinely kind came over Sharai's narrow face. "My desire isn't to be cruel. I only want to temper your expectations. Powerful people can't indulge in relationships like normal people can. But that doesn't mean you have to be alone. Surround yourself with loyal allies who understand what it means to rule. People who will use their own power to support you."

"People like you?"

"I hope so. And you can still utilize these friends of yours in the best ways possible, but remember—you'll be the only one wearing a crown. Do you know who you should trust the most?"

"Who?"

"Those who have something to gain from your victory. No one truly fights for others. We all fight for ourselves."

Nora felt she'd lost control of this conversation—if she'd ever had it. Sharai could be a powerful ally, but Nora wouldn't allow herself to be a puppet. She lifted her chin and hardened her voice. "What do you have to gain by helping me, Sharai?"

Eyes sharp, Sharai replied, "A position of power when you are queen."

The forthrightness of the request felt surprisingly comforting. Safe. Sharai wasn't here to make her feel good. She was offering a business transaction. With all the unwelcome emotions coloring Nora's other relationships, maybe an honest, straightforward alliance was just what she needed. Sharai didn't have to be likable to be loyal.

Nora took a deep breath. "If you support me in my quest for the crown, I'll give you a significant role in my government."

Sharai smiled. "I won't claim to be your friend, Your Highness. Instead, I'll swear this to you: I will do everything in my power to ensure you become queen." She held out her hand for Nora to shake.

Nora almost took it. But there was an intensity in Sharai's eyes. This was a test. Nora stared pointedly at the proffered hand, then brought her derisive gaze up to Sharai's face.

Sharai laughed. "Well done, Your Highness." She held out her hands and bowed, keeping her head down.

"You may go." They were the words of a monarch. Maybe one day such phrases would feel natural.

When Sharai was gone, Nora flopped onto her bed and stared at the ceiling. Sharai's viewpoint was cynical and harshly pragmatic. It was also realistic. The former minister wanted justice for her niece and power for herself. Nora wanted Sharai's experience. They could help each other get where they needed to be. It wasn't pretty, but at least Nora knew what to expect from the relationship.

Months ago, she'd been desperate for friends. Ovrun and Krey had filled that need. Later, Zeisha, then Sarza, had come into her life. It had been nice, feeling like she could finally relate to a group of peers. But at some level, hadn't she always known none of it would last? Even when she'd dreamed of Ovrun wearing a crown at her side, something deep inside had warned her it would never happen.

By the stone, she missed him. They'd only broken up yesterday, but the distance already yawned like a canyon between them. She hadn't yet indulged in a good, long cry.

And I can't. I need to move on, not wallow.

A leader had to be strong. There was a reason the most powerful people often lived lives of relational solitude, even when they were surrounded by others. How could a king or queen have a true, equal relationship with anyone? In the future—the near future, Nora hoped —everyone in Cellerin would be her subject. Even her husband, once she had one.

"I'd better get used to it now," Nora murmured. Her throat tightened, but she refused to let tears form.

THE STONE EATER: 4

ULMIN STROLLED across the palace lawn. Not that it could really be called a *lawn* anymore; it was nothing but dirt and dead grass. The dome's small vents let in a bit of sunshine, but it wasn't enough to keep vegetation alive. Electric lampposts scattered through the property illuminated sick and rotting plants. Mold and other fungi proliferated everywhere, giving the grounds a cloying, sickly odor.

He circled wide around the pond in the middle of the property, unwilling to get too close. The stagnant water smelled terrible these days. A guard had taken all the dackas off the pond weeks ago and released them outside the dome. The poor birds, who'd lived on that pond for decades, had been wasting away to nothing.

It's all worth it, Ulmin reminded himself as he looked directly above him. The electric lamps throughout the property didn't provide enough light for him to see the stone overhead. But he sensed its solid, comforting weight. Yes, he was sweating through his third set of clothes today, but he was safe. Who could put a price on that?

The walk to the palace chapel, which sat close to the property's entrance, felt three times as long as usual. He looked forward to wintering within the dome's warmth, but right now, summer seemed interminable. The heat made him terribly weary. His hand slipped in his pocket, emerging with three small shimshim brains. A minute later, they were in his belly. A smile tugged at his lips. This place was still sweltering, but his strength had returned.

When he stopped at the chapel door and ran his fingers along the eight-pointed metal Rimstar adorning it, deep serenity filled his heart. He entered and walked down a dark hallway toward the chapel's main room. Before he reached the door, it opened.

"Oh, Your Majesty!" The room's light illuminated Emissary Loryn's tight, gray curls as she bowed. Ulmin had been a teenager when she'd taken this assignment, and he continually marveled that she was still so spry. "I didn't hear you come in," she said.

"Care to join me in the chapel?"

"Of course." They entered the small chapel, which was lit by twenty electric bulbs. This was Ulmin's favorite place; it had to be perfect. Light was an important element in the design of every Rimorian chapel. The sun no longer shone through the expansive skylights, but electric lights were a decent substitute.

They sat in adjacent chairs in the chapel's front row. Before Ulmin had created his dome, the chapel would've been full of tourists at this time of day. He smiled at the emissary. "It's lovely being able to worship alone any time of day."

"I know you enjoy that," she murmured. "But . . . Your Majesty . . . I'm an emissary. There are only twenty of us throughout the world. Pardon my frankness, but I should be serving more of the faithful, rather than just you."

Ulmin only controlled Emissary Loryn's mind often enough to ensure she remained loyal to him. Perhaps he'd given her too much free rein. Keeping his voice level, he said, "You serve the other members of the palace staff as well."

"I do, the few who choose to worship here. But the stone . . ." She hesitated, gesturing to the small stage. Atop a wide pedestal was a thick, glass case enclosing the deep-black, broken stone that had caused Anyari's apocalypse and brought magic into the world. Every interior facet of the stone glowed with a luminous, orange light. It had broken apart along those seams after archeologists unearthed it two hundred years ago. The emissary took a deep breath and continued, "The stone belongs to the entire world, does it not?"

"In a spiritual sense, yes," Ulmin said. "But in a physical sense, it belongs to Cellerin." *To me*, he added silently.

The emissary looked troubled, but she didn't protest any further.

Ulmin smiled. "Let's talk. Really talk."

Hesitation tightened the muscles of her face. She knew about her king's faculty; everyone here did. It was pointless to resist.

Ulmin established a mental connection. "Emissary Loryn, will you ever stop obeying me?"

"No," she said, her face and tone free of guile.

Ulmin beamed. Controlled minds were incomparably beautiful. "I have shared confidences with you. Have you ever spoken of them to anyone?"

"No."

He let go of her mind, and his eyes rose to the stone. "I would like to worship."

Her shoulders drooped just a bit. "Yes, Your Majesty."

10

Ulmin dined with us tonight. He was an hour late, and he apologized profusely. He'd gotten stuck in a meeting with the Board of Ministers. Throughout dinner, he was clearly distracted.

After dessert, he and I escaped to the back porch. We discussed his meeting. I learned that, while the queen has the final say in all major decisions, she's committed to following her ministers' guidance as much as possible. It's a good policy, but it results in some long, intense debates.

As we talked, Ulmin became more and more relaxed. Within half an hour, he was almost carefree. Before he left, he whispered, "You're good for me, Ambrel."

Still no kiss. But I'm savoring his words.

-Letter from Ambrel Kaulder to Dani Kaulder
Dated Centa 27, 180 PD

NORA LIFTED and lowered the pump handle over the tub. She and Sarza shared this bathroom with Krey and Ovrun. *And Hatlin,* she reminded herself. He'd given his room to Sharai.

Growing up, Nora had enjoyed water—hot or cold—at the turn of a tap. A year ago, she would've whined if she'd been forced to tire her arm out with a pump every time she wanted to bathe.

Deroga had changed all that. There, she'd cringed each time she used a community bathhouse or outhouse. A hand-operated water pump was a huge step up. Not to mention the house's electric lights, powered by windmills.

She finished pumping and sank into the lukewarm water, basking in the glow of the amber bulb overhead. Nothing felt better than a bath after a day of hard work.

She'd spent time with orsas all her life. Never before had she realized what a chore it was to care for them. They were big, muscular, grain-eating animals. While they could travel long distances without sustenance, they expected astonishing quantities of food and water while stabled. Nora had been glad to see a bin of grain in the stable, but halfway through the day, she had to refill it from the stores in the barn. Thankfully, the pump in the stable provided easy access to water . . . which was used not only for the drinking troughs, but for cleaning the stinky stalls too. And then there were the grooming tasks. It had been a busy day.

At least she hadn't worked alone. A hired hand taught her the ropes in the morning, and Sharai worked with her all day. The former minister had wrinkled her nose at the idea of mucking out stalls, but she'd done her part.

Nora had hoped that, between the hard work and the company, she'd have plenty to distract her from her constant memories of Ovrun. It had worked, sort of. Her weary sadness remained, but she'd managed to shove it down. Over and over.

Now, as she washed grime from her body and hair, unshed tears pressed at her throat and seemed to weigh down her limbs and chest. After her exhausting day, she no longer had the strength to suppress them. Her chest shuddered with sobs, and she buried her face in her hands. All too aware of the bedrooms on either side of the bathroom, she tried to remain silent. Nonetheless, a few low cries forced themselves from her mouth, muffled by her wet palms.

Nora's mind insisted on dredging up memory after memory—of Ovrun's laughter, his adoring words, the way he'd taught her to hunt and skin shimshims. She relived their few fights and many kisses. At last, her tears stopped flowing.

Her body was even wearier than before, but it felt lighter, emptied of the emotions she'd been holding back. She sat up and quickly finished washing. Others were waiting for the bathroom.

Too tired to keep torturing herself with thoughts of Ovrun, she made a purposeful shift, reflecting on her conversations with Sharai throughout the day. They'd gotten along surprisingly well. The woman's experience with governing gave Nora a perspective none of her friends had.

In all the topics they covered, Sharai kept coming back to one point: "Utilize your companions and their skills."

The wording of it made Nora squirm. *Utilize* sounded remarkably like *use*. "I don't want to use my friends. Or future subjects. Or whatever they are," she'd replied.

"They're with you for a reason," Sharai had said. "They believe in your cause. You're not using them if they want to help you."

Nora had nodded, as she was doing now, remembering the words. She continued to mull them over as she dried off and put on a set of loose trog clothes.

She knocked on the door that led to the guys' room. Ovrun opened it. His eyes took in her wet hair, then the rest of her, before darting away.

She hadn't realized until this moment how much she missed his hungry gaze. "Tub's all yours," she said quietly.

"Thanks."

She paused. Krey was at the desk in the corner of the room, dicing up feathers. Eira had let him borrow a few carefully wrapped books from the library in Deroga. When Nora had told Sharai about their reading sessions, the woman had rolled her eyes. "The information's too dated," she'd said. "It's a waste of time."

But standing in this doorway, Nora was overwhelmed with a craving for crisp pages and soft leather—and maybe for time with a friend, though she knew that was a weakness she shouldn't indulge. "Krey?"

He looked up. "Yeah?"

"We've got about an hour before dinner. Do you want to read?"

His brows leapt up in a way that made him look like a kid. "Sure! Come on in!"

Ovrun stepped to the side, letting Nora enter the bedroom. He grabbed clean clothes and exited.

Krey put away his feathers, then brought a leather-wrapped bundle to the desk. He pulled up an extra chair but didn't sit as he unwrapped the books, grinning. "I've been dying to get back to these." He looked up, and his smile faltered. "Your eyes are all red and swollen."

Nora looked away. "You're always so tactful."

She expected teasing in response, but Krey's voice was gentle. "I know it's hard, and I won't insult you by asking if you're okay. I'm sorry you're not."

She lifted her gaze to his. "Tell me it gets easier."

He swallowed and sat. "I still miss Zeisha. But yeah. It's been well over three months. It's a hell of a lot easier." His eyes searched her face, then shifted away, fixing on the books in front of them.

Nora picked up a volume. "I've been looking forward to getting back to these too." She closed her eyes, holding the book to her nose and breathing in the old, comforting scent. Her fingertips glided across the soft binding.

"Feels like we're back in that trog library, right?" Krey's voice was almost reverent.

Warmth filled Nora. Krey was right; the books brought back the comforting thrill she'd gotten every time they'd been in the basement library. She'd loved the hours they'd spent there together. And just now, when he'd said it would get easier . . . for the first time today, she hadn't felt alone. Part of her wanted to marinate in that sensation of belonging, but she couldn't. *Rulers don't have friends. They have subjects.*

Time to focus on what mattered. These texts might hold the key to bringing down her father. "We don't have long. Let's get started." She glanced up.

Krey was watching her, an intense, unreadable look in his eyes. But she didn't have more than a half second to wonder at his expression. He shifted his gaze to his book, mumbling something unintelligible.

For nearly an hour, they didn't say a word. Nora lost herself in the books, which proved a better distraction from her grief than orsas and Sharai had been. She'd just looked up at the clock on the wall, noting that dinner would start soon, when Krey spoke.

"I know we've talked a lot about how different war was in preday times."

"Yeah, I was just reading about how to supply an army of half a million soldiers. We'll never need that information." Nora stretched her arms high above her head.

Krey's indecipherable gaze remained on her for a couple of seconds before he dropped it to his book. "Exactly." He cleared his throat. "But there's one thing I've read over and over. I don't know why it didn't sink in until now."

"What?"

He read from the book he'd chosen. " 'Short-term victories can be gained quite easily with skilled forces, strategy, and a bit of luck. In the long term, however, power can only be held through coalitions.' " He returned his eyes to Nora. "We might be able to bring down your father without a big army. But what then? Remember what Sarza said on the day of the battle for Deroga? When she told you not to take your father's crown?"

Nora nodded. "She said Cellerin wasn't ready to accept me as their leader."

"Right. They weren't ready then. And they probably aren't now. But if we can pull together a large coalition of people who support you, we can change that."

His confidence sent Nora's heart racing. This was why she needed Krey on her side. He had a head for strategy and could see the big picture instead of getting mired in details. She gave him an excited grin. "This fits perfectly with what Sharai and I have been talking about!"

Krey's jaw tightened. "I literally couldn't care less what that woman says."

"Well, you should care, because she's thinking the same thing you are. She hasn't mentioned a large coalition like you're talking about" —she noted Krey's satisfied smirk—"but she's been telling me to ally with people who feel like it's in their best interest to support me. So who should we start with?"

He shifted in his seat to face her, leaning forward. "We've made a good start with Joli's family. Her father despises the king. With Hatlin on our side, maybe we can bring in more New Therroans who live in Cellerin City. Plus, if there's any way to contact the rebels who live in New Therro, they might help."

Nora leaned in too. "What about the militia? They have great motivation to fight my father."

"I've always hoped they'd join us," Krey said. "But it's hard to plan anything involving them when they're in Deroga, and there's no room for them to stay here. Maybe we'll find a way to work with them, but we have to think bigger than a militia and some New Therroan dissidents. People all over Cellerin need to support you before you take the crown." Krey looked at the clock. "It's dinnertime. Let's discuss it with Tiam and Hatlin, see if they have any ideas."

"And Sharai," Nora said.

"Nora—"

"She's giving me solid advice, Krey. And you heard her story about her niece. I'm not saying we should tell her everything; I don't know her well enough to trust her fully. But I have a good feeling about her."

Krey raised an eyebrow and sighed. "I don't trust her even a little, but I do trust you. Do whatever you think is best, just be smart about it."

"I usually am," she said, arching a brow to mirror his.

"You are."

Nora waited for him to amend his statement with a sarcastic quip, but he just fixed his eyes on hers and asked, "You okay?"

Grief tightened her chest again. "I am. Or I will be, eventually."

He nodded. "You will. Let's go to dinner."

Working on the farm all day had been exhausting, but reading and talking with Nora had renewed Krey's energy. His stomach growled as he sat at the dining table. Varia had told them that dinner at the farm was usually late. Tiam often didn't finish his rounds until after dark. The burly farmer took his place at the head of the large table, and they all filled their plates with salad; fork-tender meat covered in gravy; and warm, brown bread speckled with crunchy seeds.

Krey's eyes shifted to Ovrun. His plate was full, but he wasn't touching his food. The former royal guard glanced at Nora, then away from her, pressing his lips together and looking at his hands.

When they'd all been eating for a few minutes, Nora put down her fork and addressed the farmer at the head of the table. "I have a question for you, Tiam. You haven't hidden your feelings about the king. We all share them to some extent—though I'll admit, mine are probably more mixed than anyone else's. But I'd like to know why you feel so strongly."

"Happy to tell you." Everyone at the table was listening, but

Tiam spoke directly to Nora. "My family's farmed this land for generations. Since long before your great-grandmother became queen. I remember my grandmother telling me how scared they were to have a monarch. But it didn't take long for Onna to prove herself to us. The previous government had gotten bloated. Expensive to run. She changed all that, even lowered our taxes. Your father was the same. Until . . ." He pressed his lips together in a little frown, and Krey knew what Tiam would say. "Until your mother died."

Krey's gaze darted to Nora. She was nodding slowly, eyes still fixed on Tiam. "What changed?"

"Before that, he cared about farmers. He'd travel around and meet with us. He made sure the roads and canals were in good repair and that our pumps were working. When the queen passed, we didn't see much of Ulmin for a while. Then he started coming around again, and he was friendly as ever. Only he didn't keep as many of his promises. Sometimes we had to pay to repair our canals, even though the government's supposed to do that. Then taxes started creeping up. My farm, it's big enough, and our ground has always been fertile. We do okay, even when it's tight. But a lot of my good friends, people with smaller farms . . ."

"They've suffered," Nora said.

"They have. And I understand what it is to lose someone, I do. But, well . . . it's been eleven years. When you get disappointed by a leader day after day, year after year, when you see your friends selling their farms because they can't afford to stay there, well, you get angry."

"I'm sorry," Nora said. "I should've seen all that, and I just—"

"Why should you have seen it? I told you, he's friendly as ever. I'm sure that's the only side of him you ever saw. You're barely more than a kid; I wouldn't expect you to know the ins and outs of how your father is ruling."

"I didn't see any of that either," Sharai said. "I was busy organizing lyster apprenticeships and trainings."

Krey's head began to feel light. Throughout the conversation, his

chest had gotten tighter and tighter. Farmers weren't the only people
the king had forgotten about after his wife died. When Krey was ten
and the orange plague ravaged Cellerin, his parents had died because
the king had refused to send antibiotics to Tirra, their hometown.
Until now, Krey had never connected that heartless act to the king's
grief and addiction.

Nora met his gaze. A wrinkle appeared in the skin between her
eyes, and she gave him a small nod. He got the feeling she somehow
knew what he was pondering. He looked at his plate, drawing in a
deep, slow breath.

"I've told you my story." Tiam continued to direct his words to
Nora. "Now I have two questions for you."

"Yes?"

"Will you rule like your father used to or like he does now?"

Nora didn't hesitate. "Like he used to. I swear it."

Tiam watched her, his gaze incisive, for several seconds. Then he
held out his arms and lowered his head in a bow.

Nora didn't stop him. She simply nodded when he met her gaze
again.

"I'll follow you," Tiam said. "I feel confident my family will too."

Varia and Joli nodded.

"What's the second question?" Nora asked.

"Pretty much the same one you asked me. Why did you turn
against your father?" When Nora didn't answer, he said, "I know it
has something to do with this militia you mentioned, but there's obviously plenty you haven't told us."

The vice around Krey's chest had finally loosened. He looked up
and locked his gaze on Nora. Could they trust these people? Then
again, did it matter? The king had controlled everyone at the palace,
plus the whole militia. Sooner or later, news of his capabilities would
get out.

Nora's countenance was calm, but Krey sensed the swirling
thoughts behind her eyes. After a long pause, she sat up straighter. In
a calm voice, she told them her father could control minds, though

she didn't explain how he did it. She recalled how she and her friends had freed the militia and defended Deroga. The king, Nora said, was strengthening his magic—something her audience had no trouble believing. They'd heard of the massive dome over the palace. "We still don't know how he's accessing so much power," she concluded.

"I never thought he was the one controlling them," Sharai said, her voice uncharacteristically quiet.

"For months," Nora said, "I thought I could convince my father to turn away from his dark magic. I wanted him to become the ruler he used to be. But"—her voice sounded choked—"too much of his mind is gone."

"So what's the plan?" Tiam asked.

Voice still wavering, she said, "Krey can tell you what we're thinking."

He explained their need for a coalition, admitting he didn't know quite what that would look like. "To start with, we're hoping the New Therroans in Cellerin City will help us." He noted Hatlin's and Sharai's nods. "We'd also like to ask the former militia members to fight on our side. I know most of them are willing to. They're some of the best magic eaters anywhere. But there's over thirty of them. They can't come to Cellerin City, because the king might find them."

"And kill them or control them again," Nora said.

"Right now," Krey said, "Deroga's the safest place for them. But they're too far away to help us."

"They need to stay close to the palace, like the rest of you are doing," Tiam said.

"There's nowhere to hide that many people," Nora said.

Tiam gave her a half smile. "You seem to think I'm the only farmer out here who's not a fan of the king."

"I'm sure you're not, but I doubt many farmers would harbor fugitives for weeks or months on end."

A smooth, low laugh flowed from Tiam's mouth. "You're underestimating how pissed off my friends are. You get your militia members here; we'll find places for them to stay."

Nora's jaw dropped. "Are you sure?"

"You bet."

Hope flooded Krey's chest. "I can fly to Deroga tomorrow morning. We'll work out a plan to get them all here."

"I'll come with you," Nora said. "I'd like to be the one to invite them out here. The sooner they see me as a ruler, the smoother the transition will be."

Krey agreed—until he considered what it would mean for Nora to come along. She'd be flying on his back.

The first time he'd carried her was the first time he'd carried *anyone*. It had been fascinating and a little weird, wrapping her body into his magic, sensing every bit of it. But he'd quickly gotten used to it.

So when he'd finally flown with Zeisha, his reaction to her had caught him off guard. His magic had melded with her body, more intimate than any touch. The first time, the second time, *every* time he'd flown with her, he'd reveled in it.

Something told him flying with Nora again would be pure torture. By the sky, he'd barely been able to keep his eyes off her when they'd sat down to read together before dinner. How was he supposed to retain his wits if he enveloped her in his magic?

Every day, Krey hoped the impossibility of a relationship with Nora would reduce his desire for her. It seemed to be having the opposite effect. If he carried her, he'd end up objectifying her, which wouldn't be fair to her—or to him. It would stoke the flames of a fire he was already desperate to extinguish.

Krey brought his mind back to the dinner table. Nora was watching him. *Oh hell, she's looking at me like I've gone insane. And maybe I have.* But his brain was still functional enough to grasp onto the one fact that might save him. "I, uh . . . I know you hate flying with me," he said, trying to smile casually and totally failing.

She cocked her head. "Is that what's concerning you? I wasn't planning to ask you to carry me." Her eyes swept over the table.

"While we're telling secrets, I guess it's time for one more. A few months ago, I befriended a dragon. I'll ask him to take us to Deroga."

The table went silent.

At last, Sharai spoke in a dry tone. "Every dethroning coalition should have a fire-breathing reptid on their side."

11

It finally happened. The conversation I've been dreading.

Ulmin asked me if I've ever been in love.

My heart pounded as I told him, "Yes. A boy back home. I don't love him now, but I used to." I was afraid to ask the next question, but I had to. "Does that bother you?"

He brought his hand to my cheek. "I don't care who's had your heart in the past. As long as it's free now."

My whole body felt suddenly light. "My heart is free. Is yours?"

"Yes. But I think it's in danger of getting stolen."

-Letter from Ambrel Kaulder to Dani Kaulder
Dated Centa 28, 180 PD

KREY SLID down Osmius's back, his boots stirring up the dust of a Star Clan street. "I can't believe you convinced me to ride on a dragon again." He patted the beast's side. "No offense."

Osmius huffed, puffing smoke out of both nostrils.

Nora slid off the dragon. "Osmius is way faster than you. Thanks to him, we beat the storm." She pointed at the gray rain clouds approaching from the east, obscuring the rising sun.

He rolled his eyes. She was right, but there was no way he'd tell her that. "Let's wake up the militia."

When they reached the men's bunkhouse, Krey knocked. A bleary-eyed militia member answered it. "You're back." He caught sight of Nora and crossed his arms over his bare chest. "Uh, hey, Princess."

"Everyone decent?" Krey asked.

"Probably not."

"I'll wait out here," Nora said.

Krey walked in with the militia member, who called, "Hey, rise and shine. Krey's here, and he needs to talk to us." They both started opening window shutters. Several groans sounded from the lumps on the beds.

When Krey had the attention of the groggy group, he said, "Sorry to wake you up. Nora and I need to meet with you. Can you get to the dining room in twenty minutes?"

He received mutters of assent, along with a few curses. "You're the best," Krey said wryly before going back outside.

He and Nora walked to the women's bunkhouse. This time, Nora entered alone. When she returned, she said, "They'll meet us, but Zeisha wasn't there. Isla said she's probably working early. Can you fly up to check the rooftop gardens?"

"Sure."

"I'll go to the dining room." Nora turned and strode away.

Krey fueled up on feathers from his pack, then flew to the rooftop garden Zeisha worked in most often. She wasn't there. He checked the other rooftop gardens, but they were all empty. He flew to the dining room and entered along with a few militia members.

"She wasn't there?" Nora asked.

Krey shook his head, frowning. Maybe Zeisha was off doing Anya things. Communing with the morning sun or something.

"Are you looking for Zeisha?" a female militia member asked.

"Yeah, do you know where she is?"

"I think she's at Kebi's place."

"Where's that?"

"It's the only house on the residential street with a teal door and shutters. I was there with her once."

"Thanks." Krey turned to Nora. "I'll see if I can find her. Don't start without me."

He took to the air, trying to let the chilly breeze cleanse him of his nerves. It had been three months since the breakup, and while much of the initial awkwardness between him and Zeisha had passed, he was still never quite sure how to act around her.

Seconds after he rose into the sky outside, a more immediate concern distracted him. The promised storm arrived, and by the time he reached the residential street, thick sheets of cold rain had soaked him to the skin. He spotted teal shutters and landed in front of the house.

Wind and rain covered the sound of his approach. The shutters were closed, but the large front porch led to a wide-open door. Krey stepped onto the porch and wrung out the hem of his shirt, as if that would prevent him from getting the floor wet. In the front room, Zeisha sat on a sofa with Kebi. They were clasping hands as Kebi talked softly. Zeisha gazed at her friend, a smile on her full lips. The type of adoring smile that, if Krey hadn't known better, would've made him suspect—

Kebi brought her mouth down to Zeisha's and kissed her. Not a quick, friendly peck, but a real, unquestionably more-than-friends kiss. Zeisha's fingers moved into Kebi's hair, tangling in the trog's tight, short curls.

Kebi caressed Zeisha's cheek, pulling away just long enough to breathe, "You're so beautiful," before resuming the kiss with even more passion. They didn't seem inclined to stop anytime soon.

Krey had been watching, frozen and open-mouthed, for at least a full minute before it occurred to him he was being incredibly rude. He coughed, but a clap of thunder muffled the sound. He knocked on the open door and called out, "Um . . . hi."

Zeisha and Kebi broke the kiss and turned, their eyes widening in unison. They let go of each other and stood to face Krey.

Despite the loud storm, an awkward hush fell over the room.

"Krey," Zeisha finally said. "It's good to see you." Even in the dim light, her deep flush was obvious.

"Can I . . . come in?"

Kebi smiled warmly. "Please do." She gestured to a chair near the couch. "Would you like to sit?"

He remained standing. "I wish I could stay"—*okay, that was a lie*—"but Nora and I were hoping to meet with the former militia members." He forced himself to gaze unflinchingly at Zeisha. "I know you don't consider yourself part of the militia, but we hoped you could come, just so you know what's going on."

"If there's a fight coming up, Kebi might want to be there. She was incredible in the battle for Deroga." Zeisha smiled at Kebi, her expression nothing short of adoring. The trog woman returned the look.

Krey blinked. *By the sky, are they in love?* He recovered quickly. "Kebi's welcome to come."

"I have an umbrella," Kebi said, hurrying out of the room.

Zeisha stepped closer. "Krey . . ." She didn't seem to know how to finish the thought.

"It's okay." Funny enough, it was. Sort of. A certain amount of disappointment squeezed his heart, but the longer he stood here, the less surprised he was at what he'd seen. Which was really odd. "We'll talk later."

Zeisha gave him a hopeful smile.

Kebi entered with the umbrella. "I only have one. We'll have to huddle together."

Krey almost laughed.

Nora stood at the front of the dining room, waiting for everyone to arrive. All the shutters were closed against the rain. Lanterns gave the space a warm, golden glow.

This meeting felt like a test. Sure, she'd spoken to the militia before . . . but now she wasn't asking them to fight for Deroga. She was asking them to fight for Cellerin and, in a very real way, for her. Most of the militia members were older than her, though not by much. What gave her the right to ask them to follow her?

The family I was born into.

Had she ever really considered how messed up that was?

But that was how this nation worked. Maybe it would change in time, but for now, who else was supposed to lead? It would be hard enough to build a coalition around her, the legal heir. She certainly couldn't ask some random person to take the crown. They were trying to avoid civil war, not instigate one.

Besides, I want to lead.

The thought caught her off guard. Just a couple of months ago, on the day of the battle for Deroga, the possibility of being queen had made her feel sick. When had she stopped dreading the idea and started embracing it?

She supposed it had been gradual. The further her father slipped into madness, the more she wanted to protect the people of Cellerin. Last night's dinner had opened her eyes to more of the ways the king was harming his country. She had to turn things around. It was worth any sacrifice.

Krey walked in with Zeisha and Kebi. He threw his head back, laughing at something Kebi said.

A lump invaded Nora's throat. *Any sacrifice* had already

included her relationship with Ovrun. Eventually, she'd also have to let go of her friendship with Krey, which had deepened over time, despite his distrust of the monarchy and her anger over his brain lysting. They'd fought through all that, coming away with something truly special.

Was it worth it to lose such a friendship?

Yes. Without question.

But by the orange sky above, it would hurt when all this was over, and it was time to say goodbye to people she'd grown to love.

She realized everyone was looking at her. Time to act like a princess.

After thanking them for coming, she got right to the point. "You all know my father is no longer capable of leading effectively. I'm inviting every one of you to help me take back our country."

Their eyes were glued on her. Most of them had gotten past their awe of her months ago. But they respected her. It was clear in the way they'd quieted before she even asked them to. The way they now listened to her with readiness, not wariness.

Fifteen minutes later, every militia member but Zeisha had agreed, enthusiastically, to relocate to the farms outside Cellerin so they could support Nora in her effort to take the crown.

Krey stood and walked toward the front of the room. Nora figured he was going to fill in some details she'd forgotten, but he didn't join her. Instead, he stopped a few mets away and held his forearms straight in front of him, palms up. His head dropped in a bow.

What the hell? The only time Krey had ever bowed to her was when he'd first arrived at the palace last year. That time, it had clearly been an ironic gesture. Now, despite his obvious sincerity, she almost laughed and told him to cut it out.

Then a chair scraped the floor. One of the militia members stood and held out her arms, lowering her head. Another followed suit, then another, until every person in the room, even Zeisha and Kebi, was standing and bowing to Nora.

In a way, it felt good. Perhaps she hadn't earned such support, but she sure needed it. And yet, as she gazed on a sea of lowered heads, loneliness smashed into her like a boxer's fist to the gut. She wasn't the only one who knew her position was changing.

"Thank you," she said, her voice sounding stronger than her spirit felt. "You may sit."

As they did so, she resisted the urge to tell them to never bow to her again. A voice spoke in her head, sounding a bit like her internal self and a bit like Sharai. *This is exactly what you need if you want to be successful. It's exactly what they need if they want to follow you.*

They spent the next few minutes discussing their transportation plans. Over the course of several nights, Osmius would carry them, three at a time.

Nora dismissed the crowd. They left in small groups, laughing and bantering. The sounds grated on her heart.

As the militia departed, Zeisha remained seated at a table with Kebi and Krey, quietly observing the room. When everyone was gone, Nora walked over.

"That went well," Zeisha said.

Nora nodded thoughtfully, turning to Krey. "I don't know why you bowed, but thank you."

He laughed. "Don't worry, it'll never happen again."

Nora smiled, but it didn't reach her eyes. "It's not raining too hard right now," she said. "I'm going to the library."

"I doubt Eira will let us bring back any more books."

"I just need one. I'm hoping she'll make an exception." She didn't explain further. "I'll see you at lunch."

Before she could leave, something inside Zeisha prompted her to speak. "Nora, I'd like to come to the farm too. I was planning to stay here, but . . . I need to come with you. I'm just not sure why."

Nora's smile was a little more genuine this time. "Of course you can come with us."

"May I come too?" Kebi asked.

Nora looked surprised, but said, "Please do. Bring your bow and arrows."

A joyful buzz filled Zeisha's chest.

Kebi stood. "Krey, I will find dry clothes for you." When Zeisha and Krey started to rise, she gestured to stop them. "You two should wait here. There's no reason for us to all go out in the storm. Nora, would you like to share my umbrella?"

Zeisha watched the two women leave. She and Krey were alone, and she was certain Kebi had planned it that way. A nearby lantern cast a glow on Krey's eyes. She saw no anger there, only curiosity. She broke the silence with five words. "I'm in love with Kebi."

Krey nodded. "I know."

"You do?"

"I suspected it when I saw how you looked at each other." He shifted in his seat. "I'm happy for you, Zei. Really."

Zeisha took a deep breath and spoke again, her voice soft and earnest. "I loved you, Krey. Don't ever doubt that. When I broke up with you, I thought I might stay single the rest of my life." She looked off toward the corner of the room, then returned her gaze to him, a small smile on her lips. "I've always thought some women were attractive, in the same way I thought some men were. But I never considered whether I could love a woman. I was in love with you. You had my whole heart. Then . . . you didn't anymore. And one day I realized Kebi had become my best friend. Not too long after that, I knew it wasn't just friendship I felt for her."

Krey laughed softly, shaking his head.

"What?" Zeisha asked.

"I had all these questions I couldn't even put into words, and somehow you're answering them."

"I'm glad."

"So . . ." he ventured, "when I found you on that rooftop and tried to convince you to give me another chance, were you and Kebi . . . ?"

A flush stole over her cheeks. "That was the day after our first kiss."

In the subsequent silence, Zeisha's mind returned to that day. She and Kebi had taken a walk at lunchtime. She'd taken Kebi's hand, weaving their fingers together. They'd stopped in the deserted street, beside the two-hundred-year-old shell of a crashed solarcar. Kebi had given her a smile full of yearning, and suddenly, their lips were pressed together.

That was a month ago, and they were still arguing about which one of them had initiated it. Whoever had made the first move, the moment had been perfect, suffused with warm sunlight and the taste of freshly harvested berries. That first kiss had been a song, driven by the beat of eager pulses under soft skin.

Krey's voice interrupted her reverie. "That was weeks before we left. Why did you keep it a secret?"

She drew in a breath, bringing herself back to the present. "I didn't want to hurt you. And . . . it seemed fast. We'd broken up less than two months before that. I didn't think you'd understand."

"Zei." He took one of her hands in both of his. "I know I didn't handle our breakup very well. But I always want you to be honest with me. And I absolutely want you to be happy."

"You're saying if I'd told you I was with Kebi when we were on that rooftop, you would've been happy?" A playful smile tugged at her lips.

"No, I would've been crushed . . . but I would've been happy eventually. And I'm happy for you now." He shrugged. "And a little jealous. But only a little."

She squeezed his hands. "I hope you find someone. You've got a lot of love to give."

He let go of her and ran a hand through his wet hair. "My love is reserved for books these days. The relationship is a little one-sided but surprisingly satisfying."

She didn't laugh or even smile. "You deserve happiness too, you know."

"I'm not so sure about that."

She opened her mouth to protest, but he held up both hands, shaking his head. "I'm an addict, Zeisha. I don't expect anyone to take that on."

"Other people have baggage too. You're a good guy, and plenty of people . . ." She trailed off. Krey wasn't listening. He was looking off into the distance, a certain helpless desire in his gaze. That desire didn't seem to be directed at her anymore, thank the sky. Had he found someone else? If so, he clearly wasn't willing to act on it.

His eyes found Zeisha again. She swallowed, then spoke. "Let someone love you, Krey."

A deep sigh exited his chest.

12

Ulmin and I spent the whole day together. First, we practiced our magic in Uncle Quin's back yard. He's experimental with his stone lysting, always trying new techniques.

"I think there's still much to learn about magic in our world," he told me. "I want to discover it all."

-Letter from Ambrel Kaulder to Dani Kaulder
Dated Centa 29, 180 PD

NORA CLOSED HER EYES, breathing deeply of Osmius's musky, slightly spicy scent. Warm air ruffled her hair and clothes.

Zeisha and Kebi rode behind her. It was Kebi's first time on a dragon, and she'd admitted to being nervous. After so many rides with Osmius, Nora was almost too relaxed. She had to remind herself not to drift to sleep. Flying on the back of a magical beast would always carry some level of risk.

But she trusted Osmius, as much as she trusted her friends. When she took the crown and everyone else moved on, would Osmius remain? Or would he settle into a life of wild solitude, far from humanity?

She couldn't ask him. She might not be able to handle the answer. But a thought insisted on drifting from her mind to his. *Why does everything have to change?*

I do not know, Nora-human, he replied, grief thick in his rich voice.

"Nora?" Zeisha called over the wind.

Nora turned her head. "Yes?"

"We need to take a detour!" Zeisha shouted.

"Where to?"

"The southwest."

One of Nora's eyebrows rose. She'd hoped for a more direct answer than that. "Is this an Anya thing?"

"Yes."

Nora couldn't come close to understanding Zeisha's new magic. She knew the basics—as the Anya, Zeisha could awaken the powers of the Well, the magic that filled the entire planet. But being the Anya also involved *listening.* Zeisha seemed to think God actually talked to her. Nora was skeptical about such an explanation, but wherever Zeisha was getting her information, she'd proven herself reliable.

"Okay," Nora called. "We'll go southwest. But we need to tell Krey first."

At her words, Osmius turned. He descended a bit, then positioned himself under Krey, who'd been flying behind them to avoid overloading Osmius.

"I don't like having a dragon under me," Krey shouted.

Nora barely stifled a laugh. She craned her neck to look at him. "Would you rather him be over you?"

"No!"

"The Anya needs to take a detour. I don't know how long it'll take."

"I need fuel and a rest soon anyway. I'll meet you back at the farm."

Nora confirmed, and Osmius turned in a southwesterly direction.

Zeisha gave occasional shouted instructions as they flew. It was at least an hour before she told Osmius to land.

When Nora's boots hit rocky, sloped ground, she asked Osmius, *Where are we?*

On a hill south of the Kamina River.

"I'll get a candle," Zeisha said.

Before she could open her pack, glowing, white light illuminated them all. Nora grinned at the white ball of fire Osmius held in his mouth. She'd seen him do this, but Zeisha and Kebi were both staring at the dragon, their mouths open as wide as his.

"Thank you," Zeisha managed.

"Why did you bring us here?" Nora asked her.

"I'm not sure yet."

Kebi smiled. "She will know soon."

They stepped back as Zeisha knelt and placed her hands on the rocky ground. "There's"—she hesitated, then continued—"old life here."

"Old life?" Nora asked.

The ground started popping. Rocks, large and small, jumped into the air, then dropped back to the ground. Nora watched, wide-eyed, as an area of ground about one-met square popped and leapt.

The ground stopped moving, piles of loose rocks now covering it. Zeisha picked up a rock and approached Osmius's glowing mouth. She beckoned Nora and Kebi over. "Look at this!"

Her two companions obeyed. Dragon fire warmed Nora as she gazed at the rock, which contained a perfect imprint of a four-toed footprint. "It's a fossil!"

"This entire hill is full of them," Zeisha said quietly. "There are

. . . memories . . . in this hill. From long before humanity's arrival on Anyari."

"I wonder if Cellerin's scientists know about this place," Nora said.

"The Well has something for us here." Zeisha's eyes were on the spot where she'd caused the rocks to dance. "But I'm not sure what." She returned to where she'd knelt before and again touched the ground. Nora was starting to shuffle impatiently when Zeisha stood. "We need to take rocks back with us, as many as we can carry."

"Should we look specifically for fossils?" Nora asked.

"No, the entire area is soaked with the planet's memories, and I awakened the Well over it all. That's what's important." Wrinkles crimped her forehead. "I'm just not sure what it means."

The women filled every available space in their packs with rocks. Nora carefully positioned them around the book she'd borrowed from the trog library, glad she'd wrapped it in thick leather. When she finished, she turned to Zeisha. "What's next?"

"I'll listen as we travel. I'm hoping by the time we get back to the farm, I'll understand why these rocks are important."

Nora nodded. Good thing her own magic was so comparatively simple. She ate ice to make ice and snow. Dragon speaking was even easier, requiring no effort or fuel. There was no way she'd have the patience to *listen* like Zeisha did.

They mounted Osmius again. As they rose into the air, the white fire he'd been holding exited his mouth as a stream of bright flames. Behind Nora, Kebi let out a frightened squeak.

Nora relaxed into the dragon's warm, smooth scales.

The next morning, Zeisha woke to dawn light streaming through the gaps in the shutters. Kebi was next to her, and Nora and Sarza occupied the other bed. All three of them were still sleeping.

Zeisha quietly dressed in extra clothes she'd brought from

Deroga. When she'd gone to sleep last night, she still didn't understand why they'd gathered the rocks. However, the voice she always listened for had spoken in her dreams. She knew more than she had the night before, though some of the mystery remained.

Someone knocked lightly on the door. Zeisha opened it. A smiling girl with wavy, medium-brown hair waited on the other side. "I'm Joli," she said.

Returning the smile, Zeisha came into the hallway. Once the door was closed, she introduced herself.

"My mother's almost done making breakfast," Joli said.

"I'm the only one who's awake," Zeisha said. "But I'm starving."

"Come with me, and we'll help my mom get breakfast on the table."

"Did Krey get in safely?" Zeisha asked as they walked.

"Yes, but later than the rest of you."

Breakfast was a cheerful affair. When Tiam found out Zeisha was a vine eater, he asked her if she'd lend her services to his crops. He usually hired a vine eater every month and was thrilled at the prospect of daily magical assistance.

Zeisha gladly agreed. When they were done eating, they ventured outside.

The day was full, and Zeisha didn't get the chance to gather her friends until after she'd helped clean up the dinner dishes. She found Kebi and Sarza on the front porch and Ovrun behind the house, gazing at the dark fields. Nora and Krey were in the guys' room, arguing vehemently about something they'd read in one of their books. Zeisha didn't ask Hatlin or Joli to join them. This meeting was only for those who knew about her position as the Anya.

They gathered in the girls' bedroom and stood around the heavy, rock-filled packs from the previous night. Zeisha described their detour the night before, then said, "According to a dream I had, these old rocks are fuel."

"We don't have any stone eaters here," Krey said.

"Not that kind of fuel. The Well has turned them into something else."

They stared at her expectantly.

"That's all I know," she said with a shrug.

"How do we find out what they're fuel for?" Nora asked.

Zeisha smiled hesitantly. "I could eat some. I don't even know if it'll work on me, but it's a start."

"That's risky," Krey said. "You know how fuel works. If I tried to eat roots like you do, it would make me sick."

"I'll only swallow a little bit. I'll be okay." They all stared at her as she knelt before her pack and undid the buckle. She set the larger rocks on the floor. When she reached the bottom, her fingers came away with a small pinch of rock powder. She put it in her mouth— and immediately spit it into her hand.

The pieces tasted *wrong*. Something inside her, something intuitive, shouted that this fuel didn't belong in her body. She looked up at the others. They all gazed back with concern. "I'm supposed to eat this," she said, just as certain as before. "But my body disagrees."

"Maybe you shouldn't—"

Before Kebi could finish her statement, Zeisha licked up the tiny rock pieces and forced herself to swallow, past her gag reflex and the sense of wrongness. The mysterious fuel went down. She stood.

"Do you feel different?" Nora asked.

"You don't look sick," Sarza said.

"I'm fine," Zeisha said, blinking slowly. "I don't feel anything at all."

"Listen, Zeisha," Kebi said softly.

Zeisha gave her a grateful smile before closing her eyes and listening. An image of plant matter, her ordinary fuel, entered her mind. She opened her eyes. "I'll be right back," she said, before rushing from the room.

Outside, she pulled some bark from a tree, stashing it in her pocket. When she returned to the bedroom, she said, "Before you ask, I still don't know what's happening. But I think this is step two." She chewed and swallowed a small piece of bark, then turned on her magic so she could make a vine.

Only it didn't turn on. Nothing at all happened.

She tried again. "My magic isn't working," she muttered, trying a third time, with the same lack of results.

"Maybe you didn't eat enough fuel," Sarza said.

"She doesn't need much," Nora said. "I've never seen a lyster more efficient than Zeisha."

Just to be sure, Zeisha ate another bite of bark. It didn't affect her at all.

Krey knelt by Zeisha's pack. He pulled out the tiniest of pebbles and swallowed it down, grimacing as he did so. "That was not meant to be eaten." Standing, he reached into his pocket and pulled out a couple of diced feathers. He ate them, then stood, watching the group.

"Yours doesn't work either, does it?" Zeisha asked.

He shook his head, eyes wide.

No one spoke for several seconds. Then Krey said, "I have an idea. Nora, don't touch the rocks."

Her hands went to her hips. "You're giving the orders now?"

"Please," he added. He gave her a smile and a dramatic bow, then left the room. When he returned a few minutes later, he handed a bowl of crushed ice to Nora. "Varia gave me this."

"Shouldn't I eat a rock first?"

"No, this is the next phase of our experiment. Just get some ice into your system and make sure your talent works as usual." He smiled, then added, "Please, Your Highness."

Nora ate a handful of ice, then blew a bit of snow from her mouth.

"Perfect," Krey said. "Now shoot ice at me."

She grinned, held up a hand, and shot a good-sized ball of ice at his stomach. Zeisha grimaced and tightened her own abdominals in empathy . . . then watched as the cold, dense ball hit an invisible wall several simmets from Krey and dropped to the wooden floor.

Everyone was silent except Sarza, who breathed a drawn-out "Daaaamn."

Zeisha grinned in realization. "It's keeping you from doing magic, but it's also shielding you from the magic of others."

"Do you think it only works on magic eaters?" Ovrun asked.

"Test it and see," Zeisha said.

Ovrun ate about as much of the fuel as Krey and Zeisha had.

Krey grimaced as his friend ate it. "It's awful, right?"

"I didn't think it was so bad. It just tasted like rock."

Zeisha tapped her lips with one finger. "It didn't feel *wrong* when you ate it?"

"Nope." He held out his arms. "Nora? Give it your best shot."

She formed another ball of ice, smaller than the one she'd sent at Krey. Giving Ovrun a hesitant look, she tossed the ball his way.

The ice hit an invisible shield and fell to the ground.

Kebi and Krey both laughed. Exhilaration came over Zeisha. She'd discovered a fuel that could protect anyone from being attacked by magic.

"It doesn't feel wrong for Ovrun to eat it because he's not a magic eater," Krey said. "It was my magic that rebelled against me swallowing that rock. Ovrun doesn't have any magic to lose."

"I wonder if it would take away Sarza's ability to have visions," Nora said.

"Sarza, why don't you try it and see if it tastes terrible?" Zeisha suggested.

Sarza put a little piece in her mouth, then grimaced and spat it out.

"I suppose that's our answer," Nora said. "If your prophetic magic doesn't want you to eat it, that probably means it works on you."

"But I always assumed my gift was different than yours," Sarza said. "I don't know much about seers, but I know they were around a long time before the stone brought magic into the world."

"I've read that seering may have been the first type of magic the stone brought us," Nora said. "We know there were seers during humanity's early days on Anyari. And we know they had access to the stone back then, before they buried it in a cave. Some historians have hypothesized that the ability to see the future came from the stone."

Sarza blinked. "I'd never heard that."

Zeisha's gaze fell on Krey, whose lips were parted, his eyes focused and thoughtful. "What are you thinking about, Krey?"

He turned to her. "How normal fuel works. It stays in your system a long time unless you do magic—then you use it up a whole lot faster. I bet we're burning up this fuel when it protects us."

To test his hypothesis, Nora happily aimed small balls of ice at him. Less than a minute later, one of them hit him right between his eyes. Zeisha was the second to lose protection. She burned up the rocks she'd eaten by attempting to use her plant magic. Before long, she could create vines again. Ovrun was still protected, so Zeisha aimed her vines at him. On her third try, her vine reached him.

"This stuff is amazing." Krey grinned at Zeisha. "What should we call it?"

"You want me to name it?"

"You discovered it!"

"Shield fuel," she said with a soft smile. She'd used the magic of the Well to shield the residential areas in Deroga. Now she was using it to shield her friends.

They were cleaning up vines and ice when a gasp made everyone stop.

"What, Nora?" Zeisha asked.

Nora's eyes were wide. "If this blocks magic . . . it should shield us from my father's control too."

The room went quiet.

Finally, Krey spoke. "We'll have to give up our own magic to be protected from him. But it'll be worth it."

"We need to break up these rocks so they're easier to consume," Nora said. "Zeisha, if Osmius takes you, can you get more?" Zeisha nodded, and Nora continued, "We'll tell everyone else in the house. Anyone who may encounter my father needs to be able to protect themselves."

"Even Sharai?" Krey said. "You really think that's a good idea?"

Nora didn't hide her annoyance. "She's on our team, Krey. The only ones who know exactly where the fuel comes from are Zeisha, Kebi, and me. We won't tell anyone else, even the rest of you."

"Not because we don't trust you," Zeisha said. "We need to protect the knowledge in case the king finds a way to interrogate someone."

Nora nodded. "We should carry it with us at all times—but we'll store the rest of it somewhere secret. We can find a place in the barn or stable where no one will come across it."

Zeisha agreed. Everyone who might fight or even meet the king needed protection from his mind magic. "We'll need to share this with the militia and anyone else who joins our coalition. But please don't say anything about how we got it. No one can know about my connection to the Well."

Kebi took her hand, lacing their fingers together. Several sets of eyes flicked down to their joined hands. Zeisha stifled a smile. Now that Krey knew about her and Kebi, there was no reason to hide it from the others. She squeezed Kebi's hand.

"We will protect your secret, Zeisha," Kebi said. She looked around the room. "Yes?"

Everyone nodded or murmured assent.

Hope filled Zeisha's heart, and she sensed it spreading through the room.

13

After dinner, Ulmin and I sat on the back porch. He said he'd like to walk through the neighborhood, but his royal guards would have to come along. I suggested we sneak out instead, just the two of us. It took some convincing, but he finally agreed.

With his knit cap pulled down and his scarf pulled up, he looked like an ordinary man. We sneaked past the guards waiting in the carriage and ran to a nearby pub, where we whispered and laughed for half an hour. No one recognized Ulmin, and that made him giddy.

We'd just arrived back on the porch when Uncle Quin came out to check on us. Ulmin and I held in our laughter until we were alone again.

-Letter from Ambrel Kaulder to Dani Kaulder
Dated Centa 29, 180 PD

OVRUN GRUNTED as the closed carriage Sharai was driving bounced along a rutted dirt street in Cellerin City. Hatlin sat across from him, handling the rough ride silently. It was Saturday night, and despite the late hour, plenty of people were out and about, socializing.

Ovrun welcomed the sounds from the street. These days, Nora filled his mind at every quiet moment. Sometimes he lost himself in thoughts of her, obsessing over what he could've done differently and wondering if he could win her back. Other times, like tonight, his worn-out heart embraced distractions such as mindless noise.

At last, Sharai parked in an alley behind a small pub.

Ovrun pulled back the curtain of one carriage window, then the other. The alley, lit by the carriage's lanterns, appeared to be empty. Thank the sky. For all Ovrun knew, there could be a bounty on his head for fleeing Cellerin City with the princess seven months ago. Best not to be seen by too many people tonight.

"If I'm not back in two minutes," Ovrun said, "it means I found who I was looking for. I'll come back to the alley in an hour."

"Be careful," Hatlin replied.

"I will. Hope your meeting goes well." Hatlin and Sharai were headed to a different pub to chat with trusted New Therroans who might join their coalition.

Ovrun stepped out. He'd just reached the pub's rear door when it swung open. He leapt back, heart pounding wildly.

A woman sneered at him as she dumped a pot of water into a gutter. "Entrance is in front."

"Yeah," Ovrun said as he rushed into the pub's tiny kitchen, ignoring the woman's protests. When he reached the door into the pub's main room, he slowed. He'd draw every eye in the place if he barreled in like a galloping orsa.

With studied casualness, he opened the door and blinked to let his eyes adjust to the dim pub. He was behind the bar. A woman holding three mugs of ale ignored him as she walked around the bar to deliver her drinks. Ovrun followed her, scanning the small room.

At a table in the corner sat a man he'd worked with as a royal guard. Lott was in his fifties and had retired shortly before Ovrun was fired. They'd always gotten along well. In private conversations with Ovrun, Lott had confided his dislike of Ulmin. Ovrun had good reason to think the man would be an ally.

One other man sat at the table with Lott. Ovrun contemplated waiting in the shadows to see if the other man would leave, but Lott looked up, met his gaze, and smiled through his thick, gray beard.

Ovrun approached. "Lott," he said, keeping his voice low. "I remembered this was your favorite pub. Hoped I'd find you here." He silently begged the man not to greet him by name.

"Ovrun!" Lott said, his voice seeming to echo through the room. "Have a seat."

Gut tightening with nerves, Ovrun did just that.

Lott introduced his friend, Kevlin, and the three men began talking. Lott didn't seem to be aware of Ovrun's adventures outside the city or his status as a wanted criminal. Ovrun mostly listened, giving noncommittal answers when Lott asked him what he'd been up to.

One theme ran through the statements of the other two men. They both hated what was happening in their city. They spoke disparagingly of the soldiers and even of the king. The more Ovrun heard, the more comfortable he became.

He didn't know these guys well enough to tell them about the dissidents hiding in farms outside the city. Instead, he asked if they'd meet with him again next week at a pub with a private back room. They agreed.

Kevlin stood. "Nearest bathroom is at the next pub over. I'll be right back."

With the other man gone, Ovrun and Lott talked a little more freely. Lott had other friends he was certain would join the cause. Ovrun invited him to bring the most trustworthy ones to their next meeting.

As he took the last swallow of his beer, Ovrun looked up at the clock. Hatlin and Sharai would return soon. "I gotta go. Tell Kevlin it was good to meet him."

"Tell him yourself," Lott said. "He just came back in."

Ovrun turned. Kevlin had indeed reentered the pub. But he wasn't alone. Two Cellerinian soldiers stood behind him.

"There!" Kevlin shouted, pointing at the table where Ovrun and Lott sat.

Both men cursed and leapt from their seats. Lott dashed toward the bar, Ovrun following. Lott circled around the bar. Ovrun was about to do the same when a server turned away from a table, stepping right into his path. He collided with her, and they crashed to the floor, along with the empty mugs she was carrying.

"Stop!" someone shouted as Ovrun pushed himself to his feet. A hand grabbed his arm. He tried to twist away.

"I'll shoot!" the man holding him shouted.

The hard muzzle of a gun pressed into Ovrun's side. He froze.

Another soldier grabbed him. In seconds, Ovrun was on the floor, pinned down by harsh hands and knees. Someone locked shackles on his wrist. Another person frisked him, quickly disarming him.

Ovrun drew in breaths as deep as he could manage, alert to any opportunity to escape. But the men holding him gave him no chance to budge, much less run.

After a couple of minutes, a woman reported, "The other guy is gone. We'll take this one to the general. I'm sure the king will want to see him."

Ovrun roared in frustration as bruising hands pulled him to his feet and dragged him into the street. Panic squeezed his lungs. If the king controlled him, the army would descend on Joli's farm. How long would it take Sharai and Hatlin to find out what had happened to Ovrun? Would they be able to get back to the farm to warn everyone in time?

I can't let him control me.

In the street, a soldier tripped Ovrun, sending him crashing into the dirt. Ovrun's arm landed in a puddle of what, based on its stench, had to be more than just mud.

"Sorry," an unapologetic voice muttered. The soldiers yanked

Ovrun to his feet again, dragged him a few more mets, and threw him into the back of an enclosed wagon. Four soldiers sat with him. The final soldier locked them in from the outside, leaving them in a stuffy space that was dark as the stone.

"Don't try anything," a female soldier said. "We're all locked in here together. You attack one of us, and Niso here'll sit on you the rest of the way to the palace."

A male soldier snorted a laugh.

The vehicle started moving. It bounced along the dirt streets, jostling its occupants. Boisterous voices from the street penetrated the wagon's wooden walls. Squeaky wheels and orsa hooves added to the clamor. Ovrun couldn't have been more thankful for the rough ride and the noise. The more distraction, the better. He had to get to the bag of finely milled shield fuel he'd been carrying in his pocket. He didn't think they'd gotten it when they disarmed him, but his shackled hands would have trouble reaching it.

The soldiers' voices filled the wagon's dark interior. Ovrun shifted forward in his seat as quietly as he could. A big bump nearly sent him flying across the wagon into the soldier across from him. He drew in a deep breath, stabilizing himself. Then he twisted, maneuvering his hands to his right front pocket.

Ovrun was a big guy. But his exercises kept him limber too. Or he thought they did. He started questioning that supposition as his muscles stretched beyond what they were accustomed to. Suppressing a deep groan, he kept twisting.

The left side of his body—arm, shoulder, upper back, chest—screamed at him. Both shackles dug painfully into his wrists. His fingers were right there, so close to the entrance to his pocket.

He twisted farther. The pain ratcheted up, shooting through his side, his wrists. Another simmet of movement, and blood ran down his left hand. A scream begged to be let out. He held it in.

His fingers dipped in his pocket. *A little more . . . a little more. Damn it, this hurts!*

The tips of his fingers grasped the rough fabric of the shield-fuel bag. Mouth twisting into a strained grin, he pinched the fabric as tight as he could and pulled. The bag wouldn't come out, not with him seated like this. Praying for smooth roads, he lifted into a half-standing position.

The bag popped out of his pocket. Ovrun held it tight behind his back, the thrill of victory giving him temporary reprieve from his pain.

"What are you doing, moving around so much?" a gruff voice asked. "Be still."

"Sorry. Bumpy ride."

He had the bag. But there was no way to get his hands up to his mouth. He cursed silently, mind racing.

Ovrun scooted forward and dropped the bag on the bench. After a quick stand, he sat again, shackled hands pressed against the planks behind him. The bag of shield fuel was now between his legs. He shimmied, moving the bag down his thighs, closer to his knees. Then he lifted his right foot and nudged the thing onto the top of his opposite thigh. More wriggling, and somehow he got it between his knees, where he squeezed it tight. Now for the hardest part.

Damn it, this would be a lot easier if I could see.

And if I wasn't shackled.

And if I'd never gotten arrested in the first place.

Ovrun lifted his feet up to the seat, drawing his knees as close to his chest as he could get them. Then, ignoring the gruff soldier who told him to stop moving, he leaned forward and brought his open mouth to the bag.

He drew the opening into his mouth like it was meat and he was a starving man. His tongue searched for the twine holding the bag closed. When he found it, he followed it to where it was tied. His teeth found one of the ends and pulled.

Sarza was being held captive and tortured.

Well, not captive, exactly. She could've left the bedroom at any point. But the torture was real. Nora, Zeisha, and Kebi were chatting. About *relationships*. And they kept trying to include her in the conversation.

She held out hope that at some point, her roommates would get tired. But they'd all slept late that morning, taking full advantage of the weekend's slower schedule. Electric light blazed in the little room.

"Did you see it, Sarza?" Nora asked.

She yawned before asking, "See what?"

"Zeisha and Kebi. Did you guess they were together before we left Deroga?"

"Uh, no." Did they really think she cared about this?

Zeisha and Kebi smiled at each other. They were sitting in bed, hand in hand, pillows between their backs and the headboard. Nora was in an armchair, cross-legged, sipping from a glass of water. Sarza had the other bed to herself for now, not that it mattered when she couldn't sleep.

"Enough about Kebi and me," Zeisha said. "How have you been, Nora?"

The princess shifted in her seat. "I—" She swallowed and schooled her face into an emotionless mask. "I'm fine."

"Breakups are never easy," Zeisha prodded.

"I'll have to do a lot of difficult things as a queen. I might as well get used to it now."

Sarza squinted. When they'd first met, Nora had been open and overly emotional. But recently, she'd waffled between normal socialization and the coldness she was displaying now.

"You know you can trust us, right?" Zeisha said.

Nora drew in a deep breath. "I'm okay. I can't wallow right now. There's no time for that."

"I wasn't asking you to wallow."

Nora aimed a bright, fake smile at Sarza. "What about you? Do you have anyone at home waiting for you?"

Now that was a loaded question. Sarza's family was doubtless waiting for her to return home from the army to bring them some money. Unless they'd gotten word about her deserting, in which case, they were probably telling everyone how ashamed they were of her. But that wasn't what Nora was asking. She was prodding into Sarza's romantic life.

"Nope," Sarza said.

"You'll find someone." Kebi said.

Sarza snorted. "I don't want to find anyone."

"I'm with you," Nora said. "I'm ready to give up on romance for a while."

"I've never wanted romance, and I never will."

The room went quiet. Sarza looked down at her hands. Why had she said that aloud?

"You've never had a crush on a boy?" Nora asked, sitting up straighter. Her mouth gaped, like it was the strangest thing she'd ever heard.

"Never," Sarza confirmed. Her breaths started coming faster. How long would this interrogation last?

"Or a girl?" Kebi asked.

"No." More words insisted on flowing from Sarza's mouth. "Not only was I the insane kid who had 'fainting spells,' I was also the one person who never giggled about kissing or crushes. I don't want to see it, I don't want to talk about it, and I definitely don't want to experience it. So if you've ever wondered why I suck at friendship, there you go. I stick out like a sore thumb in any group I'm part of."

Her voice had gotten louder as she'd spoken. Worse, her emotions had built to the point that she was about to cry. She'd already made a fool of herself. Weeping was the last thing she needed to do in front of these girls. Sarza stood and rushed from the room, then out of the house, not stopping until she was sitting on the damp lawn under the stars.

She was panting, more from emotional exertion than physical.

Refusing to give in to tears, she lowered her head, pressing her hands hard against her closed eyes. *Why did I tell them that?*

She cursed when she heard the front door open. Of course someone had followed her out here. These people didn't understand boundaries. She lifted her head. A light was now on in the dining room, and brightness streamed from two windows. Zeisha approached and sat, facing the same direction as Sarza, leaving plenty of space between them.

Eyes fixed on the dark fields in the distance, Zeisha said, "My oldest brother has always said he'd rather have friends than a lover or a spouse."

"So he's as broken as I am?" Sarza tried to keep her voice hard, but it cracked a bit.

From the corner of her eye, she saw Zeisha's head turn toward her. "Why do you think you're broken?"

Sarza laughed harshly. "Sex literally keeps our species alive. It seems pretty clear there's something wrong with someone who doesn't want it."

"Krey was raised by two aunts who are married to each other," Zeisha said, her voice gentle as ever. "They can't have biological children. Are they broken?"

Sarza didn't answer.

"I'm attracted to both men and women. One day, I may marry Kebi. Am I broken? Should I go back to Krey just so we can keep the species going?"

There was a hint of humor in Zeisha's voice, but Sarza didn't smile. "Of course not."

"What about husbands and wives who don't have kids for one reason or another? Are they broken?"

Sarza pressed her lips together.

Zeisha continued, "Think about an insect, compared to a dragon. They're both animals, but they're so different. Plants too—we've got huge trees and tiny berries and even poisonous bushes. There's so much diversity out there. So why shouldn't humans all be different

154

too? Do you really think your worth comes from whether or not you want romance? Or children? You're completely unique. Don't you think that's enough to make you valuable?"

Sarza finally turned to face Zeisha. "I've always been weird. It's never been a good thing."

"Well, I like you as you are. I'm pretty sure the other people in this house do too. We're all weird in our own ways. You fit with us just fine."

The simple statement—*You fit with us just fine*—traveled to Sarza's throat and stuck there. She swallowed past it and blinked, looking away.

"Nora wanted me to give you something." Zeisha set a leather-wrapped package in front of Sarza. "She said it's a loan, not a gift. It belongs to the trogs."

Sarza took it and ran her finger under the twine holding it together. "Why didn't she bring it to me?"

Zeisha's forehead furrowed. "She's . . . pulling away. From all of us. I don't know why." She shook her head, then smiled. "Go ahead. Open it."

Sarza used her fingernails to undo the knot in the twine. Beneath the leather wrapping was yet more leather—the binding of a book that looked terribly old.

"What does it say?" Zeisha asked.

"It's too dark to tell." *Thank the stone*, she added silently. If Zeisha saw her struggling with the words, that would be one humiliation too many.

"Let's go in!" Zeisha said, standing.

In the brightly lit dining room, Sarza ran her fingers over the letters on the front of the book. To her relief, the words were all familiar. "*The History of Seers.*"

Zeisha grinned. "You'll finally learn about your gift!"

Sarza nodded. The book was thick, heavy, and intimidating. It would take her months to read it, if not years. But her pulse sped up, anticipation making her whole body buzz. Maybe her experiences would finally make sense.

She held the book to her chest as she walked with Zeisha back to the room. "Thank you for the book," Sarza told the princess as they entered.

"It's no big deal."

Sarza sat on the bed again. Nora stayed pretty quiet, but the other girls didn't seem inclined to stop chatting. The discussion turned to safe topics—their work on the farm and the militia members who'd arrived at nearby farms the last couple of days. Sarza found herself joining in and even laughing a few times. An odd energy banished her sleepiness. *Maybe this is what it feels like to be part of a group.*

Kebi had just suggested they go to sleep when they heard Sharai's voice in the hallway. "Wake up! Everyone, wake up!"

Sarza rushed to the door and opened it.

Sharai's eyes were bright and panicked. Sweat glistened on her temples. "Come to the living room!" she urged. Sarza looked down the hall and saw that the guys had their door open too.

They rushed to the living room. Hatlin was just entering, followed by Joli and her parents.

"Where's Ovrun?" Nora demanded.

"He was arrested," Sharai said. She continued speaking over the others' gasps. "If the king controls him . . ."

Tiam straightened, every trace of grogginess gone from his eyes. "Everyone pack what you brought with you. We'll take you to one of the other farms that volunteered to host militia members. Thank the sky Ovrun doesn't know which farmers are helping us."

"I'm going with them," Joli said. Her face reddened when everyone looked her way, but she didn't back down. "I'm part of their coalition. The farm will be okay without me for a while."

Her father nodded, pride in his gaze.

"What about you and Varia?" Nora asked. "You can't stay here. If the army finds you and brings you to the king, he might learn where we are."

"I'd like Varia to go with you. But I'll stay. I'll keep shield fuel in my system at all times. If I get captured and the king tries to control me, I'll misdirect him."

"It may not fool him," Krey said. "He can feel when his mind connects with someone. He'll know something's different if it doesn't work."

Tiam's smile disappeared. "Are you sure?"

The muscles in Krey's jaw tightened as he nodded, not explaining where he got his inside information. "It'll be the same for Ovrun, if he manages to ingest the fuel he brought with him."

Sharai said, "If Ulmin knows his magic isn't working, he'll interrogate Ovrun in more traditional ways."

Nora stiffened. "My father wouldn't . . ." She trailed off, then cleared her throat, blinking rapidly. "I don't know what he'll do." Her voice was barely above a whisper. "We have to hope Ovrun stays strong."

Joli let out a short, horrified cry.

"Maybe you should leave too," Varia told Tiam, "at least for a few days."

"I agree," Tiam said. "Everyone pack quickly. I'll tell my foreman. He'll keep things running as long as he needs to."

Ovrun's gut clenched as King Ulmin Abrios entered the palace's security office, not halting until he stood in front of the bars of one of the two cells behind the desk.

"Ovrun Kensin," Ulmin said, a little smile drawing up the corners of his lips.

Ovrun bowed his head. "Your Majesty." He couldn't perform the arm part of the bow; his hands were still shackled. A met-long chain now connected him to the wall of his cell.

"Look at me," the king demanded.

Ovrun obeyed. The last time he'd seen the king was five months ago, on the night Krey had eaten shimshim brains and broken into the palace. Ulmin seemed to have aged twenty years since then. His skin was sallow and wrinkled. Bloodshot eyes with dark bags under them signaled his exhaustion.

"Where's my daughter?" Ulmin asked.

"I haven't seen her in over two months."

The king's lip twitched up. "Nice try. Step as close as you can to the bars, please."

Ovrun obeyed. The king reached into the cell. Thick burn scars on his palm were visible for a moment before he grabbed his prisoner's wrist, where the shackle had cut it on the ride over.

Despite the pain, Ovrun rejoiced silently. The fuel he'd consumed in the wagon was doing its job; his mind remained clear. He let his face slacken and his eyes glaze over.

The king's brows drew together. His eyes flicked to the royal guard at the desk, who'd been still since the king's entrance. Ulmin was probably controlling the guy right now. The king's gaze returned to Ovrun, his brows furrowing further.

It's like he can tell he's not controlling me.

Ulmin's fingers tightened painfully. "Where is my daughter?" he asked again, his voice low and dangerous.

Ovrun had planned this out. One lie for before the king tried to control him. Another for when he was pretending to be under the king's influence. In a monotone, he replied, "She flew off on her dragon a week ago. I don't know where she went."

Eyes narrowing, the king asked, "Why are you trying to gather rebels to make my daughter queen if you don't know where she is?"

Okay, so that Kevlin guy wasn't just an asshole who wanted to ingratiate himself with the army by getting Ovrun arrested. He'd also disclosed Ovrun's plans. Great. Keeping his face neutral, Ovrun replied, "She'll find us when she's ready."

Ulmin released his grip, but his incisive gaze didn't leave Ovrun's face. "I'm going to find my daughter." He took a breath. "I may instruct you to kill her with your own hands. What would you say to that?"

This was a test, Ovrun knew that. "I'll do as you ask." His expression didn't budge, but he felt sure the king could see his shirt fluttering with every frantic beat of his heart.

A small, cruel smile twisted Ulmin's mouth. He pulled up a chair. For the next several minutes, Ovrun answered the king's questions by repeatedly saying he knew nothing about the inner workings of the rebellion.

As the conversation came to a close, the king stood and stared at his prisoner. That uncertainty came over his face again. "Where is my daughter?"

Ovrun's mouth went dry. Why was the king asking this a third time? *It's another test. He tried to let go of my mind, and he doesn't know if it worked.* "I told you, I haven't seen her in a couple of months."

The king laughed, loud and long. He turned to the desk and leaned close to the royal guard on duty. They held a whispered conversation, going back and forth several times. The guard looked fully engaged, and Ovrun guessed he was no longer controlled.

As the king exited, the guard reached through the cell bars. "Give me your hand." Without a word, he removed one of Ovrun's shackles.

The guard then walked through a door at the side of the room. It looked like it led to a closet of some sort. Ovrun used the brief moment of privacy to reach into his back pocket. His fingers found the little bag of ground-up shield fuel. Just touching it made him smile. After eating some in the wagon, he'd dropped the bag between his legs again, then stood and picked it up off the bench, putting it in his back pocket. He'd have to keep an eye on the security office's front window and eat a little fuel every time he saw the king coming.

The guard returned, holding something in his hand, partially behind his leg. What was that? His hand moved, and Ovrun identified the object.

A hammer.

A terrible instinct sent panic buzzing through Ovrun's body. He felt himself backing farther into the cell. He'd been sweating since he stepped under the dome, but now he felt his skin go clammy.

The man walked up to the bars. He stood there until Ovrun met his gaze. "Listen," he said. "I have to do what the king says. I don't like it. You'll like it even less. But he'll know if I don't obey." He swallowed hard. "I'm sorry."

Ovrun's heart felt like it would burst from his chest. Eyes wide, he looked at the guard. The man was shorter than him, but his muscles strained at his uniform. His skin was as sun-starved as the king's. The tight curls atop his head were matted and wild, like he hadn't seen a barber or even a hairbrush in months. And his brown eyes—there was no cruelty there. Only dread. "What are you gonna do?" Ovrun asked.

"Put your left hand through the bars, on the floor." The hammer in the guard's hand quivered. When Ovrun didn't move, he said, "I'm not doing anything, as long as you tell the truth. I promise. But if you don't . . ." He lifted the hammer.

"Why would I give you my hand so you can smash it?" Ovrun asked.

"He told me if you didn't, I have to shoot your knee."

A sound came out of Ovrun, some combination of a gasp and a choked cough.

"Just tell the truth," the guard said. "Please."

Ovrun felt like he was floating. Somewhere in his mind, he knew he was hyperventilating, but he couldn't stop. On feet that felt both heavy and weightless, he shuffled to the front of the cell. He knelt and put his hand through the bar. In a burst of stubborn rage, he slammed his palm on the floor.

The guard knelt on Ovrun's hand, holding it in place, leaving the fingers exposed. "Where's the princess?"

He stuck with his first lie. "I haven't seen her in months."

The hammer came down on Ovrun's index finger. A bone snapped.

The pain was twice as excruciating as Ovrun had imagined it would be. He refused to scream.

"Where's the princess?" the man asked again.

The same answer brought the same result. This time, a deep grunt exited Ovrun's mouth.

"Another lie, and I have to move on to the second finger. King's orders." The guard was breathing hard now. He turned desperate eyes on Ovrun. "Come on, man. Where's the princess?"

"It's been months since I saw her—I swear!"

The hammer came down again.

The cracking of bones assaulted Ovrun's ears. Dark spots filled his vision. He smelled his own sweat, tasted the sourness of fear. And his sense of touch—he'd give up his ability to ever feel anything again if only it would save him from another swing of the hammer. Every time the metal connected with his hand, unspeakable pain shot up his arm.

Perhaps two minutes later, three of Ovrun's fingers were broken, two of them in two places each. The guard asked his question again, and when Ovrun opened his mouth, lie number two came out. "She flew away—she flew away—on her dragon—a week ago. Please, stop. Please!"

"Oh, thank God," the guard said. With a flick of his wrist, he sent the hammer sliding across the floor like he never wanted to see the thing again. "Tell the truth faster next time, and you'll save yourself a lot of pain."

Ovrun drew his hand back into the cell and cradled it against his chest. He turned away, but not to hide his weeping. He didn't care if the guard saw that. No, he was hiding a smile so wide, it caught several of his tears.

They believed me. Oh, thank the sky, they believed me.

14

It snowed last night! My new friend Reymi came over this morning. Then Ulmin showed up earlier than expected. The three of us got into a snowball fight that left us cold, wet, and laughing our heads off.

Reymi went home, leaving Ulmin and me alone. He took both my hands, and it started snowing again. The moment turned magical, like I'd drunk a potion made of laughter and ice and the touch of his hand. I wanted Ulmin in a way I hadn't before. I saw the same desire in his eyes.

Why hasn't he kissed me yet? Maybe he's trying to build up my anticipation.

It's working.

-Letter from Ambrel Kaulder to Dani Kaulder
Dated Centa 30, 180 PD

"THE FARMS we're staying at are good sources of soil, stone, plant matter, and animal blood. It takes more effort to get ice and feathers, but we're doing okay. Lately, we've been training with firearms, though we don't have enough ammunition to . . ."

Nora tuned out the female militia member. She knew how the frequent drills and trainings were going; she often took part in them.

Since moving to a new farm four weeks ago, Nora had stood in this barn twice a week, facilitating meetings with her team of key leaders. The gatherings were training her for the many administrative tasks in her future . . . or what she privately called *the boring stuff*.

Shuffling her feet, she scanned the benches before her. For a split second, she sought out Ovrun. Then her mind caught up with reality, and the anxious briars in her belly, planted there the day of his capture, dug in deeper.

She had no doubt her father had brought Ovrun to the palace. Was he in pain? Clearly he hadn't talked, as no one had invaded Joli's family's farm. Did that mean he was dead? Or was he fooling the king or enduring torture?

Around the table at nearly every meal, Nora, Joli, and Krey tormented themselves by asking those unanswerable questions. Even Zeisha, who was usually so peaceful, sometimes joined in on their anxiety-ridden conversations. And Sarza listened to it all, her furrowed brow the only testament to her worry.

It was now thirty-three days since Nora had ended things with Ovrun. When he'd first been arrested, she'd thought his absence would further stoke her desire for him.

That hadn't happened.

In fact, she missed his companionship more than his kisses. He was the royal guard who'd always treated her as a person rather than a princess. She no longer imagined him by her side as she ruled the kingdom, but she couldn't fathom living in a world robbed of his steady goodness. Nora was coming to the conclusion that their friendship had been deeper than she'd realized, and their romance more shallow.

Was she an awful person for slowly getting over a guy who might be currently fighting for his life? That question often dug into her mind when she tried to sleep. She missed Ovrun desperately, but not in the way she'd expected to. To make things worse, any level of *missing him*—romantic or not—went against her resolution to emotionally detach from her friends. But she couldn't seem to think herself out of her misery.

Enough of this. Nora blinked hard to shift her mind back to the meeting. The militia member was talking about lyster training she'd scheduled for the next day.

Tuning out the report, which she'd already heard privately, Nora's eyes returned to the group. Krey sat on the front bench. He looked engaged, but she knew his mind was spinning with strategies. The two of them had read all the books they'd brought from Deroga and were now working their way through the texts again. Too many nights lately, they'd stayed up late, discussing strategies and sometimes waking others with their loud debates.

Next to Krey sat Sarza, whose occasional visions had proven invaluable to the group. She'd cautioned Tiam not to trust one of his neighbors, lest the man betray them to the king. Later, she'd advised Sharai and Hatlin to contact a particular New Therroan man who'd turned into a strong ally in the city.

The third person on Krey's bench was Joli. Despite a less-than-positive relational history with her, Ovrun had vouched for her loyalty. They'd gradually brought her into more discussions, and she'd proven to have an excellent mind for details, helping Nora and Krey think through the practicalities of their strategies. Nora's trust in her had grown so much that last week, she'd brought Joli to live at this very farm, where all the young leaders—Nora, Krey, Sarza, Zeisha, and Kebi—were staying.

The young woman finally wrapped up her report and returned to her seat. Nora smiled. "Thank you for that. Kebi, please update us on weapons training."

As she listened to Kebi's report, Nora continued her scan of the room. Next to Joli sat her father, Tiam. With efficient confidence, he'd brought together nearby farmers to help their cause. A dozen of them now hosted people who'd joined the coalition, mostly former militia members. Tiam and Varia were back home now, since Ovrun clearly hadn't disclosed their location to the king.

Zeisha sat in the second row, looking as serene as ever. She was still unsure what role she'd play in taking down the king, beyond keeping everyone stocked with shield fuel. The space next to Zeisha was empty; Kebi had been sitting there before joining Nora on the stage. When she wasn't helping in the farmhouse garden, Kebi trained their team of rebels in archery.

Another bench held Sharai and a New Therroan from Cellerin City. As the army continued trampling on freedoms, more New Therroans in the capital had joined the cause. Most still lived at home, ready to fight at a moment's notice. But eight of them who wanted to be more involved had moved out to the farms.

Three talented lysters from the militia rounded out the planning team, sharing a bench in the front row.

Just as Kebi returned to her seat and Nora opened her mouth to ask if there were any other items to discuss, a door at the side of the barn swung open, and Hatlin walked in. He'd left the previous night for Cellerin City and was just now returning.

"Do you have a report?" Nora asked.

He stood in front of the group, addressing the whole team. "Turns out one of my old friends joined the army. Problem is, he thinks occupying the capital is wrong. Plenty of other soldiers agree."

Nora's heart beat faster. "How strongly do they agree?"

Hatlin's mouth widened into a smile. "Well, my friend's dedicated enough that he wants to live out here with us. Want me to bring him in?"

"Please do."

A minute later, a man in his forties with medium-brown hair and a dark goatee stood before Nora. His hands trembled as he performed a bow, and when Nora thanked him, he kept his head down.

165

"You can look at me," she said, holding back a smile.

He swallowed as he did so. To her surprise, she didn't have to prod him to speak. "Your Highness, what the king's doing is wrong. I've been patrolling the streets of Cellerin City, and . . . the people, they're scared of us. They're my neighbors, and they hurry across the street when they see me coming. I'll fight for you. Others will too. You just let us know what to do. We want our country back."

"Sharai," Nora said as everyone left the meeting "I'd like you to stay."

"Of course, Your Highness."

Krey caught her gaze on the way out, raising a cynical eyebrow. He didn't seem to understand why Nora kept seeking the former minister's advice.

She'd tried to explain it to him. Over the last month, Sharai had grown on Nora. The woman's pragmatic, matter-of-fact outlook was refreshing. She reminded Nora of Dani, someone who'd always challenged her and spoken the truth, even when it was hard to hear. Sharai carried with her the essence of the palace. Of home. Nora hadn't realized how much she needed that.

And the woman wasn't without a soft side. She'd actually gotten emotional when she'd reunited with her niece in the militia. Krey said she'd faked it, but Nora swore she'd seen a real tear on Sharai's cheek.

"Have a seat," Nora said.

When they were both settled on a bench, Sharai said, "Things are looking up."

"I'd hoped we could bring some of the army to our side," Nora said, "but I didn't expect Hatlin to be the one to make it happen."

"I'll admit, I'm impressed with him. In fact, I've been surprised by the competency of many members of your team, including your friends." Seeing Nora flinch, Sharai drew her brows together. "What is it?"

"You're the one who told me, 'Rulers don't have friends. They have subjects.'"

A smile spread across Sharai's face. "Is that why you've been so uptight lately?"

Nora bristled. "Uptight?"

"Ever since I arrived. I'm not criticizing you; it's simply unexpected. When I worked at the palace, you were immature, seeking fun above all else."

"First you call me uptight, and now you say I'm flighty?" Maybe she wasn't so fond of Sharai after all.

"Used to be flighty." Sharai's eyes locked onto Nora, demanding honesty. "Do you disagree with my assessment?"

Nora opened her mouth, but nothing came out.

"Princess." Sharai sighed. "When I told you rulers don't have friends, I was making a point. A queen must make hard decisions. She can't be too close to the people she rules, or she'll lose her objectivity. I never expected you to be all business, all the time."

"What are you saying?"

"Guard your emotions, always. Don't forget who you are. But let your people see that you're human. Have a little fun. Fake it, if necessary."

Nora stared at Sharai, the last person she'd have expected to give such advice. Have fun—or at least pretend to? Every bit of her body rebelled against the idea. "I'm uptight," she snapped, "because an important member of my team was arrested a month ago, and he may be dead."

Sharai's eyes locked onto Nora's. "I know." She took a deep breath, clearly considering her next words. At last, she spoke. "I'm not heartless, Your Highness. I won't tell you to simply get over it. But you're distracted. Your preoccupation with Ovrun's absence is doing him no favors."

Nora's mouth went dry as the truth of Sharai's words hit home. If Ovrun was alive, the surest way to find and rescue him was to take down the king. For Ovrun's sake—and for that of everyone suffering under the leadership of Ulmin Abrios—Nora had to find a way to let go of the unknowns and focus on what she had control over.

Sharai leaned forward, her gaze intense. "Dozens of people at these farms are risking their lives to follow you. You must show them they're as important to you as Ovrun is. They respect you already, but to remain loyal, these rebels need more. Convince them you want to be here with them. Make them love you."

"How am I supposed to do that?"

Sharai pressed her narrow lips together, looking off to the side thoughtfully. Then she nodded, turning back to Nora. "You need to connect with your followers, and you all need relief from the constant tension you've been working under. Fall will arrive next week. It's been a good summer harvest. It's time to throw a party."

Nora glanced at the clock, then gasped. "We have to go!"

Krey looked up from his book, then stood and stretched. "Time flies when you're planning a revolution."

It was true. The clock's hands always seemed to move more quickly when they were in Krey's room, huddled over books. Rising, Nora looked down at her clothes—loose, black pants and a shapeless, gray shirt. "I remember when I wore a new, custom-tailored outfit to every party."

"Do you miss that?"

She was about to say no, because it seemed like the right answer. Then she remembered the feel of finely woven fabric hugging her skin. Longing filled her chest. "So much," she admitted.

Krey grinned. "Let's go."

They exited the little farmhouse, then crossed to the same barn they used for leadership meetings. It was Quari 1, the first day of fall. The last big party Nora had attended was nearly three months ago, when the trogs had come together to celebrate. That party had started out fun, but Nora had been melancholy by the end of it. As soon as she walked into the barn and heard the first strains of music, she made herself a promise: tonight, she'd enjoy herself.

Since meeting with Sharai a week ago, Nora had channeled her anxiety about Ovrun into an intense focus on training and strategy. She'd encouraged Krey and the others to do the same. But her tension —from Ovrun's absence and the very real stress of planning a revolution—remained. This party, she was convinced, was more a necessity than an indulgence. Surely some real fun would give her the energy to keep going.

The barn was filled with nearly a hundred people—Nora and her rebels, plus the farm families who were hosting them all. Dozens of hanging lanterns cast golden light around the room. Tables covered in cheerful cloth held a stunning quantity of food and beverages. A few members of farmers' families played music at one end of the room. Herb-scented candles swathed the room in a mild, pleasant scent and kept biting insects away.

Despite the music, only a few people were on the dance floor. Sarza was one of them; it seemed she'd gotten the dancing bug after the party in Deroga. But most of the partygoers were eating and chatting. Nora found herself swept into a conversation with a militia member while Krey headed for the food tables.

Some time later, Nora and dozens of others were sitting on the freshly swept wooden floor playing a raucous game of Guess What. A New Therroan crawled on all fours in front of the group.

"Orsa!" someone from his team shouted.

"Yes!" The New Therroan stood and scanned the left side of the room, where the other team sat. His eyes lit up, and he bellowed, "Your Royal Highness, you're up!"

Nora groaned but followed it with a smile. She felt surprisingly free tonight. She'd stayed away from the barrel of beer one of the farmers had brought, but now she wondered if the tart punch she'd gulped down was alcoholic. Stepping over knees and feet, she made her way to the front of the room, where she leaned close to the previous contestant so he could speak in her ear.

"Wind," he whispered.

She straightened, giving him an incredulous look. "You get *orsa* and you give me *that*?"

He shrugged, and everyone laughed. When he went to his seat, Nora began by blowing, letting her cheeks puff out.

"Blowing out a candle!" someone from her team shouted.

She shook her head. *I need another tactic.* With a shrug, she moved as if the wind were blowing her, leaning one direction, then another, then twisting, letting her dark hair whip around.

Her team shouted a few guesses: "Dancing!" "Turning!" "Drunk!" That last one, which applied to more than a few people in the room, made everyone laugh.

Nora continued leaning and twisting. It did feel a bit like a dance, and she found herself moving in time to the music, her eyes scanning her team. Out of forty people, none of them could guess this?

Her gaze found Krey. He sat at the edge of the group, watching her, mouth slightly open, head tilted. It was an expression she'd seen on him before, though it had been months—and back then, he'd directed it at Zeisha. But the look couldn't mean what Nora had always assumed it did, because back then, she'd interpreted it as . . . no, it couldn't be.

There was no way Krey West was looking at her with desire. Right?

Whatever the expression signified, it was gone in an instant. Krey sat up straighter, closing his mouth, a hint of sarcasm in his slightly lifted brow.

Nora realized she'd frozen in place. Refocusing, she tried to channel the wind. She moved more violently than before, attempting to literally shake off the odd feeling Krey's expression had given her. Thirty seconds later, she was opening her mouth to forfeit her turn when Krey shouted, "Wind!"

Nora stopped moving. "Yes!"

He gave her a half smile.

She scanned the other team and chose a female militia member as the next contestant. Mind muddled by the oddness of whatever she'd seen on Krey's face, she leaned close and whispered the first word that came to mind: "Farmer."

Nora eyed the place where she'd been sitting, but she didn't want to step over everyone to get to it. Better to find a spot at the edge of the crowd. Her mind a little fuzzy—surely that punch was spiked—she found a spot, not realizing until her butt hit the floor that she'd walked straight to Krey and was now sitting next to him.

"Good job," he said quietly.

"Thanks." She tried to pay attention to the game, but Krey, who was looking straight forward, drew her gaze. They'd spent a lot of time together lately, poring over books and considering strategies. Nora tried to keep her emotional distance, as she did with everyone else.

But that was difficult with Krey. She was too comfortable with him. Sometimes late at night, when sleepiness overcame her anxiety over Ovrun and her studied professionalism, Krey said something that got her laughing so hard, she had to smash her hand against her mouth to stay quiet. A couple of times, they'd fled his room to go outside and give their late-night giddiness free rein.

As much as Nora tried to keep up walls, as much as Sharai told her to remember who she was, sometimes all she wanted was to relax into the relationships she'd spent months cultivating. She missed Ovrun's friendship constantly. Nothing would feel right until she knew he was safe. But she couldn't deny the distinct comfort her other friends brought her—especially Krey.

Friendship. That was all she'd seen in his expression. She was sure of it now. He'd probably been holding back laughter; she knew she'd looked like a fool.

Everyone started clapping. The game must be over. Krey turned, too quickly for Nora to pretend she wasn't staring. One of his eyebrows arched as a small smile played at his lips. "What?" he asked.

And maybe it was the punch, or the atmosphere, or Sharai telling her to let loose. Whatever the reason, Nora allowed herself a moment of vulnerability. "I'm really glad you're my friend."

A dizzying mix of emotions flashed across his face. She thought she read disappointment there, and more of that look that couldn't possibly be desire, and maybe some relief. A confused smile settled on his lips. "What's gotten into you tonight?"

Partygoers were walking all around them, streaming to the food tables and dance floor. "What do you mean?" Nora asked.

"You've seemed . . . like your old self. Less uptight."

There was that word again. Nora felt heat enter her cheeks. "I'm trying to figure out how to be a crown princess while also planning to take down my father. Pardon me if I look like I don't know what I'm doing, but I don't."

He held his hands up in surrender, but he was smiling. "You're doing better than I would."

It was too nice of a night to stay annoyed. "Yeah," she said, "you'd make a crappy princess."

They both laughed, then sat in silence. Nora's gaze wandered the room, and when she spoke, she kept her voice low. "I can't be carefree like I used to be. Since Ovrun's capture, it's been even harder to let loose. You know that as well as I do. But Sharai said I need to let people see me having fun every once in a while."

His voice turned thick with incredulity. "This is all Sharai, isn't it? She's forming you into the leader she thinks you should be. And tonight, the only reason you're having fun is because she told you to! Has she given you written permission every time we laugh late at night too? As long as you read for three hours straight, you're allowed to have fun for five minutes?"

She scowled. "Don't be an ass!"

"I'm just calling it as I see it."

"You don't get it, Krey!" A harsh sigh exited her chest in a huff. She'd just told him how glad she was to have his friendship. Now here he was, reminding her he didn't understand her better than anyone else did. And why should she expect him to relate to a future he'd play no role in? She took in his stiff shoulders and tight mouth. *He's mad. Well, good. So am I.*

Finally, he spoke. "You shouldn't listen to anyone who says you have to turn into someone else to be a queen. You're smarter than that."

She rolled her eyes. "That's not what I said." Pushing herself to her feet, she looked down at him. "If lecturing me is on your agenda, move it to another night. There's music and food, and I'm gonna enjoy myself if it kills me." She stomped to the dessert table. Sugar could fix anything.

As she loaded a plate, footsteps approached behind her, and somehow she knew it was Krey. He stood close enough that she felt his warmth all along her back. She stood still as a statue as he leaned in and spoke in her ear.

"I'm really glad you're my friend too."

Her anger vaporized. Every muscle in her body loosened, and emotions she couldn't identify flooded her heart. She turned to find Krey watching her, his eyes intense. A corner of his mouth turned up in a hopeful smile.

"I'm about to eat way too much cake," Nora said. "Then, I seem to remember you promising you'd dance next time you had a chance. I let you off the hook when we had our little goodbye party in Deroga. So are you up for it tonight? Or were you planning to brood in the background again?" She lifted her chin, challenging him with her gaze.

He laughed. "I'll dance, since you asked so nicely."

"Great. We'll both dance like fools. And tomorrow, if anyone asks why I was acting so un-queenlike, I'll blame it on the spiked punch."

Krey's smile turned confused. "The punch is nonalcoholic."

She blinked. "How . . . weird." Maybe the slight giddiness she'd felt all night was just hunger.

One way to find out. She dug into her cake, laughing at the look Krey gave her.

THE STONE EATER: 5

ULMIN STOOD before one of the two cells in the security office, staring down at Ovrun Kensin.

The young man had been here for over a month. Captivity hadn't been kind to him. His dark, wavy hair was shaggy and tangled, and he stank, despite occasional sponge baths and weekly laundering of his clothes. His muscles were less prominent, not for lack of exercise—according to the guards, he performed frequent calisthenics—but due to his restricted calories. Shadows under his eyes testified to his lack of sleep.

Then there were Ovrun's hands, which had suffered through many interrogation sessions. However, Ulmin had quickly realized that, while pain had its uses, relief did too. All Ovrun's fingers had been broken repeatedly, then healed by a blood lyster Ulmin brought in every few days. The healer always did her best, but sometimes she couldn't fully mend the bones. A couple of the boy's fingers were now crooked.

According to the guards, Ovrun's fear had grown more and more palpable. He knew how much that hammer hurt and how good healing felt. Yet he still insisted on lying every time, until he was in too much pain to resist telling the truth.

Ulmin hadn't wanted to resort to torture, but Ovrun hadn't given him a choice. His mind was different in some inexplicable way. Ulmin couldn't feel it when he controlled it. From the start, he'd known this was likely a fluke. No one in the world could match Ulmin in magical strength. An ordinary boy like Ovrun, who wasn't even a lyster, couldn't hope to resist the pull of his king's mind. But just in case, Ulmin had tested his prisoner. As Ovrun's hands turned puffy with swelling and purple with bruises, Ulmin became convinced that the stories Ovrun told while being controlled were true. He'd last seen Nora when she flew away on a dragon. And he had little information on the resistance.

Ulmin could've told the guards to stop the torture. It was no longer necessary. But he'd grown so impressed by the young man's strength . . . and more determined than ever to break him. How marvelous it would be if Ovrun, a young man with supreme mental and physical strength, became truly loyal to his king?

So their conversations had shifted of late. Ulmin had been looking forward to this one all day. He'd consumed more brain matter than was strictly necessary before walking into the building. Magical strength was fairly rushing through his limbs and, more importantly, his mind.

Smiling at Ovrun, he said, "Come close." When the boy obeyed, Ulmin wrapped his scarred hand around the boy's fingers. Due to his inability to sense Ovrun's mind, Ulmin always established a physical connection. His smile grew wider when Ovrun's face slackened. "Tell me what you feel," the king said, "when guards come to interrogate you."

"I get scared." Ovrun's voice was flat. "I know how much it'll hurt."

"I'm so sorry. If you told them the truth the first time they asked a question, they wouldn't need to harm you."

"I know."

"Have you considered that?"

"Yes."

Ulmin paused, brows raised. He'd asked that question a few times. Ovrun had never answered affirmatively. "You've considered telling the truth? No pain required?" His lips curled into a small smile.

"Yes."

"That would make me quite happy."

Ovrun nodded.

Ulmin licked his lips, gazing thoughtfully at his prisoner. Sometimes if he planted an idea in someone's mind while controlling them, the thought remained in their subconscious when they came back to themselves. "The more you speak the truth, the more I'll trust you. Eventually, I would like you to live in the palace dorms instead of this prison. I would like you to work for me. To work *with* me."

Another slow nod from Ovrun.

"Would you enjoy that?" Ulmin asked.

"Yes."

"What do you want more than anything, Ovrun?"

"I want to stop feeling pain."

"I can do that for you. I can protect you like no one else. Do you believe me?"

The young man's tired eyes stared at Ulmin. People being controlled rarely hesitated in their responses. When they did, it was because their minds were busy working out new truths. Ulmin waited.

"I believe you," Ovrun said.

Ulmin did his best to release his control over his prisoner's strange mind. He knew it had worked when Ovrun sat up straighter and looked around in confusion.

"Ovrun," Ulmin said, leaning toward the bars of the cell, "where is my daughter?"

Ovrun's head bowed. His shoulders slumped. He stood there for a long, silent moment, before lifting his chin to look in the king's eyes.

"The last time I saw her," he said, his voice rough and tired, "she was flying away from Deroga on a dragon. It was a week before I got arrested. She said she'd come back when she was ready to lead her rebels. She wants your throne, Your Majesty." He swallowed hard. "There's . . . so much I regret. I never should've worked with her. If I knew where she was, I'd tell you."

Ulmin nodded and gave the young man the most fatherly smile he could muster. "I know you would." He released his control of the guard's mind. "Have someone bring in a tub so this young man can take a proper bath. Get him some meat too." Turning back to Ovrun, he said, "No hammer tonight."

Ovrun buried his face in his hands. His shoulders shook with sobs.

15

Ulmin and I went on a carriage ride after chapel services again. This time, he sat across from me in the carriage, barely looking at me. When my knee bumped his, he jolted, like I'd shocked him.

After half an hour of no conversation, I couldn't stay quiet. "What happened to you? Yesterday, we shared a beautiful moment. Today, you're as cold as the snow."

His shoulders slumped, and when he looked up at me, I saw real fear in his eyes. "What happens if this doesn't work?" He grabbed my hand and held it tight, like I was his anchor. "What I feel . . .it's stronger than I anticipated, and I can't expect you to reciprocate."

I leaned forward, pressing my forehead to his. "What if I want to reciprocate?"

He stood in the jostling carriage and sat next to me. Then he held me in his arms so tightly that I could feel his racing heart.

-Letter from Ambrel Kaulder to Dani Kaulder
Dated Centa 31, 180 PD

———

KREY HAD BEEN awake for at least an hour when dawn's light crept through the cracks between the shutters. With a quiet groan, he sat up. It was useless to try to get more sleep; his mind was too awake. It didn't help that outside, birds were grumbling loudly, like they wanted everyone else to join them in rising early.

He slipped on some loose pants and opened the shutters, then padded over to the desk. This room was way smaller than the one where he'd stayed in Joli's house, and there was no electricity. But having a space to himself was a worthwhile tradeoff. Most of the time. On mornings like this one, when his thoughts scurried like shimshims through his mind, he wished he still had a roommate to distract him. *God, protect Ovrun,* he breathed, as he did every morning.

Sighing, he opened a book full of exhilarating accounts of battles and started reading where he'd left off. He'd gotten through two paragraphs before he realized he wasn't retaining any of it. He raked his fingers through his tangled hair. *I made a fool of myself last night.*

Nora had caught him staring at her during that damn game of Guess What. He'd tried to wipe the slobbery, dopey look off his face, but he knew she'd seen it. Then she'd told him she was glad he was her friend. The only thing worse would've been if she'd said she cared for him like a brother. He let himself chuckle at that, though it wasn't really funny.

Crisp memories from the rest of the night sparked in his mind. They'd argued, and he'd told her he was glad she was his friend too, and she'd thought the punch was spiked (what the hell was that about?), and they'd danced. And danced. And danced. Certain he couldn't handle holding her close for minutes on end, he'd made sure they were dancing in a group of friends, keeping it light, changing partners frequently. Still, he'd found himself gazing at her longingly again, like some pathetic character in a romance story. And he was pretty sure she'd caught him doing it.

Yep, he'd made a fool of himself. Hopefully she'd assumed he was drunk. He knew the truth—he hadn't touched the beer.

Why was he worried about her opinion, anyway? It wasn't like she'd spare any thoughts for him today. She was way too busy trying to become some sort of badass, emotionless leader. After her brief foray into having fun, her walls would surely be back up this morning.

Which was a good thing.

Really.

A sharp knock sounded. Krey crossed the room and opened the door. Nora, Zeisha, Kebi, Sarza, and Joli stood there, all clad in pajamas.

"It's Sunday," Krey said. He hadn't expected anyone else to get up for at least an hour.

"I had a vision," Sarza said. "I wanted to tell all of you about it at once."

Krey's eyes widened. "Come in." He opened the shutters and returned to his desk chair. Sarza took the second chair, and Joli sat on the bed. Nora, Zeisha, and Kebi settled on throw rugs on the floor.

"Someone needs to go to the chapel at the palace," Sarza said.

Nora's brows drew together. "It's covered by the dome. No one can get in there."

Sarza shrugged. "There's a way. We just have to figure it out."

"Who should go?" Kebi asked.

"I don't know." Sarza briefly rubbed her temple, like she was in pain. "The figure in the vision was fuzzy. I think that means we can decide ourselves."

"Let me get this straight," Krey said. "Someone needs to visit the chapel at the palace. Only it's totally inaccessible, and we don't know who should go."

Sarza shrugged. "You got it. And I don't think we should tell anyone outside this group, so it needs to be one of us."

"Do you know why we're supposed to go there?" Nora asked.

"Not yet."

Krey looked around the group, seeing on their faces the same grogginess, excitement, and confusion he felt. "What do you think, Nora?"

She sat up straighter. "I trust Sarza. That means we need to figure out how to sneak one of us into a stone dome. Who has ideas?" Her eyes, though sleepy, were hard and focused. Back to business for the crown princess.

"It's too bad we can't tunnel under the dome," Joli said. One of the militia's dirt eaters had tried just that a couple of weeks earlier. He'd found that the stone extended underground, all the way to the bedrock.

Krey said, "We need to convince the emissary at the chapel to let someone in."

"Whatever story we tell will have to be good enough for my father too," Nora said. "The rebels in Cellerin City told Hatlin that no one can enter the dome without the king's permission. The good news is, my father worships almost every day. If anyone can convince him of anything, it's his own personal emissary." She said the final phrase with a sneer.

"What does the king want?" Zeisha asked.

Nora turned to her. "What do you mean?"

"What does your father want more than anything in the world? If we have to convince him of something, we need to know what motivates him."

Nora bit her lip. After a time, she spoke. "I almost said *power*. But he already has that. He's afraid of losing it . . . of losing everything. What he wants most is to feel safe. That's why his army is occupying both New Therro and Cellerin City. He wants to be sure no one will challenge him. And he clearly built the dome to protect himself and his power."

Krey nodded. "You convinced him to leave Deroga by telling him Zeisha would tear apart his palace and his land. He couldn't stand the thought of being vulnerable."

"Ever since my mother died, he's dreaded the unexpected. He tries to mitigate every possible risk. It's why he's a brain lyster. Letting people think for themselves is too risky."

Krey nodded slowly, eyes fixed on Nora. She'd lost both her parents—one to death, one to madness. But right now, her jaw was set against any pain she might feel.

Zeisha said, "We need to convince your father that letting someone into the chapel will make him safer."

Ideas flew around the room. Some were promising enough to discuss in depth, but nothing seemed quite feasible.

After perhaps an hour, Joli broke a lull in the conversation by saying, "I think we're making this too complicated. Would your father ever let a pilgrim visit the chapel?"

"I doubt it," Nora said. "It's been closed to visitors since the dome went up."

Silence fell again. Krey's knee bounced up and down as he considered Joli's suggestion. Finally, he turned to Nora. "It'll have to be just the right pilgrim."

"What do you mean?"

"He's currently ruling his nation through fear. Surely he realizes it would be better if people actually wanted to be loyal to him. Do you think admiration would make him feel more secure in his power?"

"Maybe," Nora said. "What are you thinking?"

"Well, he's pretty proud of his position as the keeper of the stone, right?"

"*Proud* isn't a strong enough term," Nora said with a short laugh.

"So we send in someone who's in awe of the stone. Someone who admires him because he's protected it for so long. A pilgrim, like Joli said. But it can't be just anyone. We need to also offer him another type of security—an alliance with another country."

Nora tilted her head. "Keep going."

"One of you—someone the king has never met, of course—can reach out to the emissary, claiming to be Rimorian clergy from a neighboring nation. You'll say you're on a pilgrimage, and not only do you hope to see the stone; you've also been instructed by your nation's leaders to establish a religious alliance, hoping it'll lead to a political one."

"We'd have to choose a country we're not already allies with," Nora said. "That rules out Cruine, Lerenor, and Banth."

"What about Newland?" Krey asked.

Zeisha shook her head. "The Rimorian religion is outlawed there, remember?"

"Oh, that's right." Newland's so-called prime minister was really an autocratic dictator.

Nora said, "Only one nation makes sense—Rimoria." It was a large nation hundreds of clommets southwest of Cellerin. The large Therro Desert separated the countries.

"That's perfect," Joli said. "It's a theocracy. Their government was formed on Rimorian principles. My aunt is from there. She was happy to get away."

"Cellerin isn't allied with Rimoria?" Krey asked Nora.

She rolled her eyes. "No, they've never deemed us righteous enough to trust us. If my father heard that a member of the clergy from Rimoria was hoping to establish groundwork for an alliance, that would excite him. Their population is bigger than ours; they'd be a powerful ally. And they're far enough away that it would be tough for him to check up on the story." She turned to Sarza. "What do you think?"

"My gut tells me it's a good idea."

"Great," Nora said. "Let's figure out who'll play our fake member of the clergy, and then we can hammer out the details."

"It can't be you, obviously," Krey said, "or me or Zeisha. The king can control me on sight, and the same might be true for Zeisha. We know he spent time with the militia."

"That leaves Kebi, Sarza, and me," Joli said.

"I'll do it," Sarza said.

"Why you?" Nora asked.

Sarza squared her shoulders and lifted her chin. "Because it'll be dangerous. Kebi has Zeisha to think about, and Joli has her parents."

Krey's mind filled in the blanks. *And you don't have anyone.*

Zeisha said softly, "You've got friends too."

Sarza dropped her gaze to the blanket she was sitting on. "Yeah. Well . . . it should still be me. My ability will guide me. Nobody else has that."

"If the king comes near you," Zeisha said, "you'll have to eat shield fuel. It'll block your abilities."

"I know. Hopefully I can fulfill the prophecy without actually meeting him." Sarza's chin came up again, and she locked her gaze on Nora. "I want to do this. Please." She drew in a deep breath and let it out. When she spoke again, her voice was strained. "A year ago, I didn't know what it felt like to have a purpose. Now I do. That's because of the people in this room. I'm not very good at saying thanks. So let me do this. For the group."

"And if you don't make it out?" Nora asked.

"I'm afraid of plenty of things. Dying's not one of them."

Coming from most people, that statement would be bluster. But Krey believed Sarza.

Nora studied the seer for a long moment before finally saying, "Okay. It's you." All professionalism, she turned to Joli. "You're the detail person. Grab some paper and a pencil. Let's make our plans."

16

Today, Ulmin took me to the chapel at the palace.

I spent a long time looking at the stone. It's unlike anything I've ever seen. The black is deep and otherworldly. In the sunshine that streams in through the skylights, the stone's orange surfaces shimmer, almost like they're alive.

What caught me off guard, though, was Ulmin's reaction to it. He doesn't worship it. That practice would be too close to heresy. But he takes deep pride in being one of its keepers. He honors it for its power— to bestow both death and magic. He said it's not just a stone to him. It's a symbol of who the people of Anyari used to be, who we are, and who we could become.

-Letter from Ambrel Kaulder to Dani Kaulder
Dated Barna 1, 180 PD

By the light of a single candle, Sarza put on a dark-green Rimorite dress belonging to Joli's aunt. It was over the top in its modesty. The neckline, fastened by way too many buttons, went almost up to her chin. Long, wide sleeves swallowed her hands. Billowy fabric extended to the floor, somehow making her look even thinner than she already was. A black scarf covered her short hair.

Sarza frowned at herself in a dirty, full-length mirror. *I can't believe Rimorite pilgrims wear dresses like this. It would suck to travel in.* But since she'd supposedly done just that, she and others on her team had taken turns wearing the garment every day for two weeks without washing it. It had mud on the bottom hem, sweat stains under the arms, and a stench that made Sarza wrinkle her nose.

"I'm honored to meet you," she said to her dim reflection. Joli's aunt had worked with her to get the drawling Rimorite accent just right.

After making sure she'd put the letter from the palace and a bag of shield fuel in her pockets, Sarza blew out her candle and exited the dingy room she'd been renting in a Cellerinian pub for the last week.

During that time, she and the emissary at the palace had sent messages back and forth, something Sarza couldn't have done from the farm without giving away the rebels' location. Joli had ridden an orsa to the city every night to meet with Sarza and get a status update. Last night, Sarza had finally shared some good news: the king had approved her for a morning visit.

The dark stairs squeaked as Sarza descended into the pub's main room, which smelled of dust and last night's cooking. Even the cook wasn't up this early in the morning.

It was hours before Sarza was supposed to arrive at the palace to meet with Emissary Loryn and the king. By arriving early, she hoped to be in and out before the king even got up. *If the guards let me past the gate.*

Cellerin's quiet streets glowed with dim light from streetlamps. A chilly autumn breeze grabbed Sarza's oversized dress, sending the hem swirling around her hurried feet. To avoid tripping, she lifted it off the ground. It would take at least an hour to walk from the pub to the palace, which was west of the city. As she traveled, she drew in deep breaths, trying to stay calm. She hadn't had any further visions, so she was depending on her gift to provide guidance when she got there.

Once Sarza exited the city, stars and a half moon provided barely enough light to navigate by. She was just getting worried that she'd missed the stone dome when she realized it was right in front of her.

The structure was awe-inspiring. Sarza had imagined a perfectly round dome, like one covering a dinner plate. Instead, it was a rectangle with rounded corners, one of which she was standing next to. It connected two straight walls: one paralleling the street, the other bordering the forested area east of the palace. Both walls rose at slight angles, disappearing into the dark sky.

I probably shouldn't touch it, she thought, even as she reached up to do just that. Her fingertips, then her palm, connected with cool stone. Sarza wasn't sure what she'd expected magically created stone to feel like, but it seemed the same as stone quarried from the ground. The large, rectangular pieces were smooth, and she couldn't feel any mortar between them. Maybe magic held them together.

She resumed her walk, brushing the stone with her fingertips as she followed it down the road. Before long, she reached the front entrance.

Royal guards stood on each side of a metal gate that was large enough for a wagon to pass through. Lanterns sat at their feet. Each guard brought a hand to the gun at his waist as she approached. She stopped a safe distance from the first guard.

"State your business," he said.

"I have a letter." Her voice emerged as a drawl that almost made her laugh.

As soon as her hand went to her pocket, the guard grabbed her arm. "None of that." With a brisk touch, he frisked her sides, then stepped back. "I'll take the letter now."

Sarza glared at him, biting back an insult, then pulled out the folded paper.

He picked up his lantern with one hand and took the letter with the other. After a quick moment scanning it, he looked up, a smirk on his lips. "Rimorite clergy? Sorry I had to frisk you, Aunt." Members of the Rimorite clergy were traditionally called *Aunt* and *Uncle*, but it sounded ridiculous coming from someone who was at least ten years older than her. "This letter says the king wants to meet you mid-morning. Why are you early?"

"I sent the emissary a note, telling her I'd come before dawn for a time of quiet worship."

He squinted, reading the letter again. "Come on, I'll walk you in. We'll see what the emissary has to say."

"Thank you."

He approached the entrance, carrying the lantern. A couple of mets inside the dome, there was a fence, topped with razor wire. It, too, was gated. A guard stationed inside the grounds unlocked both gates. Sarza's escort led her inside and turned right, walking along the fence.

The area smelled of mold and moisture. In less than half a minute, Sarza was sweating. "By the stone, it's hot in here."

The guard laughed. "Yeah, and you're right, it's *by the stone*—and I mean the stone above us, not the one in the chapel. The dome traps the heat. Now you see why I get stationed outside the gate as often as I can. It's hard to sleep at night. At least it's cooler now than it was during the summer."

Despite the heat, Sarza shuddered. She couldn't imagine living in here. Was Ovrun under the dome? If so, he must be miserable. She'd never met someone who liked the outdoors as much as he did.

After a few minutes walking through the stuffy air, the guard held up his lantern, revealing a building whose side wall extended all the way to the fence. "The chapel's front door is in the fence," the guard said. "It used to be the public entrance. I'll take you to the back." He led her around the building and knocked at the door. Nobody came. "Probably still asleep." He knocked again.

After a couple of minutes, the door opened, revealing an elderly woman with tightly curled, gray hair. She wore the gray tunic, slacks, and scarf of an emissary. Bands of blue and black, Cellerin's royal colors, lined the scarf's edges. Her eyes took in Sarza's ridiculous costume. "Senita," she said, "you're early."

Sarza tried not to flinch at the fake name she'd given. "I'm sorry, I thought you knew I wanted time alone to worship."

"Perhaps you did mention that." The emissary turned to the guard. "Please alert the king that our guest is here."

The guard turned to obey.

"There's no need to wake him," Sarza blurted, barely remembering her accent. "I can meet him at the time we set."

"He will want to know. Come in." The woman stepped to the side and closed the door behind Sarza. "I'm sorry the hallway is so dark. The electricity in this building is reserved for the chapel itself." She led Sarza down the hall and opened a door. At the flick of a switch, bright light flooded the room.

From her conversations with Nora, Sarza knew the guard and king might return from the palace, on the opposite end of the property, as soon as twenty minutes from now. She needed to figure out why she was here . . . then leave before the king got the chance to touch her.

Despite the time crunch, she stepped toward a pedestal on the small stage. She was no Rimorian, but the black stone—the cause of Anyari's apocalypse—filled her with awe. Light glimmered off the orange edges of its broken pieces. No wonder pilgrims traveled for weeks or months to visit it.

"Please don't touch it," Emissary Loryn said, "even the case. It's alarmed for your safety. I've seen two people who touched the stone, then died within a day."

"I understand." Sarza pulled her attention away from the glorious, terrible artifact in the glass case and smiled at the emissary. "Thank you for allowing me to visit. I've traveled for weeks to see this."

"Would you like a few minutes alone to worship?"

An urge—or what the book she'd been slowly reading called a *premonition*—overtook her. This woman wasn't supposed to leave. "I'll worship alone after meeting the king, since he's on his way."

"Very well. Would you like to have a seat?"

"That would be lovely."

They sat in the front row and chatted about how Cellerinian and Rimorite clergy might begin connecting with each other. Sarza was only half focused on the conversation. Under her cool exterior, her thoughts raced. *Why am I here? What am I supposed to learn? When will the king arrive? Why didn't I look at the clock on the wall when we came in?*

The swarms of questions weren't doing her any good. As the emissary talked, Sarza forced her breathing to slow. After a minute or so, another premonition hit her. The emissary was trustworthy—but the king controlled her at times. And he could arrive any minute. It was time to be frank. And very cautious. Anything she said might later be repeated to Ulmin.

"Emissary Loryn," Sarza said.

The woman flinched, obviously not used to being interrupted. "Yes?"

"I have to leave very soon. I'm . . ." Sarza took a quick breath, letting her urges guide her. She dropped her fake accent. "I'm not who you think I am. I'm sorry I lied to you." The emissary's mouth dropped open, but Sarza kept going. "We don't have much time. I know the king controls people, including you. I know you may have to tell him all this later. That's okay. I'll be gone by then. I need you to listen to me. No one should be allowed to control people. Someone has to stop the king. But we don't know how he's gotten so powerful or how to fight him."

The woman's breathing had quickened. Eyes wide with intense fright, she said, "I'm committed to obeying my king."

"I know." Sarza sucked at empathy, but she tried to give the woman an understanding smile. Continuing to follow feelings that could be either panicked instincts or mild premonitions, she held her hand to her belly. "I have to go. I'm feeling ill."

Emissary Loryn took Sarza's hand, giving her an inscrutable, intense look. "Do not, under any circumstances, go in my office."

Sarza's breath stopped in her throat. Something important was in that office, though Loryn didn't dare say it openly. "I won't." Sarza squeezed the emissary's hand. "Thank you."

She fled into the dark hallway. The first door she opened led to a small bathroom. Next, there was a broom closet, then the emissary's bedroom.

When Sarza's hand fell on the fourth doorknob, the sound of another door opening broke the silence of the hallway. Someone was entering the building. Sarza froze. Between her and the open door were perhaps ten mets of dark hallway. She held her breath and looked over her shoulder, wishing desperately she could disappear into the shadows.

A figure, cloaked in the dome's darkness, walked in. Sarza closed her eyes, lest some glimmer of light reflect off the frightened tears that filled them.

Perhaps the visitor was walking at a normal pace, but to Sarza, it seemed each quiet footstep took an eternity. Every muscle in her body tightened as she anticipated hearing King Ulmin's voice. Feeling his hand on her skin. Losing her mind to his control.

A door squeaked open. A bit of light shone through Sarza's eyelids.

The door shut with a click. The footsteps stopped.

Sarza's eyes flew open, her head swiveling to look behind her again. The hallway was dark and empty. The visitor had entered the chapel. She drew in a deep breath, unwilling to give in to the panicked sobs building in her chest. She turned the knob, opened the door, and slipped in.

Her pulse pounded in her neck, face and palms. She hadn't held her breath for long, but she couldn't stop gulping air. A light drew her gaze. It came from a tiny glass window, several simmets tall and as long as her forearm, built into the wall. On the other side was the chapel stage.

The window made sense; the emissary would want to be sure visitors didn't disturb the stone. That little piece of glass would reveal something important to Sarza. She'd never been more certain of anything.

The king and Emissary Loryn stood between the chairs and the stage, talking. The emissary appeared to be in control of her own mind. This was the first time Sarza had ever seen King Ulmin. He looked older than she'd expected, the wrinkles on his forehead turning more pronounced when he lifted his brows in response to something the emissary said.

They both stepped onto the stage. As they got closer to Sarza's little window, she stepped back, just in case. From her new position, she still had a good view of the stage.

Emissary Loryn knelt slowly behind the pedestal that held the stone. Sarza's eyes narrowed as she watched the gray-clad woman take a key from her pocket and open a panel. She reached in, moved her hand a bit, then shut the panel door and stood. With a nod to the king, she stepped away from the pedestal.

King Ulmin approached, reaching out both hands. The second he touched the glass case around the stone, Sarza flinched, expecting to hear an alarm.

Nothing happened. Emissary Loryn didn't look at all surprised. Sarza's gaze darted down to the panel again. *The emissary turned it off.*

Grinning broadly, Ulmin lifted the glass case and set it on the floor. His wide eyes turned almost feral. He reached out both hands and grabbed two pieces of the stone.

Sarza tried to stifle her gasp. Did the king have a death wish? Her breathing halted as bright-orange light traveled from the artifact's pieces to the king's hands. The luminescent glow swirled up his arms, then covered his shoulders, his neck, his entire head. His broad chest swelled and collapsed as he took several deep breaths.

Emissary Loryn's expression didn't change. A heavy, harsh sureness settled into Sarza's chest: *This is normal for both of them.*

After half a minute or so, the king placed the stone's pieces back on the pedestal. The orange magic enveloping his arms, neck, and head faded away as he replaced the glass case. Emissary Loryn returned to the little panel and repeated her actions from before.

The king stepped off the stage. When the emissary finished her task, he beckoned her to join him. As soon as she stepped in front of him, her whole body slackened, her mind clearly controlled.

Sarza's stomach tightened. She stepped closer to the window again, hoping to read their lips. She didn't get the chance. Pressure filled her brain. Anticipating the vision she knew was coming, she dropped to the floor. As soon as she sat, the vision began.

She saw herself standing from this very spot on the floor and running from the chapel building into the night. In the vision, she held up the skirt of her ridiculous dress and sprinted nearly to the front gate. Just before she arrived, she released her dress and slowed to a demure walk. She thanked the guards and left. The gate wasn't too far from the southwest corner of the dome. Sarza walked that direction, rounded the corner, and darted into the darkness. Behind her, someone shouted. Before anyone could get to her, Osmius landed in front of her. Sarza climbed on his back, and he lifted into the air just as guards rounded the corner of the dome. They shouted and shot, but Osmius flew her to safety.

The vision faded to nothing, then gradually lightened as a second scene began—another option. The book she'd been reading would call this a *potential prophecy*.

This scene started as the first had. Sarza stood from her spot on the floor. But instead of leaving, she turned to the bookshelf behind

Emissary Loryn's desk. With a suppressed grunt, she heaved it away from the wall. She reached into the narrow space, scraping her hand against the bookshelf's wooden back. Her fingers found a small book, not much larger than her hand. She slipped it in her pocket. As before, she fled the building.

Again, she sprinted, then slowed and exited through the gate. She turned right and hurried toward the corner of the dome.

She heard the same shout as before, but this time, she was closer and could make out the words. "Arrest that woman!"

Sarza ran, royal guards from outside and inside the dome pursuing her. Faint lantern light outlined their bows, and she was certain they had guns too.

The vision ended. Post-vision pain swelled in Sarza's brain. She ignored it. She had a choice to make. Something inside her told her that book was important. She might not be able to escape the guards. But it was worth the risk.

Without hesitating, she pushed herself to her feet and dashed to the bookshelf behind the emissary's desk.

Cold stone pressed into Nora's elbows, belly, and thighs. Krey lay on one side of her, Kebi on the other, both propped as she was on the curved top of the palace dome.

Guards stood at the gate below, but Nora's perspective didn't give her a good view. Osmius flew in the dark sky above, high enough to remain unrecognized. He'd been sharing his sight with Nora since they'd arrived a couple of hours ago. Thanks to his excellent night vision, she'd seen plenty of details as Sarza approached the dome and entered. Now, Nora, Krey, and Kebi all anxiously waited for the seer to exit.

Nora had been hesitant to bring Osmius. He hated flying near the palace, fearing the king would see him and capture his mind. But there was no better way to travel secretly than high in the air, on a dragon's back. Besides, Nora doubted her father would glimpse Osmius. The king wouldn't want to leave the safety of his dome.

He'd better not, considering that Krey was vulnerable to mind control too. But, unlike Osmius, Krey truly wanted to be here. Of everyone who knew about this mission, he had the best aim with a handgun. Plus, his flying ability could end up being an asset. Nora had agreed he should come.

They'd named Kebi as their second team member since she'd trained with a bow for over half her life and had performed well in the battle for Deroga. She'd spent the last week further honing her archery skills, even shooting arrows while flying on Krey's back, in case such a feat would be helpful during their mission.

No one had wanted Nora to come along; they thought the future queen should stay hidden. But she'd insisted. This was her fight, more than anyone else's.

Through the dragon sight in her mind, Nora saw movement at the gate. "I think she's coming," she whispered.

The gate opened. Sarza exited and turned toward the corner of the dome, nearly running. As she drew closer to safety, Nora's heart lifted with hope.

Then everything fell apart.

A running figure approached the gate within the dome. Nora recognized her father an instant before he shouted, "Arrest that woman!"

Sarza began running. The two outdoor guards lifted guns and chased her. Four more guards—two with guns, two with bows—joined them. Krey and Kebi had jumped to their feet as soon as they heard the king. Kebi ran along the dome's curved top as Krey flew low above it, both of them headed toward the corner Sarza was desperately trying to reach. Nora followed. While she had ice and a gun at her disposal, her primary role was to observe using Osmius's sight and to pass along any helpful information.

She watched Sarza round the corner. Through her own eyes, she saw Krey land. He could aim better with his feet on solid ground—or, in this case, stone. He and Kebi took aim at the corner Sarza had just passed, ready for the guards to appear.

All at once, panic rushed into Nora's body. In the space of a single second, her mind flashed with images of those her father had taken from her. Faylie. Taima. Ovrun. Now, he'd take Sarza. Nora was the only one who could end his tyranny. She'd always known that. It was time to stop expecting others to fight her battles.

Acting on pure instinct and some unstoppable urge, Nora stopped next to Krey and Kebi, who'd just halted, their weapons trained past the dome's corner, where the first of the guards was about to turn.

"STOP!" Nora shouted.

Kebi and Krey froze. With Osmius's sight, Nora saw two guards turning the corner, getting nearer to Sarza at every moment.

"I'm the crown princess of Cellerin!" Nora screamed to the guards on the ground. "I command you to stop!"

Two of them halted and looked up. The others didn't react at all, continuing their pursuit. It was like they hadn't even heard her. In a gut-dropping instant, Nora realized the guards couldn't follow her commands if her father was controlling them.

And that wasn't her only mistake. She'd just shouted so loud, her father had surely heard her.

Osmius! Nora cried.

I am coming, he replied.

One of the guards who'd halted now sprinted back toward the gate, doubtless to report to Ulmin. Krey followed, shooting. In the darkness and chaos, his bullets missed their marks.

The other guard who'd stopped was still staring at the top of the dome. All four remaining guards—the ones Nora assumed were controlled—continued their pursuit. Kebi shot arrows at them in quick succession. Nora disconnected from Osmius's vision and aimed balls of ice at the guards. Two of them fell, though she couldn't tell who'd hit them.

After a few moments that felt like a lifetime, Osmius dove from the dark sky. Rivers of white-hot fire exited his mouth, creating a long, tall, burning fence between the guards and Sarza. The guards shot bullets and arrows, but they couldn't see their quarry. Osmius descended further, grabbing Sarza with his front claws and flying off with her, eliciting a scream.

A bullet from below smashed into the stone near Kebi. "Middle of the dome!" Nora shouted. She, Krey, and Kebi stopped their attack and ran that direction.

Osmius's voice reached Nora's mind. *I must go so the king does not see me. Tell Krey to carry you. Meet me in the forest.* He sent a picture to Nora's mind: the clearing where he and Taima had both landed on the night Krey used his brain-lysting faculty on the king.

"Take us both!" Nora told Krey. "It won't be a long flight."

He grunted and knelt. Without a word, Kebi climbed on his back. Nora stood in front of him and locked her arms around his neck. She didn't have anywhere to put her legs, as Kebi's were around his waist. "Hold me tight!" she said.

Krey's arms crushed her to him, and he lifted into the air, flying toward the back of the dome. Away from the king. He'd told Nora dozens of times that when he wrapped her in his magic, she was safe. But for the first time ever, her back was facing the ground as they flew. Terror, hot and acidic, burned her insides. She shoved the feeling to the side, giving Krey gasping instructions to land in the forest clearing.

He suddenly changed direction and adjusted his angle sharply upward at the same time. Nora squeezed her eyes shut and buried her face in his chest.

"Sorry," he muttered. A few seconds later, he leveled off. "Guard. Outside the dome."

After a short, frightening flight, they reached the clearing, where Osmius was waiting, Sarza on his back. Krey landed, and both his passengers hopped off. "Quick!" Nora gasped, knowing her father would send guards to search the area. Without another word, she and

Kebi climbed up. Krey lifted into the air first, followed by the great dragon.

Osmius ascended high into the darkness, then waited for Krey to catch up. They flew together through the night air.

No one spoke. Not aloud, anyway. When they were halfway to the farm, Osmius's deep, resonant voice entered Nora's mind, every word imbued with fury. *You announced your presence. You forsook the plan. Nora-human, by the stone, what were you thinking?*

THE STONE EATER: 6

"What do you mean, *They're gone?*" Ulmin roared.

The guard didn't flinch. "We think the dragon flew off with the Rimorite pilgrim. We assume he carried your daughter to safety too."

"And whoever was with her," Ulmin muttered. "She certainly wasn't shooting a gun and a bow at the same time."

"Yes, Your Majesty."

If only I still had a feather lyster on staff. After that boy Krey had controlled the palace's flying guard, Ulmin had been unable to trust the woman. Krey might've somehow planted treason in her mind. Once Ulmin created the dome, it hadn't seemed so important to have someone flying above the palace. He'd done away with the feather lyster; she was buried now in the palace garden. It was time to find another flyer, someone he trusted.

Ulmin released the guard's mind and hurried back toward the chapel. Fury sent heat through his body. His joints crackled in an alarming fashion as he rushed along the uneven ground, but his fuel and the stone's magic filled him with energy.

Breathe. Think.

Emissary Loryn had been one of his most faithful servants for his

199

entire reign. Years ago, after his wife's death, he'd tried to kill himself by eating animal brains. Instead of falling dead, he'd discovered his ability to control minds. Immediately, he'd been addicted. With help from his chef, he ate just enough brain matter to satisfy his need, but he didn't use his new faculty. In his mind, his new magic was horrific. Evil. His need for such a dark fuel added shame to the desolation he was already drowning in.

Ending everything hadn't worked, so he sought comfort for his grief elsewhere. He tried discreetly inviting a woman over but couldn't bring himself to walk her past the front door of the residence. Overindulging in alcohol was no better; it made him ill and turned him into an ineffective leader. Going for long runs through the chapel grounds helped until he injured his knee.

At last, he turned to books. The history of religion and of the stone had always fascinated him. He read book after book in the palace library, numbing his grieving heart with knowledge. Frequently, he visited Emissary Loryn to discuss what he was learning. They built a mutual trust, and one day, the emissary brought out a small book.

"An early emissary wrote this," she said, "a generation after The Day. We've lost the author's name, but we know they shared the knowledge only with the Abrios family, who then passed it on to the emissary's successor. At some point, the knowledge became restricted to the clergy assigned to this chapel. By studying our world's magic and history so deeply, you've proven yourself worthy of the truth, Your Majesty. I only ask that you not remove the book from my office. You're welcome to come here and read it whenever you like."

She handed him the little volume, and it changed his life.

When he felt ready to use the knowledge in the book to strengthen the magic he'd been given, Emissary Loryn refused his request. She'd known nothing of his darker faculty, but even enhanced stone magic was, in her mind, too dangerous to play with. After months of trying, he'd at last convinced her that he'd use his new power for good. She'd given him access to the stone. Because she'd trusted him.

When did that change?

Earlier this morning, Ulmin had arrived at the chapel, only to be told the Rimorite visitor was feeling ill and had left early. He took the opportunity to draw power from the stone—his highest form of worship. Afterward, he sensed some nervousness in Emissary Loryn. So he captured her mind and asked her questions.

She came clean about the traitorous pilgrim who'd likely spied on Ulmin as he touched the stone. By lying to the king and distracting him, Emissary Loryn had helped the rebel escape. Why had she turned against the king she'd served so well?

His heart compressing with the agony of betrayal, Ulmin opened the Rimstar-adorned door and continued into the main chapel. Emissary Loryn was sitting in the front row, seemingly waiting for him.

He lowered himself to the chair next to hers, fixing his eyes not on her, but on the stone. "What changed?" He kept his voice low and allowed her mind to remain her own. "Why did you turn against me? Please tell me the truth."

Her voice was quiet. Hollow. "You've always known you could trust me. I'd been loyal for years. Yet you embraced the magic of brain lysting. Then you started controlling me. You've changed from the man you used to be."

He swiveled his head slowly, bringing his gaze to hers. "Just weeks ago, you told me you were still loyal to me. I know it was true, because I . . ." *Because I had possession of your mind when you said it.*

"I was loyal, because at the time, I didn't see any other option. I hoped you'd finally see the error of your ways. I was loyal until someone came in here and told me people are working to bring you down. It gave me hope."

Ulmin felt tears enter his eyes. He let them spill onto his wrinkled cheeks. "You were the one person I trusted."

"If you only trust one person, how many do you think truly trust you?"

He blinked. She wasn't usually that frank unless he forced her to be.

"Stop," she whispered. "Stop eating brain matter. Stop touching the stone. It's not too late."

He laughed softly. In the past, his conscience had gotten the better of him, and he'd tried repeatedly to wean himself from his dark fuel. Months ago, he'd sworn off all such fruitless attempts. These days, he could only go a few hours before his desire had him sweating and panting like a madman. The smooth, indigo substance found in animal skulls was the only thing that calmed him. And as for the stone . . . it had made him who he was. It was the greatest gift he'd ever received. Why in the world would he turn away from that?

There was no use explaining all that to the emissary. She'd chosen which side she was on. He respected her enough to believe her decision was final. Leaning closer, he asked, "Do you want to be aware?"

"Of what?"

He grasped her wrist hard enough to make her wince. "Do you want to be aware? When I kill you?"

She squeezed her eyes shut. A single sob convulsed her chest. But it only took a few seconds for her to rein in her emotions. She brought her newly hardened gaze to his face. "Yes, I want to be aware."

Along with the brain matter he'd eaten before leaving his residence, Ulmin had also drunk some water with pulverized stone mixed in. He gave the woman next to him a single nod, then lifted his hand.

A stone spike exited his palm, entering the soft flesh where her chin met her neck, traveling far enough to reach her brain.

Emissary Loryn's eyes went blank. Her taut muscles relaxed. Ulmin caught her and lowered her gently to the floor, shaking his head. "This was so unnecessary," he whispered as he closed her eyes.

17

After dinner, Ulmin and I sat on a bench next to the palace pond, chatting and laughing. After a lull in the conversation, he said, "I'm glad we're friends, Ambrel."

The words hit me like a punch to the gut. "Is that what we are? Did you bring me out here to tell me we're just friends?"

"I don't think you understand. I don't have friends. I have parents and tutors and people who pretend to be friends so they can get something from me. I've always wanted a true friend. And I've wanted a wife too. I hardly dared to hope they'd be the same person."

His hand found mine, and I kept my eyes on the pond, grinning like a fool.

-Letter from Ambrel Kaulder to Dani Kaulder
Dated Barna 2, 180 PD

THE SKY SHIFTED from black to dark gray as they flew to the farm. Krey landed in a fallow field, followed by Osmius and his three passengers. Before the dragon's dark form lifted off again, Krey approached him. "You risked yourself to save Sarza. Thank you."

He thought he saw Osmius nod.

"Let's gather in the girls' room and talk," Nora said.

Krey nearly pulled Nora off to the side to ask what the hell she'd been thinking back at the palace. If she'd stuck with the plan, he and Kebi would've done their best to protect Sarza as she escaped. While the guards tried to figure out where the bullets and arrows had come from, Nora's team could've taken more care in their escape, timing it to the patrols of perimeter guards. But by announcing her presence atop the dome, Nora had put her team in danger. And now her father knew she was nearby, working actively to take him down.

The only good thing about her actions was that Krey had discovered he could still wrap Nora in his magic without turning into a lecherous creep. He could fly with her again . . . as long as their lives were in danger and he was furious enough with her to distract him from her body. Great.

With effort, Krey shoved down his bubbling anger. Everyone would want to know what Sarza had seen and heard. He'd have to wait until later to give Nora a piece of his mind.

The group walked to an old barn the farmers had converted into a bunkhouse for their grandkids to sleep in when they visited. Nora, Kebi, Zeisha, Sarza, and Joli were all staying there, while Krey used the single guest room inside the house.

Nora opened the door. Zeisha and Joli were playing a board game by the light of the fireplace. They stood and rushed to the door.

Zeisha pulled Kebi into a tight hug, stifling a sob against the trog's chest. After a couple of minutes, she turned to the others, wiping her eyes. "I'm so glad you're all okay."

"Barely," Krey muttered.

"Let's gather by the fire," Nora said. Krey took off his jacket and sat between her and Kebi. When everyone was settled, Nora turned to Sarza. "Did you get any information about Ovrun?"

"No. I'm sorry."

Krey's heart dropped. He, too, had held out hope that Sarza's gift was leading her to the chapel to rescue Ovrun.

Nora's face twisted with disappointment, but she swallowed and asked Sarza, "What happened inside the dome?"

The group sat, spellbound, as Sarza told her story. Krey held his breath when she described the orange light that had enveloped the king's arms and head as he touched the stone. "I think he's getting his power from it," she said.

"I've grown up hearing that anyone who touches the stone dies," Krey said. "I guess the royals and Rimorians have been keeping some secrets."

"There's more," Sarza said. She went on to describe a vision she'd had that led her to a book hidden in the emissary's office. With a hint of drama, Sarza pulled a small, leather-bound book from her pocket.

"What is it?" Nora breathed.

"I haven't had a chance to look." Sarza shoved it toward Nora. "It's from your palace, you take it."

Krey had a ridiculous urge to snatch it from Sarza's hand. Instead, as Nora took the book, he leaned closer to her. She moved it to her other hand, farther from his gaze. He leaned even closer, and she pulled it farther away, smirking.

"I'll let you read it with me," she said, "but grab a lantern. This fire isn't giving me much light."

Krey lit a lantern and set it between them. True to her word, Nora held the book so he could see it too. When she opened it, the scent of old dust wafted out. The ink on the first page was faded but legible.

"What does it say?" Sarza asked.

"It's titled *The Stone*. It's handwritten, and there's no author listed." Nora carefully flipped through the pages. "It's pretty short.

Anyone up for story time?" Grinning at their enthusiastic responses, she started reading.

The Stone was a journal written by a nameless Rimorian emissary who'd acted as the stone's keeper in the decades after The Day. The first three entries contained short observations about the artifact, such as how sunlight interacted with its broken orange faces.

Nora began reading the fourth entry.

"We know the stone kills those who touch it. Today, we learned of an exception to the rule. A pilgrim came to visit the stone. He shoved me out of the way, then removed the glass case and grabbed a piece of the stone.

"I screamed, but the man did not fall. Orange light covered his hands. He dropped the stone and ran from the chapel.

"I assume he will die."

Nora turned the page. "This is dated the following day," she said, before continuing her reading.

"The pilgrim returned today. He confided in me that he was trying to take his own life yesterday. When the stone brought light into his hands, he feared he'd made God angry.

"He told me he has a gift allowing him to manipulate the ground."

Nora looked up. "This was before scholars had settled on which magical terms to use. He was probably a soil lyster." She resumed her reading.

"After touching the stone, he ate a bit of dirt to distract himself from his depression. He then experienced greater power than

ever before, creating deep furrows across a large piece of unin-
habited land.

"Perhaps all who are gifted with magic are immune to the
stone's power to kill. For them, the stone may be a friend, not a
foe. However, I am terrified to think what would happen if this
knowledge became widespread. Those with magic could use
their gifts to destroy entire communities. Wars might be fought
over the stone."

"Can I see that?" Krey asked. Nora handed him the book, and he
turned to the previous entry. After skimming it, he handed the book
back. "Why do you think the light only covered his hands? Sarza said
it traveled all the way to Ulmin's head."

"A dirt eater only has magic in their hands," Zeisha replied.
"Ulmin has magic in his hands and his head. The stone makes both
his talents stronger."

"That explains how he made the dome," Krey said. "And why his
mind talent is so powerful. Do you think he let Faylie touch the stone
too?" His eyes turned to Nora. Faylie, the mind-controlled militia's
Overseer, had been her best friend. Nora had killed her to free the
militia.

A swallow rippled through Nora's throat, but her voice was
steady. "I can't imagine my father telling anyone about this. It would
be too easy for someone to use their enhanced power against him."

"We could keep discussing this," Sarza snapped, "or you could
read the secret book I risked my life to get."

A smile tugged at Nora's mouth. She returned to the book, again
reading it aloud. The emissary wrote that she'd invited the man to
stay at the small chapel for a time to explore his strengthened skills.

The stone's magical enhancement only lasted a few days after
touching it. However, the pilgrim could easily top off his power by
touching the stone again. In time, he'd discovered he could carry a
small piece of the stone with him, drawing power from it for several

weeks. Eventually, it lost its effectiveness until he returned it to the other stone pieces.

"Maybe when your father visits the militia, he brings a piece of the stone for Faylie to touch," Kebi said.

"I still can't imagine him sharing such a secret," Nora said.

"Keep reading," Sarza insisted.

Nora read page after page of entries that told them nothing new. Then she struck gold.

> "The pilgrim has now been here three years. Last month, he became a member of the Rimorian clergy. He is a good man who has found his purpose.
>
> "He has kept his promise to protect the secret he discovered. We have only shared it with two members of the Abrios family.
>
> "Yesterday, a young woman who lives in this area visited the chapel. Her toe caught on the threshold as she exited. The pilgrim grabbed her wrist to keep her from falling.
>
> "She looked up and asked what he'd done to her. She said she felt a jolt of power in her hands. He assured her he'd done nothing.
>
> "I heard the exchange, and I remembered that the young woman has the same magical gift as the pilgrim. He and I took her on a walk. She ate fuel and discovered that her magic was enhanced as well, though not to the same extent as the pilgrim's.
>
> "We did not reveal the source of her new power, and she agreed not to display her strengthened magic to anyone. She promised to report back to us on how long her gift remained altered."

Nora turned the page. "The next entry is dated over a month later."

"For several weeks after being touched, the young woman continued to experience increased power every time she ate dirt, though the pilgrim didn't touch her again. However, if he went days without touching the stone, her power receded along with his. And her magical strength always returned to its normal level at night, when the pilgrim was asleep.

"The woman's power decreased somewhat over time, and at the six-week mark, it dropped sharply and soon fell to her normal level. If the pilgrim had touched her again, perhaps he would have renewed their shared magic. She, however, was glad to be rid of it.

"I have nearly reached the end of this book's pages, and I hope we have discovered all we need to know of the stone. We will protect the object itself and the terrible secrets it contains."

After making sure the rest of the pages were blank, Nora closed the book. "I think—no, I *know*—my father forced Faylie to become a brain lyster, then shared his power with her so she could control the entire militia at once. I doubt she ever knew how he'd gotten so much strength."

Krey nodded. "And when the two of you took your two-hundredth-anniversary tour, he must've brought a piece of the stone with him. That way, he could keep drawing on its power and sharing it with Faylie from a distance."

His mind returned to the day he'd first met Nora and her father in Tirra. He'd considered himself so superior to royalty, not realizing he and the king had the same dark secret. *Nora deserves better.* He wrote that phrase inside his mind, in large, block letters. It had become his mantra of late.

Nora's eyes narrowed thoughtfully. "My father can obviously control when he shares his enhanced power. Otherwise, he'd be passing it along to every stone lyster he shakes hands with."

"He grew up working with magical masters," Krey said. "He's gotta be way more skilled than the pilgrim in the book was. I doubt he's ever had any trouble determining exactly who he wants to give power to."

Zeisha sat up straighter. "I just thought of something. According to the book, when power is shared, it decreases over time. That must be why Girro helped Faylie while the king was on his tour. I'm sure she got weaker while Ulmin was gone."

The room went silent. Girro was the brain-eating trog who'd helped Faylie control the militia for several weeks. He'd lost his mind completely in the process.

Joli, who'd remained silent since they'd all gathered, said, "I used to wish I was a magic eater. The more I hear, the more I'm glad I'm not."

Zeisha nodded, then yawned. "It's past dawn. As much as we'd all like to sleep, we'll be expected at breakfast." Their hosts didn't know about their nighttime adventure.

Krey's stomach was ready for food, but it would have to wait. He stood with the others and tapped Nora's arm. "Can we talk?"

She must've seen something in his eyes. "Osmius has already told me all the ways I screwed up; now I get to hear it from you too?"

He shrugged, giving her a *what did you expect?* look.

She sighed. "Let's go outside."

They put on their jackets and exited into the chilly autumn air. The book had distracted Krey from the events at the dome, but as he strode to the side of the renovated barn, his anger flared back to life. As soon as they stopped, Krey spat, "We had a plan!"

"We did."

"Why did you ignore it?"

She spread her arms wide. "I don't know!"

"Well, there has to be a reason you announced your presence and put the rest of us in danger! And now your father knows you're coming after him! How long do you think it'll be before he figures out where you are?" He was yelling by the end of his tirade.

A harsh sigh left Nora's throat. "I honestly don't know why I did it! I was fine with the plan, but then I saw you and Kebi running with your weapons, and—" Her mouth snapped shut, and she stared at Krey, her brows furrowed.

He drew in a deep breath. If he didn't get his temper in check, she wouldn't want to tell him anything. "And what?" he asked, gentleness and frustration warring in his voice. "You saw us running, and what?"

She was breathing quickly through her nose. When she spoke, her voice trembled a bit. "I was standing up there, thinking about Faylie, Ovrun, and Taima. My father took them all from me. And while I watched, he was about to take Sarza too." She blinked, her eyes glistening with tears. "If I don't stop him, he'll keep tyrannizing our country. It's all up to me. I guess that responsibility hit me all at once. I felt like I should be the one to act. So I did."

He stepped closer, just as a tear slipped from her left eye. Before he realized what he was doing, he reached up and wiped it away, his thumb gliding across the scar on her cheek.

Nora drew in a short, sharp breath.

"Sorry." He dropped his gaze and wiped his wet thumb on his pants. A swallow, and he met her gaze again. "It's not all up to you. I don't know if that thought came from Sharai or from your own mind, but it's a lie."

"It didn't come from Sharai, and it's not a lie." A tear slid down Nora's other cheek, and though Krey's hand twitched, he didn't wipe it away this time. She continued, "I'm the only one who can legitimately take his crown. I'm not trying to be dramatic. It really is all up to me."

"Is it?" His voice was thick with skepticism.

She nodded, pulling her bottom lip between her teeth.

"So should the rest of us leave?" His anger was building again, though he tried to control it. "Are you planning to go to the palace and do this thing on your own? Nora Abrios, the savior of Cellerin, the loneliest queen in the world?"

She squeezed her eyes shut, and he cursed himself for hurting her. "That's not what I mean." Her gaze met his, challenging him. "I know I can't do it all alone. But I wish I could."

"Why the hell would you say that?"

"Because once the fighting's over . . ." She stepped back, pressing herself against the side of the barn. Her hands came up to her mouth, and she drew in a shuddering breath, then let it go.

Krey's anger faded again. She was so close to crying, and he was so close to stepping in and holding her. *Bad idea.* He locked his knees, pressing his boots into the ground.

Nora spoke again. "Once the fighting's over, I'll be alone. Zeisha and Kebi will live their storybook romance in Deroga. Sarza will find something to do, maybe work at a tailor shop. Ovrun—" She clenched her jaw for a moment, like that was the only way to prevent a sob from escaping. "If we save Ovrun, he'll find a way to work on a farm, his own or someone else's. And you?" Though tears still filled her eyes, she smiled. "You'll go off and change the world. Because that's who you are."

"And you think you'll be alone."

She shrugged. "I'll have Dani and my orsa. That's how it always used to be. It was enough."

"Was it, though?" he asked softly.

A sound—it could've been a hiccup but was probably a suppressed sob—formed in her throat. She looked down and whispered, "No."

"Nora." When her expectant eyes met his, he briefly lost his breath. Her pink cheeks, her glistening eyes, her parted lips . . . why did she have to be so beautiful? He pulled air into his lungs. "Whatever I do with my life, I'll make room for your friendship. If you tell the royal guards to let me past the gates, anyway." He tried to smile, and it must've been successful, because the corners of her lips turned up.

"You will?"

"How could I not?" he asked, hoping she didn't catch the passion behind the words.

"Sharai says—no, Krey, don't give me that look! Just listen. Sharai says all my relationships will change when I'm queen, because everyone will be my subject. Even my husband, when I get married. He'll be the king, but I'll still be the one in charge. She says monarchs don't have the same types of friendships other people have."

"Sharai's an idiot."

"I know you don't like her, but she's helped me a lot. She's got way more experience leading a country than any of the rest of us do."

"I refuse to believe a queen can't have friends. That's just stupid."

"I don't want to believe it, but I suspect it's true."

Krey shook his head. "We don't even know when you'll become queen. Let's focus on today." That was certainly what he needed; the thought of Nora being holed up in a palace while he lived a life separate from hers was tearing him up. "You've gotta stop blocking out the rest of us. Yes, you're the only one who can legitimately take the crown. But that doesn't mean you have to fight alone. Let us help you. That's what we're here for."

Nora stared at him silently for a long moment. Then a deep exhale came from her mouth, like she was releasing something she'd been holding onto. He didn't think she'd let go of Sharai's ridiculous words yet, but maybe she'd at least let her friends help her fight for the crown.

"Thanks," she said. "For being there."

Krey smiled. "Any time." He turned to walk to the house for breakfast.

"Wait," Nora said.

He pivoted to see her standing there with her arms wide. *Damn it, again?* The hug right after she and Ovrun had broken up had nearly killed him. But he couldn't leave her hanging, not after telling her he'd be there for her. Krey walked into her embrace, holding her tight, way too aware of her softness pressing into him and the scent of her hair and her warm breath on his neck. *Damn it, damn it, damn it.*

He pulled away before his body could betray just how much he enjoyed her closeness. "Let's go to breakfast," he muttered, already striding that direction.

18

"Have you ever seen a dragon?" I asked Ulmin as we walked, hand in hand, through the palace grounds.

He laughed. "I've seen large birds and tried to convince myself they were dragons." He pointed toward the palace fence. "I've heard there are unicorns in the forested area east of here. I think I spotted one when I was a little boy."

"Let's go look for one," I said.

"Now?"

"Why not?"

And that's how he ended up skipping meetings to wander through the woods with me all afternoon (trailed by an annoying guard, of course). We didn't see any unicorns, but the day was magical.

-Letter from Ambrel Kaulder to Dani Kaulder

NORA WATCHED Krey walk toward the house. Her cheek felt warm where he'd wiped a tear away. He'd dropped his hand just as she'd been about to reach up and cover it with her own.

She'd liked the feel of his thumb on her skin. She'd wanted to touch him back. What was that about?

It reminded her of when she'd first met him. She'd found him attractive—striking, rather than handsome. He'd intrigued her with his magic, his willingness to stand up to her father, even his sarcasm.

Not long after that, she'd kissed him in the palace garden . . . if a brief touch of the lips, followed by him pulling away and asking what the hell she was doing, could actually be called a kiss. Once he'd calmed down, he'd told her about Zeisha.

Her crush had dissipated pretty quickly after that, especially when she'd reconnected with Ovrun. Now that she'd ended things with him, her overly romantic heart must be on the prowl again, looking for its next defense against boredom.

That had to be all she'd felt when Krey touched her cheek. Then at the harvest party earlier in the month, when her silly, boy-crazy mind interpreted his glances as gazes of desire. And just now, when his arms came around her, and she feared he'd feel the pounding of her thrilled heart against his chest.

She'd always wanted adventure and excitement. Add in the rebound effect of a break-up and the stress she'd been under since Ovrun's capture, and it was clear she wasn't truly attracted to Krey. She just missed having someone to touch, to distract her from reality. She'd recover from this stupid infatuation as quickly as she had the first time.

Except this is different. I know him now. Really know him. Krey could rile her up faster than anyone. He called her out on her stupid decisions, and he expected her to do the same for him. Yet he had a gentle side that kept catching her by surprise. He'd known just the right words to say when she'd blurted out her fears today.

They'd spent so many hours together lately, delving into old books, getting way too excited about strategy, giggling together when they were too tired to do anything else.

He's my best friend.

Warmth filled her chest, even as goosebumps sprouted on her arms and legs. When had he become her best friend? How had it happened, when she'd tried so hard not to let anyone get close?

Even without Krey standing here, she could picture him perfectly. He was the same height as her, with hair that perpetually needed cutting. His jaw was strong, his nose a little big, his eyes sharp and passionate, his lips, well . . . *really nice.* He had the body of a runner—lean, long muscles in his arms and legs.

Striking, she thought again.

Those wiry, strong arms had felt amazing wrapped around her. And his eyes, when he'd told her he'd remain her friend, had locked onto her, like they'd never let her go. Then there was that thumb, calloused and gentle, setting her nerves alight as it skimmed across her scar. By the sky, she could stand here all day, getting lost in the memory of those sensations—

"No!" She said it aloud, following the word with a brisk shake of her head. Crushes and best friends and racing hearts had only been acceptable when she'd thought her coronation was decades away. Krey's promises were nice, but they came from a hopeful eighteen-year-old who wasn't ready to look reality in the face. It didn't matter how much they both wanted to continue their friendship; her crown would still push them apart.

Time to let go of fantasies and act like an adult and a future queen.

Ignoring the tightness in her chest, she squared her shoulders and walked toward the house for breakfast.

217

By evening, Nora was fuzzy headed and exhausted, having spent all day in the stable with no one to talk to. After dinner, she and her friends trudged to the large, open barn to wait for the rest of the key leadership team.

Krey said, "I've been thinking all day. We can assume the king forced the emissary to tell him everything Sarza said. Plus, he knows Nora was there. That means he knows she's actively planning to take him down."

"He probably already knew," Nora said. "With more and more New Therroans and soldiers in the capital changing their allegiances, I'm sure there are rumors."

"This is different," Krey said. "One of your rebels infiltrated your father's palace grounds. He may not have much more information than he did before, but how do you think he'll react to her making it past his guards?"

"Not well." Despite the realization, Nora couldn't seem to drum up the proper amount of concern in her sleepy state. A massive yawn exited her mouth. Every other person in the circle followed suit. "You're right, Krey," she said. "Sarza's security breach is exactly the type of thing that would panic him."

"That's what I thought too," Krey said. "Ulmin will be warier now. The army will probably crack down on the capital even more than before."

"How does this change our plans?" Kebi asked.

Krey shrugged. "What plans? We're building a coalition of New Therroans, disloyal soldiers, and former militia members, but we still don't have a strategy for taking down the king. And we need one. Before he starts acting even more insane." His gaze fell on Nora. "Sorry to—"

"Don't apologize for calling him insane. I know it's true." She drew in a long breath. "Let's start by agreeing on one thing: we need to keep Sarza's trip to the chapel secret. Anyone who finds out will ask too many questions. The information in that little book can't spread further than this circle."

"You're not going to tell Sharai?" Krey asked, his gaze piercing.

She'd considered it as she worked today. The former Minister of Lysting could advise them on how to prevent others from taking advantage of the stone's power. But Nora couldn't justify telling anyone else. "The more people who know this secret, the more likely it is to get out. We have to tell the rest of our leaders something, though. This meeting needs to light a fire under us."

"Fire is good," Krey said. "A plan is better."

Nora nodded, but didn't respond. The militia's three representatives were entering the building. She stood to greet them. Over the next half hour, the rest of the key leadership team arrived. Nora somehow found enough energy to run the meeting.

Much of the news the leaders shared was good. The rebels scattered among farms continued training in magic and weapons. More New Therroans in the capital were begging Hatlin and Sharai for a chance to fight against the king, hoping it would lead to freedom for their people. Army dissidents, anxious to devote themselves to a more compassionate leader, held secret meetings throughout Cellerin City.

There were problems to solve too. A militia member was pregnant; one farmer regretted letting people stay on his land; and a couple of dissidents had asked to transfer to different farms. Nora tried to guide the group to fair conclusions as quickly as she could.

That done, she squared her shoulders and ensured every eye was on her. "You should all know that my father recently became aware of our growing strength."

Several leaders spoke at once. Nora raised her eyebrows, waiting for the room to go quiet. She turned to Sharai. "You had a comment?"

"What precisely does he know, Your Highness?"

"All I can say is that we're in greater danger than ever because my father has greater reason to fear us than before."

People shifted in their seats, clearly uncomfortable with her vague answer.

Nora nodded at a militia leader who'd raised his hand. He stood. "Princess, we spent months with our minds controlled. We're following you because we thought things would be different. Now you're keeping secrets from us?"

Defensive anger sprouted in Nora's chest, but a deep breath calmed her. "Thank you for sharing your concern. Let me be clear: you're free to follow me or not. I won't retaliate if you leave. That's the difference between me and my father. I'd like to tell you everything I know, but I'd be putting you at risk if I did. When I'm your queen, I'll have to decide what information I can share and what burdens I need to carry alone. I'm asking you to trust me to do that now."

The young man narrowed his eyes. "I could tell you I'm walking to the palace to reveal everything I know, and you wouldn't stop me?"

Nora hesitated, but only for a moment. "Every day, any of the rebels on these farms could turn on me. That's the risk of giving people freedom, isn't it? So yes, I'd let you go, but I appreciate your warning. If I hear you've fled, I'll protect my people."

The young man still didn't look happy, but when he spoke, the challenge had left his voice. "I'm not going anywhere, Your Highness." He sat again.

Nora found Krey in the audience. He gave her a miniscule nod and a half smile. A raised hand caught her attention. "Yes, Sharai?"

"I have a suggestion. May I come forward to speak to the group?"

Nora wouldn't allow just anyone to do such a thing. However, she and Sharai still met frequently, though they lived on different farms. Their respect for each other kept growing. "Please do," Nora said, beckoning her.

Sharai stood and approached. "We're building a coalition, but it's primarily centered on the capital. Citizens throughout the rest of our land might've heard the king is occupying New Therro and Cellerin City, but how does that affect them? More importantly, why should they support an eighteen-year-old queen if she steals her father's crown?"

Nora bristled at that, but she knew it was true.

"We don't just need allies who will fight," Sharai said. "We need a populace who will cry out in joy when they hear that Nora Abrios is queen. Our people must love her so they'll want to serve her."

She turned to speak directly to Nora. "I've long thought you should tour the nation, generating excitement and building support. I hesitated, knowing word would get back to your father. Now, however, you say he's aware of the danger we represent. I guarantee you, he's already doing whatever he can to root out our rebellion." The corner of her mouth lifted, her keen eyes turning bright. "It's time for you to go public."

"He'll hunt me down if I do that," Nora said.

"He will." Sharai's thin lips spread into a wide smile. "But he can't catch up if you're flying on a dragon."

Nora stood, arms crossed against the evening chill, watching the sky.

Last night, when she'd asked Osmius to take her on a tour of Cellerin, he hadn't given her an answer. Instead, he'd told her to meet him the next night, in the same fallow field where he'd landed after the trip to the palace.

She hadn't been waiting long when he arrived, his wings sending cold ripples through the air as he descended. *Nora-human*, he said once he'd landed, *come here.*

She stepped toward his dark silhouette. Osmius lowered his broad head to her, and she hugged the underside of his wide neck. Maybe he sensed the shame she felt after her bad call at the palace. Maybe he wanted to assure her that all was well between them. Whatever it was, she drew in his strength. *Thank you.*

He lifted his head. *I shall take you on a tour of the land, but it would be unwise for me to take you alone,* he said. *In order to remain safe, you should surround yourself with others who are willing to protect you. Unfortunately, the more people I carry, the slower I fly.*

I've been thinking about that, she replied. *Two of us can ride on your back. I'll bring Krey and Hatlin along, because they can fly on their own. If things get dangerous—*

Osmius interrupted, *Turn around, Nora-human.*

Nora obeyed, blinking into the thick darkness.

I shall share my sight with you, Osmius said.

A moment later, Nora had the strange experience of seeing herself from the back. But that wasn't all she saw. She stepped back with a sharp gasp.

Several mets away stood two dragons, one the size of Osmius, the other nearly as large as Taima had been.

"He-hello," she said, forgetting that she didn't need to speak aloud.

Greetings. Somehow, Nora knew the thought came from the larger dragon, a female whose smooth voice was higher pitched than Taima's had been.

The smaller creature remained silent, lowering its head and releasing a smoky huff.

Despite the slightly muted colors of Osmius's night vision, Nora could tell that the larger dragon had golden scales, while the other's coloring was the deep reddish purple of wine.

Oddly enough, the smaller dragon didn't have the basket-weave skin of a reptid. Instead, its scales were oval-shaped, with the bottom edge of each overlapping the scale below it. Its nose was long and tapered, and sharp horns shaped like lightning bolts emerged from the sides of its head. While it still had the compound eyes of an Anyarian animal, they matched its skin in color and were quite small. Its neck was long, and its muscular tail rested on the ground behind it, unlike Osmius's stubby tail.

The dragon's voice, male and breathier than Osmius's, inserted itself into Nora's mind. *Osmius, you did not tell me the human would stare.*

Nora dropped her gaze. *Pardon me. I . . .* She looked over her shoulder. Using her own vision, she could barely make out Osmius's head. *I have a lot of questions.*

Shall we sit? Osmius said. *You may climb onto my back so that when you share my sight, it is not too jarring.* After a pause, he added, *It shall also show our new comrades that I truly trust you.*

I take it they couldn't hear that last sentence?

Correct. Once she was on his back, he said, *These two dragons will come on our journey if you wish them to.*

With a smile, Nora said, *I would be honored.*

The larger can easily carry three passengers, Osmius said. *In order to travel quickly, we smaller dragons shall each carry two.*

Thank you, Nora said. *I do have a question. I won't ask you to reveal your true names, but what can I call you?*

You may call me Gild, the female dragon said.

It suits you.

The male sounded bored. *I care not what a human calls me.*

Nora refused to be offended. If anyone had the right to be arrogant, it was a dragon. *How about Vin—short for* Vinaceous? *It means "wine-colored."* She'd seen the term in a book once and loved the sound of it.

As you wish.

Nora directed her next question to all three dragons. *So . . . how do you know each other?*

Osmius replied, *Apart from mated pairs, dragons are generally quite solitary. However, we support one another if humans endanger us. This morning, I approached Gild and Vin. I explained the king's current state of mind and your desire to remove him from power. Knowing his history of dragon enslavement, they agreed to assist you.*

Vin spoke again. *I am only willing to carry passengers because I know the king has abused dragonkind. After our journey, I will never again allow such a travesty.*

Thank you both, Nora said. *You have no idea what this means to me.*

I am honored to help, Gild said, her voice melodic. *Osmius has spoken highly of you, Princess.*

Nora grinned. *Don't tell him I said this, but you may be the nicest dragon I've ever met.*

I heard that, Osmius growled.

Oops.

I assume you would like to know why Vin differs from other dragons you have seen, Osmius said.

Yes, please. Nora had been hesitant to ask. The finer points of dragon etiquette were beyond her.

As I have told you, I was formed from a shimshim. However, shimshims are not found through the whole world.

And dragons are, Nora replied, seeing where his story was going.

On The Day, dragons emerged on every continent, from a different animal each time. Across the world, on the continent of Vallinger, they were formed from small phibians called telminas.

Nora had never heard of telminas, but all phibians were adapted to live both on land and in the water. Now Vin's differently shaped scales made sense; phibians had similar skin. Telminas probably had horns, pointy noses, and long tails, just like this dragon. *Do you breathe fire?* Nora asked.

Vin's mouth opened, and a short burst of fire emerged, stopping mere simmets from Nora's face. She swallowed. *I guess that's a yes. Do you have to eat mushu leaves first?*

I do, when I am on this continent. My body is capable of using any of the world's fire fuels.

Why are you so far from home?

Twenty years ago, I settled here. In another twenty years, I may be ready to leave. I wish to know the whole world, not merely the place where I was formed.

If you don't mind moving, Nora asked, *why are you helping me instead of leaving this place behind?*

She somehow sensed the dragon's anger before his message reached her mind. *I will not allow a human to drive me from my home. Remember that, future queen!*

I will. Thank goodness her telepathic voice was calmer than her real one would've been.

When will you be ready to leave, Nora-human? Osmius asked.

An hour before sunrise Saturday. That gave her just over two days to prepare. *We'll meet you here.*

Vin's wings snapped out. He lifted into the air at a terrifying speed.

Nora swallowed. *Thank you, Osmius,* she said as she dropped to the dirt. *And thank you, Gild.* The female dragon lowered her head and breathed deliciously warm air on Nora.

I'll be honored to fly alongside you, Vin. Nora sent the thought into the air, knowing it would reach the dragon's mind. He ignored her.

19

Today, I watched Ulmin speak to volunteers at a charity that feeds the hungry. The people clearly love him. He's charming and earnest and, most of all, confident.

Dani, I wanted to drag him off that stage and get him somewhere private and demand he kiss me.

(You don't show anyone these letters, right?)

> -Letter from Ambrel Kaulder to Dani Kaulder
> Dated Barna 4, 180 PD

THAT WAS A TERRIBLE IDEA! Vin's voice pierced Nora's mind.

From where she sat, propped against Osmius in a grassy meadow, Nora squinted into the sky. The reddish-purple dragon was fast approaching. *What happened?*

As soon as I drew close enough to be identified as a dragon, the townspeople retrieved weapons.

Nora swallowed. *What kinds of weapons?*

Bows and blades.

Well, that was better than guns, but it still wasn't good.

A few minutes later, she was standing in a circle with the rebel leaders she'd chosen for the trip. No one had been surprised when she decided to bring her entire inner circle: Krey, Zeisha, Kebi, Sarza, and Joli. Krey hadn't appreciated the inclusion of Sharai as the last member of the team, but Nora had refused to budge. With her experience working in the monarchy, Sharai brought legitimacy to this trip.

Now, however, Krey was pinning a snarky, *I-told-you-so* look on Sharai. She'd been the one to say two members of their party should fly in on a dragon's back and land in a town square with no notice whatsoever. A dragon, she'd said, would engender respect and a healthy dose of awe. The passengers could then announce Nora's visit.

Krey had argued that since dragons rarely flew within sight of humans these days, someone below might get scared and attack, killing the dragon or its passengers. Vin scoffed at that, informing Nora that his skin was far superior to that of local dragons, thick enough to protect even from bullets.

Hearing that, Nora had agreed to the plan, but only after Vin assured her that if things went south, he'd do all he could to protect his riders. They certainly didn't have bulletproof skin. She'd sent Sharai and Sarza as her representatives—Sharai because the town's leaders would probably listen to a former Minister of Lysting, Sarza because you never knew when one of her prophecies would prevent a disaster.

Nora cleared her throat, drawing Krey's attention away from Sharai. "We'll move on to Plan B. Sharai and Sarza will approach the town on foot and announce my visit. Please be careful."

The two women were gone about an hour and a half. A smile of victory crossed Sharai's face as she approached Nora. "They're ready to welcome you and your dragons."

"Really?"

"They balked at first. I told them if fire-breathing dragons truly wanted to attack a town, they'd likely succeed. The people decided they'd rather be on a magical creature's good side."

Nora grinned. Krey could say what he wanted about Sharai; the woman knew how to get things done. "Sarza, any visions or premonitions?"

"Nothing."

A nervous thrill shot through Nora, making her fingers and toes tingle. "Let's go."

Once she'd mounted Osmius, she looked down at herself. She wore clothes befitting a traveling princess: blue pants and a black tunic, both fitted, and low, black boots. The midday sun was pleasantly warm, but she pulled on her black, hooded coat. It would be cold in the sky.

Sharai had insisted Nora needed professional clothes when speaking to the people of Cellerin. One of the farmers helping the rebels had purchased two outfits, both in Cellerinian blue and black. Another had quickly tailored them. Nora didn't want to admit to anyone how amazing it felt being clad in soft, expensive fabric and leather again.

After a quick flight, all three dragons landed without incident in the town square. Their seven passengers dismounted. Nora's eyes scanned the square. A small group of men and women stared at her. When the dragons returned to the sky, more townspeople emerged from the buildings.

A man who appeared quite young introduced himself as the mayor. He bowed, and everyone else followed suit.

Nora stood straight, her shoulders back. "Thank you for your warm welcome. I'm here to tell you what's really happening in Cellerin."

Krey watched Nora speak. Following Sharai's advice, she was calmly telling the townspeople that her father had found a way to control minds . . . and that he was losing his own. Ulmin was using his ability too often, Sharai had argued, for it to remain a secret. Nora should expose the truth before someone else did. Sharai had also suggested Nora be open about her desire to take Ulmin's crown. Some patriotic citizens might consider this treasonous, but the fire-breathing beasts flying overhead would surely discourage any attacks.

Krey had scoffed at Sharai's strategy. This time, however, the woman's instincts had been on target. Damn it.

As Nora spoke of her father's ability to capture minds, a shocked silence fell over the crowd. She didn't describe where his power came from; she'd do all she could to protect that dangerous secret. But she didn't mince words as she described his growing insanity. Her speech exuded passion, grief, and strength.

Krey shifted his attention to the listeners. Some had crossed their arms, wary of Nora's message. But many nodded, and all were captivated.

When Nora stopped talking, she and the mayor held a short, private conversation. Then he turned to speak to the entire group. "Do you remember when King Ulmin sent workers to build our first windmill?" He pointed at a wooden windmill, barely visible over one of the square's buildings.

Most of the audience confirmed it with nods and murmured words.

"That was thirteen years ago. I was fifteen. Do you remember when the king sent workers to build our second windmill?" A pause, then: "Of course you don't. He said he'd do it, and he never did. Do you remember when we had a terrible drought and sent a delegation to the king? He gave us promises of assistance—promises that did nothing to fill our bellies. Do you remember . . ."

As the mayor went on, the crowd hung on his every word, as they had with Nora. Krey could see how this guy had gotten elected. In a speech so smooth it seemed he'd practiced it, he gave many examples of how the king hadn't fulfilled his commitments to the town. Krey blinked back tears when the man spoke of not having enough medicine during the orange plague epidemic.

"Do you remember?" The mayor's voice was still loud enough for everyone to hear, but it had taken on a somber tone. "Do you remember asking your spouse, your neighbor, your parents, 'Why?' Why, we wondered, would a king who'd always been faithful to us, suddenly ignore us?" He turned to Nora. "At last we now know why. Thank you, Your Highness. I can't speak for my people . . . but I'm ready for a change."

Krey let his gaze sweep over the crowd again. Many arms that had been crossed now hung loose. Lips that had been pursed were relaxed. Eyes that had held cynicism were now full of trust.

Nora spoke to them again, committing to bring justice back to the land and to remember the citizens her father had forgotten.

She sounded like a queen.

It must be close to midnight. Nora was too keyed up to sleep. She'd visited three towns in one day, a feat only made possible by the dragons. Now, she was wrapped in a blanket, sitting on a dark plain. Gild was a few mets away, having completed a successful hunting trip. Osmius and Vin were still searching for prey and for the mushu leaves that fueled the fire they breathed. Most of Nora's team members slept in tents around a dying campfire.

Thank you for coming with us, Gild, Nora said. *You, Vin, and Osmius made this possible today.*

We are not the ones who captured the hearts of Cellerinians in three towns. There seemed to be a smile in Gild's sweet voice.

Yeah, but you carried us there. And you gave me courage, knowing you were flying up there, ready to protect me.

I should thank you for inviting me on this adventure. After two hundred years of hunting and soaring through the clouds, I was terribly bored. Musical laughter traveled from Gild's mind, and Nora couldn't help but join in.

All three communities they'd visited had invited the princess and her party to stay with them, but Nora had decided in advance that they'd only camp outside. She'd found a lot of support today, but her father had loyalists everywhere. It would be far too easy for someone to attack her in her sleep. She had, however, accepted food before leaving the last town.

Nora pulled her blanket tighter around her, breathing in the crisp air and basking in the silence. She'd spent so much time planning and strategizing lately. Today had given her a glimpse of the big picture, and her heart still thumped hard with the thrill of it all. She'd had a purpose for a while, but it had been theoretical. Now it was rich with the faces of hopeful citizens she'd spoken to, people who believed she could improve their lives. Now she knew who she was fighting for.

Rapid footsteps approached. It had to be Krey, who'd taken the first watch shift. "Hey," Nora said softly.

He stopped, the pale starlight barely outlining his silhouette as he squatted near her. He was panting lightly; he must've been jogging around the camp. "Why are you awake?" he asked.

"I can't sleep. Why are you running?"

"To keep myself awake."

She laughed softly. "I'll take this shift. I'm not tired."

"Actually, can we talk? I've been thinking about something."

"Sure, have a seat."

"Can we go a little farther from the group?"

She nodded, then realized he couldn't see her. "Okay." She stood.

Krey led her to a spot under a tree, near enough for him to keep an eye on the campsite, far enough that no one would overhear their soft voices. They sat next to each other in the dirt. Nora wrapped herself in her blanket again. "Aren't you cold?"

"Yeah, it's keeping me alert." She heard his long intake of breath, then his sigh. In a low voice, he said, "I've been thinking about the stone. Once you're queen, do you think you should hide it? Somewhere no one will ever find it?"

"No!" The word shot from her mouth of its own volition.

"How do you really feel about it?"

She couldn't see his wry smile, but she could picture it. "Krey, the stone . . . it's part of my inheritance. It doesn't *belong* to my family, but we've kept it safe ever since The Day. And we don't just protect it; we create an opportunity for people to visit it. It's unthinkable to hide it away."

Krey didn't respond, and Nora appreciated him mulling over what he'd said. For several minutes, the only sounds were small shifts of their bodies on the cold dirt.

At last, Nora said, "I know the stone is dangerous. I wouldn't trust any lyster—even myself—with its power. It's just . . ." She turned her head, barely able to make out the shape of him.

He turned too. "Why are you giving me that look?"

"You have no idea what look I'm giving you."

"Yeah, but I know you're giving me one."

She laughed, feeling suddenly warmer. "It's strange to hear you talking about hiding the stone."

"Why?"

"Well, you're religious."

It was his turn to laugh. "You think I'm one of those people who worships a stone that caused an apocalypse?"

"I don't think you worship it. But a lot of Rimorians, especially lysters, honor it."

"I don't. I mean, it's powerful, but it's still just an object. If someone's taking advantage of its power, maybe we should make that impossible. Pretty sure the stone can't do anything to stop us from burying it or dropping it in the ocean."

Nora bit her lip, considering his words. "Power isn't always a bad thing. The stone is a symbol of humanity rising again after so many people died. Can we take that away from people?"

"I don't know." His voice was soft, thoughtful. "Symbols are important."

She stared at his silhouette, wishing she could see his expression. "Why do you believe in God?" The question slipped out before she was sure she wanted to ask it.

There was a long pause, but Krey didn't turn away. Finally, he said, "Humans traveled to Anyari from a planet preday scientists never found. Their journey was farther than we can imagine, but I'm sure it was nothing more than a tiny blip, compared to the size of the entire universe. There are so many wonders out there—black holes and galaxies and nebulae. There are planets we could survive on and planets where we'd burn alive if we even got close to them. All that makes me think maybe there's a God, some sort of creative force behind it all."

Nora shook her head. "Science explains the formation of the universe and the evolution of life. I don't have to tell you that; I'm sure you've read as much about it as I have. Probably more."

"Yeah. Nature makes me consider God's existence, but it doesn't convince me."

"What does?"

His voice lowered. "All the stuff we can't see. Selflessness. Generosity." Nora thought she heard him swallow before he continued, even softer than before. "The ability to appreciate beauty. God's got to be behind that, don't you think?"

Warmth rushed through Nora again. *I could talk with him like this forever.* As soon as the thought ran through her mind, she caught herself. *None of that.* She dropped her blanket, letting the crisp air run over her shoulders and neck. Gaze now fixed on the darkness beyond them, she said, "All those things you mentioned are great. But they're no less real than death and injustice. Is God behind all that too?"

Apparently she'd broken whatever spell had fallen over them, because out of the corner of her eye, she saw Krey turn away from her. "Is that why you don't believe?" he asked.

Nora blinked. She hadn't been ready to talk about her rickety relationship with faith. But he'd opened up to her; she'd force herself to do the same. "My mom was murdered. My dad has become my enemy. Yeah. The ugliness in the world is why I don't believe."

"That's fair."

Relief softened muscles Nora hadn't realized she'd tightened. She'd expected Krey to go into debate mode. She pulled her blanket around her again. "I think a part of me always knew my dad was a hypocrite," she said quietly, eyes fixing on the orange remnants of the fire. "I saw him go to the chapel every day, but I almost never heard him pray. He taught me about ruling with fairness and justice, but we know how well he's been doing with that. Why would I want to share my father's faith when that's what it looks like?"

"That type of faith is worthless." An odd hardness had come into Krey's tone.

Nora turned her head again. The taut lines of Krey's jaw were visible in the starlight. "Glad we agree on that."

He faced her again, gentleness returning to his voice. "It's not my job to say whether your father truly believes. All I know is, I'm not interested in an elitist faith that's made for royalty. I hate the palace chapel. I don't care that the stone is there. I hate that even before there was a dome, the chapel's Sunday services were closed to anyone who wasn't 'blessed' enough to work for the royal family."

His words were strangely refreshing. Nora had always felt that way, though she'd never said it aloud. "If my dad's brand of faith is the wrong one, what's the right one?"

The slight breeze they'd had all night turned into a cold wind. Krey's shadowy form shivered. "Get over here and share my blanket," Nora said.

"I'm okay."

"Don't tell me you still need to be cold to stay awake. You know very well conversing with me is more invigorating than any breeze." He laughed. As she waited for his response, she found herself breathing shallowly, her body tense with the desire to hear him say—

"Okay." Krey scooted closer and took one end of the blanket, pulling it around him. The side of his body pressed against hers—shoulder-to-shoulder, knee-to-knee.

Nora's first thought was that she wished he'd put that firm arm around her. Her second thought was, *You are an idiot, Nora Abrios, and you should've let him get his own damn blanket.*

"So," Krey said, "you asked what I think is the right kind of faith?"

Oh, thank the sky for Krey's logical mind. He certainly wasn't giving a second thought to how his arm felt, pressed against hers, and how easily they could reach over and take each other's hands, and—"Uh, yeah, that's what I asked."

"Well, I figure if there is a God—and let me make one thing clear, yes, I'm a Rimorian, and I pray, but I'm cynical enough to question my belief in God on a regular basis. Anyway . . ." He drew in a deep breath. "If there is a God, he's clearly a lot more powerful than I am. And . . . I don't think he keeps that strength to himself. I'm an addict, Nora. I still crave my fuel every day. I depend on someone stronger than me to help me say no."

"Go on," she said softly.

He faced the fire again. "If God is powerful but still takes care of people like me, then I figure those who believe in him should use their power to take care of others too. I mean . . . if we want to be like God, we should give what we've got to others. That might be money or food; or it might be knowledge or magic. I guess what I'm saying is, if there's a God, I think he's generous."

Nora completed the thought. "And those who claim to worship him should be too."

"Yeah. I can get behind a faith where we take care of the people around us."

Nora mulled over his words. She'd grown up with a faith that was centered around dressing up once a week to attend a boring chapel service. She'd never considered that spirituality could be based on generosity. "You know," she murmured, "I don't know if I'll ever believe in an all-powerful being that we can't see. But if I do, the faith you just described is the only one I'd want to buy into."

He didn't answer, but it was a nice sort of silence. Nora finally broke it. "So, about the stone." His shoulder shook as he laughed softly. "You thought I'd forgotten that's what you wanted to talk about, right?" she asked.

"Never."

"Whatever. Anyway . . . I'll think about what you said. It's not something I can decide lightly. And if you have any more input, I want to hear it."

"It's a deal."

The edge of Krey's hand lightly brushed against her knee. She moved her own hand just enough to catch his pinky finger with hers. He let out another little chuckle. And he didn't let go.

It's just one finger, Nora thought. *Totally appropriate touch for two friends.* But she was thankful that the darkness hid her smile.

THE STONE EATER: 7

THE PALACE GROUNDS felt empty as Ulmin strolled through them, his way lit by occasional lampposts. Plenty of people were in the dome, but most of them were asleep. Ulmin was waking earlier than ever these days, drawn from sleep by hunger—for fuel, not food.

He slipped a tiny brain, no bigger than the pad of his thumb, from his pocket. Bringing it to his nose, he inhaled and smiled. Inkbird, one of his current favorites. He popped it in his mouth and chewed, his lips curving into a satisfied smile.

This time of morning, when he could still glimpse stars through the dome's vents, he could almost imagine the heat away. It *should* be cool. It was Quari 16th, over two weeks into the autumn season. But the thick, warm air under the dome was wonderful in its own way, reminding Ulmin to appreciate his great creation.

He hadn't made the dome alone; he'd shared his enhanced magic with two other stone lysters. When a member of the palace staff had escaped by tunneling under the dome, the two lysters had assisted with extending the stone far beneath the ground. They'd been honored to help their monarch build this wondrous work of art that would last for generations.

If only the capital's citizens had such loyalty to their king. To be fair, some did. Ulmin reveled in the letters he received, thanking him for bringing order to their city. Far more people, however, grumbled about the soldiers in the street. Army officers kept bringing Ulmin word of these selfish malcontents. Then there was the young traitor, an ally of Nora's, who'd pretended to be a pilgrim. Was Nora even now building an army to take down her father?

Ulmin shuddered. When Faylie had lost control of the lyster militia, he'd vowed to never share his mind magic with another. He'd chosen to limit his mind control to those within his palace grounds, workers he could keep close tabs on.

His citizens' current discontentment and outright rebellion had changed his mind. The only way to keep a populace safe, to keep a *nation* safe, was to control minds. Just because Faylie had failed didn't mean other Overseers would. Especially if Ulmin had entire teams of them.

But not just anyone could be an Overseer. Ulmin could only share his heightened mind magic with fellow brain lysters, and finding such people was terribly difficult. Few lysters were lucky enough to process brain matter as fuel, rather than poison.

When Ulmin had begun looking for his very first Overseer, he'd procured two lysters, criminals with no known friends or family. They'd both died when he fed them brain matter. Ulmin would've kept testing such "safe" subjects, had Nora's best friend Faylie not seen one of the bodies being carried away. She'd asked questions, too many for her own good.

Ulmin had panicked. He'd controlled her mind and given her brain matter to eat, planning to tell her mother he'd found her dead. Only she hadn't died. She'd become a brain lyster, nearly as good at controlling minds as he was.

It had been a true joy, capturing Faylie's mind. Teaching her to do the same to others. Sharing his strength with her. Her faculty had expanded to accommodate every new lyster who joined the militia. Ulmin hadn't even minded paying her mother a truly shocking sum to move out of the country and stay quiet—and, later, paying someone to kill her when she attempted to contact her daughter. Faylie was his prize for all his sacrifices, all the work he'd put into his own magical abilities.

Everything had worked so well until Nora had turned against her father and her former friend, manipulating the militia so they'd begin serving her. His own daughter had brought months of work and years of planning to a halt in one devastating day.

"This time," Ulmin muttered, "it will be different." Hearing his voice, a caynin loped up and nudged his hand with its flat snout. Ulmin laughed softly, crouching and scratching between the animal's huge ears. "This time," he told the beast, "we'll have many Overseers, all sharing my magic. I'll send them into Cellerin City. They'll keep their identities secret, capturing minds through handshakes and such. Word will spread. Citizens will know their minds could be captured by anyone at any time. They'll see the value in loyalty, and we'll know peace at a deeper level than ever before. Right, my friend?"

The caynin's forked tongue emerged and licked Ulmin's forearm, beneath his rolled-up sleeve. The king chuckled again and stood. "Go, you slobbery thing. Do your job and keep me safe." The animal ran off.

As soon as Ulmin had come up with the plan, he'd known it was solid . . . except for that nasty problem of finding Overseers. How was he to discover who could tolerate brain matter without killing the vast majority of lysters he tested?

He'd first tried with the two stone lysters who'd helped him build the dome. Both were now buried in the palace garden. Ulmin had moved on, asking his army officers to send him magical soldiers who caused problems . . . those who started fights or expected special treatment as lysters. They'd come to the palace, one after the other, to be tested. Six had died over the course of three weeks.

Last week, he'd had a breakthrough. He'd given a lyster a minis-cule amount of brain matter, a tinier piece than he'd ever used before. The young man got ill for several days, rather than dying. Then he recovered. Ulmin had always been taught there was no safe amount of brain matter to eat. Apparently that was false, like so many other things he'd learned about magic.

Best of all, Ulmin had tested the same tiny amount of fuel on himself, and he was confident it wouldn't be enough to allow a brain lyster to control anyone. Hopefully that also meant it wouldn't establish an addiction. When he discovered brain lysters by using these miniscule doses, he could keep their names in his back pocket, so to speak, until he was ready for them.

Next week, his people would test lysters in the army. They'd discover which ones could tolerate consumption of brain matter. Ulmin would get a list of those names. His future Overseers.

"Your Majesty?" a voice called from several feet away. "Are you all right?"

Ulmin looked up. In his musings, he'd somehow made it all the way to the front gate. Someone was laughing, and he spent several seconds trying to find the source before he realized it was him.

Odd that he hadn't heard himself until now. That made him laugh harder. After a time, he turned his smiling face to the young man. "I couldn't be better. It's a lovely morning in our stone home, isn't it?"

20

After Ulmin's speech yesterday, he spent a full hour chatting with people. I've also noticed how often he engages his guards in conversation. He knows their names and makes a point to ask about their families. They all stand up straighter when they see him coming, but he jokes around with them, putting them at ease.

Remember Mom telling us, "Leave the maid alone; she has work to do"? Well, today, I spent a few minutes talking to Uncle Quin's cook. She has a family and a full life outside her job. I'm embarrassed to admit that surprised me. Now I wonder about our staff back home, the ones who don't live with our family. What do you think their lives are like when they leave our house each night?

-Letter from Ambrel Kaulder to Dani Kaulder
Dated Barna 5, 180 PD

As soon as he heard the king's laughter, Ovrun tried to shrink back into the shadows inside the palace gate. *Don't look over here,* he begged silently, dropping his head, hoping Ulmin wouldn't notice him.

Shiny, black boots approached. "Ovrun!" The king was no longer laughing, but his voice was full of cheer.

Ovrun let out a silent sigh and held out his hands, keeping his head bowed. "Your Majesty."

"How are things this morning?"

Ovrun dropped his arms and looked up. "Uneventful, Your Majesty."

"Always a good thing, right?" The king clapped Ovrun on the arm. "Walk with me, son."

Ovrun nodded and joined the king. By the sky, he hated these walks. If only he had a weapon, he could attack Ulmin. But he was the only royal guard who didn't carry a gun, bow, or blade.

He'd spent a lot of time mulling over where he now stood with the king. The best analogy he could draw was that Ulmin saw him as a loyal pet—like a caynin who'd been abused and was so relieved not to be kicked anymore that now he loved his master more than anything. A pet, of course, didn't get weapons or important responsibilities. His owner just liked to dress him up in guard clothes and take him on walks.

Ulmin seemed to truly believe he'd gotten all the information he could from his prisoner. He never tried to control Ovrun anymore, preferring the natural conversation he got from a loyal, untouched mind. Hopefully the king would never seek to seize his mind again. The day Ovrun had put on the performance of his life—pretending the torture had broken him—was the day he'd consumed his last bit of shield fuel. If Ulmin ever tried to control him again, Ovrun would disclose everything he knew about his friends. The possibility made bile rise in his throat.

"How are things among the guards?" Ulmin asked.

These days, he didn't just want the truth from Ovrun. He could get that from anyone. When he talked to his human pet, he wanted real dialogue, sprinkled with just the right amount of gossip and colored with wide-eyed loyalty. The conversations were a new kind of torture for Ovrun.

"Things are good," he said. "I'm always amazed . . ." He trailed off, chuckling. "Never mind, it'll sound silly."

A lamppost nearby shed light on the wrinkles Ulmin's grin brought to his cheeks and eyes. "Go ahead, be silly! Tell me!"

Another laugh. "I'm always amazed at how different things feel from when I worked here before. It was just a job back then. To be honest, sometimes we guards would have bad days, and we'd complain, just like you do at any job. But now, everyone is positive all the time." That was true. Nobody dared whisper against the king. Mind-controlled interrogation was a powerful deterrent.

Ulmin briefly rested his hand on Ovrun's back. "You don't know how delighted this makes me. I want that type of contentment, not just among my workers in the palace, but across our whole land."

"I'm honored to serve under such a good king." Ovrun stretched the fingers of his left hand, then squeezed them closed. His new nervous habit. Two of the fingers closed less than halfway; they hadn't healed properly.

They walked for a minute or two before the king spoke again. "Ovrun." His voice had lost its lightness.

"Yes, Your Majesty."

"You know I speak with the other guards often. They tell me their true feelings."

"Yes, Your Majesty," he said. "As I do."

"It's different with them than it is with you. They're loyal; I have no doubt of that. Yet most of them follow me because they fear me. They don't trust me the way you do. How can I encourage them to trust me, Ovrun?"

"Your Majesty," he said, "your kindness, it . . . it means the world to me. I used to be afraid of you too—oh, damn it, I shouldn't say that, I'm—"

"It's okay," Ulmin said gently. "Please be honest."

"Okay. I used to be afraid, and I don't know when it changed. Gradually I started seeing all the good you do. You've given us this safe place to live. You gave me my job back. Even these walks . . . I see you as a person now, Your Majesty, not just a king."

"You still think it's kindness that made the difference?"

They'd had this conversation over and over. Ulmin thought he'd gained Ovrun's loyalty through torture. He probably hoped his former prisoner would advise him to start breaking all the staff's fingers. *Not gonna happen.* "How could anyone not follow you when they've seen this side of you?" Ovrun asked.

The king nodded slowly. They were on the short walking loop they often took, and they'd almost reached the gate again. He stopped and faced Ovrun, gripping his arm. "You know Nora quite well, don't you?"

Dread came into Ovrun's chest. "Yes, Your Majesty."

"Do you think she's still coming after my crown?"

Ovrun's brows drew together. By the stone, he hoped so. And oh, he wished he could be with her when she confronted him. Not *with her* romantically; his weeks here had confirmed how much he hated royal life. Even without a dome over his head, the palace, with its politics and procedures, would be an awful place to live for years on end. But what he wouldn't give to be part of Nora's team, working every day to get her a crown she deserved to wear.

The grief of being separated from everyone he cared about, of being stuck in a stifling dome, of constantly pretending to love a king he despised, hit him all at once. Tears came to his eyes.

"Did you hear my question?" Ulmin asked.

A sob broke free, filling the space between Ovrun and the king.

"Oh, dear boy!" The king's other hand came up, and now he was gripping both of Ovrun's sweaty, uniformed arms. "What is it?"

Ovrun couldn't hold back the tears, so he surrendered. But the part of his mind that was constantly focused on his goal—to protect his friends—whispered to him that he had to justify this show of emotion. "I . . . I . . . " He couldn't seem to speak.

"It's okay, son. Have a seat." Ulmin guided Ovrun to sit on the warm, dead dirt. Kneeling before him, Ulmin said, "Calm yourself. Breathe. Then you can tell me."

Ovrun took the advice, drawing deep, shaky breaths, broken by sobs. In a couple of minutes, he was able to talk. "Your Majesty . . . I'm sorry."

"As I said, it's fine. Tell me what you're thinking."

"It's Nora. I . . . I don't know if she still wants your crown. I just wish . . ." Ovrun let more tears turn his voice thick. "I wish she saw you the way I do. If only she knew how good you are for our nation. She . . . she's young, Your Majesty. Even younger than me. I hope you'll be kind to her when you find her. Please . . . she's got a good heart, she's just . . . impulsive." That part was true, though less than it had once been.

The king tilted his head, eyes narrowing. "I'm sure you miss her."

Ovrun's chest tightened with fear. He was always trying to find the right balance between truth and lies. Had he gone too far in pleading for Nora's safety? "I miss who I thought she was, Your Majesty." He met the gaze of the man in front of him, letting his eyes fill with what he hoped looked like fervent admiration. "Before I knew who you really are."

"Oh, son." Ulmin's shoulders dropped as he sighed. "I miss who I thought she was too." He stood. "Let's get you back to your post."

Ovrun rose, and they returned to the gate. A couple of guards gave him curious looks—he'd been close enough for them to hear his loud sobs—but he ignored them.

"It was a pleasure speaking with you," Ulmin told Ovrun.

Ovrun gave him a big smile. "You too!" If he'd only let his tongue hang out of his mouth, he'd look just like the king's favorite caynin. By the stone, it was hard not to hate himself after these interactions.

As Ulmin turned away, a woman outside the gate called in an out-of-breath voice, "I have a message for the king!"

Ulmin halted, stepping farther into the shadows but clearly listening.

"What is it?" a guard outside the gate asked.

"The princess—she and several others rode dragons into my town yesterday. She's traveling around, building support. She's planning to steal the crown!"

Ovrun stiffened.

Ulmin turned to the highest ranking guard, who stood near Ovrun. He spoke softly. "Once I'm safe at the palace, let her in. Take any weapons she's carrying, and find out what she knows. When you're done, lock her in one of the security office cells. I'll speak with her there."

As he walked away slowly, Ovrun heard him murmur, "If she's gone public, I have to do the same. We'll find her, and we'll stop her. We'll find her . . ." He shook his head, seeming to realize he was talking out loud. Squaring his shoulders, he walked briskly through the thick, warm air toward the palace.

21

Ulmin invited me to spend all day at the palace with him. When we arrived, he had a surprise waiting: two master lysters—soil and stone—waiting to tutor us. I ate more fuel than I've ever done in a single day before. But I also learned more in eight hours than I used to learn in weeks of magic classes back home.

-Letter from Ambrel Kaulder to Dani Kaulder
Dated Barna 6, 180 PD

NORA WOKE with a gasp from a dream in which she'd poked her head inside the large oven in the palace's residential kitchen. She groaned and flipped over, then realized she was genuinely hot. Which made no sense on an autumn night.

A blast of steamy air puffed into her tent, ruffling her hair and practically searing her scalp. She sat up, muttering, "What?" and bumped her head against . . . something. Her hands came up and contacted a warm, rock-hard substance.

Next to her, Sharai woke, mumbling. Nora ignored her, because the voice in her head was louder. *Get up. Now.* It was Vin.

All at once, Nora knew it was his skin she'd connected with, his breath that had nearly broiled her. *Why the hell is your head in my tent?* She usually tried to stay on his good side, but after such a rude awakening, she didn't have any politeness to spare.

I called, but you did not wake. He sent a picture into her head: fifteen riders on orsaback, some of them carrying torches. *They are approaching us,* Vin said. *You must move. I shall return to the air to keep watch.*

At once, Nora was wide awake. She'd been traveling for over two weeks now. According to reports they'd gotten in several towns, Ulmin and a group of guards were tracking them. Taking advantage of the dragons' speed, Nora's party had kept their route unpredictable. So her father had changed his strategy too. No one had heard from him in a full week. Krey suspected the king was hiding somewhere, waiting to hear that Nora was close.

How much time do we have? Nora asked Vin.

Very little. Leave the tents here. Go!

Nora cursed. "Sharai, wake up! Grab our blankets and bags. We have to go." When she was sure Sharai had heard, she darted from her tent and spoke to Joli, who was on watch duty. The two of them woke the others. Moments later, the team rushed to Osmius and Gild and crowded onto their backs. Both beasts lifted into the air.

Osmius, please take the lead, Nora said, sharing the thought with all three dragons. *Find us another campsite, far from here.* She shifted her thoughts, sending them only to Vin. *Why were you awake?* With all the flying the dragons did, they weren't expected to keep watch at night.

I woke feeling hungry. I took to the air to hunt, and I saw the group.

Thank the sky for that.

A few minutes later, Vin spoke to her again. *When we arrive at our new camp, I shall have a gift for you.* His tone was a bit ominous.

A gift?

Vin sent a memory to her mind. He was flying high, surveying the camp and surrounding area as Nora and other tiny figures rushed to the dragons. Perhaps half a clommet away, the king and his party had just dismounted. Two of them remained with the orsas while the others walked toward the camp. Orsa hooves were too loud when you were trying to be clandestine.

Movement in the scene caught Nora's eye: a feather lyster, flying off to the side. So that's how her father had targeted them in the middle of nowhere. As she watched, the lyster changed direction, speeding directly toward the camp.

She saw Osmius and Gild rise into the air, carrying Nora and her friends. She knew this was a memory, knew she was safe, and yet her heart pounded as her father's feather lyster flew over the tents her team had vacated moments before.

Then the perspective in her mind shifted so fast, Nora nearly threw up. Vin was diving from the sky at a terrifying speed. His strong claws extended and grabbed the feather lyster out of the air.

The memory ended. *Did you kill him?* Nora demanded. They'd all agreed to keep violence to a minimum. She wanted the populace to trust her, not fear her.

No, I am holding him carefully so you may interrogate him.

That didn't excite Nora as much as Vin seemed to think it would. Her only experience with interrogation was when she'd confronted a spy in Deroga. It hadn't gone well. She sighed and spoke to Osmius. *Let's find a place to land so Vin doesn't accidentally crush that flyer.*

He alighted behind a hill, followed by Gild. Everyone dismounted. Osmius held a ball of white fire in his mouth, illuminating the area. Vin soon arrived, dropping a wide-eyed, hyperventilating man into the grass and pinning him there with a single, large claw.

"Take your foot off him," Nora said aloud.

Vin's maroon, faceted eyes fixed her with an expression she assumed was a glare.

"Vin, he can't even talk to us until he catches his breath. Let him sit and calm down. He knows if he tries to run, he won't get far."

Vin did as she'd asked, but not until after he'd puffed hot air onto his prisoner.

The man sat up. He was probably in his fifties, with silver hair and whiskers. A round belly pressed against his buttoned coat. He was panting, clearly terrified.

"Breathe," Nora said. She came closer, and a smile took over her face. "Master Kadin?"

He nodded.

She let out a short laugh. He was one of the most talented feather lysters in Cellerin and had often visited the palace. He'd always been kind to her. "Sorry to meet you under these circumstances." Seeing that he was still too panicked to talk, she said, "I have no desire to hurt you. Really."

At last, he calmed enough to ask, "What are you going to do to me?"

"Ask questions." She sat in the dirt in front of him.

"You know I can't answer any."

She sighed. "I suppose my father will find out everything that happens here if you return to him? Whether you choose to tell him or not?

Kadin's lowered eyes were all the answer she needed.

"You don't have to be controlled by him anymore. Stay with us."

A long sigh filled the space between them. "Nora . . ."

"That's Your Highness to you, Kadin." The voice belonged to Sharai, who'd approached quietly.

"Your Highness," Kadin repeated, performing a bow. His gaze lifted to Sharai, then returned to Nora. "I'm impressed you've got a minister with you."

Sharai's presence boosted Nora's confidence. Maybe a master lyster would listen to the former Minister of Lysting. "She doesn't work for my father anymore," Nora said, her voice calm and firm. "He fired her months ago, because he's lost his mind."

Kadin didn't try to defend the king. He simply said, "If I stay with you, he'll kill me."

"Not if I take his crown."

Kadin chuckled. "You and what army?"

"You might be surprised."

"Your Highness, don't do this. If you confront your father, you'll lose. Don't underestimate the power of the loyalty he's built up over the years."

"Don't underestimate the power of the truth. I've visited dozens of communities in the last two weeks. Do you know how many mayors didn't allow me to enter their towns? *Three.* We know some people will remain loyal to a madman who's controlling minds and forgetting about his responsibilities to his subjects. But not many."

"He has an army, Nora!"

When Sharai tried to correct his casual address this time, Nora held up a hand to stop her. "I know he does. But an army is just people. If given the chance to follow a better leader, I think they'll say yes." She leaned forward, propping her elbows on her knees. "Stay with us, Kadin."

He shook his head. "I can't. Not willingly, anyway."

She sighed, sensing nothing she said would break through this man's fear of his king. *Vin, please pick him up again. Do your best not to injure him. Drop him off safely a couple of clommets away from my father. While you're gone, the rest of us will find another place to camp tonight.*

Moving remarkably fast for such a large beast, Vin grabbed Kadin around his middle, eliciting a scream.

Nora stood. "Go back to my father. Tell him I won't stop until I'm wearing his crown. If he wants to make this go easier, he can surrender it to me."

"He'll never do that," Kadin said through panting breaths.

Nora's throat tightened. "I know." This might be the only chance she had to send her father a message. She'd want to look back and know that she'd tried. "Tell him anyway."

"Please don't let him leave yet!" Sharai cried.

Nora turned.

"A word, Your Highness?" Sharai asked, her eyes wide in the light of Osmius's white fire.

Brow furrowed, Nora asked Vin to stay. She led Sharai off to the side, where no one would hear them.

"He has information," Sharai said softly. "He could tell us what the king's plans are, how many people guard him at night, how likely—"

"But he won't," Nora said.

"Not willingly."

Nora blinked. Was the woman she'd grown to trust—and even sort of like—suggesting torture? "There are lines I won't cross, Sharai."

To her surprise, Sharai smiled. "I know. That's why I follow you. All I'm suggesting is that you threaten him. He's scared to death of that dragon. Use that fear."

Nora looked down, considering the advice. It was pragmatic. Efficient. Maybe even wise.

All at once, a scene from a recent nightmare returned to her mind. She'd seen her father as a red-eyed, horned monster, carving up Ovrun with a sickle. She'd woken up terribly frightened, not of the dream's hyperbolic elements, but of the truth underneath the symbolism. Her father was indeed a monster, albeit without horns. And it was entirely too possible he was really terrorizing Ovrun in one way or another.

Nora's eyes found the former minister again. "Sharai, I trust your experience. Most of the time, I agree with your advice. But you're talking about ruling by fear. I know someone who does that, and I don't like the results." She sent a message to Vin: *Go.*

When the dragon's wings snapped open, Sharai spun around. "Wait—!" Then she caught herself, her mouth snapping shut. The dragon soared away, carrying Kadin.

Sharai turned to Nora. "I want you to win."

"So do I. But not like that." She couldn't quite read Sharai's expression. She hoped it was grudging respect. "Come on," she said. "Let's get back on the dragons and find a safe place to sleep. I have big plans for tomorrow."

22

Today was <u>Q</u>ueen Onna's birthday, so she reserved an entire restaurant for "a quiet family dinner." She invited Uncle <u>Q</u>uin and me to join them.

Our carriage arrived at the same time as Onna and Ulmin's. As I stepped out, a man on the sidewalk looked me up and down with the creepiest eyes you can imagine and said, "I'll show you a better time than you can get at this place."

Before I could respond, Ulmin pushed through his guards and grabbed the man by his lapels. He said three words: "That's enough, asshole." Then he sent the man away with a glare that was sharp enough to cut someone in half.

I'm falling for him. Hard.

-Letter from Ambrel Kaulder to Dani Kaulder
Dated Barna 7, 180 PD

NORA WAS the first to wake the next morning, which pissed her off. Her body had grown too used to rising with the sun. After tossing and turning a bit, she sat up, cocooning herself in her blanket. Osmius, bless him, had found a cave in the side of a hill for them to stay in. It was a good alternative to the tents they'd left behind.

Bits and pieces of the last sixteen days of travel flitted through her tired mind. Tales of her tour had spread throughout Cellerin. All over the land, eager eyes gazed at the sky, wondering if they'd be the next to meet the princess and see the dragons.

Nora hadn't been lying about only three communities turning them away. In fact, most visits ended with at least some of the populace bowing. In the past eleven years, citizens outside the capital had suffered more than the naïve princess in the palace had ever realized. People were hungry for change.

Nora's gaze swept across her sleeping companions. They'd all played their roles on this tour. Sharai offered experience and royal legitimacy. Sarza's visions often guided them to their next location. Krey's knack for strategy was invaluable. Plus, Nora appreciated his friendship more than she wanted to admit. Joli had good instincts about connecting with rural populations, and she used her organizational skills for numerous tasks, like stocking supplies, recording the names of community leaders and their reactions to Nora, and scheduling nightly watch shifts. Kebi carried her bow, acting as a loyal guard. And Zeisha brought a calming influence to all of them. Perhaps at some point she'd even tap into the Well's power, but only if she could do so secretly. Sharai and Joli still didn't know of her abilities.

Gradually, everyone woke. The humans relaxed while the dragons hunted. Then they all took to the sky again.

It was their longest leg of travel yet. Hours later, they landed well outside of their next destination: New Therro. Visiting the occupied city was an important part of their strategy, and after almost being caught last night, Nora hadn't wanted to wait any longer.

When she became queen, making peace with New Therro would be one of her top priorities. She'd once hoped the negotiations would be easy. After all, she'd built goodwill by getting New Therroan men released from the Cellerinian Army after the battle for Deroga. But that was months ago. Since then, her father had oppressed their city in ever-crueler ways. For all Nora knew, whatever trust they'd given her had dissolved long ago.

A quick, surprise visit wouldn't win over every New Therroan. But at least Nora could extend her hand in peace. Maybe that would set the groundwork for a positive relationship with them.

Nora's team would need a new approach for entering New Therro. If Sarza and Sharai tried to waltz in and tell the army that Nora wanted to speak to the city's inhabitants, they'd be arrested. Before leaving the caves this morning, Nora and Krey had spent hours planning. Vin had agreed to fly her into the city tonight. He'd assured her he could briefly carry four people and still fly at a good speed, so she'd asked Krey, Kebi, and Sharai to come along.

Thanks to a block of ice Osmius had fetched from atop Cellerin Mountain yesterday, Nora and Krey would be prepared to defend themselves with something less lethal than bullets. Krey would also fill up on feathers, and Vin and Kebi would have fire and arrows at the ready. Still, flying into the city presented far more risks than any of them were comfortable with.

Nora lowered herself from Osmius's back. Her feet had barely touched the ground when Krey dropped down beside her. "Nervous?"

"We aren't leaving for hours. And then all we'll have to do is fly under the cloak of night into a city occupied by hundreds of soldiers who'd like to arrest me. Why would I be nervous?"

He came to stand in front of her. One side of his mouth lifted in a smile. "You'll do great. And you'll be safe, if I have anything to say about it." He gave her a wink, then turned to join the others.

Warmth filled her chest as she watched him go.

Theoretically, being a feather eater should take away the fear of flying on a dragon. If Krey fell off the beast's back, he could fly under his own power. Somehow, the knowledge didn't help. Soaring through the air on a huge reptid—no, a huge phibian this time—was far from natural.

Vin's four passengers overlapped on his back, like extensions of his scales. Sharai was in front, with Kebi hanging onto her, followed by Nora. Last was Krey, his chest draped over the princess's rear end, cheek pressed against her back, arms reaching around her to hang onto the dragon's scales. Being this close to her would've been way too nice at any other time. Now, when he feared for his life, lying on Nora was just awkward. He kept his eyes squeezed shut, trying not to think about how far down the ground was.

"Sorry I'm sweating on you," he told Nora.

She laughed, her back vibrating against his cheek. "With my coat on, I can't tell."

"Good. If I lose my dinner, it won't soak through."

"You're disgusting."

Yeah, this was the opposite of romantic. *Which is a good thing*, he told himself. But such reassurances weren't working these days. Damn it.

"Getting close," Nora said.

Krey forced his eyes open. New Therro seemed to have an inordinate number of street lamps, probably so the army could better patrol at night. All that light would make the dragon in the sky less visible. But once they landed, Nora would want to be seen.

Hatlin knew the area far better than Sharai, who'd rarely visited, despite her New Therroan heritage. He'd sent them on this trip with a crude, hand-drawn map of the city. The plan was to land on the rooftop of a low-end apartment building. According to Hatlin, most of the army occupiers stayed in nicer neighborhoods than this one. There might be some foot patrols, but if luck was on Nora's side, she'd have a little time to talk to New Therro's residents before getting run out of town.

They entered the airspace above the city, staying high enough that residents and soldiers were unlikely to see them. The dragon stopped directly over the residential street where they planned to land.

"Vin says to hold on tight!" Nora called.

Krey cursed, squeezing his thighs and gripping Vin's scales tighter with his fingers.

Vin pointed his head downward and took a nosedive toward his target. Krey bit back a scream as the force of the movement tore his legs off the dragon's back. His first instinct was to let go and fly under his own power, but he was holding Nora down. If he let go, she and those in front of her might do the same.

The dragon's scales felt like slate on Krey's cramped fingers. A sharp edge broke the skin of the middle finger on his left hand. He sucked in air, breathing past the pain, not loosening his grip.

The dragon leveled off as quickly as he'd entered the dive. With a jolt, they landed on a flat roof.

Thank you, thank you, thank you, God. Krey scrambled off Vin's back, sliding down the beast's hip to get to the blessedly solid surface of the roof. He sucked on his bleeding finger as Nora, Kebi, and Sharai dismounted in quick succession.

Nora must've been talking to Vin, because the dragon stepped to the edge of the roof and painted the sky in orange flames. A couple of voices below cried out.

"Good evening!" Nora called. "I am Princess Ulminora Abrios. I have a message for you. Please tell your friends and neighbors to come outside or open their windows!"

She didn't give them long to obey before she started talking. As she'd done in other Cellerinian cities, she acknowledged her father's dark magic and poor leadership. However, she quickly moved on to addressing New Therroan concerns. She made it clear she would allow them to govern themselves if that's what they chose.

Krey could only half listen to her. He was scanning rooftops and the street below, looking for anyone who might try to attack them. He knew Kebi and Vin were doing the same. There were a couple of soldiers in the street, but they didn't seem eager to fire on their princess, especially with a dragon standing next to her.

After a brief speech, Nora asked Sharai to talk to her people. Just as the former minister began, Krey's eyes caught movement in the air. He squinted. Had he imagined it? His instincts told him he hadn't. He scurried to the back of the roof and leapt into the air, ascending quickly and scanning the area. There—a feather eater, flying just beneath a roofline, headed toward Nora.

"Not today," Krey muttered, pursuing the flyer.

The man was flying low over the building next to Nora's perch when Krey caught up. He shot two dense balls of ice in quick succession. Both hit the other feather eater square in the head. A grunt left the man's mouth before he crashed into the peaked roof. He rolled awkwardly along the shingled surface, clearly unconscious.

Krey zoomed down and caught the man as he was about to tumble two stories to the ground. It was tempting to allow it, but Nora had repeatedly insisted that violence was a last resort. And she was right, no matter how much Krey wanted to take out anyone who'd try to attack her.

He incorporated the man into his magic, carried him a few streets away, and dropped him on a roof. With a length of rope he'd brought just for such a purpose, he tied the unconscious man's hands tightly behind his back. Seconds later, he was standing with Nora again. Sharai was just finishing her short speech.

"Soldiers are all around the building," Kebi whispered. "Some go inside. It will not take long for them to reach the roof."

Nora had just started speaking again. Interrupting her wouldn't look right. Instead, Krey approached Vin and asked him to tell her it was time to go.

Nora wrapped up her speech. A few people cheered as she and her team flew away on Vin's back. Two gunshots sounded, but none hit their mark.

Time would tell if the visit had been worth it. But they were getting out alive, and the person who'd gotten closest to reaching Nora was unconscious on a roof. Krey would be happy about that . . . once he got off this damn dragon.

―――――

"You need to go back!" Sarza said.

Krey had just slid off Vin. He shook his head, trying to rid himself of the remaining nausea from the journey. "What?"

"I had a vision. You need to go back to New Therro."

"All of us?"

"Just you."

Nora stepped closer. "What's going on?"

Sarza released a short, frustrated groan. "I don't have time for this. Krey needs to fly back to the city."

"Where?" Krey asked at the same time Nora said, "Alone?"

"Yes, alone." She turned to Krey. "I'll give you directions to the building."

"Why?" Nora asked.

"There's something important there. That's all I know."

Moonlight reflected off Nora's wide eyes. "It'll be dangerous, Krey. Are you willing to go?"

"Your wish is my command."

She gripped his arm. "I'm not wishing or commanding. This isn't safe."

Krey covered her hand with his own. His smile disappeared. "I'll go. I want to."

As he shoved diced feathers in his mouth, Sarza gave him detailed instructions to avoid sentries and make it to his destination.

He repeated it all back to her, then asked, "How do I get back?"

"Um . . . go back the way you came? I don't know, my vision didn't show me that."

Krey wanted to ask if she was joking, but she clearly wasn't. "I better go." Unfortunately, he'd have to ride a dragon again. Sarza had insisted the time saved would be worth it. At least this time, Osmius could carry him. Krey felt marginally safer on the gray dragon's back than on Vin's.

"Be careful!" Nora said as Krey mounted.

Osmius carried him to the grassy hills north of the city. The location brought back painful memories of the concussion Krey had gotten when he'd crashed here before the battle for Deroga. Thank the stone he was rested and fueled up this time.

He thanked Osmius and took to the air under his own power. Sarza's directions served him well, guiding him past sentries outside the city, then along quiet, shadowy streets.

He landed outside a small pub. As Sarza had told him to do, he walked in the front door and got a beer, then sat at a table in a shadowy corner, keeping an eye on a muscular woman at the top of the basement stairs.

Within two minutes, the woman stepped to another table and bent down to talk to someone. *That's the only time you'll have access to the stairs,* Sarza had said. No wonder she'd told Krey to take a dragon. If his trip had taken longer, he would've missed this chance.

Leaving his beer on the table, Krey hurried to the stairs and ran down them as quietly as he could.

"Stop!" the woman called.

Krey brought his hand to the knob of the door at the bottom of the stairs. It didn't turn. This was where Sarza's vision had ended. Krey was on his own now. He knocked hard as the woman pursued him, her footsteps echoing on the stairs.

The door remained closed. Krey turned as the woman reached him, trying to push her away. But she was frightfully strong and quick, grabbing both his arms. Despite Krey kicking and squirming, she pulled him up the first stair, then the second.

He shot ice from both hands, but with her holding him, he couldn't aim it. One of the frigid balls hit his opposite arm, while the other smashed into a stair.

Where the woman gripped his left wrist, his skin lit up with pain. "Fire beats ice, frost eater," she growled. "Get up the stairs, or I'll really burn you."

He did the only thing he could think of. "It's Krey!" he bellowed, desperately hoping someone he knew would be in the basement.

The woman continued dragging him.

He tried again, loud enough to sear his throat. "It's Krey!"

The door opened. Krey craned his neck, seeing a goateed man of average height and build. Oh, thank the sky, it was Wallis, a New Therroan rebel. An ally. Of sorts, anyway.

"Let him in," Wallis said.

"Can I burn him first?" the woman asked. "Just a little?"

"We've got an audience." Wallis pointed to the top of the stairs. "Let him in."

The woman released Krey's wrists. He fell on his backside, then slid down to the bottom of the stairs, grunting the whole way. He'd be sore tomorrow.

Wallis helped him up, barking at the onlookers at the top of the stairs to mind their own business. When both men were in the basement, Wallis slammed the door and bolted it. Without a word, he led Krey around a corner into a lantern-lit room.

There were tables, but the room's eight residents were all standing, ready to move. T, the slight man who led the New Therroan resistance, pinned Krey and Wallis with an expectant glare.

"He made a scene!" Wallis nearly shouted. "We've gotta get outta here before someone tells the army to investigate!"

T spoke to the group in the airy, tenor voice that Krey had always found odd coming from a rebel leader. "Location two! Take different routes. Krey, you're with me."

Men and women pushed past Krey to exit the way he'd entered. T grabbed Krey's arm. "Come on."

There was a bit of a logjam on the stairs. As the room's residents reached the top, they walked briskly through the small space, heads down. Some exited through a side door, while others entered the kitchen.

"Act casual," T muttered as he led Krey to the side door.

As T opened it, a voice boomed from the pub's front door. "Everyone stay still, by order of the king!"

T pulled Krey through the door. The soldier shouted again, and rapid footsteps followed.

"Run!" T said.

"Fly!" Krey replied, drawing the smaller man into a tight hug and wrapping him into his magic.

T gasped as Krey lifted about a met off the street and flew into the shadows. To his credit, the rebel leader recovered quickly. "Turn here!" he hissed.

Krey obeyed, flying between two buildings. "Let's get you onto my back," he said, landing. He squatted, and T jumped on. "Where to?" Krey asked.

"Straight. I'll direct you. Stay low; the army's got two flyers."

Krey almost laughed. One of the feather eaters was probably still tied up on a rooftop. T's quiet instructions took them between buildings and down unlit streets. They halted behind a dark house. T inserted a key in the lock, and they slipped inside. He led Krey to a living room, then lit a single lantern, which adequately illuminated the tiny, unfurnished space.

It also illuminated T's fierce gaze. "You nearly got me arrested," he spat. "Why are you here?"

"A seer told me to come."

T's eyes widened, but he didn't follow up on the claim. "We heard that the princess and Sharai visited on a dragon tonight. Were you with them?"

"I was. Who were you meeting with tonight?

A rapid knock in an intricate rhythm sounded at the back door. T left the room, returning with a woman from the pub basement. "No names," he told Krey. "All you need to know is, these are people I trust."

The meeting's other attendees, including the ash eater who'd guarded the stairs, came in over the course of the next several minutes. When the last one arrived, T expelled a sigh. "Thank the sky."

They all sat on the floor, and T turned to Krey. "Tell us why you're here."

"I honestly don't know."

"We heard that the princess claimed she'll give New Therro independence if she becomes queen."

"It's true. She's more than willing to negotiate."

T snorted. "We've seen how the royal family *negotiates*."

"So has Nora. Listen, T, I know you don't want to trust royals, but you know Nora fought for your soldiers to get released from the army. You have every reason to believe her. If New Therro wants to remain part of an improved Cellerin, she'll make sure you're treated well. If your province chooses independence, she'll make it happen. Either way, she'll get the army out of here as soon as she takes leadership."

T pressed his thin lips together, his neatly trimmed goatee twitching as he did so. His eyes bored into Krey. At last, he said, "I don't entirely trust her, but I'm inclined to think she'll do better than her father has."

"Good. Then I need to know what's happening on your end." Seeing T's hesitation, Krey bit back an angry retort. Keeping his voice level, he said, "I risked my life to fly here. Give me something."

T nodded once. "We have a robust resistance within the city. Mostly New Therroans, but a couple dozen Cellerinian soldiers are now on our side too."

"Are you planning to drive the army out of town?"

One of the women snapped, "Hard to do when they've got the guns and the food!"

T nodded. "Our resistance never meets in cells of more than ten people. However, despite all our attempts at secrecy, some rebels are invariably discovered. When army officers find them, they kill them and punish the whole city by reducing rations."

Krey cursed softly, scanning the group. They all looked thin and weary.

"We tried sabotage early on," T said. "We set off explosives at their headquarters—at night, mind you, when no one was there. They paid us back in blood. Lots of it." He clenched his teeth, the closest thing to an expression of rage Krey had ever seen on him.

A chuckle broke through the tension. Krey looked towards its source, a young man wearing a full beard instead of a goatee. "I don't even think we need to sabotage them," the man said. "They're doing a pretty good job of it themselves."

"What do you mean?" Krey asked.

"They held a banquet for magic-eater soldiers last week. Almost everyone got the runs for four solid days. Or maybe *solid* isn't the right word for it."

"Food poisoning?" Krey asked, grinning.

T wasn't amused. "We have reason to believe it was on purpose. One of the soldiers loyal to us helped prepare the meal. He saw a fellow soldier making bite-sized rolls. As she formed them, she added a tiny dot of some substance in each one. And there's a rumor the same thing happened in Cellerin City. On the same night."

Krey's brows drew together. "That does sound suspicious. Do you know anything else about it?"

"We've heard they all ate the rolls at the same time," T said. "The officers set it up as a symbolic moment. A single soldier can make the nation stronger, just like a single bite of bread makes a person stronger, or something along those lines. They ate the bread, and most of them immediately got sick."

Cold suspicion sent a chill across Krey's body. "Did the soldier who told you about this mention what the poison looked like?"

"It was glossy and navy blue, and the baker only put one miniscule piece in each roll. She used tweezers to be precise. Anyarian brain matter is the only poison we know of that fits such a description, but it's said to be fatal at any dose."

All at once, Krey could smell the dark fuel—not in the room, but in his memory. His mouth watered, even as nausea invaded his gut. Ulmin had discovered a nontoxic amount of brain matter. He was looking for brain eaters. Krey swallowed to keep from puking, then spoke in a low voice. "You said most of them got sick. How many didn't?"

"Just one," T said. "Out of a couple dozen."

"Any idea how many didn't get sick in Cellerin City?"

"There are a lot more troops there. I heard seven didn't get sick. And two died the next day."

"Damn." Ulmin now had the names of eight more brain eaters. Did they know about their powers yet? Had they eaten enough to get addicted? He shuddered.

"What are you thinking, Krey?" T demanded.

Krey had never told T how Ulmin had gotten his mind-control power. He couldn't share it with this roomful of people now. But he had to prepare someone for what might be coming. "Can I speak with you alone?"

T sent the others into the kitchen. Krey kept his voice low. "Those eight magic eaters may start controlling people," he said. "Just like the king does."

The smaller man fixed his intense eyes on Krey. "Brain matter fuels his talent?"

Krey had known T's sharp mind would make that leap, but somehow he'd hoped it would take longer. "Yes. And no one can know. Can you imagine if every magic eater in Cellerin decided to eat a tiny bit of brain matter to see if it works as fuel for them?"

"I agree. We may need to kill the soldiers who didn't get sick."

"I doubt you'll be able to. They'll be heavily guarded." Krey swiped his palms down his face. Would Ulmin share his power with these new brain eaters? Was he planning to create more Overseers? "This is bad."

"What do we do about it?" T asked.

Krey sucked in a deep breath. "Nora's got to take the crown. As soon as she can." He returned T's stare. "She's committed to supporting New Therro. I hope your people will do the same for her."

"Many people have supported the princess since the battle for Deroga. But for others, anti-royalty sentiment has never been higher."

"She's on your side," Krey said. "Please make them see that."

"I'll do what I can. And you'll need a way to communicate with me." T gave Krey an address where he received mail. They discussed a simple code to use in their correspondence.

Then T sent four members of his team to escort Krey through the city. They scouted out his route a few blocks at a time, occasionally distracting soldiers to ensure that Krey could pass safely by.

When they reached a building at the northern edge of New Therro, Krey thanked his escorts, then took to the air again. He quickly flew above the range where sentries on the ground would see him.

In minutes, he reached Osmius. "I hope you don't mind giving me another ride. We need to get back fast." He climbed on the dragon's back and closed his eyes as they shot through the cold evening air.

23

I ate dinner with Ulmin at the palace tonight. It was particularly cold, and even the building's ingenious heating system didn't keep all the chill out of the residence.

The queen is out of town. So after dinner, Ulmin took me to his quarters, something he'd never dare with his grandmother there. We sat in front of the fire in his sitting room, talking softly.

And he kissed me. Finally.

I know you, Dani. I know you want details.

But I'm afraid I can't give any. I'd feel silly telling you that his lips were soft and urgent and perfect and that I swear I got drunk from the taste of him. It would be outright embarrassing to admit how badly I wanted to lead him through the door to his bedroom. And as much as I enjoy the descriptions in a good romance novel, I wouldn't dare write about how his hands tangled in my hair, and his breath was hot on my *neck, and we ended up lying on the floor, holding each other, warm for the first time all night.*

I'd never say any of that, so you'll have to settle for this:

Ulmin kissed me. And I don't want to ever let him go.

-Letter from Ambrel Kaulder to Dani Kaulder
Dated Barna 8, 180 PD

NORA PACED AROUND THE CAMPFIRE, arms crossed against the chill.

"Hey," a voice said softly.

Nora turned to see that Joli had joined her. "Hi."

"I think he'll be okay," Joli said.

"Who?"

"Krey." The firelight illuminated Joli's smile.

"Of course he will." Nora wished she didn't sound so defensive.

They walked in a slow circle, passing by all the others. Zeisha and Kebi were huddled together under a single blanket, chatting softly. Sarza sat close to the fire, gazing thoughtfully into it.

Sharai was wrapped in her blanket, trying to sleep. As Nora and Joli strode by, the former minister spoke. "Krey is fine, Your Highness. You realize he's too stubborn to get caught, right? Get some rest."

Nora laughed softly. That was about as motherly as Sharai ever got.

"How about we sit?" Joli said.

"Sure." Nora lowered herself to the ground and cocooned herself in her blanket.

Joli brought over a blanket and joined her. "You know . . ." she began softly.

Nora groaned inwardly. She wasn't in the mood for a conversation. She'd been perfectly happy pacing and checking in with Osmius every couple of minutes for updates on Krey.

Joli continued, "We met a couple of months ago, and we've never really talked."

"That's true." In her mind, Nora said, *Osmius?*

Still nothing, the dragon replied, a hint of annoyance coloring his tone.

"It seems weird for us not to talk," Joli said, "considering we have something big in common."

Nora looked over to find Joli smiling wryly. "You mean, we both broke up with one of the hottest guys in Cellerin?"

Joli laughed. "Yep. I'm tired of not talking about it. And clearly you need a distraction tonight."

Osmius? Nora said again.

By the stone, Nora-human, I shall reach out the moment I see him again. Let Joli distract you.

Are you listening in on my conversation with her?

Yes.

Gild's voice reached Nora. *He shall return soon. I feel sure of it.*

Nora huffed. *Are my personal interactions safe from anyone?*

"I'm sorry. It must not be a good time," Joli said.

"What? Oh—no, I was talking to Osmius and Gild." Nora felt her lips curve up. "Osmius told me to let you distract me. And maybe I will. If both dragons stop eavesdropping."

Laughter—deep from Osmius, melodic from Gild—reached her mind. *Done*, Osmius said. Gild echoed him.

Nora scooted until she was facing Joli, instead of the fire. Joli did the same. "So," Nora said, the crackling flames nearly stifling her quiet words, "you want to talk about Ovrun?"

Joli's blanket-covered shoulders lifted in a shrug. Her chin trembled the slightest bit, and she shifted her eyes to gaze into the darkness beyond the camp. "I'm really worried about him."

"Me too. And I wonder if people expect me to be okay, because we're not together anymore . . . but I still care about him."

"Exactly," Joli said.

"What—" Nora began, then halted. She hardly knew Joli, besides the fact that she was an organizational whiz who'd proven herself steady and trustworthy. "Never mind."

"Ask me anything, Nora."

"Okay. Do you mind telling me what happened between you and Ovrun?"

Joli blinked. "I . . . figured he'd told you."

"He said you broke it off with no explanation."

Sighing, Joli pulled her knees up to her chest. "He must think I'm such a bitch."

Nora couldn't help but smile. "Can you imagine Ovrun ever calling anyone a bitch?"

Another soft laugh. "Not in a million years." Joli turned her head to gaze at the fire. As the silence stretched out, Nora considered reaching out to Osmius again. Then Joli said, "Living on a farm, there's this closeness that families develop. There's not a lot to do in the evenings, so we spend our time together."

Nora nodded, not sure where this was going.

"When Ovrun told me he was becoming a royal guard, and I told my father . . ." Joli let out a groaning sigh. "You've met my dad. You know he despises the king. He was so disappointed in Ovrun. And I didn't want him to be disappointed in me."

"So you broke up with Ovrun to keep the peace at home?" Nora said.

Joli sniffled and wiped her nose on her knee. "It was the stupidest, most selfish decision I've ever made. And then I was too embarrassed to fix it. Plus, I was afraid if I went back to Ovrun, my dad would never forgive me."

"How old were you?" Nora asked.

"Sixteen."

Nora reached out and squeezed Joli's arm. "I don't know about you, but I barely know what I'm doing at eighteen. I was totally clueless at sixteen." They both laughed softly. "You made the best choice you could at the time."

"Maybe. I hope I get the chance to explain to him someday." Joli let out a loud sigh. "What about you? Why did you end it with him?"

Nora twisted the blanket in her hands. "It's kind of ironic, I guess. You broke up with him because you thought he might spend the rest of his life at the palace. I broke up with him to keep him from doing that."

The skin between Joli's brows drew together. "What do you mean?"

Nora smiled. "You've seen him work on the farm. Do you really think he'd be happy penned up on the palace grounds? Wearing starched shirts? Discussing policies and diplomatic relations? I ended things with him because I don't think our futures fit together. It was as simple as that."

"We've got to find him." Joli choked on the words. "Can you imagine how miserable he is, imprisoned under that dome? If he's even still . . ." She let out a little yelp, maybe a sob.

"I know," Nora whispered. The same thoughts still tormented her every day, though she'd been doing her best to put them to the side when she needed to focus on other things. And while it was nice to talk to someone who understood, jealousy's sharp claws were digging into her gut. Joli still cared for Ovrun. Maybe a lot.

Staring at the fire, Nora berated herself. What was her problem? She didn't want Ovrun, but she didn't want anyone else to have him either? She gritted her teeth. *Joli's not the selfish one here.*

"Any word about Krey?" Joli asked, her voice level again.

Nora pulled the blanket around her even tighter. "No." She brought her gaze back to Joli, who was peering at her closely. Probably trying to figure out what Nora's feelings were for Krey. *Well, that makes two of us.*

"You okay?" Joli asked.

"Yeah. Or maybe no. I'm just . . . stressed out."

"Is there anything I can—"

Nora's back went rigid. Osmius had just called her name. "Hang on," she told Joli. *Yes?*

I see him, Osmius said. *Flying toward me. I shall tell you what he says when he arrives.*

"Thank the stone," Nora said aloud, her lips broadening into a giddy grin. She relayed the information to Joli.

Before long, Osmius was in her mind again. *I shall carry him back. He says we must hurry.*

Relieved to have something to talk about besides her stupid, irrational feelings, Nora stood, waking Sharai and telling everyone what Osmius had said. Once again, she paced. When the dragon landed, she rushed over to them, arriving as Krey's feet hit the ground. "You were gone a long time!"

"I've got news." His tone was dark.

"Do you want me to gather everyone?"

"Hang on." He took a step closer. In a low voice, he told her what he'd learned in the city.

A particularly strong curse word flew from Nora's mouth.

He gave her the tiniest smirk. "My feelings exactly. I wanted you to have the details, because we need to be careful what we say to the group."

He was right. Sharai and Joli didn't know how the king's mind-control talent worked. "Walk with me," Nora said.

"Yes, Your Highness."

"Stop that," she said, but she was smiling.

They strode beyond the light of the campfire, then halted. "We have to stop him before he gathers his new brain lysters," Nora said. "Otherwise, he could end up with eight more Overseers."

"Exactly what I was thinking."

"We know where he was a day ago. We need to find him on the road and stop him. Whatever it takes."

In the darkness, she could barely see Krey nod. "I agree. He's more exposed out here than in the palace. Not that I'm looking forward to facing a bunch of mounted royal guards."

"Don't worry," Nora said with a grin. "We've got dragons. Come on, let's go talk to the others." Krey took a step that direction. On a whim, she grabbed his hand. "Wait."

He turned slowly. "Yes?" His voice was strangely soft.

Something about that word—and the feel of his fingers on hers—set her heart racing. She stepped closer. "I'm glad you're safe."

"Me too."

They stood silently, close enough that Nora heard every one of his quick breaths. Hers were coming just as fast. *He's just a friend,* a faraway part of her brain protested. But her instincts were louder than her reason. Her body moved on its own, leaning in, her lips parted, begging him to cross the remaining few simmets between them.

"Nora," he said softly, his breath brushing against her lips, his fingers slipping in between hers.

She closed her eyes.

All at once, Krey dropped her hand, nearly flinging it away. Her eyes flew open in time to see him take a rapid step back. "We better get back." He was breathing hard. "Your Highness."

This time, the honorific didn't sound remotely sarcastic. It was respectful and somber, almost sad. Like nothing else could have done, those two words brought reality crashing into Nora.

The discussion they were about to have with the group . . . it wasn't just any conversation. They'd be talking about how to make her the queen. Not at some time in the indefinable, distant future. No, as soon as they could find her father.

Within the next few days, if all went well, Nora would make several irrevocable barters.

Princess for *Queen.*

Your Highness for *Your Majesty.*

Friends for *subjects.*

This national tour had felt like a vacation of sorts. It had been easy to pretend she could hang onto her friendships. She'd even flirted with Krey, just a bit, and sometimes she convinced herself he was doing the same.

But it didn't matter what he said about coming to visit her once she was queen, or what Sharai said about how she could still cut loose every once in a while. It didn't matter what anyone said, because Nora knew the truth.

When her father's band of gold encircled her brow, everything would change.

"Are you coming?" Krey asked from where he still stood, an arm's length—or maybe an entire world—away.

"Yeah." She squared her shoulders. "Let's go figure this out."

THE STONE EATER: 8

ULMIN SAT IN BED, propped up on pillows. He was staying at the finest inn the town of Ravind had to offer . . . which wasn't all that fine. But his bedding was soft, and he was close enough to the Therro Desert that the autumn weather was mild, even with no fireplace in the room. It would do.

He reached a hand into the right pocket of his pajama top and withdrew a small piece of stone. Cradling it in the center of his palm, he gazed at it in wonder. Two of its faces were deep black, smooth and warm. The other edges were broken, coated in a luminescent orange substance.

Orange light flowed up his arm with an electric-like buzz. It ventured onto his neck, then his head, then down his other arm. Power, tangible and intoxicating, filled his hands and brain. He groaned with pleasure.

Reluctantly, he dropped the stone back in his pocket. He wasn't sure if touching it too often drained its power more quickly, but he didn't want to risk it. Right now, he was full to the brim with its strength. When he next fueled up, he'd have as much magic as he needed.

While his body was strong now, his head felt suddenly fuzzy. Lately, if he didn't consume his dark fuel consistently enough, his mind seemed to slow. It was his body's way of reminding him to remain connected to his gifts.

Ulmin pulled a small bag filled with dried brain matter from his left pocket. He preferred fresh, but on a trip like this, he made do. He pinched some out and shoved it in his mouth, barely chewing before swallowing it down. Blissful clarity flooded his mind.

"Guards!" he called.

The door opened. "Yes, Your Majesty?" a female guard said.

"Send in Ovrun."

"One moment, Your Majesty."

At first, Ulmin had wondered why he felt so drawn to Ovrun. Then one day, it had hit him. Ovrun knew Nora. And by the stone, Ulmin missed his daughter.

He gripped his bedding hard, squeezing his eyes shut to prevent tears from bursting forth. Nora's flight from the palace had been as sudden and shocking as Ambrel's death ten years earlier. Adding to his grief was the fact that Nora had *chosen* to betray him. Then she'd dug the knife deeper, dismantling his militia and fighting with the trogs against him. Now, she was touring the nation to turn his own people against him.

Did she have any idea how much that hurt? How much he still loved her?

In the early days after Nora's disappearance, Dani and Ulmin had spoken often of how empty the house felt and how worried they both were. Then, with no warning, Dani had turned cold. Ulmin had captured her mind and interrogated her, learning that Nora had visited the palace. His daughter knew he was a brain lyster. She wanted to stop him . . . and Dani was on Nora's side.

Another betrayal. Knowing how disloyal Dani was, Ulmin had hesitated to leave her at home during this trip. However, some of his most trusted guards were at the palace, guarding her quarters. They all knew the consequences if their loyalty slipped while he was away.

With Dani no longer a reliable ally, Ovrun was a breath of fresh air. He cared for Nora, and he was deeply devoted to his king. Ulmin had found immense relief in their talks of late, in knowing that he didn't need to control Ovrun anymore. The young man's loyalty was firm. Even Ovrun agreed the torture had been worth it. Sometimes truth only came through pain.

A knock sounded at the door. "It's Ovrun, Your Majesty."

"Come in."

Ovrun entered, bleary eyed but dressed in his guard uniform. He bowed respectfully.

"Have a seat, son. Pull the chair up to the bed." Ulmin watched Ovrun lift the heavy desk chair and carry it over. He was a strapping young man; no wonder Nora had apparently fallen for him. For the first time, a thought occurred to Ulmin. Maybe Ovrun was the key. Surely he could convince Nora of the truth.

Ulmin smiled as Ovrun sat. "Do you remember in Deroga, when I told Nora she could do better than you?"

"Yes, Your Majesty."

"I don't often apologize, but I must say . . . I regret that."

"Thank you." Ovrun's face was unreadable.

"You told me your relationship with her ended shortly after that battle. How would you like the chance to be close to her again?"

Ovrun's eyes widened. "Sir?"

"If we find her . . ." Ulmin chuckled. "Pardon me, *when* we find her, my heart's desire is to prepare her to be a good queen. In the past, I made the mistake of holding back knowledge from her. I wanted to let her enjoy her childhood, rather than seeing the ugly side of ruling. I created a girl with naïve, idealistic notions of what a nation should be. When I bring her home, she'll need a great deal of education." Ulmin leaned toward Ovrun. "She'll also need a partner who sees the truth and can help her see it too. Someone who can one day become a good king. Someone like you."

"Your Majesty." Ovrun swallowed. "I'm honored, but I'm content in my current role . . ."

Ulmin cut him off with a raised hand and a smile. "I know you are. That's why I can trust you with more." He wasn't under any illusions about Ovrun's ability to lead a country, but if the young man could direct Nora's heart back to her father, that would be enough.

A sharp rap sounded at the door. "Your Majesty! An urgent message!"

"Come in."

The female guard entered and bowed.

"Yes, yes, what is it?" Ulmin asked, suddenly annoyed. His fingers twitched, aching to enter his pocket for fuel.

"Sir, a letter from the mayor of Elda."

Elda was a town less than fifteen clommets away. From what Ulmin had heard, Nora had attempted to visit them a week ago, and, they'd refused to let her enter. Far too few communities had responded in such a way, and he appreciated those who had. He took the letter from the guard and ripped open the envelope.

As soon as he read it, a low laugh formed in his chest. The mayor had heard the king was nearby and was inviting him to speak to the loyal citizens of Elda. Ulmin couldn't say no to that. He turned to the guard who'd handed him the letter. "Send a rider ahead to tell the mayor we accept. As always, we'll ride at night."

24

Dani, what was I thinking?

What seemed perfect last night is humiliating in the light of day. I threw myself at the crown prince. I convinced myself I was falling for him, but I've known him less than two months. Now I'm questioning everything. Maybe I only fell for the idea of him, for the thrill of being chosen by royalty.

And Ulmin? For all his sweet words, how do I know he really cares for me? He's probably making the best of an arranged marriage he doesn't even want. How can I trust anything he says when neither of us has a choice in who we marry?

I made a fool of myself yesterday, telling him I wanted him, saying no one's ever made me feel the way he does. I imagine him laughing as my carriage departed, carrying away a starry-eyed, silly girl.

I sent him a message saying I can't see him due to a headache. It's not a lie.

I gave a big piece of my heart to him, and I wish I could take it back.

-Letter from Ambrel Kaulder to Dani Kaulder

Dated Barna 9, 180 PD

KREY SQUIRMED in the tall grass, accidentally elbowing Nora. "Sorry," he whispered.

"It's okay. I wasn't asleep."

"You should be. The dragons will tell you if they see anything."

"I'm afraid I won't wake up."

He laughed. "Vin can always come breathe on you again."

"No thanks."

He could hear the smile in her voice. Despite her words, her breaths grew as slow and even as the others in their group. Krey needed rest too, but his mind wouldn't allow it. Their plan had too many holes. And he didn't know how to fix it.

The day before, they'd flown back to the area where they'd nearly encountered the king two nights ago. The dragons had landed outside a nearby town that had recently welcomed them with open arms. Sarza and Sharai had quietly visited the mayor, who'd given them good news: rumor had it the king was nearby, in the town of Ravind. The mayor agreed to write a letter in the name of the mayor of Elda, inviting the king to visit. He even knew someone who could forge his fellow mayor's seal. He'd promised to have the letter delivered after dark.

Nora predicted that in order to be safer, her father would travel to Elda at night. As soon as darkness fell, Osmius, Gild, and Vin had flown their passengers to a spot off the road leading out of Ravind.

All three dragons were now circling far too high for anyone on the ground to spot them. They'd tell Nora if they saw the king and his people. From there, they had more strategies and contingencies, but everything would likely go out the window once they confronted the king. Krey's stomach churned as he reviewed all the things that might go wrong and how he'd respond if they did.

Nora shifted, letting out a small sigh, drawing Krey's attention. By the stone, she perplexed him as thoroughly as the upcoming confrontation did.

What had he been thinking the night before? She'd stood near enough for him to feel her breath, and somehow, he'd gotten it in his head that she wanted him to kiss her. He'd almost done it too. Looking back at it, he realized how stupid he'd been. Of course they'd stood close; they were talking quietly. She'd only taken his hand because she was glad he was safe.

But as soon as her skin touched his, he'd been done for. Like an idiot, he'd woven his fingers with hers and had nearly thrown all his pent-up desire into a kiss that probably would've resulted in her slapping him.

I've eaten brain matter. I loved the power it gave me. Part of me wants to experience all that again. And none of that is gonna change. It didn't matter that Nora's intelligence made Krey's heart beat faster, that her laughter turned him on in a way he didn't know laughter could, that her round hips and full lips annihilated his rationality.

None of that mattered, because she needed someone trustworthy to help her rule her country. And that wasn't Krey. His cravings weren't strong these days, but they certainly weren't gone. They might overwhelm him at any moment. He'd gone back to his dark fuel once. Who was to say he wouldn't do it again?

He shifted from his side to his stomach. His coat made a crappy pillow.

"You need sleep too." Nora's whisper barely reached his ears.

"Yeah. Sorry to wake you."

"It's okay. I'm not that tired." She touched his arm. "By the stone, Krey," she breathed in his ear, "you're tense."

He heard her sit up next to him. Then two hands found his tight shoulders and started kneading them. Even through the fabric of his shirt, her touch was warm and terrible and wonderful. Krey's muscles loosened as his heart raced.

He should tell her no, but this was a thoughtful gesture. It would be rude to push her away. Nora was just being kind. She knew he needed to relax if he was going to be effective when the king came. So he slowed his breathing down, trying not to think about who was touching him, urging his mind to go still.

Somehow, he drifted off.

───────

When she was pretty sure Krey was asleep, Nora reluctantly took her hands off his shoulders and lay on her back. The rest of the group was quiet.

Touching him had been a bad idea. She'd told herself the only reason she was doing it was to help him get the rest he needed.

I'm a terrible liar. Even when I'm lying to myself.

Ever since their quiet encounter outside New Therro nearly twenty-four hours ago, Nora had tried—again—to settle into a new way of thinking. Time to get over her childlike crush. She might become the Queen of Cellerin tonight. She had to prepare for the realities of ruling.

Except she couldn't stop thinking about how she wished he'd closed that miniscule gap between their lips. Today, despite frequently reminding herself to act like a queen, not a hormonal teenager, she'd felt more drawn to Krey than ever. As they'd traveled, he'd pushed past his fear of dragon flight to talk with her about their plans for tonight. And even with the wind devouring many of their words, she'd had the same thought she got when they read books: there was something so *right* about them strategizing together.

When they'd landed, she'd repeatedly caught herself staring at him. Her attraction was both undeniable and confusing. Nora had dated Ovrun, who was pretty much temptation personified. One of her fears after breaking things off was that she'd never find a "normal guy" attractive.

Yet somehow, Krey, with his wiry muscles and smaller frame, his smirk and kind eyes and sharp jaw, captivated her utterly. She wanted him in ways that weren't the slightest bit *friendly*. She'd touched him tonight because it was what she'd longed to do all day. Because the darkness had given her courage. Because it felt *safe*, with him on his stomach and her kneeling next to him, his shirt between her hands and his back, plenty of space between their lips.

This is so stupid. She stared at the stars overhead. *I'm torturing myself for no reason.* Whatever feelings she'd developed, she couldn't act on them. She had to settle for Krey being her friend . . . and she still doubted whether that was possible in the long run.

One thing was certain: Krey couldn't ever sit at her side as king. She couldn't expect him to love her if she was ruling over him. He was too strong, too self-assured for that.

Nora closed her eyes, trying to focus on the confrontation she hoped was coming between her and her father. It seemed less scary and convoluted than her feelings about Krey. The cool breeze teased her skin, and sleepiness fell over her again.

Nora. It was Gild.

Nora sat up. She'd actually gotten a little sleep, thank the stone. *I'm awake.*

A single rider on orsaback is galloping toward you. Despite the urgency of her message, Gild's voice was calm and soothing. *He shall reach your position in perhaps ten minutes. Several clommets behind him are fourteen riders, moving more slowly. I assume the king is one of them.*

Nora reached out to Osmius. *You need to land.*

I am coming now.

Has anyone seen Kadin? My father's feather lyster?

Vin's breathy, deep voice reached her mind. *If he is in the air, I shall find him. Again.*

Nora shook the shoulders of Krey and Sharai, the two people she was sleeping between. "It's time," she said quietly.

The message passed through their small group. "It's time."

Nora and Krey fueled up with ice and, in Krey's case, feathers, all provided by the mayor who'd allied with them. Zeisha had plenty of grass to eat, though she'd do all she could to avoid using her magic in combat.

Nora shoved one more bite of ice into her mouth, groaning at her full belly. "Sarza?" she called softly. "Any visions? At all?"

"Nothing."

The rider shall reach you soon, Gild said.

Nora drew in a deep, calming breath. "Let's go." Together, their entire group crouched and ran to the road. Krey, Zeisha, and Sharai crossed to the other side. They all dropped to their bellies.

The sound of a running orsa met Nora's ears. "Here we go," she whispered. She catalyzed some fuel and listened as the hoofbeats neared.

The moon overhead shed just enough light for her to see the silhouette of the orsa and rider. As they approached, Nora shot dense balls of ice at the animal's torso. She knew Krey was doing the same.

The orsa let out a bellow. It slowed but didn't stop. Nora continued aiming ice at it, with the same result.

A moment later, the animal fell on its side, throwing its rider.

"Got it," Kebi murmured as they stood and rushed toward the moaning royal guard. Nora's heart dropped. She'd hoped Kebi wouldn't need to shoot the orsa.

The man didn't seem to be seriously injured, but he was stunned enough to be easily subdued. Leaving the others to tie him up, Nora rushed to the orsa.

"*OHH-AHH*," it bellowed, pain clear in the cry.

Nora cursed, holding back tears, and rubbed one side of its squat snout. Her other hand gently stroked its chest, stopping when it encountered the arrow lodged there. "Oh, by the sky, I'm sorry." If only ice had been enough to bring it down.

"Can I put it out of its misery?" Sarza asked.

Nora stood and turned away, sniffling. "That would be good."

Moments later, the animal's voice went silent. Nora coughed, trying not to sob as the sweet, strong smell of Anyarian blood filled the air.

"It's done," Sarza said softly.

Nora was glad she couldn't see the yellow blood on the seer's knife. She pulled in a quick, deep breath and spoke loud enough for everyone to hear. "If he's tied up, let's go."

"Almost done," Krey called.

When he finished, they ran down the sides of the road toward the place where they planned to confront the king.

Vin's voice rang out in Nora's mind. *I have the flyer.*

Excellent, Nora said. *Bring him to us.* She reached out to Osmius and Gild. *Where are you?*

Osmius said, *I took all your packs to the location we discussed. Now Gild and I are waiting by the road.* He couldn't let the king see him, so he wouldn't be part of the coming confrontation unless Ulmin was killed or rendered unconscious. They'd talked about giving Osmius shield fuel but had agreed the risk was too great. He was a creature with magic in his very essence; an anti-magical substance might harm him.

At least they had two dragons who could help them defeat the king. Assuming everything went as planned.

Which Nora knew it wouldn't.

They reached their destination. Vin dropped Kadin, the flyer, at their feet. Nora gave the man a quick, heartfelt apology. Then Krey squeezed his neck until he passed out. They gagged him and tied him to a nearby tree.

Nora called out, "Everyone but Zeisha, eat your shield fuel!"

Zeisha needed to keep her ability to connect with the Well, just in case. The day before, Nora had pulled her to the side, asking if she could reduce the king and his guards' oxygen as she'd done in Deroga. Zeisha concluded it would be too difficult while they were riding galloping orsas. If she was to use the Well, she'd have to figure it out on the fly.

"Sorry, I can't eat it," Sarza said.

"Why not?" Nora asked.

"I finally had a premonition."

"What did you learn?"

"That I'm not supposed to eat shield fuel."

Nora groaned but couldn't argue with the seer. She was kind of jealous; she didn't want to eat the stuff either. Not only would it take away her ice lysting power; she'd also discovered it kept her from communicating with dragons. But she couldn't risk her mind being stolen by her father. After sending the dragons a quick *Talk to you later*, she fought her gag reflex to get down two swallows of shield fuel. "Everyone get in position," she commanded quietly.

She, Sharai, and Sarza climbed onto Vin's back. Krey, Joli, and Kebi mounted Gild. The dragons hovered on either side of the road, far enough back that the king's group wouldn't see them. Zeisha settled in the tall grass away from the road, ready to connect with the Well if the right opportunity came along.

Nora had warned Joli and Sharai that they might see magic that they couldn't explain during this confrontation. Joli didn't seem to mind such secrecy, but Sharai had seemed genuinely hurt.

"I want to help you," the former minister had pleaded. "When you don't share things with me, you're tying my hands."

"I wish I could tell you more," Nora had replied. Sharai's experience and connections had been invaluable as they traveled Cellerin together. But the secrets Nora was keeping—about Zeisha's gifts and the stone's capabilities—seemed to have put a wall between them, and she wasn't sure how to tear it down.

Nora's entire group was armed. Kebi carried her bow, Sarza her knife. They each had two loaded guns, but they'd agreed to injure, rather than kill, when possible. Above all, they'd do everything they could to avoid killing Ulmin. Regicide was no way to establish goodwill with the public. And while Nora hadn't said it aloud, she wasn't sure she could handle another parent's death, even knowing who he'd become.

Waiting was torturous. But it wasn't long before hoofbeats—many more than before—reached Nora's ears. The riskiness of what they were about to do slammed into her, and she gulped down several panicked breaths.

When the orsas had nearly reached Nora and her friends, she slapped Vin's side. He and Gild lifted into the air. They each flew in a large half circle at top speed. Streams of orange fire exited their mouths, creating a flaming fence around the king and his people, crossing the road and extending into the grass beyond. Cries rose up from the mounted guards, and orsas bellowed as they stopped, crashing into one another, sending some of their riders tumbling to the dirt road.

The fiery circle had a diameter of about thirty mets. Taking advantage of the chaos within, both dragons landed in the circle, releasing their passengers and rising back into the air. Shots sounded, but both dragons escaped.

Nora pointed a gun at the guard nearest her, who was sitting atop his orsa, mouth gaping at the flaming fence. She shot him in the hip. He cried out, falling to the dust. Nora held back a grimace and looked for another enemy.

It was time to take her father down—and take his crown.

25

I knew I couldn't avoid seeing Ulmin forever, so I agreed that he could visit me today. It was a bad idea. Now we've had our first kiss and our first fight.

As always, my face wouldn't let me hide what I felt. As soon as we were on the back patio together, Ulmin asked me what was wrong. Somehow I ended up accusing him of faking his feelings to make the best of a difficult situation. I took my fear and turned it into fact, then threw it in his face.

He denied it. And if he'd just stayed calm and assured me he cares about me, I think I would've been okay. But instead, he got as angry with me as I was with him. He told me the reason he'd waited so long to kiss me was because he was afraid I'd hurt him, and now I'd proven him right.

It was a quiet fight; we didn't want to be overheard. But it's amazing how much soft words can hurt. I don't really think he was faking his feelings, and I know I don't want to hurt him. But now we've both said cruel things, and we can't take them back.

-*Letter from Ambrel Kaulder to Dani Kaulder*
Dated Barna 10, 180 PD

Five civilians and a princess against thirteen royal guards and a king. It sounded bad.

But Nora's team had two dragons on their side. In Krey's mind, that definitely improved the odds.

The dragons' roles were simple. Vin would fly just above the combatants, depending on his thick skin to protect him as he breathed well-aimed fire at guards. His goal would be to debilitate, rather than kill. Gild would fly high above, using her excellent sight to monitor the battle. From that perspective, she could guide Vin to where he was needed most. She was vulnerable to gunfire and stone missiles, but she might be able to dive in and help once most of the enemy was out of the fight.

Meanwhile, Krey and his friends would do their best to disarm and subdue the guards, then capture the king. Carrying him, they'd escape on dragons.

Krey had known the plan wouldn't be as simple as it sounded. Fights were never clean and easy. The first seconds of the confrontation confirmed it.

Flickering firelight illuminated the king's guards, some of whom had fallen from their orsas, as they scrambled to surround their monarch. Krey would have to be careful with his gun. One errant shot could kill the king.

A flicker of motion caught Krey's eye. His instincts told him to dive low, thus avoiding the swipe of a knife. Krey lunged and connected with the guard's leg. The man went sprawling, his knife flying from his hand.

Krey was about to shoot him in the leg when he saw another guard taking aim, this time with a gun. He rolled, getting off a shot that hit an orsa instead of the guard. Krey shot the orsa again, this time on purpose. The beast fell on the second guard, pinning him down. Krey spun, looking for the first guard, but he'd gotten away.

Nearby, Kebi fought with a guard, attempting to push him away with her bow. *Now would be a good time for a dragon to help us out,* Krey thought. Vin was overhead, but he wasn't breathing any fire. Krey immediately saw what was wrong. With friend and foe so close together, even Vin's excellent aim might hit the wrong person.

Those thoughts went through his mind in a half second, even as he leapt to his feet and dashed to help Kebi. He didn't make it. He spotted a guard taking aim at him. A quick spin brought him behind an orsa.

Krey slipped into the calm, eerily focused mindset he'd found during the militia battle months ago. Everything was chaotic and quick, but his reactions sped up too, his mind and body working in sync. Seeing that the guard aiming at him had gotten distracted, Krey ran to Kebi, taking down her guard by slamming a pistol against the man's temple.

The fight couldn't have been going for longer than ninety seconds when Krey heard the king's voice. He was shouting at his guards not to use their guns unless they had to. Was he afraid to get shot himself, or did he still have some measure of concern for his daughter? Maybe both.

The gunshots slowed, but didn't stop. Despite the close quarters, Vin got in a couple of well-aimed spurts of fire, taking down two more guards. The sight sent hope surging in Krey's chest.

But Nora's team was taking casualties too. The guard must've injured Kebi before Krey got to him. She was on the ground, moving, but no longer fighting. Nora, who was still on her feet, had blood pouring down the side of her face.

Krey circled around an orsa and spotted a female guard facing away from him. He put her in a headlock. As he waited for her to lose consciousness, he spun around, lest anyone else attack him. His eyes fell on Joli, just as a thin, short stone spear shot into the back of her shoulder, penetrating deep. With a cry, she fell.

Behind her, Ulmin stood, hand raised, an insane smile stretching his mouth open.

Krey dropped the female guard, hoping she was unconscious. He lunged toward the king. Another guard, whose firelit eyes held the glaze of mental slavery, tackled him. By the time Krey escaped from the man—he wasn't even sure how he'd done it—there was an orsa between him and the king.

Nora had no idea if they were winning. She hadn't brought down any guards since that first one. She'd been injured by a good, old-fashioned punch to the face. Her cheek was bleeding, though her adrenaline kept her from feeling any pain.

Mostly, she'd woven in and out of huge, skittish orsas, trying to avoid injury and find an opportunity to contribute to the fight. Preferably without dying. A blast of fire caught her eye. Thank the stone, Vin had managed to aim at a guard, whose forearms were now flaming. The woman dropped to the ground with a scream.

Nora's single second of preoccupation allowed a large, male guard to swoop in and grab her, binding her arms to her body. Panic and anger sent strength through her limbs. She kicked backward, her boot connecting with his leg. He continued to hold on, dragging her toward the center of the fight.

No, no, no, it can't end like this!

It didn't. A punch sounded, and the guard grunted and toppled. She fell on top of him, then pulled away and swiveled to take in her surroundings, swearing to herself she wouldn't get distracted again. But she broke her vow immediately when she saw who'd taken down the guard.

Ovrun.

He grinned and disappeared behind an orsa.

Nora ducked behind another orsa, peeking to take in the scene at the center of their makeshift fighting ring.

Her brief thrill at seeing Ovrun disappeared in an instant, replaced by cold fear. At least six guards were surrounding her father, fighting ferociously against Nora's people. Her team had started this thing outnumbered. They'd agreed that they had to get the upper hand right away if they were to win. That hadn't happened.

The king's guards, who'd started out shocked by the sudden attack and dragon fire, were now focused. Some fought with clear-eyed, intelligent fierceness, others with the fearless actions of the mind controlled. Vin's attacks were sporadic and mostly ineffective. Nora didn't think there was any way to reach her father now, but she had to try. She rushed out, gun in hand, to join the melee.

Zeisha could see nothing through the flaming wall the dragons had created. But she didn't need to see, she needed to listen.

The voice that guided her, the one she heard more than ever these days, told her the fight inside the flames wasn't going well.

I want to help.

An image entered her mind: the old man she'd known as the Anya, creating a fence of swirling dirt. Certainty filled her heart. She needed to do something similar, though less drastic. Why, she didn't know. But she had no time to question it.

She sprinted to the tall fence of flames and knelt as close to it as she dared. She placed one hand on the ground and raised the other into the cool air. Her unique magic flowed from her heart, to her hands, to the ground and air. It traveled underneath and through the flames, into the circular battleground. She couldn't see what she was doing, but she sensed it. The dirt under the feet of the combatants stirred to life, rising in fine clouds.

At the same time, she sent a burst of magic through her raised hand, guiding the dirt to fly around haphazardly. Immediately, the people inside began to cough. The sound made Zeisha frown; she'd never before used the Well in a harmful way.

The voice in her heart told her all was as it should be. There would be no lasting harm.

Zeisha nodded and sat back, letting the Well continue its work.

Sarza's knife was more useful than a gun in such close quarters. At the start of the fight, she'd gotten engaged in hand-to-hand combat with a guard who was as well trained as she. They were still going at it, so evenly matched that neither could get the upper hand. She'd taken a cut to her forearm and given the guard one on his bicep, but they could both still fight, even with blood dripping from their wounds.

From the corner of her eye, she saw a second guard aim a gun at her. Cursing, she threw herself to the ground, eyes still pinned to her original opponent's knife. Just as she hit the dirt, intense pressure overtook her brain. *Not now!* Desperate to get away from her enemies, she scurried and skidded between an orsa's legs, somehow reaching the other side of the beast without getting trampled.

Her vision began.

It was a potential prophecy, and thank the stone, it was short. Sarza came back to herself with a gasp—and drew in a mouthful of fine dust.

She coughed hard. Swirls of dirt were all around her. She closed her eyes reflexively, but not soon enough to keep the dirt out of her eyes. The noise of the fight had mostly stopped, replaced by coughs.

The dust didn't surprise her. She'd seen it in her vision. Now she had a choice—keep fighting with the others as best as she could, or follow a far more dangerous path.

Sarza had never minded a little danger.

Eyes barely open, she untied one of her boots and yanked it off.

Next was her sock. She slid it onto her hand, just as she'd seen herself do in the vision.

Then she ran, one foot bare, the other booted, through distracted guards and allies, until she reached the center of the mass of people. Through her squinting eyes, she saw Ulmin Abrios, bent over, coughing.

As if in a dream, Sarza slipped her sock-covered hand into the front pocket of the king's pants. He reached out to stop her, but she punched his arm hard.

Still coughing, she pulled a small rock out of his pocket, thankful for the sock protecting her hand. She had no idea if touching the stone would kill her or increase the strength of her prophetic gift. Neither option appealed to her.

A single step, and she was out of reach of the coughing king. Several more steps, and Sarza reached the other person she'd identified in her vision: Krey. He was rubbing his eyes with one hand and coughing hard, like everyone else.

Embracing the burn in her eyes and the rebellion of her lungs, she pulled the sock off her hand, turning it inside out so the object she'd just stolen was now captured within it. She spoke, voice eerily calm, in Krey's ear. "The stone's in your pocket." Cough. "Don't touch it."

The second the sock left her hand, she turned. This was the moment where the vision had stopped. The king was distracted by dust. Maybe she could use her knife to subdue him. Coughs racking her body, she reached into her pocket for the bag of shield fuel. The premonition that had led her to remain unprotected was gone. She wasn't about to let the king take her mind.

Just as she pulled out the bag, sudden, piercing heat entered her back. The bag of fuel slipped from her fingers. Her brows drew together, her mind growing fuzzy. Had she gotten stung by something? A female guard was standing next to her, coughing and staring right at her, her hand reaching out as if to touch Sarza's back.

Then that same heat—along with shocking, agonizing pain—

reached the front of Sarza's body too. She looked down. Something sharp was pressing against the front of her shirt.

Her addled mind whispered one word: *Knife.*

She fell to the ground.

As soon as dust rose into the air and started flying around, Nora knew it was Zeisha's doing. Immediately, coughing replaced most of the fighting.

Vin! Gild! Nora called in her mind. *This is a good time to attack!* Then she remembered they couldn't hear her. Hopefully they could see through the dust, with their excellent eyesight.

She coughed harder, tears streaming from her squinting eyes. A guard, hacking like his lungs were falling apart, lurched toward her. She sidestepped him, and a flame shot down from the sky, igniting his arm. If Nora hadn't been coughing, she would've laughed. Dragons were amazing.

Avoiding another coughing guard who was still trying to fight, Nora wove her way through people and orsas toward her father. At last, she saw him—just as a guard nearby stabbed Sarza in the back.

"NO!" Nora screamed.

Her father, who was coughing as hard as anyone else, turned her way. With a wide grin, he lunged for her.

Gild dove at a steep angle, golden skin glimmering, fire aimed at the king's arm. Ulmin leapt back, avoiding the attack. But Gild was flying too quickly to pull up immediately. Nora ducked, lest the dragon's strong front claws scrape against her head.

Her father didn't seem to have that fear. The same wild smile on his lips, he reached up. Despite the dust in her eyes, Nora saw her father's fingertips brush against the shimmering scales of Gild's foot. The dragon froze in midair, just above the king.

Tears falling down his wrinkled cheeks, Ulmin spoke between coughs. "This creature is mine."

Dread burst open in Nora's chest, shooting panicked energy into her limbs. Gild's head turned downward, her mouth opening wide. Following the line of the dragon's gaze, Nora saw Krey. She didn't have to be a seer to see the future—Gild, now under the control of Ulmin, would incinerate Nora's best friend.

Hacking harder than ever, she charged toward Krey, knowing she wouldn't get there in time.

A mass of shimmering, dark scales slammed into Gild, sending the golden dragon crashing into Ulmin. He fell to his knees. In the flickering light of flames, Nora saw Vin grab the larger female dragon's neck within his sharp front claws, pulling her up and away from the fight. Fire streamed from Gild's mouth, dissipating harmlessly into the air.

Nora rushed forward. This was her best chance to get her father, while he was huddled in the dirt.

She didn't get the chance. Gild broke free, diving toward Nora, who threw herself down. Above, Vin latched onto Gild's long neck yet again, yanking her away. A guard launched himself at Ulmin, protecting the king's body with his own.

All at once, a strange wind drew the dirt away. The battleground went dark. From her position on her belly, Nora looked around, panicked. The wall of fire was gone.

Then it hit her—Zeisha must have used the dirt to squelch the fire. That meant one thing. The voice within Zeisha, the power behind the Anya's magic, had determined it was time for this fight to end.

And they'd lost.

Nora shook off her despair and stood, crying, "Retreat! Retreat!"

She ran, stepping on fallen bodies, hoping none of them belonged to Sarza, who might already be dead. The thought brought a painful lump to her throat, but she kept running anyway, shouting in a strained voice, "Retreat!"

Someone next to her cried out and fell, and despite the lack of words, Nora recognized the voice. She halted. "Krey!"

"Go!" he grunted. He was obviously fighting someone, though all Nora could see were dark, moving silhouettes.

She aimed a hard kick at what she hoped was a guard's butt or, better yet, his groin. The man let out a low, choked groan and toppled off Krey. Nora couldn't help but grin. "Come on!" she said, somehow finding his hand in the dark. She pulled him up, and they ran together, dodging orsas and a few guards.

As she ran, Nora cried out for Ovrun, desperate to find him so he could escape with them. Krey joined in calling for him, but he didn't respond.

Above, both dragons roared. Their flames briefly lit up their own fighting forms and the still-chaotic landscape below.

Nora and Krey had to fight their way out; now that the dust was gone, the remaining guards were determined not to let them leave. They'd just broken free from two guards when something massive struck the ground nearby with a crash that shook the dirt beneath Nora's feet. One of the dragons must've fallen.

Moments later, strong claws grasped Nora and Krey around their waists, lifting them from the ground. They both screamed. Nora grabbed the claw holding her. It was covered in oval-shaped scales. Thank the stone—it was Vin. Gild was probably lying on the ground nearby. Hopefully still alive.

The flight lasted only a minute or so, but it would take far longer for the king's people to cover such a distance. Nora found herself dropped unceremoniously on the ground, right next to Osmius. The team's packs were tied together and draped around his neck. Zeisha was already on his back. She looked up just in time to catch a glimpse of Vin's departing form.

By the orange sky, Nora needed her dragon-speaking ability back. She screamed at all three dragons in her mind, hoping her attempted use of magic would burn up her shield fuel.

Osmius nudged her with his nose, pushing her toward his back. She took the hint and climbed up, still crying out to him in her mind. Krey mounted after her.

Vin soon returned carrying Joli and Kebi, both moaning in pain.

"Osmius, can we get some light?" Nora asked aloud.

He created a white ball of fire in his mouth. Its light illuminated a stone spike in Joli's shoulder and a large gash on Kebi's leg. Vin gently deposited them on Osmius's back. Now there were five people on the gray dragon.

"Should I get down?" Krey asked. "Vin can come get me after he picks up Sharai."

Nora didn't want to risk leaving him behind. Plus, being crowded might not be a bad thing. The injured women would need to be held securely as they flew. "Osmius," she said aloud, "we need to go to a healer. Can you carry five of us—even slowly?"

The ball of fire in Osmius's mouth moved as he nodded.

Nora, Krey, and Zeisha arranged themselves, using their own bodies to carefully cover Kebi, who was now in shock, and Joli, who appeared ready to pass out. "Let's go!" Nora said.

Osmius quenched his fire and rose into the air.

"Osmius," Nora said, "Ovrun was with the king! Can you please tell Vin? Send him a mental image of what Ovrun looks like? Maybe he can pick him up along with Sharai."

With everything in her, she wanted Vin to look for Sarza too. If the seer was still alive, perhaps a healer could save her. But Sarza had been lying near the king. There was no way for Vin to get her without risking being touched by Ulmin. Besides, being carried in a dragon's claws would certainly hasten Sarza's death, rather than saving her life.

At least they could get help for Joli and Kebi. The mayor who'd assisted them had given them directions to an excellent blood lyster. As Osmius flew that direction, Nora continued to send out telepathic cries, blocked by her shield fuel. She was reciting a poem she'd learned years ago when a voice entered her mind.

Why do you scream, Nora-human?

Nora laughed aloud. *Oh, thank the stone, I burned up my shield fuel!* She reached out to Vin. *Is Gild okay?*

She fell. I believe she is merely unconscious.

Good. Are you on your way?

I am. I do not, however, have your friend.

She'd known Vin probably couldn't get Ovrun, but her chest ached with the knowledge. Ovrun had been traveling dressed as a guard. His fellow guards had surely seen him helping Nora's team. What kind of punishment would that earn him?

Vin's voice turned low and foreboding. *I also did not retrieve Sharai.*

Why not?

When I returned, she was speaking with the king. Nora could almost feel his anger warming her. *She did not appear to be a captive. I believe her loyalties have shifted.*

"Damn it!" Nora whispered. Had Sharai faked her side of the relationship they'd built? Maybe she resented not being in the inner circle. Or had it been a pragmatic decision, made in the moment she'd realized their attack on Ulmin was unsuccessful? Krey had always said Sharai's goal was to ally herself with the winner, whoever it was. Maybe he'd been right.

And maybe Sharai was right too. Nora was clearly fighting a losing battle. Her father was still free. One of her allies was most likely dead. The king now controlled sweet, gentle Gild. Then there was Ovrun. For some reason Nora couldn't fathom, he'd been traveling as one of the king's guards . . . but they'd lost their chance to rescue him. Could this get any worse?

Vin cried out, his voice panicked and fierce. *Gild is attacking me!* An image invaded Nora's mind: fire and claws, teeth and scales. Then the picture disappeared.

Nora cursed again, then called to Krey and Zeisha, "I've been talking to Vin. I have a lot of bad news."

26

The morning after an emotional night is the worst. I woke with my eyes gummy and swollen from crying. My mind screamed that I'd just messed up an amazing future. To make it all worse, I'm having trouble figuring out why we were fighting.

Apparently the queen wants Ulmin and me to work it out, because she sent a carriage to fetch me for lunch. She's an excellent conversationalist, but today Ulmin and I were both quiet. I couldn't stop thinking about how I wished I could fix things with him.

When my mind's full of the things I can't say, I have trouble saying anything at all.

-Letter from Ambrel Kaulder to Dani Kaulder
Dated Barna 11, 180 PD

OSMIUS LANDED in a meadow behind a little cottage. "I'll get the blood lyster!" Nora called. She ran to the house and knocked loudly enough to wake even the soundest sleeper, not letting up until the door opened.

A man of about thirty stood there in pajamas, holding a candle. His eyes widened when he took in Nora's appearance. Her cheek must look worse than it felt. "Come in. I'll heal you."

"There are two others who need it more." Nora pointed behind her.

"I'll get my fuel." He turned.

"You'll need a lot!" Nora called.

He emerged with a clay jug. "I take it we're going to that light?"

Osmius had a ball of white fire in his mouth again. "Yes," Nora said. "And I should warn you, *that light* is dragon fire."

The man's mouth dropped open.

"They don't have time for you to get freaked out about it," Nora said.

He blinked once, then nodded, all business. They ran to Osmius. It only took half a minute, but the healer was breathless as he looked up at the dragon.

"You'll need to climb on his back," Nora said. "They're bleeding, and we didn't want to move them."

Krey dropped to the ground to make more space on Osmius's back. The healer lifted the jug to his mouth. Nora looked away as he fueled up, nearly gagging as she heard him swallowing what she knew was thick, yellow blood. When he finished, she showed him how to use the edges of Osmius's scales as handholds and footholds.

The healer climbed up. Osmius bent his neck to direct the light on the injured women. Zeisha showed the healer the wounds on Joli's shoulder and Kebi's leg.

A few seconds later, he stopped. "My magic—it's not working."

"Damn it, the shield fuel is blocking it," Krey said. "We should've thought of that."

After a quick conversation, they determined the best way to burn up Joli's and Kebi's shield fuel was for Zeisha and Nora to attack them with magic. Zeisha began shooting vines at Joli.

The ice in Nora's pack was a solid block. Osmius attacked it with his claws, and she ate the broken pieces as fast as she could. When she'd eaten a couple of handfuls of fuel, she climbed halfway up Osmius's back and began aiming ice at Kebi. Krey kept handing up additional handfuls of ice until she insisted she couldn't eat more. He began eating it himself so he could burn up his shield fuel by attempting to use his magic.

Small balls of ice left Nora's hands, one after another. When each ball got close to Kebi, it changed direction, gliding over an invisible shield before dropping to Osmius's back. Zeisha's vines did the same as they approached Joli. After several minutes, a vine finally hit Joli. The healer began working on her, and Nora continued targeting Kebi until the trog's fuel stopped protecting her.

She dropped to the ground and sat next to Krey, both of them coughing occasionally. They handed the jug of fuel to the healer when he requested it for a refill. Krey successfully got his own magic working again. His knee bobbed up and down as they continued to wait.

Vin's voice entered Nora's mind. *I . . . cannot . . .* His weakness was unmistakable. *I . . . am . . .* He trailed off.

Vin, are you injured? Nora asked. *What happened?*

He didn't answer.

VIN!

The responding silence seemed just as loud as her telepathic cry. Her breaths came faster, and her pounding heart threatened to break her ribs. *Osmius, we've already lost Gild, and Sarza and Sharai, and Ovrun—again! We can't afford—*

SILENCE. Osmius's voice erupted in her mind, before softening. *Breathe, Nora-human.*

She sucked in a deep breath, though it took effort.

Come to me, Osmius said.

Nora walked to him, and he lowered his head. Warmth puffed

from both his nostrils, rustling her hair. It would've made her giggle if she hadn't been so stressed.

Despite all that has happened, Osmius said, *we must plan our next steps. Let us assume your father has information from Sharai and that he has a dragon at his disposal. What will he do?*

Nora groaned audibly.

No time for that. The dragon's gentle voice belied his words. *What will he do? Breathe and think, Nora-human.*

She obeyed, and the truth hit her in an instant. It should've been at the forefront of her mind as soon as she'd heard Sharai was gone, but she'd been too distracted to think clearly. *Sharai will tell my father everything. He may take Gild to search for us from the air. Then . . . oh, Osmius, Sharai will lead him to the farms! He'll arrest them, or kill them all—Hatlin, the militia, the farmers, everyone. We have to go there. We have to warn them—but Gild is faster than you! We'll be too late!* Her breathing picked up its pace again. *We can't let him get to the farms, but there's no way—*

Yes, Osmius interrupted. *We must warn those at the farms. It may not be too late. Perhaps something will delay the king.*

But he'll force Gild to attack them! All those innocent families!

We shall do all we can do. We must trust it will be enough.

It won't!

Still, we shall try.

We have to find a place for everyone but me to hide. You can't take us all to the farms; we're too—

Breathe, strong princess.

The gentle words filled her mind, resonating against her anxiety, chipping away at it. As she worked to slow her breathing, the healer climbed down. "They'll both be okay, but the one with the shoulder wound will be very sore. It'll take some time for her to fully heal." He took his jug from Nora and lifted it to his lips for one more swallow. After setting it on the ground, he gestured to her cheek. "May I heal you?"

"Actually, we need to go—"

"Your eye may swell shut if I don't heal you. Please, I'll be quick."

She nodded. Immediate relief flooded her cheek when he touched it.

After several seconds, he removed his hand. "I'm glad you got here when you did tonight. Your friend with the shoulder injury lost a lot of blood. She'll be exhausted."

"Thank you. I can't pay you, but I'll come back another time—"

He held up his hands. "I have a paying job as a painter. I don't charge for healing."

"Thank you." She let out a short cough that turned into an extended, deep one.

"Are you ill?" the healer asked.

"We all breathed in a lot of dust tonight."

"I can heal that too, if you'd like."

"We really don't have time—"

Your lungs need healing, Osmius said, his voice firm.

"Please make it quick," she told the healer.

"Turn around." He put his hands under her shirt, over her ribs. Nora hadn't realized how congested her lungs still felt until she coughed out a stream of foul-tasting mucus, and her breathing cleared. The healer slid his hands from her shirt, and she turned. "Thank you."

"You're welcome, Your Highness." Seeing her raised eyebrows, he smiled. "The dragon gave it away."

"His lungs need healing too," Nora said, pointing to Krey, "along with the two women you already healed."

He drank more fuel and got to work. Nora updated the others on Vin's message and on her plan to fly to the farms with Osmius, once the rest of them were safely hidden from sight.

When the healer finished, Nora and Krey thanked him, then mounted Osmius. He took to the air to search for a hiding place.

Joli and Kebi were awake, but no one spoke as they flew. Nora ruminated over the absolute disaster this evening had been. Sharai,

Sarza, Ovrun, Gild, and now Vin . . . all valued allies and friends, all dead, captured, missing, or working for the enemy.

She'd fly with Osmius to the farms and try to warn the people there. But in her heart, she knew it was too late.

Too late to save the rebels. Too late to bring down her father.

Too late to bring justice and peace to Cellerin.

───────

Krey was crammed with four others on a dragon's back, yet he wasn't scared. He was too fixated on the sock-wrapped stone in his pocket. It was small but held a weight far beyond its size.

What the hell am I supposed to do with it?

He and Nora had known her father would be traveling with part of the stone, and they'd discussed what to do with the object if they captured him. Nora had been firm in her belief that one person should never have that much power. She'd vowed that no one on her team would ever touch the stone. They'd protect it until they could return it to the other stone pieces in the chapel.

She'd told Sarza, Zeisha, Kebi, and Joli of her decision. They'd all seemed to agree with her. So why had Sarza stolen the thing? And why had she given it to Krey of all people—Krey, who'd already shown his willingness to dabble in magic's dark side?

He could almost hear it calling to him. What could he do with enhanced magic? Fly faster and farther than a dragon? Create ice cold enough to turn Ulmin's stone dome brittle? The possibilities danced in his mind, but he did his best to shut them out. *That's not who I am. I have to get rid of this thing.*

Maybe he should drop it right now, let it plunge to the ground. It would sit in that sock, losing its power due to its separation from the other pieces. Holding Osmius tightly with his left hand, he slipped his right hand in his pocket—then pulled it out. He couldn't do it. The stone was far too valuable to drop it in the middle of nowhere.

Its power continued to call to him. "What am I supposed to do?" he breathed, too quietly for anyone but God to hear.

Cool wind blew over him, and with it came clarity. Now that the stone was in his pocket, there was no way he could keep such knowledge to himself. He'd tell Nora. She'd make sure he didn't do anything stupid with it.

He half hoped she'd say they should use it. They were in far worse shape than they'd been a couple of hours ago. Maybe the stone's magic could turn the tide, helping them stop Ulmin from gathering his new Overseers and further devastating his nation.

The thought made Krey's heart thump harder, anticipation and terror warring in his chest. Ulmin's use of magic was wrong. Evil. Dangerous.

Could they borrow his magic without becoming like him?

Nora's voice interrupted his dark thoughts. "There's a deserted farm below us," she called. "We'll drop you off, and then I'll go to the farms with Osmius."

He'd talk to her. But it would have to wait.

THE STONE EATER: 9

Controlling a dragon was mentally taxing.

But oh, it was worth it.

As the huge, golden beast fought with the smaller dragon, Ulmin kept a portion of his mind connected to the reptid, even as he handled the other urgent matters fighting for his attention.

"Pursue my daughter and the other traitors!" he shouted to his guards. Coughs overtook him. When he recovered, he grabbed a female guard who was running past him. "Take an orsa back to Ravind. In my name, instruct the mayor to provide us with a healer and two rested orsas for the two of you to ride. Hurry! Go!"

"Yes, Your Majesty."

Ulmin's knees suddenly felt weak. He pulled two tiny brains from his pocket and downed them, sighing as familiar strength filled him again.

The ground shook. A dragon must have fallen, though Ulmin couldn't tell which one. It was dark as the stone out here. He scrambled to one of the uninjured orsas, digging in the saddlebags and pulling out a small lantern, oil, and matches.

When he'd lit the lantern, he turned to find his dragon, but his attention was arrested by a skinny, one-booted girl lying in his path.

The girl who'd stolen the stone from his pocket.

Roaring with anger, Ulmin knelt. She was unconscious, a knife blade protruding through her belly, her chest barely moving. Her blood soaked into the knees of his pants as he frantically went through her pockets.

She didn't have the stone.

He scrabbled in the dirt. Had she given it to someone else? Thrown it away? Panic squeezed his heart as he dug through her pockets again.

"Your Majesty," someone said.

"Not right now."

"Your Majesty."

He glanced up. Sharai—the traitor who'd joined his daughter's side—was standing over him. He'd seen her during the skirmish, doing her damnedest to stay out of it all. He leapt to his feet and extended his hands, whether to strangle her or control her, he didn't know.

She scurried out of his reach. "Please—listen to me. Then you can do whatever you want with me."

He took in her narrow face, peeking over an orsa's back at him. By the sky, he hated her—that short hair that was now messy and shaggy; those wide eyes; that stupid, thin mouth that had pledged loyalty to him over the years and had lately done the same to Nora. "Put your hands up," he said. "Come over here."

She walked around to stand on his left, hands in the air. He moved the lantern to his right hand and grabbed the base of her neck with his left, establishing a connection with her mind. "Are you going to kill, injure, or betray me, or help anyone else to do so?"

"No."

"Follow me." Letting go of her neck but retaining control of her mind, he stepped past orsas and over injured guards, scanning the area and quickly finding a dragon—*his* dragon—on the ground. The other dragon was gone. Ulmin sent urgent messages to the golden beast's mind, demanding that it rise. It tried, legs shaking, before again falling.

"You will rise as soon as you are physically capable of it!" he screamed. "You will fly from here and search for those you allied yourself with." Unlike other brain lysters, Ulmin could retain a connection with a controlled mind over quite some distance. Now that he had the beast in his mental grasp, he could continue to guide it even if it flew out of sight. He'd need to prevent it from flying too far, however. Dragons had stronger minds than humans. The king continued, "If you find our enemies, you will kill them. The people and the dragons."

All at once, he realized what he'd said. One of those *people* was his daughter. He opened his mouth to tell the dragon to spare Nora.

His teeth snapped shut. Nora had attacked him.

Again.

Earlier tonight, he'd naïvely imagined molding her into the princess and future queen she needed to be. It was time to stop lying to himself. She was no longer his daughter. She was his enemy. Nothing he did would change that.

Still, he wanted to see her. To tell her goodbye. To ask why she'd turned against him. Then . . .

Then he would be a man and kill her himself.

Through a tight throat, he spoke to the dragon. "Kill everyone but Nora. Bring her to me. Now GET UP!"

The massive, stupid beast tried, but it still could not stand. Ulmin shook his head in disgust and turned to Sharai. He frisked her, confiscating two guns and extra bullets. When he was done, he released her mind. "Talk."

She blinked, looking around in confusion before meeting his gaze. "I'll tell you everything. I only ask that you consider making me part of your government again."

He would've laughed if he didn't despise her so much. "You're a traitor, and I can get the truth from you whether or not you want to share."

"That would depend on you asking the right questions. You may get more information if I talk willingly."

That was true. "Perhaps you can convince me to trust you again." The lie emerged smoothly, followed by a cough. "I invite you to do your best to try."

She nodded, all business. "Nora's been working with a seer. She's bleeding out over there, and if you can't get a healer here fast, she'll die."

Ulmin's mouth dropped open. "Show me."

Sharai led him to the young woman who'd stolen his stone. Ulmin knelt and released a short, relieved sigh when he saw that she was still breathing. He looked up at Sharai, whose face was ghoulish in the lantern light, all sharp lines and shadows. "She's a seer?"

Sharai nodded.

Ulmin allowed himself a small smile as he placed a hand on the girl's face, establishing a connection with her mind so that if she woke, he could control her. By the stone, that healer had better get here fast. With a seer and a dragon on his side, what couldn't he do?

"Tell me everything," he commanded Sharai.

Information flowed from her mouth as freely as water from a tap. Ulmin listened, but his eyes were flitting across the area. When his dragon at last rose to its feet, Ulmin hushed Sharai and ran to the creature. "You know your instructions! Go!" It lifted into the air.

Not a minute later, fire from two fighting dragons lit up the sky some distance away. Ulmin let out a joyful cry. He reached out his mind to determine if the second dragon was the gray one he'd once held captive. It was not. He sent fierce mental pressure to his dragon, instructing it to fight to the death. The other creature could not be allowed to return to Nora. Where was she amassing all these damn reptids, anyway?

Before long, the blood lyster arrived. Ulmin stood over her as she knelt by the seer, muttering about the severity of the injury. She drank copious amounts of thick, yellow blood as she slowly removed the knife from the girl's gut, repairing tissue along the way.

The healer let out a frustrated groan. "My talent wasn't meant for injuries this severe!"

Ulmin knelt by her. "If you want to leave this place alive, you will succeed in this task. Do you understand?"

"Yes . . . yes, Your Majesty."

He hovered over her as she worked. At last, the knife was out, and the wound on the girl's belly was closed. "She will wake soon," the healer said.

Ulmin stood. Giddy laughter bubbled in his chest. He held his belly as his entire body rejoiced. The seer—*his* seer—would live. The dragons were still fighting, closer to him now. He calmed himself and sent a mental instruction to his dragon, commanding it to fight even harder. The beast roared in return. Ulmin was certain it would win this battle.

Joy sent lightness throughout his body, and he looked around for someone to share it with. Someone he could trust. "Ovrun! Come here, son."

When the young man didn't come, a bit of dread slithered through Ulmin's insides. "Ovrun?" He hurried through the area, stepping around orsas, ignoring questions his people sent his way. "Ovrun! Ovrun, my boy!"

Cold with fear, he kept searching as the healer took care of all the injuries, big and small. At last, she approached the king, asking if she could heal his lungs from the dust he'd inhaled. He nodded, barely noticing her cool hands on his back. He was too busy scanning the area for the hundredth time.

Ovrun, the one person Ulmin had dared to believe was truly loyal, was gone.

27

Ulmin showed up on Uncle Quin's doorstep after dinner tonight. "Can we talk on your porch?" he asked. "My grandmother insisted I come work things out."

It wasn't the greatest start to a conversation. And for a long time, it didn't improve. But fighting is tiring. After a couple of hours, we gave in and started listening to each other.

He told me again how afraid he is of losing me, not because he doesn't trust me, but because of how much he already cares for me. I told him I want to give myself over to my feelings for him, but I can't stop questioning the whole process and how little control we have over it.

After a long, difficult talk, we made a commitment . . . to friendship. I hope it'll turn into more, but that's what we both need right now.

-Letter from Ambrel Kaulder to Dani Kaulder
Dated Barna 12, 180 PD

WHERE ARE YOU?

Osmius and Nora had just taken to the air after dropping off the others when Vin's voice entered her mind. Heart racing, she replied, *We're flying! Are you okay?*

I escaped from Gild.

Oh, thank the stone. Renewed hope loosened the bands of tension circling her chest. *Osmius, can you send Vin directions to the barn?*

I am doing so now, Nora-human.

Nora's thoughts swirled, fogging up her brain like the dust Zeisha had stirred up. *Where were you? Why didn't you answer me earlier? We thought—*

It was a hard fight, he interrupted. *Never before have I been so weak. I needed to hunt to replenish my energy. It was difficult to say even a few words to you. I have eaten now, and my strength is returning. I shall catch one more meal before coming to you.*

Are you injured?

I have a gash in one wing, but it shall heal.

Nora was hesitant to ask, but she had to. *What about Gild? Is she dead?*

No! Vin's voice was shockingly strong, resonating with anger. *I would never kill another dragon. She is merely fatigued. She fought with a frantic energy, far more than she would have used were her mind not manipulated. In the end, she fell from the sky, unconscious. We were flying quite high, and I caught her with my claws so the fall would not kill her. In Vallinger, when a dragon becomes exhausted to the point of losing consciousness, they remain asleep for hours. Osmius, is it the same for dragons here?*

It is, Osmius said. *When Gild wakes, she will need food, as you did. But she is strong. She shall recover fully.*

Relief, as cool as the autumn wind, rushed over Nora. The thought of her father controlling Gild still sent nausea burning through her stomach. But at least the gentle, golden dragon wasn't dead. And thanks to Gild's exhaustion, Nora's father couldn't immediately attack the farms.

Nora again considered their strategy. Flying Osmius to the farms had never been an ideal plan. One glimpse of the gray dragon, and her father would capture his mind again.

Vin's mind, however, wasn't subject to the king's control. If Vin carried Nora, she'd have the freedom to help the rebels until the moment someone spotted Gild and Ulmin in the air. Then she and Vin could fly out of sight. Nora shared the idea with both dragons.

Vin, Osmius said, *do you have the strength for such a trip?*

I shall, when I have eaten again, he replied. *I can go without rest for some time if my belly is full.*

Happy hunting, then, Nora said. *We'll see you when you're done.*

Osmius turned back toward the barn where the others were staying. *Flying with Vin is a wise choice, Nora-human, though I always prefer to carry you myself.*

You're a big softie.

He responded with a growl.

Despite the long night, Nora's limbs filled with sudden energy. Vin's message didn't fix everything that had gone wrong tonight. But she had every reason to think they'd get to the farms on time. A soft, relieved laugh burst from her mouth.

As they landed at the barn, Osmius said, *I shall hunt, then return.*

Sounds good. Nora dismounted and ran inside. The old building was lit only by a couple of candles. Kebi and Joli were both resting peacefully, but Krey and Zeisha were awake. Nora huddled with the two of them and laid out the new plans.

Krey's smile got wider the longer she talked. When she was through, he said, "The grumpy dragon came through for us."

Nora laughed. She and Krey got into a deep discussion about the best way to evacuate the farms. At some point, Zeisha bid them goodnight, joining Kebi and Joli on the floor.

After some time, Krey said, "Before you leave again, there's something I need to tell you." Candlelight bounced off the planes of his face. He looked as serious as she'd ever seen him.

"What is it?"

As Krey drew in a deep breath, Osmius spoke to Nora. *I have returned.*

"Hang on for just a minute," Nora told Krey. "Osmius is back." She sent the dragon a message: *That was a quick hunt.*

Now we shall see if I can fit in the barn doors. Will you open them, please?

Nora passed along the message to Krey, and they crossed to the double doors, pulling them open. She expected the light of Krey's candle to fall on a dragon. Instead, it illuminated a very familiar set of wide shoulders and a joyful grin.

Nora screamed and threw herself into the newcomer's arms. "Ovrun! You're here! How are you—oh, you're here!"

He laughed and gave her a squeeze, then let her go. "I ran off at the same time the rest of you did," he said. "After I'd been wandering around for a long time, a weird-looking dragon with a long tail landed next to me. It grabbed my shirt with its teeth and put me on its back. The next thing I knew, we were in the air. We landed pretty quick, and Osmius was waiting. The other dragon picked me up again and dropped me on Osmius's back. And here I am. You'll have to get the rest of the story from him." He looked over his shoulder at the gray dragon.

Wiping her eyes, Nora spoke aloud to Osmius. "You told me you were hunting!"

Vin found Ovrun and asked me to pick him up. I considered telling you, but I thought you needed a joyful surprise.

Krey hugged Ovrun. "You have no idea how good it is to see you, man. You've got a lot to catch us up on."

Zeisha walked up, grinning. Apparently she hadn't been able to sleep through Nora's squeal.

As she hugged Ovrun, Osmius spoke to Nora. *I would still like to hunt. For prey this time, not stranded humans.*

Okay, I'll see you when I get back from the farms.

Osmius lifted off.

Nora quickly updated Ovrun on Sharai, Sarza, and Gild, then shared her plan to return to the farms with Vin. "I know we're all tired, but before I go, can you give us the short version of what you've been through?"

They found a spot across the barn from Joli and Kebi. In a low voice, Ovrun told them of being captured and tortured, then somehow entering the king's trust. He showed them his fingers that hadn't healed properly. Nora went numb as he spoke, her heart unable to process how far her father had fallen.

"I have a lot of questions," Krey said, "but they'll have to wait. Nora, I still need to talk to you before you leave."

"Ovrun, if you're hungry, we have food," Zeisha said.

"That would be great."

The two of them strolled away.

Krey sat directly in front of Nora and spoke softly, his words meant only for her. "Like we suspected, your father was carrying a piece of the stone. Sarza stole it during the skirmish and put it in my pocket."

Nora wasn't sure what she'd expected him to say, but that certainly wasn't it. She swallowed, trying to moisten her dry mouth. "Did you touch it?"

"No." He leaned toward her, which sent her heart racing for reasons that had nothing to do with their conversation. "I'll be honest, I considered it. But it would turn me into someone I'd be ashamed of. I know it would."

His words warmed her, while also sending a spear of pain into her chest. Resisting such a temptation took strength. Why couldn't her father have done it? He was strong too . . . wasn't he?

"I considered dropping it off Osmius's back and not telling anyone," Krey said. "But I couldn't do that either. Sarza risked her life to take this from the king. Maybe she had a vision or something, I don't know." He shook his head. "We don't have time to talk about all that. I'd like you to take it."

"Me?" Nora drew back.

"For better or worse, your family is supposed to care for the stone. I don't trust your father, but I do trust you. You should have it."

"I—wait! How can you get it out of your pocket without touching it? Did Sarza touch it?"

He smirked. "She put it in her sock. I hope you're not too grossed out by Sarza's foot sweat."

Nora let out a nervous chuckle. "Congratulations, Krey, you've managed to make an otherworldly, magical artifact sound totally disgusting."

He reached in his pocket, then placed a warm, cloth ball, surprisingly light, in her palm. His hand closed over the object, his fingers wrapping around hers. "Will you take it?"

"You don't think I'll be tempted to touch it?"

"I know how badly you don't want to be your father." His voice was so low, so close. "Like I said, I trust you."

Her fingers brushed against his hand as she closed them around the sock. "Your trust is a bigger gift than this stone."

The soft words hovered between them. Krey was still for a long moment. Then he let go of her hand and leaned back, crossing his arms. "Anyway . . . when you get back, we can talk more. Maybe one of us will have an idea of what we should do with the stone by then."

Nora blinked, thrown by the sudden shift in atmosphere. She slipped the sock-covered stone into her pocket. "When I get back, things will be fast and furious until . . . everything changes." Lonely dread filled her. How much longer did she have with Krey, the feather-and-ice lyster who'd flown above her in his town square, then somehow become her best friend? How much time did she have with Ovrun and Zeisha and the others? With Osmius? Suddenly needing to get away, she said, "I've gotta talk to Ovrun before I go."

"Yeah . . . of course. See you soon." Krey stood and walked into the barn's darkness, leaving the candle sitting next to Nora.

Her decision to talk to Ovrun had been impulsive, born out of the sudden weirdness between her and Krey. But as she walked toward the wall he and Zeisha were sitting against, she realized she really did want a moment alone with him. This was her chance to speak the things that had built up in her heart for the last two months.

As she approached, she contemplated the least rude way to ask Zeisha to leave. But once again, Zeisha's intuition saved the day. When she looked up and saw Nora, she picked up her candle and stood, yawning. "I need some rest."

Nora watched her leave, then sat next to Ovrun. She set the candle between them and leaned her back against the wall, turning her head toward him. His shoulders were broad as ever, and his wavy hair was longer than before. He shifted to look at her, the candle's amber light dancing in his eyes, and she tensed, anticipating the surge of desire he'd always elicited in her.

It didn't come.

"Hey," she said, giving him a genuine smile.

He returned it. "It's good to see you, Nora."

"Listen, I'm not sure how long I have. And I've been wanting to talk to you."

His silhouette stiffened a little. Was he afraid she'd throw herself at him? Or that she wouldn't? She pressed forward. "There's one thing I've regretted, ever since the day I ended things with you. I said . . ." She had to stop and breathe; just the memory of that moment pained her. " 'Why would I want a man who isn't strong enough to stand up for what he really needs?' I remember the exact words."

"So do I," Ovrun said softly.

Nora briefly squeezed her eyes shut, lacing her fingers together in tight regret. "I'm so sorry. I didn't mean it; I just wanted to convince you I was serious. I was pushing you away. But I didn't mean it."

"I know you didn't." His voice was low and so very kind. "But you were right."

"No I wasn't!" It came out as a shrill cry, bouncing off the barn's floor and walls. She brought her volume down. "Calling you weak— nothing could be less true!"

A sigh left his chest. "I let myself get lost in you. I shoved down my own dreams. I loved you; I really did. But if I'd married you and become king, one day, I would've regretted it. And . . . I would've been good to you, I know that. But I don't think I would've been good *for* you."

Exhausted, relieved tears sprang to Nora's eyes. She impatiently swiped one off her cheek. "Do you really believe that?"

"Trust me, I've had way too much time to think about this, stuck under that dome. You need someone who won't just love you. You need someone who'll stand up to you too. Someone who'll be excited to get up every morning. Not just because you're next to him, but because he cares as much about ruling this land as you do."

She unfolded her hands, spreading them wide in frustration. "How am I supposed to find someone like that?"

Ovrun laughed softly and placed a warm hand on her knee. "You're a lot of things, Nora . . . but you aren't stupid."

She stilled, an odd tingle taking over her cheeks and hands. Was he saying—?

Ovrun started coughing. He let go of her knee and turned to the side.

Grateful for the distraction, Nora said, "You should ask Krey to fly you to the healer we visited earlier tonight. We all got our lungs healed."

Ovrun got control of himself and turned back to her. "I'll do that." He let out a short laugh. "But I'm not letting you change the subject so easily. I saw the friendship you and Krey were building before I got taken. I saw you talking in the corner just now. And like I said, I've had a lot of time to think. Tell me you only see him as a friend, and I'll shut up. But be honest."

Honesty. She owed him that much. But there was no way she could honestly say she didn't have feelings for Krey. She bit her lip, then released it with a harsh sigh. "Whoever I marry will be king, but he'll also be my subject. I can't . . . I can't do that to someone I care about."

"So you'll marry someone you don't care about? Do you have any idea how ridiculous that sounds?"

"Well, when you put it that way . . ."

"Hey, you're the one who—"

Nora interrupted Ovrun. "Hang on. Vin just called my name." *Yes?* she asked the dragon.

I have fed and shall arrive shortly.

I'll be ready. Aloud, she said, "I swear I'm not avoiding this conversation, but Vin is on his way back."

"Let me ask you one more question. Before I got taken, you were pulling away from all your friends. What was that about?"

"I . . ." She could spend an hour explaining this, but all she had time for was brutal simplicity. "I realized it'll be impossible to have real relationships with people I'm ruling. I've been trying to prepare myself for that."

"Did you get that idea from your father?"

"You said you only had one question."

"I lied," he said with a short laugh.

Nora shrugged. "Well. . . yeah. I've spent a lot of time considering the sacrifices my father had to make through the years." Although, come to think of it, Sharai had been the one to claim the king had kept himself distant from his subjects. Was that even true? Who had her father really been before he'd lost the love of his life?

"One more question," Ovrun said. "Don't answer it; just think about it as you fly. Why are you trying to be like your father when you've always said that's the last thing you want?" He reached out and gave Nora's knee a squeeze. "It really is good to see you again." He stood and started walking toward the others, leaving Nora alone in a maelstrom of confusion.

"Wait!" she called, leaping to her feet and running to him. She grabbed his arm. "I'll think about it—I will. But let me give you something to think about too."

"Fair enough."

She lowered her voice. "There's a girl across the barn you need to talk to. You need to ask her why she ended things with you."

"I got over Joli a long time ago. We're fine."

"She's not fine."

Ovrun stilled. "She's not?"

"No. So talk to her. And maybe . . ." A grin took over her face. "Maybe get to know her again."

"Don't get any thoughts in your head, Nora. I never loved her. It was, well . . . honestly, I don't think it was ever more than a crush between us. We called it a relationship. But it wasn't deep."

"Okay. But have you changed in the last two years?"

"Of course."

"Ever think maybe she has too?"

Satisfied with Ovrun's silence, Nora smiled, released his arm, and walked to where she'd set down her pack. She grabbed it and said her goodbyes. As she walked outside, she became aware again of the lump in her pocket. She gripped it through the fabric of her pants. Her smile, which had lingered on her lips after her conversation with Ovrun, disappeared.

Yes, she'd have a long time on Vin's back. And maybe she'd ponder Ovrun's words. But first, she had to figure out what to do with the object she was carrying. A piece of the stone that brought magic into the world. The same artifact that caused the apocalypse.

Somehow she knew this small piece of it would affect the coming fight. What would it bring this time—freedom or destruction?

28

"I want you to know I trust you," Ulmin said, "so I'd like to tell you something."

When he took my hand, I thought he'd say something sweet—maybe tell me he wants more than friendship. Instead, he told me a secret . . . about international politics.

I'm sure it sounds unromantic, but it was what I needed to hear. It showed me he still wants me to be part of his life. Part of his future.

-Letter from Ambrel Kaulder to Dani Kaulder
Dated Barna 13, 180 PD

———————

As VIN LANDED in an expanse of golden grain at the farm where Hatlin was staying, Nora waved at several militia members working in the field. The morning sun was gloriously bright in the pale-orange sky. In the past, the dragons had been wary of flying over inhabited areas during the day. But during Nora's tour of Cellerin, they'd had to put aside their caution.

Nora gave Vin's deep-red scales a pat before sliding from his back. She asked a militia member where Hatlin was, then ran off toward the field behind the farmhouse. It wasn't far, but her legs were terribly heavy. During the flight, only her racing thoughts had kept her from drifting to sleep. Unfortunately, she hadn't reached any conclusions about her best friend or the stone in her pocket.

As she approached, Hatlin looked up. "Nora! You're back!"

She halted, panting. "Sharai defected to my father. I'm sure she's told him everything by now. He has a dragon, and he may fly here in a few hours. We have to get everyone off these farms."

His eyes widened as she spoke, but all he said was, "We'll make it happen."

"Great. We should send all the farmhands home—I'm assuming most of them have family in the city. As for the rebels, I was thinking—"

"Nora. I said we'd make it happen."

"What does that mean?"

He grinned. "You think we've been doing nothing since you left? We've got an evacuation plan. We'd arranged for our people to ride in wagons, but . . . you didn't happen to fly in on one of those dragons, did you?"

"Vin brought me."

"You think he would mind ferrying some passengers?"

"Great minds think alike."

———

Nora watched Hatlin give orders to militia members. They rushed off to saddle orsas and visit nearby farms. He also sent messengers to the city to spread the word to New Therroan dissidents there. Sharai knew who many of them were, and they'd need to hide or join

Hatlin's group. "It's all just like we've done in our drills," he told Nora.

"I had no idea you were so organized."

He laughed. "I had lots of help."

"Can you update me on the plan?"

"Our team's been gathering supplies—everything we need to live in the wild for a couple of weeks. They'll bring it all here in wagons. The plan was to use the wagons to evacuate our people too. Instead, we'll have everyone carry what they can, strapped to their backs. Vin can fly them out, a few at a time."

"Where will he take them?"

"We've found a place near the river. It's not far from here, but it's off the beaten path. There's plenty of trees to hide us. But then . . . well, we had another idea too. A couple of us scouted out the woods east of the palace. We figured some of us can relocate there—at night, of course. If we're camped out by the palace, it'll make it easier to support you when you're ready to take your father down."

Suddenly, Nora was laughing—harder than she should've, but that was the exhaustion. When she caught her breath, she realized Hatlin was looking at her like she'd lost her mind. "I would've never considered camping right under his nose like that," she said. "But it's brilliant. There are streams in there, right?"

"Yep, and even a little pond. Plenty of water." Hatlin's broad shoulders had a proud set to them.

Her smile faded. "My father's got a dragon now. If he sends her out to keep watch over the area, she'll see you."

"Yeah, but she can't talk to him, right?"

"No, he's not a dragon speaker. He might have someone ride her, though, so they can report back."

"Then it's not a problem. We knew the king might have a feather eater scouting the area. We already planned for it. The trees are thick where we're gonna stay, and we've got dark clothes. We'll rest during the day, staying hidden. At night, we can come out."

Nora nodded slowly. "A human won't be able to see you in the dark, and if the dragon spots you, she can't say anything about it. How many of you will be there?"

"Less than forty—just the former militia and others we've been working with on the farms. If rebels from the city join us, they'll stay here, by the river."

"This might be doable if you're careful. It's dangerous though."

"Everyone already knows that. If they're willing to take the risk, I say you let them. You don't know when the right time will come to attack. You'll need people there, ready to back you up."

Nora nodded. "Okay. Leadership suits you well, Hatlin."

He smiled. "I know Vin might be tired after carrying everyone to the river. Think there's any chance he can take a bunch of us to the woods by the palace after dark tonight too?"

"I'll ask him. As long as he has some time to rest and hunt first, I doubt he'll mind."

Hatlin's brows drew together. "You need rest too—you look exhausted. How about you ask Vin to take you to the river now, while everyone's gathering up? I'll come along to give him directions. We'll bring a tent and some bedding. Then Vin and I'll spend the next few hours getting everyone moved."

The thought of lying down sounded heavenly, but Nora shook her head. "I shouldn't leave before everyone else."

"That's absolutely what you *should* do. If your father gets here sooner than you expect, you can't be here." Seeing her about to protest, he held up a hand. "You do realize we're all here to support you, right? To protect you until we can make you our queen? So take a damn nap. You need one."

She gave him a soft smile. "Thank you, Hatlin."

Nora hadn't expected to sleep long, but her body had other plans. She didn't wake until the sun was setting. Maybe the sound of the nearby river had blocked out the clamor of rebels arriving. A peek outside her tent revealed more tents and people surrounding multiple campfires.

Nora ventured out and approached a group of former militia members. "Did everything go smoothly?"

One of the young women laughed. "Yeah, just as the last group was leaving the farms, they saw another dragon way off in the distance. I heard our dragon flew so fast, the people he was carrying almost fell off!"

Nora's heart leapt into her throat. The people she was talking to had no idea it was her father on the other dragon.

She wandered the camp until she found Hatlin. They ate dinner together, along with other members of her leadership team. She updated them on the events of her two-and-a-half-week tour.

When full darkness fell, Vin began carrying rebels to the woods by the palace. With his first group on his back, he reached out to Nora. *Shall I fly over the farms?*

Her chest tightened, but she didn't have the privilege of looking away from whatever her father had done. *Yes, please.*

A few minutes later, an image entered her mind. She squeezed her eyes shut and covered her mouth, grinding her teeth together to prevent herself from crying. Her father, taking full advantage of the dragon under his control, had attacked with fire, striking every farm that had allied with Nora. Dozens of fields and structures were ablaze, and flames even extended to the fields of some farmers who hadn't taken in rebels. Joli's family's farm was the worst, its details invisible past black smoke and orange flames.

Emotion thickening her throat, Nora spoke to Hatlin and the others, describing what Vin had shown her. They began a quiet discussion about how they'd share the news with the farmers.

Vin's voice reached Nora's mind again. *I have dropped off the first group and am flying high over the palace now. I see no sign of Gild. However, something is happening at the stone dome you've spoken of.*

Can you show me?

Her mind filled with the image of the back of the dome. A new stone platform protruded near the top. It was large, with a low wall on one side. As she watched, a massive stone brick appeared on top of the low wall. Then another, and another. *What is it?*

I know not. I must return to carry another group.

Nora stared at the campfire, considering what she'd just seen. Her father was home, using his enhanced magic again. It looked like he was creating a room on the side of the dome . . . a room big enough for a dragon.

He was building a cell for Gild.

———

Morning hadn't yet dawned when Vin and Nora returned to the abandoned barn. Despite the early hour, everyone was awake. Their sleep schedules must be as messed up as Nora's. She smiled to see Osmius sitting in a corner, silently watching her enter.

Her friends were sitting in a circle, huddled in blankets. Nora gave them a full update. Joli sobbed when she heard about her farm. But a certain hope covered the group when Nora told them some of their allies were waiting near the palace to help them.

"If Gild and your father are back at the palace," Krey said, "we don't have to worry about them finding us. Anyone want to sit around a fire outside instead of freezing in here?"

The reaction was enthusiastically positive. They broke up some old crates and built a campfire. As the sun peeked over the eastern horizon, they ate dried berries and meat for breakfast.

Nora stood. "I've been spending a lot of time on a dragon's back. I'm going to take a walk."

"Can I join you?" Krey asked.

A little thrill shot through her. She shrugged. "Sure, if you want to."

They strolled to the dilapidated farmhouse and walked around to the front of it, out of sight and earshot of the others. Krey tested the porch railing, then leaned against it. Nora did the same. He said, "I've been strategizing nonstop since you left, except when I was sleeping. Even then, I was dreaming about what we should do. I have an idea."

Eager to hear it, she took one of his hands. "What is it?"

He looked down at their hands but didn't pull away. Nora became very aware of the warmth of his fingers on hers. A giddy tingle made her shiver. *You're eighteen, not twelve*, she chided herself. *Get a grip.*

Krey ran his thumb over her knuckles. "What if we went back to some of the towns that supported us? We could ask them to send people to the capital—anyone who's willing to fight for you. They could spread the message to nearby communities too."

"We don't have time for any more traveling," Nora said. "We have to stop my father before he gathers his new Overseers."

He frowned. "It's too late for that. He's already back at the capital. He's probably gathering his new Overseers as we speak."

Nora's shoulders fell. "You're right. Damn it, that's why we needed that attack on him to work. I don't even want to think about what this means. Eight people like Faylie?"

He sighed. "I know."

There was no time to get mired in melancholy. She met his gaze. "If we try your strategy, do you think people will say yes? Will they fight for us?"

Krey smiled, and Nora could've sworn the sun itself got brighter. "Not *us*, Nora. *You*. They love you. I don't know what the result will be, but hang onto that truth—a whole lot of people believe in you. They'll fight for you."

By the sky, she wanted to hug him for saying that. She didn't, though. Ever since her conversation with Ovrun, she'd twisted her mind inside out, trying to convince herself a relationship with Krey was a good idea. But she couldn't justify it. Krey deserved more than a messed-up romance with a future monarch.

She dropped his hand. It was time to focus on goals she could actually meet, not dreams that would never come true. Folding her arms, she resumed walking, more briskly this time. As Krey scrambled to catch up, she said, "If a bunch of people travel to the capital, the soldiers there will notice. Where are they supposed to stay? How will we communicate with them?"

"I was wondering the same thing, until you reported back. How many people do you think could fit in the area by the river?"

"A few hundred at least, if they cram together. Plus there are plenty more trees at other spots along the river." She stopped, too excited to keep walking, and faced Krey. And despite her resolution to keep her distance, both of her hands somehow found his. "This might actually work." All at once, her heart dropped. "Except we still don't know how to get into the dome. We could storm the entrance, but they'll pick us off as we come in. I don't want a bunch of people to die for me, not if we can avoid it."

He squeezed her hands, making her heart leap in her chest. "I have an idea for that too. I think I may know a way for us to use the stone Sarza stole."

"Tell me!" Her traitorous body stepped closer to him.

"It's a little odd."

"The best ideas usually are."

I trust him absolutely, Osmius told Nora.

She was sitting in a patch of sparse grass in front of the gray dragon. His head rested on the ground, and she gazed into his golden, faceted eyes, wishing she could read his emotions in them. *I don't know Vin very well. Not like I know you.*

I do not know him deeply either. Yet I am certain he is trustworthy.

Is it because you're both dragons?

That is much of the reason. In my two hundred years, I have heard of only one dragon whom some might consider evil. Her mate had been killed for sport. She then spent decades hunting humans.

Nora pictured her father, shooting that terrible spear of stone at

Taima. Shame warmed her cheeks and neck. *A human killed your mate too.*

We all respond differently to grief. Perhaps if I had not already met people like you, I would have turned vengeful as well.

Nora leaned forward and rested a hand on the side of his face. *You'd risk humanity's future on Vin?*

While your phrasing is a bit dramatic, yes. I would. He is the safest choice, since I need to stay away from your father.

Nora turned to Krey, who was sitting about a met away. "Osmius says we can trust Vin."

"And what do you think?"

"I agree with him. Let's talk to Vin."

Krey's mouth widened into a grin. "If he says yes, we'll have to test it out."

"I can't wait."

The next morning, Krey climbed on Osmius, along with Nora and Ovrun. Osmius took to the air, followed by Vin, who carried Zeisha, Kebi, and Joli. It was time for part two of their tour of Cellerin.

Today's flight would take them a good portion of the morning, even at dragon speeds. It was a clear day, warm for mid-autumn. Traveling east, they passed over the southern portion of Cellerin's inhabited lands. Most of the area was wilderness, but they saw a few lakes surrounded by lush trees. To the south, Krey caught glimpses of the golden dunes of the Therro Desert.

They landed in the center of a town that, while small, was larger than any nearby communities. Its citizens had welcomed them warmly on their first visit. The mayor met them in the square and bowed to Nora.

"Thank you," Nora told her. "My advisor and I would like to meet with you privately." She gestured to Krey.

Krey's eyebrows rose a bit, but he tried not to give any other outward sign of his surprise. He'd assumed Nora would handle these meetings alone. She was certainly capable of it. Apparently he was now officially her *advisor*. He considered the term, deciding he rather liked it.

Once in the mayor's office, Nora explained their plans to confront the king. She then asked the mayor to send fighters to the capital and to ask nearby communities to do the same. Not releasing the woman's gaze, she waited for a response.

After a long pause, the mayor said, "We'll fight for you, Your Highness. And we'll spread the word. I don't know how many will go —I won't force it. But things in this nation need to change. We trust you to make that happen."

A small smile pulled at Nora's lips. "I'm honored." She turned to Krey. "Would you like to explain our other request?"

He leaned forward. "Mayor, I can't tell you why I need this, but I can assure you it's important. Do you have any stone eaters in the area?"

After a much-needed bath and an early lunch, all in the town's tiny inn, Krey climbed on Vin's back behind Nora. A quick flight brought them to a house where a wide-eyed, fourteen-year-old girl sold them a slab of magical stone she'd used her talent to create.

They returned to the air. Vin carried the stone between his front claws. It was roughly square, about a met to each side and half a met thick. They landed out of sight of any structures or people. Vin set down the slab, and Nora and Krey dropped to the dirt.

He watched her chew on a cuticle before catching herself and clasping her hands together. "Let's do this." She reached toward her pocket.

"Gloves," Krey said quickly.

She nodded and swallowed. "Thanks." She put on a pair of thin leather gloves and knelt in the dirt. Carefully, she pulled the sock-wrapped parcel from her pocket, then turned the sock inside out and let the stone tumble a few simmets to the ground, too cautious to touch it even with her gloves.

Nora was gazing at Vin, and somehow, Krey knew she was talking to him. The wine-colored dragon stepped closer and, without hesitation, set one of his front claws on the stone, covering it completely.

Orange light traveled up the dragon's front leg, then raced across his chest and up his neck. Nora stepped back to Krey, her arm brushing against his. The light continued to spread across Vin's body until his entire form glowed orange, like the broken faces of the stone.

Vin removed his claw from the stone, and the orange glow faded to nothing. Nora carefully put the stone back in the sock, then in her pocket. "Okay, Vin," she said aloud. "Let's see what you can do."

The dragon stood before the stone slab and opened his mouth, sunlight reflecting off his incredibly sharp teeth. Fire rushed from him in a loud *whoosh*.

Krey had never seen a dragon breathe fire like this—bright blue and so brilliant that he had to squeeze his eyes shut. An after-image of the stream of fire seared his eyelids.

The noise continued for several seconds, then ended abruptly. Krey opened his eyes. He followed Nora as she approached Vin.

Dragon fire could burn through wood, flesh, and even bone. It could not, however, destroy stone. So Krey had suggested they might enhance Vin's fire-breathing magic in the same way Ulmin increased his own power.

He hadn't dared hope it would work this well. In front of Vin was a charred crater. The magically crafted stone was gone, utterly incinerated by the dragon's blue fire.

"Wow," Krey breathed.

A few stronger words came out of Nora's mouth.

"Vin," Krey said, "how do you feel about doing the same thing to the king's dome?"

Nora laughed. "He says it would be a dream come true."

29

"We captured a spy today," Ulmin told me. "My grandmother has to decide whether to imprison him."

"Is there any other option?"

"We could extradite him. But if we do, he'll be executed for getting caught." He let out a long sigh. "One day, all these decisions will be on my shoulders."

If I become queen, I'll have to help him make those calls. I can't imagine holding lives in my hands.

-Letter from Ambrel Kaulder to Dani Kaulder
Dated Barna 15, 180 PD

"THANK YOU, SARZA."

Sarza flinched, looking around. She was in King Ulmin's large office, sitting on a comfortable couch. The last thing she remembered was him walking into the room where she was staying. He'd caught her eye. Then . . . nothing.

Now he was seated across from her, smiling. "As always, I enjoyed our conversation. It was very insightful."

Sarza's throat tightened as images of Nora and the rest of the team filled her mind. How had her words betrayed them today? Her gift had never felt like more of a curse.

The king's interrogations weren't the only reason she hated her magic more than ever. The day before the battle, Sarza had read some of the book Nora had loaned her. The chapter was titled, "The End of a Seer's Life." In the same matter-of-fact tone used in the other chapters, the book had informed her that seers eventually lost their minds, finding it impossible to distinguish between imagination, prophecy, and reality. Only those who died early avoided such a fate. Sarza had read the passage over and over, hoping she was misinterpreting it. But the words were clear.

Horrified, she'd tried to put the information out of her head. Now she wished she could share the weight of it with someone. Was this really her life? Mental slavery to a king, then eventually joining him in his madness?

"A guard will escort you out," Ulmin said, his voice a welcome distraction.

As Sarza stood, she glanced at the dark window. She'd only been in this place for four days, but she already hated its perpetual night and still, stale air. At least it was cooler than when she'd visited the chapel.

King Ulmin opened the door. As always, she considered attacking him. But she'd have to knock him out immediately, or he'd take her mind. Plus, there weren't any weapons in here—no fireplace pokers or heavy vases. Not even a letter opener. Sarza absentmindedly patted her pockets, wishing for her knife.

The king held out his arm, blocking her from exiting. "I bet you wish you had some shield fuel in that pocket, don't you?"

335

She glared at him, refusing to answer. Of course he knew about shield fuel now. Between her and Sharai, there wasn't much he didn't know. Thank the sky only Nora, Zeisha, Kebi, and Osmius knew exactly where shield fuel came from.

Ulmin smiled at her and handed her over to a guard outside the door.

The man led Sarza down the hallway, not speaking a word. He unlocked another office with a sign on the door reading, "Dani Kaulder." Sarza stepped inside her daytime prison.

She wasn't the only inmate. Sharai sat in the corner, as restless as ever. Sarza tried not to smile. Had the former minister thought the king would welcome her back with open arms? She'd played both sides, and now no one trusted her.

The room's other occupant was Dani, King Ulmin's sister-in-law. She sat at her desk, head tilted slightly to the side, her face placid. For some reason, King Ulmin kept Dani controlled all day, every day. Sarza had quickly learned that trying to converse with someone whose mind was enslaved was a losing prospect.

Sharai, on the other hand, started frequent conversations with Sarza, trying to convince her to trust the king. The woman was clearly in this room as part of Ulmin's strategy to get Sarza onto his side. The king himself had also been surprisingly nice to Sarza— keeping her out of a cell, giving her good food, and pretending to like her. None of it was convincing Sarza to change her loyalties, and none of it would. If she had one talent beyond prophecy, it was stubbornness.

The afternoon passed slowly. At six, Ulmin entered. "Sharai," he said, "I'll have a dinner tray sent up."

"Thank you so much, Your Majesty." She bowed humbly.

Ulmin raised an eyebrow. Even as he tried to change Sarza's loyalties, he seemed to be constantly testing Sharai's. He even made her sleep in this office, on the floor without a pillow.

The king walked Dani and Sarza to the kitchen in the residence for a quiet meal, not even hiding the animal brains he ate alongside his small portions of meat and vegetables. Sarza didn't eat much. Her gut was still sore from the knife wound. After dinner, a guard escorted the women to Dani's room.

When it came to her sleeping arrangements, Sarza wasn't sure what the king's game was. Did he not want to assign extra guards to guard a private bedroom? Did he think she'd appreciate not being forced to sleep alone?

Dani's room smelled a bit of smoke, and gray smears stained the walls and furniture. Sarza remembered Nora talking about a dragon burning up part of the palace, months ago. The living room looked and smelled brand new. Couldn't Ulmin have renovated Dani's rooms too? Was he too insane to think of it, or did he just not care?

Dani brushed her teeth and put on her pajamas, her glazed expression never changing. They both went to bed early, Sarza on the couch in the sitting room, Dani in her own bed.

Some time later, Sarza woke from a dream. She'd been hanging out with Nora, Krey, Ovrun, Joli, Kebi, and Zeisha. *Her friends.* For once, she hadn't felt like an outsider. She'd relaxed and laughed and told stories.

When she woke in the dark room, breathing the dome's dank air, she sat up and started weeping, her body heaving with uncontrollably loud sobs.

The door to the hallway cracked open. "Is everything okay?" a male guard asked.

"I'm . . . fine!" Sarza practically shrieked between gulping breaths.

The door swung closed. Then Dani's door opened, and she emerged with a candle, setting it on a table by Sarza. She knelt in front of the sofa. Her expression was clear, her brows furrowed. Concern practically bled from her eyes. "Oh, honey," she said, holding out her arms.

It was the first time Sarza had seen Dani in her right mind. Her shock stalled her sobbing. The king must not be able to enslave her while he slept. Sarza fell into Dani's outstretched arms, then started crying again.

"I'm so sorry," Dani said softly in her ear. "I know it's hard. I'm so sorry."

As she calmed, something occurred to Sarza. The woman holding her had no idea who she was. She pulled away and wiped her eyes, first with her hands, then with a handkerchief Dani fetched for her. "I'm sorry. You don't even know who I am, and here I am on your couch—"

"Shh." Dani shook her head, and there was a certain intensity to the action. A message. *Don't tell me anything.*

"Why?" Sarza whispered.

Another shake of the head, accompanied by a gentle smile. Dani took Sarza's hands, rubbing her thumbs gently along the younger girl's skin.

Sarza's breathing slowed further. She wasn't sure why Dani wouldn't talk, but she could guess. Ulmin would likely find out if they had any conversations of merit. Would he punish them? Possibly. Was his constant daytime control of Dani a reaction to something she'd done in the past?

Letting go of the unanswerable questions, Sarza let Dani's soft touch bring her peace. Her eyelids got heavy, and she smiled and lay down again.

Dani gave her hands a squeeze before returning to bed.

30

You'd better be glad you're home, because if you were here, I wouldn't know whether to hit you or hug you! I can't believe you didn't tell me Mom was coming. When I walked into the dining room for lunch, there she was, Ulmin next to her, both grinning.

I know I've only been gone a little over a month, but seeing her is just what I needed. I probably won't write for the next two weeks while she's here. She'll update you on everything anyway.

By the way, she and Ulmin got along like they'd known each other for years. I can't tell you how happy that makes me.

-Letter from Ambrel Kaulder to Dani Kaulder
Dated Barna 16, 180 PD

———

KREY CAUGHT Nora's eyes across the campfire. "Where to next?"
She swallowed her last bite of lunch. "We need baths and beds."

He looked around the group. Nora was right; they were dusty, their clothes smelling of smoke. The last time they'd bathed was four days ago, in the town where he and Nora had met the stone lyster.

Since then, they'd traveled almost nonstop. As before, they'd camped in the middle of nowhere each night. The first community had supplied them with tents, and every town since had offered whatever other supplies they needed, including fresh clothes. But nothing could beat a bath.

"Do we have time to take a break?" Joli asked.

"We need to make time," Nora said. "We'll all think more clearly if we're rested and clean. Besides, it won't exactly be a break. We're headed to an area we haven't visited at all yet. I happen to know there are plenty of brave people there. It would be good to have their support."

Nora's expression was unreadable until her gaze caught Krey's, and the corner of her mouth twitched. Hope made his heart leap. "What area?" he asked.

She gave in and grinned. "We're going to Tirra. Krey and Zeisha's hometown."

"Yes!" His eyes found Zeisha, who was sharing a joyful smile with Kebi.

"If we pack now and get out of here," Nora said, "we can be there mid-afternoon. I think we have enough food for tonight—"

"My Aunt Min will insist on feeding us," Krey said.

Nora laughed. "She can cook for six extra people with zero notice?"

"She could cook for the whole army with zero notice. And it would taste amazing."

"My family will want to help with the meal too," Zeisha said.

"Well, then." Nora stood. "Let's get to it."

She walked to her tent and knelt to pull a peg out of the ground. Krey approached and squatted behind her, laying a hand on her shoulder. When she turned, he got lost in her dark eyes for a moment before remembering why he was there. "Thank you."

THE STONE EATER

An adorably awkward laugh exited her mouth. "What are friends for?"

The words were like a sudden rainstorm on a sunny day. "Yeah, well—uh, thanks." Krey was standing and turning away before he even finished talking.

The roads to Tirra ran through the steep foothills around Cellerin Mountain. They were narrow, winding, and poorly maintained. Nora remembered traveling them the year before. It had seemed to take forever.

Amazing what a difference air travel made. After an easy trip of several hours, Osmius and Vin landed outside Tirra, dropping off their passengers. As Nora walked toward the city with Krey on one side and Zeisha on the other, her stomach clenched, and she couldn't pin down why. Maybe because she'd met Mayor Ashler of Tirra on her trip here nearly a year ago, and the woman had seemed to be a big fan of the king.

She suspected, however, that her nerves had a different source. She might meet Krey's aunts today. The opinions of two random women in a small city shouldn't concern her. But for some reason, she wanted the women who'd raised Krey to like her. *Needed* them to like her.

Focus. All that's secondary. Tertiary, even. Or more. Quadrary? Quadratic? Doesn't matter. Focus on getting support. On taking down the king.

Her gut twisted further.

As they entered the town, Nora's mind returned to her first trip here, in her father's steamcar. People had lined the streets, cheering them on. Today, she, Krey, and Zeisha—the three who might be recognized—wore hooded coats and kept their eyes down. No one paid them any mind.

In the town square, they turned toward Mayor Ashler's office, where Ovrun and other guards had whisked Nora after Krey interrupted their royal ceremony by flying above it. He'd then built a huge ice slide . . . and fallen when it broke to pieces beneath him. Nora snorted at the memory.

"What's so funny?" Krey asked.

"That slide you made. And how you fell when it broke."

He glowered at her. "That was a serious injury. My ass still aches on damp days."

She sobered immediately. "Seriously?"

He broke out in a loud laugh. "No!"

Nora shoved him and continued toward the office.

Mayor Ashler wasn't as enthusiastic as some of the other mayors had been, but she came around when Krey and Zeisha spoke. In the end, she agreed to spread the word to her own people and those in nearby communities, encouraging anyone willing to fight for Nora to travel to the capital. The journey would take at least a week, longer for those without orsas. Hopefully Nora's fight with her father would be over by then. But if it wasn't, she'd certainly need the reinforcements.

The mayor walked her guests back to the lobby, where three women and one man, all middle-aged, waited. Behind them stood two young men.

A joyful shriek exited Zeisha's mouth. At the same time, Krey drew in a gasp. Zeisha rushed to the man and woman on the right, while Krey practically tackled the two women on the left.

In between giddy greetings, Zeisha's dad explained that one of the mayor's assistants had come to fetch them. When the initial thrill died down, one of Krey's aunts, a plump woman with short, tight black curls, smiled broadly. "Dinner is at our place tonight."

Nora caught Krey's gaze. *Aunt Min?* she mouthed.

Beaming, he nodded.

Dinner was as amazing as Krey had predicted. Aunt Min and Aunt Evie—who insisted on being called by those names—welcomed them warmly. Zeisha's family was quieter than Krey's, but they couldn't wipe the smiles off their faces all night.

The house where Krey had lived after his parents' deaths was beautiful. Bookshelves lined the walls of the dining room, living room, and hallway. Nora was almost surprised not to see any in the bathroom. Evie was a fashion designer, and the classic lines and exquisite details of the window coverings, furniture, and artwork conveyed her aesthetic. The whole house even had electric lights, having recently been connected to the town's wind power.

After dinner, they spread out in the large living room. Nora settled in a cozy chair by the fireplace, enjoying the loud conversation and laughter.

Her eyes drifted to Ovrun. Since escaping, he'd been quieter than usual. His eyes often took on a haunted look, and Nora knew that was when he was remembering her father's torture.

She'd had several good conversations with him, keeping her commitment to rebuild their friendship. But Joli had been there for him even more consistently, talking softly with him long after sundown each night. The two of them had clearly worked out some of their issues while Nora had traveled to the farms. Now, they were sitting on a small couch together, chatting with Zeisha's brothers.

The joyful atmosphere abated when Krey announced that they'd have to leave before midnight to get back to the capital while it was still dark. Nora braced herself, expecting the two families to beg them to stay longer.

Krey's Aunt Evie, a slender, tall woman with long, glossy, black hair, spoke. "If you're planning to travel for much of the night, you should get some rest now." Her smile was a little wobbly, and Nora appreciated her all the more for the effort.

Zeisha left with her family, along with Kebi. Krey showed Nora, Joli, and Ovrun to separate guest rooms, explaining that his aunts had expanded the house years ago so they could host groups of traveling scholars.

As Nora waited for her turn in the bathroom she and Joli were sharing, someone tapped on her bedroom door. "Come in," she said.

Evie entered and set a large, wooden box on the desk next to the door. "Nora," she said, since Nora had put a stop to all the *Your Highnesses* hours ago, "Krey told me you enjoy wearing my designs."

A slow smile spread across Nora's face. Yes, she'd told him that, way back when they'd first met, when he thought she was nothing more than a spoiled brat. He remembered? "I do."

"If you have room in your pack, I'd love to send you home with a couple of pieces."

Delight surged through Nora. During her nine months away from the palace, she'd slept on a warehouse floor, in an abandoned home, in tents, and on the ground. Makeup hadn't touched her face in months. She'd gotten way too good at peeing outside, and she'd even suffered through her period last week while camping. All in all, she'd adjusted to life on the run better than she would've ever expected.

But damn, she missed shopping.

Just then, Joli tapped on the open door. "I'm done in the bathroom."

Evie turned. "Nora's about to choose some clothes to take with her. I was headed to your room next. Would you like to go through them together?"

Joli's cheeks dimpled. "Sure!"

"If you find something you love and it's the wrong size, let me know. I may have smaller or larger options in another box. Take as much as you like." Evie closed the door behind her.

Nora pulled the lid off the box and dug her hands into the soft fabrics, letting out a blissful groan. Thank the stone they'd taken baths before dinner; she'd never have dared put her stinky, dusty limbs in these clothes.

She and Joli each found a top and bottom to take with them.

After changing into the pajamas Min had loaned her, Nora held a pair of exquisitely soft leggings to her cheek, sighing. She'd never take fine textiles for granted again.

"I'd better get some sleep," Joli said, slipping out.

Nora brought the clothes back to Aunt Evie in the living room. She went to the bathroom and brushed her teeth, then returned to her room.

But when she opened the door, the walls were light gray instead of bright yellow. The bed had a red blanket on it, not a green one. And Krey was standing there, wearing pajama bottoms and an unbuttoned pajama top.

"Oh—I—oops!" Nora sputtered. "I'm so sorry. Wrong room."

She started to pull the door closed, but Krey grabbed the edge of it. "Wait," he said quietly. "I was just thinking about . . . well . . . can you come in for a minute?"

Her upper chest went tight, and an inexplicable flush found her neck and cheeks. "Sure." She stepped past him into the room.

Nora had seen Krey without a shirt on before, but this felt different. He began buttoning it from the bottom up, and her eyes drifted to the space between the two pieces of fabric. His skin looked so smooth, stretching over lean muscles she could barely see the edges of.

Nora told herself she should look away, but her eyes remained fixed on him, shifting from his chest to his slender fingers as he finished the task. She lifted her gaze and found him watching her, a tiny smirk on his lips, one of his brows lifted. Nora coughed and crossed her arms. "What did you . . . uh . . . want to talk about?"

In a low voice, he said, "Things are gonna get intense in the coming days. And I wanted to tell you, I appreciate you letting me be part of this."

Her brows drew together. "Part of what?"

"Everything. Reading old books and traveling and strategizing with you. It's been really . . . really good. Thank you."

A short laugh exited her mouth. "Why wouldn't I want someone who's smart and insightful on my team?"

He sighed. "I fell into the exact trap your father did. After I ate those shimshim brains, I didn't think you'd ever trust me again."

She stepped closer, eyes locked onto his, shocked at the shame she saw there. Her hand found his, and she squeezed it tightly. "Krey West, you are not my father."

"Clearly not, I was only a few months old when you were born, and—"

"Shut up, I'm being serious." She waited for the little smile to leave his mouth. "You do realize you did everything right, right? Or—not everything. Eating those shimshim brains was stupid. But after that, you were honest with all of us. You've told us when you're struggling with cravings. You even gave me that piece of the stone because you wanted to be sure you didn't misuse it."

He interrupted, "Yeah, but I—"

"No, no buts! Your buts will be the same ones we all have—but I could've done better. But I'm not perfect. I don't care about all that. You're one of the most trustworthy people I know. Let go of your shame, Krey. You've earned my confidence."

He blinked and swallowed hard. "Do you mean that?" he asked, his voice low and throaty.

"Without a doubt."

One of Krey's hands still held hers, but he lifted the other to cup her cheek. She pressed into his palm, soaking up his warmth. Suddenly, she was ultra aware of the open door behind him, of how easily someone could walk by and see them. But she couldn't bring herself to move.

"You have no idea what that means to me." Krey's eyes dropped to her mouth. His thumb traced her bottom lip. "You're so beautiful."

Her heart pumped wildly. Where had that come from? When Krey's eyes found hers and she saw the unmistakable heat in them, she let out a whispered curse.

Krey laughed softly, and it was somehow the sexiest sound ever. "What's wrong?"

She covered the hand on her cheek with her own. "What's wrong is, if all goes according to plan, I'm going to be queen."

"And that's a problem because . . . ?"

Nora pulled his hand off her face. She kept hold of him, her thumb brushing across his knuckles. Not because it was a good idea, but because she couldn't bring herself to let go of him entirely. "Because if—hypothetically—I had feelings for someone, someone who was intelligent and strong and an amazing leader in his own right—hypothetically, if that happened, I could never act on it."

He released her hand, then brought both his own hands up, resting his fingertips just below her ears. His touch slid gently across her skin, stopping at the back of her neck, where he rubbed her tight muscles. The action was exactly what she needed and exactly what she shouldn't allow. Yet here she was. Unmoving.

"Hypothetically," Krey said, "why couldn't you act on it?"

"Because next time I get into a relationship, I'll go into it actually thinking about my future."

Krey moved his hands inside the collar of her pajamas to press his fingers into the knotted muscles at the base of her neck.

Trying to ignore how good it felt—and failing utterly—Nora continued, "Eventually, I'll get married. My husband will be my subject. There's no marriage of equals when you're a monarch. I would never do that to—" She almost said *you* but caught herself. "To someone I cared about."

Krey dropped his hands to his sides. His eyes remained on her face, his thoughts swirling in them. The building tension had nearly driven Nora mad by the time he spoke again. "If I'm honest with you, will you do me the same favor?"

She didn't like where this was going. But she'd just told him she trusted him, so she nodded.

"Here's my honesty." Though they weren't touching, his intense gaze warmed her skin, her eyes, her very bones. "You're beautiful and smart and funny, and I've tried to think of you as just my best friend, but it's no good. If friendship is all you want from me, fine. But I'm telling you right now, I want to give you more."

She could hardly breathe but managed to whisper, "What do you mean by *more*?"

That smile she loved came over his face. "Did I say *more*? I meant *everything*."

Nora stopped breathing.

Krey's smile faded. "Your turn. Tell me the truth, is it just me? Or have you fallen as hard as I have?" His eyes begged her to say yes.

Her throat was tight. She couldn't remember how to speak. She nodded and managed a strangled, "Mmm hmm."

A small laugh rumbled in Krey's chest. He stepped even closer, and his voice took on the firm confidence she knew so well. "Your Highness, I'm secure in who I am. I fully trust your leadership ability. When you become queen, I'll gladly be your subject. I'll bow to you and serve you and do absolutely anything I can to support you." His eyes took on a passionate intensity, and without looking away from her, he lifted his right foot and kicked. It connected with the bedroom door, which swung shut with a *click*. He lowered his voice. "As long as we're equals behind closed doors."

His words—their pure logic and tempting promise—took her breath away. It couldn't be that simple, could it? But why not? Who was telling her she couldn't truly love, couldn't have an equal partner? Was she still listening to Sharai? And her father?

Why should someone else determine the most important relationship in her life?

"Oh, Krey," she breathed.

His slow grin was sweet and more than a little cocky. "Yeah?"

"I would tell you how perfect what you said was, but your head would get too big."

He threw that very head back and laughed. Nora joined him. Then a beautiful silence, taut with possibility, replaced their laughter. In one quick movement, Krey grabbed Nora's waist and pulled her close.

Her breaths quickened. She laid her hands on his chest, slowly sliding them up until they were behind his neck. His lips were temptingly close, and she nearly closed the gap and kissed him—but all at once, she stopped herself.

Nora had been kissing boys for years. The groom's son, and a young ash lyster who'd visited the palace, and that one grandson of a diplomat, and, of course, a certain royal guard.

She'd even tried to kiss Krey once. But that was before . . . everything. Before traveling and fighting and reading and laughing together.

Before he'd become her best friend.

Krey's eyes were deep pools of longing. Nora dropped her gaze.

"What is it?" he asked.

She looked up at him again. "This is just so . . . weird."

His lips curved into a little smile. "I know, right? Let's try something. Put your hand on my heart."

She trailed the fingers of her right hand lightly along his neck, taking her time, holding back a giggle when he drew in a quick breath. Then she pressed her palm on the left side of his firm chest. His heart was beating so fast, she was surprised his shirt didn't tremble with it.

His right hand slid up her back, teasing her neck just as she'd done to him, and when she shivered, he didn't suppress his own laughter. He hovered his palm over her upper chest. "May I?"

"Yes." It was more a breath than a word.

He pressed his hand over her racing heart and gave her a delighted smile. "Close your eyes."

She did.

"Just breathe," Krey said.

Nora pulled in a deep breath. She'd never taken much notice of Krey's scent, but now, she couldn't get enough of it. Beneath the soap from his bath was something familiar and alien and altogether tantalizing, something purely *Krey*.

As she continued to inhale his scent, she became aware of his warm breath, falling on her lips. The awkwardness she'd felt dissolved into mist, replaced by a deep need—to know Krey in ways she'd hardly dared dream of. To pair the smell of him with the taste of him.

"Nora," he murmured.

His mouth on hers caught her by surprise, but she recovered instantly, softening her lips to match his. And oh, by the sky, his mouth was warm and urgent, generous and demanding. Krey's hand left her heart and slid around her shoulders, pulling her closer.

She tangled her fingers in his hair and teased his bottom lip with her tongue. He responded with a low moan, deepening the kiss, and she lost herself in the taste of him. When he guided her farther into the room, it was like a dance, and when he pressed her to the wall, she barely noticed the painting that rattled against the plaster.

Krey's lips left hers, finding her ear, her neck, the hollow between her collarbones. Nora briefly tried to catch her breath, before resigning herself to never breathing normally again. She gave in to the giddiness, running her fingers along his back and neck and through his hair. Then his mouth found hers again, and they drowned in another kiss, more delicious than the first.

They were both panting when he pulled his lips off hers and pressed their foreheads together. Then he tugged her away from the wall and drew her into a tight, perfect embrace, burying his head in her neck. "I've wanted to kiss you for months now," he murmured. "I tried really hard to convince myself it was a bad idea."

"That makes two of us." Arms still around his neck, she stepped back, putting a few simmets of space between them. For several long seconds, she drank him in—his body, slim yet trained for endurance through his frequent runs; his eyes, full of trust and intelligence; the stubborn, firm set of his shoulders. "Krey, you're so . . ." She paused, then smiled. "Striking."

One of his dark brows rose. "Is that a good thing?"

She ran a hand along the sharp line of his jaw. "A very good thing."

"Good, because"—he shook his head slowly—"I need to learn to write poetry just so I can tell you how beautiful you are. And damn, Your Highness, can you *kiss*."

She let out a delighted laugh.

He pressed a frustratingly chaste kiss to her lips. "We really should get some sleep. We're leaving in a couple of hours."

"Yeah." She pressed her palms to his warm cheeks, the action almost desperate. "Everything just changed between us."

"I know."

"Do you think you'll regret it?"

He pulled her into one more tight hug and whispered, "Not a chance."

31

Mom is leaving today, so I'm sending this letter with her. I know she'll update you, but you need to hear this story in my words.

During the last two weeks, my friendship with Ulmin has taken the sweetest turn. Hands held under the table, secret glances, whispers that make me blush.

Last night, we bundled up against the cold and walked to the back porch. I was watching the snowflakes come down when he said my name.

I turned, and he was on his knees. "Marry me," he said. "I love you. Please, marry me."

My whole body went hot, and I don't know exactly what I said, but I know I said "Yes" and told him I love him too. And I do! I love him with everything in me.

When he'd put a ring on my finger (wait until you see it!), he stood and *finally kissed me again. It was just as perfect as the first time, except that it got cut off too early when the door opened.*

Mom has always had a knack for interrupting at the worst moments, have you noticed?

-Letter from Ambrel Kaulder to Dani Kaulder
Dated Barna 30, 180 PD

———

KREY'S SLEEP was less than restful, but in the best of ways. Nora's lips, hands, and heartbeat populated his dreams.

At last, he rose and turned on the light, squinting against its brightness. According to his wall clock, it was only a little past ten-thirty. Aunt Evie had volunteered to wake them all at eleven.

Krey dressed and brushed his teeth. Then, an embarrassingly large grin on his face, he approached the door next to his and tapped gently.

A muffled, "I'm up, Aunt Evie" floated through the door.

"Can I come in?" Krey asked quietly.

"Oh!" Nora sounded more awake now. "Yeah."

He slipped into the dark room and pressed the door closed. Heart pounding, he made his way to the bed. His hand found Nora's shoulder, then her face. He leaned over and placed a soft kiss on her lips. "Good morning."

"It's morning?" She pushed herself up with a start. Her forehead knocked against Krey's, causing them both to moan.

"I didn't mean *morning* literally."

"Well, you said *morning*. And I'm awake now. Can you turn on the light?"

He did. Nora was squinting, her whole face screwed into a melodramatic frown, pieces of glossy hair stuck to her cheek. Krey bit his bottom lip, but it didn't suppress his smirk.

"Don't look at me like that," she mumbled.

He sat on the bed next to her, pulling her into his side. "What, like you're beautiful?"

"Like I'm a groggy mess, and you wish you hadn't kissed me with that freshly-brushed mouth."

He pressed a kiss to her temple, lightly rubbing a hand along her arm. "I'd never regret kissing you." After a short pause, he added, "But you are a groggy mess."

She pulled away, then shoved him hard, nearly sending him tumbling off the bed.

"A gorgeous groggy mess!" he protested, using a pillow as a shield when she tried to push him again. "The most beautiful groggy mess I've ever seen, I swear by the stone."

She couldn't hide her smile, and the sight of it did something wonderful to his insides. "Your hair's sticking up," she said, "but you still look good. Really good."

All at once, he was terribly aware of the bed they were on and how close she was to him. His voice dropped. "My aunt will be waking everyone"—he looked up at the clock—"in fifteen minutes. I just wanted a little time with you."

"Hang on," Nora said, getting out of bed. She looked back at him with a stern expression. "Don't move." She slipped out of the room and returned a couple of minutes later, hair brushed, the promise of mischief in her eyes. Returning to the bed, she sat next to him and kissed him with a mouth that tasted of toothpaste. When she pulled away, she asked, "Better?"

"Hey, I wasn't complaining in the first place." He pulled her in for another kiss, but she broke it off quickly.

"I was thinking," she said, sitting back and taking his hand in hers, lacing their fingers together, "we can't tell anyone about us yet."

Krey's eyes left hers, all his insecurities from the past months shoving to the forefront again. "Okay, yeah—that's fine." He could hear the tinge of pain in his voice but didn't know how to get rid of it.

"I know people will think it's a bad idea, with my history. Plus, it might be hard on Ovrun—"

Another quick kiss shut him up. "That's not it, Krey, not even sort of. Our entire team trusts you." A rueful grin took over her mouth. "And as for Ovrun, he actually told me to give you a chance."

Krey's brows leapt up. "Seriously?"

"Yeah. I think Zeisha will be okay with it too. She seems really happy with Kebi."

A low laugh left his chest. "When I found out about Kebi, Zeisha basically told me to get over myself and let someone—" He paused.

Nora's gaze flicked down to his lips as he licked them nervously. "Let someone what, Krey?"

He swallowed. "She said I should let someone love me."

A soft smile stole over Nora's mouth, and her eyes danced with unspoken promises for the future. "That girl is full of good advice."

That damn uncertainty was back, like a knot in his belly. "Why don't you want to tell anyone about us?"

A frustrated sigh exited her mouth. "I didn't say I don't want to, I said we can't. If people know about us, it may get back to my father, one way or another. You know how he used Ovrun against me in Deroga. I won't put a target on you like that."

"So you trust me; you just don't want me to die." The knot in his gut untied itself, and he grinned. "Now that, I can get behind."

Suddenly, her lips were on his again. Between kisses, she spoke. "I want . . . to tell . . . the world about us, Krey." Another long kiss. "We will, as soon as we can."

Something in the back of his mind tried to remind him that they needed to get out of bed and prepare for their trip, but he swatted the thoughts away, holding her closer, entranced by her mouth, by all of her.

A tap on the door elicited a gasp from Nora, who pulled away, eyes wide. In a slightly strained voice, she called, "I'm up, Aunt Evie."

"Are you dressed?"

"Yes, of course!" she responded quickly, as if she had to defend her honor to Krey's aunt.

Krey winced, and a quick glance at Nora showed him she'd realized her error too. Aunt Evie wasn't accusing Nora of being naked with a boy; she was just asking if she could come in. If Nora had claimed to be getting dressed, the door wouldn't even now be swinging open, and the woman behind it wouldn't be blinking at the two of them, mouth agape.

"Good morning?" Aunt Evie said.

"Good morning," the room's occupants replied. Krey's body thrummed with awkward tension, and he could tell Nora was in the same state.

"Nora, I wanted to wake you and let you know that Min packaged up some food for your team."

Evie's gaze shifted between them, and Krey knew there was no way he'd convince his aunt that he'd entered this room for a friendly, platonic chat.

She let out a short sigh, her shoulders dropping a bit. Amusement and resignation battled for prominence in her half-smile and furrowed brow. "You both have good heads on your shoulders," she said. "Make sure you use them."

"We will," Krey mumbled, as Nora replied, "Yes, ma'am."

Evie took a couple of steps into the room. "Min and I have missed you, Krey." Her voice wavered a bit. "I suspect we're going to continue missing you for a long time. But this . . ." She gestured between the two of them. "if you're smart about it, I get the feeling it's a good thing."

Before he could think how to respond, she was out of the room, closing the door behind her.

"You'd better get back to your room before anyone else sees you," Nora said.

Krey nodded, taking her hand and giving it a quick squeeze before getting out of her bed. At the door, he turned. "She's right, you know. This is a good thing."

Nora's smile warmed him as he returned to his room to gather his things for their trip.

———

Several hours later, Osmius and Vin spiraled through the darkness and landed. Once everyone had dismounted, Nora lit a lantern. It illuminated grasses to the north and trees to the south. The sound of the river met her ears.

Osmius and Vin left to find a place to rest. Nora led her team along a narrow path through the trees. Before long, the lantern illuminated several tents that seemed far more closely spaced than the last time Nora had been here. "Anyone awake?" she called.

A few minutes later, she and her team were huddled with two male farmers and one female. "First," she said, "how many people are staying here?"

The woman grinned. "Farmers, rebels from the capital, or people from around the country who've come to support you?"

A relieved laugh bubbled from Nora's chest. "Oh, thank the sky, they're actually coming!"

"There are about fifty farmers," the woman said, "and seventy-five New Therroans and Cellerinian soldiers who joined us when you came back to warn us. Plus about three hundred people from all over the country, but that number is growing fast. Honestly, Your Highness, it's crowded. We're just glad they brought their own food."

"There'll be more," Nora said. "We'll find other places for them to hide. What have you heard from Hatlin?"

"The king has a gold dragon that keeps watch over the area by the palace, including the forest. It takes some breaks, but it's in the air most of the time. Someone rides on its back."

"Does the dragon ever leave to hunt?"

"No, Your Highness."

"They must be feeding her at the palace. Does she take a break at night?"

"Yes, Hatlin said they never see her from about eleven at night 'til four in the morning."

That fit with what Ovrun had said, that the king wasn't sleeping much these days. Five hours of sleep left him nineteen hours a day to control Gild. Nora shuddered, then turned her attention back to the woman. "Has anyone gotten a look at the prison they built for her? Is it open on the outside?"

"Someone sneaked over there a few days ago. There's some sort of stone door on huge hinges. Looks impenetrable."

The hint of a smile pulled at Nora's lips. "We . . . might have a way to get in there. But first, we need some rest. We brought our own tents. Tomorrow, Vin will fly to the forest by the palace." Her smile got bigger. "If all goes well, by the end of the night, we'll have three dragons on our side again."

Sarza woke with a loud, deep gasp. The pressure in her head was intolerable. She squeezed her eyes shut, buried her head into Dani's couch cushion, and waited for the coming vision.

She was in the sky, watching the domed palace. The scene was dark, yet Sarza could make out every stone.

A huge, closed-in room stuck out from the rear of the dome. At the front of it was a stone door with massive hinges.

As Sarza watched, Vin soared into view, flying riderless. He was headed directly for the protruding room. He stopped in front of it and painted the door with a thick stream of shockingly blue fire that burned through the thick stone. It was gorgeous . . . and terrifying.

When Vin stopped, Sarza peered into the cave. Along each wall were what looked like two large lumps of charcoal. Human-sized lumps. A breeze entered the cave, dispersing the black substance. Not charcoal, but ash. It scattered through the cave, some of it blowing into the open dome beyond.

In the center of the cave, Gild, the great, golden dragon, was rising to her feet. Immune to her fellow dragon's fire, she was unharmed. Below her were pools of melted metal. The remnants of her chains.

The vision ended.

Sarza sat up, then rushed to the bathroom, barely making to the toilet before she lost her dinner. She continued to heave. The book called this torture *PVS. Post-Vision Syndrome.*

When she was done, she grabbed her toothbrush, reflecting on what she'd seen. The vision was what the book she'd been reading called *immutable.* Sarza couldn't change it.

A premonition came to her as she scrubbed at her tongue: *This will happen tonight. Soon.* Sarza gasped, nearly choking on her toothbrush. She gripped both edges of the sink and spat out her toothpaste.

If she and Dani could get up to Gild's cave . . . if they could somehow hide near it, away from the blast of that blue fire . . . they could ride Gild out of the palace dome. But how would she convince Dani, who didn't even know Sarza was a seer? Should she tell her what she'd seen? *Could* she tell her?

She opened her mouth to speak the vision. Her teeth shut of their own accord, her throat tightening. Okay, forget telling Dani. This was a secret vision, what the book called a *shrouded prophecy.* She couldn't speak it even if she wanted to.

Sarza never saw herself in immutable or shrouded prophecies. She could decide how to react to the events she'd seen.

In seconds, she had a plan. She rushed to Dani's room, flipping the switch on the wall. Painful light penetrated her skull, which was already pounding. "Dani, wake up!"

Dani sat up, squinting. "What is it?"

"Do you trust me?" Sarza asked.

She swallowed, waiting for the answer. Several times since Sarza had arrived, Dani had gotten up and sat with her in the middle of the night. Once, they ate cookies the chef had given them. Another night, they silently played a board game. They never said much, but every time, Dani gave Sarza a tight hug before going back to bed. Despite the strangeness of it all, these late-night meetings were the most normal part of Sarza's miserable life. That had been enough to instill trust in her. Did Dani feel the same?

"I do trust you," Dani said.

"Then if you can get us out of this house, I'll get us out of the dome."

Dani blinked several times, her gaze wary. Sarza thought she understood her concerns. If this didn't work, Ulmin would be furious. He might kill them both.

"Let's get dressed," Dani said.

They did, quickly. Dani whispered a few instructions, and they hurried to the door of her quarters.

As soon as it opened, a female guard stepped in front of it, hand on her gun. "What's going on?" Her eyes fell on Sarza, who was holding her middle and grimacing.

"Cramps," Dani said. "Nora used to get them too. I'm sure there's some medicine in her bathroom. We'll be right back."

She tried to step into the hallway, but the guard grabbed her arm. "I'll come with you."

Sarza's heart dropped, but she followed Dani and the guard down the hall. The guard led them into Nora's quarters, flipping on the light to illuminate another smoke-stained room.

Sarza pushed the door closed and followed Dani through Nora's sitting room and into her bedroom. She held her gut and released a miserable moan. Once in the bathroom, Dani got a chance to breathe three words—"Get her gun"—before the guard followed them in.

Dani opened a door to a closet Sarza would've expected to be filled with linens. Instead, its shelves were crammed with cosmetics, jewelry, and handbags. She rolled her eyes.

"It's on the top shelf," Dani told the guard. "I can't reach up there. Can you get it?"

The guard wasn't much taller than Dani. She glanced at Sarza, who hunched even lower, muttering, "I hope this stuff works."

With a sigh, the guard stood on her tiptoes, propping her left hand on a lower shelf and reaching up with her right.

Sarza sprang into action, grabbing the guard's gun from the holster at her hip. The guard managed a short shout before Dani clapped a hand over her mouth.

The guard was well trained, but Sarza's years of knife drills had given her impressive dexterity. She pulled the woman into a head-lock, cutting off her ability to cry out. Ignoring the boot pummeling her shins, she told Dani, "Grab some scarves! Fast!"

Dani did, and between the two of them, they soon had the guard gagged and tied up.

"Come on!" Dani said.

Sarza shoved the gun in the rear waistband of her pants and followed Dani. They ran through Nora's quarters and into a small room with chests on the floor on either side. Nora's icehouse. Several locks had been installed on the door to the outside. Dani threw the bolts, then stopped. "There are caynins. Follow me out, and stay very close to me for the first few seconds. They'll trust you when they know you're with me."

She opened the door. Light from Nora's bedroom fell on the perked-up ears of two waiting caynins. Sarza followed Dani out of the icehouse, shuddering when the caynins sniffed at her. She'd never liked the beasts. Even the docile ones had double rows of sharp teeth, and she was certain the palace's caynins had been trained to be the opposite of docile when necessary. But Dani's presence protected her.

After a sprint along the fence surrounding the palace residence, the two women reached the gate. Dani unlocked it, and they emerged into the bright-white light of security lamps.

"Take my hand!" Sarza said.

Dani did. They ran, panting. Sarza tried to ignore the occasional caynin that approached. It didn't take long to reach the fence at the back of the property.

As they continued to jog, Sarza kept her eyes peeled for some sort of access to the dragon's prison. She let out a too-loud sigh of relief when light from a lamppost shone on a stone staircase that looked like someone had shoved up against the fence. This had to be it. Sarza looked up, seeing a dim light breaking through the dome's darkness. She started climbing, trusting that Dani would follow.

At the top of the fence was a stone landing that extended over the short gap between the fence and the dome. The staircase turned again, continuing up the inside of the dome. Sarza's heart pounded. Even if the stairs weren't made of stone, she'd be convinced the king had created them. No sane person would've made this dark staircase with no railing. The dome's slightly concave wall pressed against her on one side, like it wanted to nudge her off the drop-off on the other. Ignoring the cold fear in her belly and the continued pounding in her head, she asked Dani, "You okay?"

"Yes," Dani said breathlessly.

Sarza's thoughts spun, creating a plan. *We'll wait near the top of the steps until I see the dragon fire. Then we'll shout so Gild hears us. She'll fly us out of here.* This might actually work. She took the steps a little faster.

Something caught her eye below—the swinging light of a lantern. A sound reached her ears: footsteps, two sets, heavier than Dani's.

"Another shift in paradise," a man said.

The second man laughed.

Sarza's breathing turned panicked as she picked up her pace. *We're so close. We're so close.*

The dim light above illuminated a wide landing that led to the massive opening into Gild's cave. Sarza could barely make out the outline of the dragon.

Her heart pounded so hard, it hurt her chest. A guard, holding a mostly shuttered lantern, stepped onto the landing. "We thought you two were never gonna make it!" he called.

For a terrifying moment, Sarza thought he was talking to her and Dani. But no—they were shrouded in shadows. He was speaking to the lantern-lit guards below.

Sarza's mouth turned dry, her thoughts racing. Could she and Dani push the relief guards down the stairs? Would Dani dare do such a thing?

Then a simple fact occurred to her: *I have a gun.* The realization sent a frantic, electric charge through her arms, spurring her to action.

She moved her hand to her waistband. Her fingers closed around the gun's handle and began pulling it free. The guard above stepped back into the cave.

Blinding blue fire—even brighter than it had appeared in the vision—seared Sarza's eyes. She lurched, both hands darting to her eyes, instinct screaming at her to protect her sight. The gun slipped from her fingers, tumbling into the blackness beneath her. Her panicked mind let loose with a silent roar.

Two terrified voices cried out from the cave. Desperate to protect herself from the dragon fire, Sarza ducked as low as she could on her step. Even with her head hidden in her arms, violently intense blue light pierced her closed eyelids.

The men's cries turned to tortured screams. Scorching heat blasted over Sarza. The guards in the cave didn't scream for long. Sarza pictured the lumps of ash she'd seen. She swallowed, barely avoiding heaving.

When the bright light disappeared, Sarza uncovered her eyes and grasped the next step with a sweaty hand. She'd crawl to the top, as quietly as she could. They could still do this. She heard movement in the cave; Gild was probably about to leave. When she got a little closer, she'd run to the top and call her back.

A man barked, "Stop. I saw you both. I've got a gun on you."

The voice was right behind them. As Sarza and Dani had huddled on the stairs, protecting themselves from the light and heat, one of the relief guards had closed in.

Sarza squeezed her eyes shut, letting her forehead fall to the stone staircase. Something powdery settled on her hand, and she knew it was ashes from an incinerated human.

"Please don't shoot us," Dani said.

"If you both come down, I won't have to."

Sarza considered scrambling up the rest of the steps. If Gild returned quickly enough . . . but no, the guards would hear her and follow, possibly pushing Dani to her death in the process. Sarza couldn't risk that. She pressed a hand into the stone of the dome. It was still warm from Vin's fire.

This dank, depressing place was her home. For the rest of her life, most likely. However long that was.

"No need to shoot," she said, scooting around to face downhill. "We're coming." In the light of their captor's lantern, she caught Dani's gaze. "I'm sorry."

THE STONE EATER: 10

ULMIN ABRIOS HAD ALWAYS LOVED his sister-in-law.

Now, however, it took everything in him not to send a stone bolt into her heart.

Sarza, the skinny, ungrateful seer—at least he understood her. Of course she'd tried to escape when he was sleeping. He should've predicted that.

But Dani? He'd given her a home for eleven years, ever since Ambrel died. And this was how she repaid him? Attempting to leave on the back of his dragon?

He sat on the front of his desk, gripping its edges so hard, it was a wonder the wood didn't crumble. Dani and Sarza stood before him, faces blank, both controlled. "How did dragon fire burn through my stone?" Sarza's mouth moved with a response, but he bellowed over it. "My dragon escaped! TELL ME HOW!" The scream abraded his throat. This time, he listened for Sarza's response, though he knew what it would be.

"I don't know."

Breathing heavily, he lowered his voice. "Do you have any ideas?"

"Vin isn't from here." Her tone was flat, matter of fact. "He's a phibian. Maybe his fire is hotter than reptid-dragon fire."

Ulmin suspected the truth was far darker. This very girl had stolen a piece of the stone from his pocket, then handed it off to that boy Krey. She hadn't connected the dots, but he had. That dragon's fire wasn't natural.

Who else had touched the stone and enhanced their powers? Was that stupid boy Krey even now controlling dozens of people? Would he create his own Overseers? Or was Nora planning to fill his dome with ice, freezing him to death? Fiery anger burned in his chest, coming out as a wordless roar that made the guards at the door flinch.

A tremble entered two of his fingers. He was all but certain the movement was too small for anyone to notice. Still, he grasped his guards' minds and sent all his mental captives a silent instruction to look away.

This is not weakness, he told himself as the tremble grew to encompass his whole hand. *It's simply my body's signal that it needs fuel.* Perhaps he needed food too; he hadn't eaten since the previous morning. He'd deal with that issue later. Heart racing with anticipation, he pulled a handful of tiny brains from the container on his desk and ate them so quickly that he nearly choked. Strength filled his limbs again.

He turned to gaze out his window. Perhaps he should bring soldiers to the palace. He'd avoided such a move until now. While he could easily keep tabs on his staff, how was he to trust dozens or hundreds of troops? But Nora's rebellion was strengthening . . . and now, his own dragon was gone. He needed more bodies surrounding him, people who would die to protect him.

The thought shot fear through his limbs. *I can't trust them. That's why the dome is here. It will keep invaders out.*

Unless dragon fire penetrates the stone again. The thought sent nausea burning through his gut.

He stood taller, resolve cutting through his fear. He'd bring troops to the palace. He despised taking risks, even calculated ones, but he had no choice. *I must protect myself. My palace. My stone.*

First, however, he had to deal with the women in front of him.

Ulmin released Sarza's and Dani's minds along with those of his guards. "Don't move a muscle," he told the two women. His voice was deathly calm now. "You've both betrayed me. You'll be locked in neighboring cells in the security office. Sarza, my people will limit your food intake, your ability to sleep, and your access to chamber pots, in an effort to increase the number of your visions." He should've done that earlier. He knew how seers worked. Mess up her routines, her comfort, and she'd have more visions. Instead, he'd tried to lure her in with kindness. A stupid thing to attempt. Fear and pain and magic—those were the only ways to control someone. He should know that by now.

He shook his head, bringing himself back to the moment. "When you have a vision or even a premonition, you will tell a guard immediately."

Her eyes hardened. "And if I don't?"

The question delighted him. "I or one of my Overseers—" He laughed when Sarza's brows leapt up at that word. "I can see my daughter has told you about the Overseer she knew. I have eight of them now, all staying here at the palace. Their skills are growing rapidly. It's quite impressive. I or one of them will control you frequently, throughout the day, at unpredictable intervals. We will interrogate you. If we learn that you have not been open with us, you will watch as Dani, in her right mind, endures torture."

Tears filled the girl's dark eyes, and her entire body stiffened. Leaning forward, he smiled and whispered, "Bet you wish you hadn't made friends with each other." He'd been furious when, during an in-depth interrogation, they'd revealed their late-night hugs and snacks. But the horror now splashed across Sarza's face made all that worth it. "You will help me take my daughter down," he said. "Then, if you're helpful enough, I might let you stay locked up forever, helping me rule my kingdom. What would you think of that?"

A tear rolled down her cheek. Ulmin laughed, then stood and brought his hands together in a single clap. "Guards, you heard my instructions for these women?"

They nodded.

"Then take them! And when you're done, escort my Overseers to my office. They'll find themselves busy in the coming days."

He watched them leave, and when the door shut, he indulged in a good chuckle. Having eight Overseers available to him at all times was simply delightful.

His plan had been to send them into the capital to keep the peace. When he'd learned of his daughter's growing rebellion, however, he'd reconsidered. Why risk revealing his greatest weapons to Nora? No, he was better off keeping them here, close by, ready to send them out to battle for him when he needed them most. They could practice on the troops he was bringing here.

Nora was attempting to win the nation's hearts. She'd find out soon how ineffective her strategy was.

The hearts of citizens were useless . . . when the king could steal their minds.

32

I know I've broken my letter-a-day vow, but I had no idea how much work it is to plan a wedding. We have less than five weeks, and with all the to-do lists engraved on my brain, I've almost forgotten my name.

I got Ulmin to myself for a little while tonight. We sat on a couch in the palace living room, and I told him if I'd known how little I'd see him while planning our wedding, I would've either said no or demanded an elopement.

He kissed me, which was nice. But then he held me close for an entire half hour. We said nothing at all, and it was exactly what I needed.

-Letter from Ambrel Kaulder to Dani Kaulder
Dated Wolf 6, 180 PD

IN THE OPEN land to the north of the rebel camp now known as Riverside, Nora sat against Osmius's chest, distracting herself by chatting with him. Krey was dealing with his own nerves by running, despite the dark, cloudy night.

I have her!

As soon as Vin's voice entered Nora's mind, she let out a joyful scream and jumped up to hug Osmius's broad neck. *Are you okay, Gild?* she asked.

Yes. Tired, but healthy.

Krey's footsteps drew near. "I heard you scream. Did you get some news?"

"Gild is free!" Nora pulled Krey into a tight hug.

Vin's voice reached her mind again. *I am leading Gild to a place where she may sleep. However, I have a concern to share with you. After I rescued Gild, we flew over Deep Forest so I could show her the camp. However, we saw no rebels.*

None at all, Gild echoed.

Nora's forehead screwed up. Deep Forest was the camp by the palace. She let go of Krey. "Vin said they didn't see the rebels. It's the middle of the night; Hatlin's people should've been visible."

"Do you think your father found them?" Krey asked.

He did not, Vin told Nora. *Remember, I returned one of Hatlin's messengers to Deep Forest before I rescued Gild. I did not at that time fly over the camp, but when I landed in the clearing, two rebels emerged from the trees.*

Nora passed the message along to Krey.

Osmius's voice, low and hesitant, penetrated Nora's mind. *I know of one way dozens of people could hide from dragon sight. It is highly unlikely, and yet I can think of no better explanation.*

Nora spoke aloud, so Krey could hear her part of the conversation. "Now I'm intrigued, Osmius."

Many months ago, you mentioned a rumor of a unicorn living in the forest by the palace.

Nora smiled. She'd told Osmius that on the day he'd shown her the kingdom's magical places. They'd seen a pack of unicorns in the

Kamina Forest, and she'd laughed with him about the stories she'd grown up hearing. "Keep going."

Unicorns are highly intelligent. They communicate with each other, but never with other species. However, they do touch the minds of other creatures.

"How?"

They cast illusions.

"Are you saying a unicorn is hiding the rebels?"

"Wait—what?" Krey asked.

"I'll update you in a sec."

Perhaps, Osmius said, *but they live in packs. If there is one, there are likely at least four.*

"Why would a herd of unicorns protect our people?"

Vin's voice intruded on the conversation. *That is an excellent question. Unicorns are not in the habit of involving themselves in human affairs.*

That is true, Osmius said. *However, they are likely observing the rebels and know they are enemies of the king. The unicorns could be protecting them to prevent Ulmin from attacking the forest.*

"Good point," Nora said.

Perhaps. Skepticism was thick in Vin's voice.

Additionally, Osmius continued, *Unicorns have a strong sense of ethics. Perhaps they know your people are in the right.*

Nora chewed on her lower lip. "If they're ethical, I assume they're peaceful?"

The dragon's laughter bounced about her mind. *Only if they are left alone. When they are attacked or their way of life is threatened, they do not hesitate to protect themselves, even if that means killing other creatures. Carnivores have been known to hunt them. It is difficult to defeat unicorns, but their illusions break down at very close distances. When an enemy occasionally gets close enough to see what is real, the unicorns attack with their poisonous horns.*

"Poisonous?" Nora repeated, incredulous.

Next to her, Krey muttered, "What the hell are those dragons telling you?"

Generally fatal, Osmius replied.

Nora shuddered. "Should I tell the others?"

Tell only those you trust most. If the unicorns feel threatened, they may flee. Worse, they may fight.

"Thank you, Osmius." Silently, she added, *I'd better update Krey. He's squeezing my hand so hard, I'm afraid he'll snap off my fingers.*

The next night, Nora prepared to move to Deep Forest with her friends and two hundred rebels. Osmius, Gild, and Vin would carry them. Joli had once again proven her organizational prowess, creating a travel schedule and a simple system that minimized transition time on the ground.

When Nora arrived, Hatlin pulled her to the side. "A scout spotted three hundred Cellerinian Army troops marching to the palace this morning."

Nora wanted to scream. If she and her two hundred rebels had moved to this forest just a day earlier, they could've attempted to stop the soldiers from entering the dome. Perhaps she wouldn't have dared expose herself through such an attack, but it would've been nice to have the option. Now all those troops were in the palace, acting as a living shield for her father.

Shaking off her frustration, Nora turned to welcome the next group of rebels, flying in on Gild's broad back.

Shortly after sunrise, a feather lyster soared above the trees, approaching from the direction of the palace. Nora recognized him as Master Kadin. For a moment, she regretted not killing him in their last encounter. There was no way to completely hide hundreds of people in the forest, and it was one thing to hope unicorns were protecting them. It was another thing to truly believe it. She held her breath, watching him.

As Kadin passed overhead, he didn't react at all to the scurrying rebels beneath him. Hours passed with no response from the palace. The rebels murmured amongst themselves, coming to the conclusion that the feather lyster was secretly on their side. Nora let the assumption stand.

Secretly, she marveled at the truth. Unicorns had to be protecting Deep Forest. That meant she could bring even more of her supporters to this place.

In many ways, the rebels were no match for the king's army. They hadn't trained together. They carried a discouragingly large variety of weapons, from pitchforks and sickles to swords and bows. The former militia had guns, but limited ammunition.

Nora's band of rebels, however, had been growing. Every day, people showed up to fight for her. Hundreds had arrived in Riverside the day before, and they spoke of thousands more behind them.

The rebels told Nora the same stories over and over—about how disenchanted they'd become in the last eleven years. How ready they were for a leader who remembered her people.

Nora and her team spent hours discussing their next step. Waiting, they agreed, was the best plan. Before long, their sheer numbers would give them the advantage against trained soldiers. At least that's what Nora hoped.

Every day was full of strategies that shifted quickly enough to give Nora whiplash. Soon, nearly a thousand people occupied Deep Forest. They weren't even trying to hide from Kadin, who frequently flew overhead. The camp at Riverside overflowed with eight hundred more rebels. And Nora's supporters kept coming.

She sent messengers on dragons to meet arriving rebels, directing them to camps on Cellerin Mountain and in additional wooded areas along the river.

Night after night, Zeisha flew on a dragon, gathering more shield fuel. Bored rebels were happy to grind it up, and volunteers rode dragons to distribute it among the camps. "If the king's people attack, eat this," they instructed. "It'll protect you from their magic."

After several days had passed in an exhausting blur, Nora and Krey grabbed a moment alone, hidden behind some thick trees. "It all feels out of my control," she murmured.

"It is." He was standing behind her, rubbing her tight shoulders. His lips moved to her ear. "It's a movement, Nora. You can't determine all the twists and turns it'll take, but you're still the leader. These people believe in you."

She gave herself two minutes to relax into his touch before they rejoined the group to deal with the next crises, victories, and adjustments.

That afternoon, Ulmin got word of one of the hiding places by the river. He sent three hundred troops to deal with it. Nearly fifty rebels were killed, and they only took down a dozen Cellerinian soldiers. Vin saw the skirmish and dove into it. The soldiers, most of whom had never seen a dragon, fled. All three dragons relocated the remaining rebels.

Nora's people were surrounding her when she heard of the attack. She had no choice but to let them see her cry. It seemed to make them love her more.

A week after returning to the capital, Nora got news from Osmius that a group from Tirra would soon arrive.

The same night, she received a letter. Nora and Krey read it by candlelight. New Therroan rebels had convinced a hundred Cellerinian soldiers to join them in a rebellion. Together, they'd driven out the troops still loyal to Ulmin. Over a thousand people, New Therroans and soldiers alike, had left the city and were camped in the hills north of the capital, awaiting Nora's orders. She'd have to send a messenger on a dragon to guide them to a safer hiding place.

"What do you think?" Nora asked Krey.

"I think it's time."

"I agree. In two days, we'll gather our best people. Vin will burn a hole in my father's dome. We'll send word to all the camps to converge on the palace."

"And we'll fight," Krey said, "until we take our nation back."

That night, it felt more like winter than autumn. Despite her coat and blankets, Nora was shivering in her tent when she heard Krey outside, asking to enter. The militia member guarding her wouldn't allow it.

"Let him in," she called. The two of them had kept their secret. It had been easier than she'd anticipated; with everything going on, they'd barely had time to see each other. But tonight, she needed him to hold her.

He lay on his side behind her, pulling her close to his chest. After a few whispered words, Krey's breaths slowed. Nora timed her own breathing to match his, drifting into a deeper slumber than she'd enjoyed in days.

They warmed each other's sleeping forms until screams woke them at dawn.

33

Tonight was my engagement ball. I know you wanted to be there, and I'm praying as hard as you are that the weather clears so you can travel soon.

Honestly, you didn't miss much. The best thing I can say is that the room looked amazing. I think Uncle Quin is rather proud of his beautiful ballroom, since the palace itself doesn't have one!

But everything else went wrong. My dress was too tight because, as always, I eat when I'm stressed, and my measurements have changed. I only got to dance two songs with Ulmin; the rest of the night, I was passed around like an appetizer tray.

Then, just as guests were leaving, a young man from an important New Therroan family begged for a dance. I said yes, and he spent the entire song coughing on me. While I'm sure he wasn't trying to spread germs, it felt like an attack.

If I get sick, he's uninvited to the wedding. Back me up here, please.

-Letter from Ambrel Kaulder to Dani Kaulder
Dated Wolf 9, 180 PD

SOMEONE THREW Nora's tent flap open. "Come with us, Your Highness."

Despite the distant screams, Nora recognized the voice of one of the militia members who guarded her tent. "What's going on?"

"I don't know. We need to get you to safety."

"Make sure you get the rest of our leaders too," Krey said.

"Their guards are waking them now. Let's go."

Tension buzzed through the air as militia members led Nora and Krey through the trees, following some path Nora couldn't see. They'd been drilling daily for a time such as this.

As they rushed through the dim light of dawn, they passed other rebels, running toward the sounds of battle. Guilt drove a knife into Nora's gut. Running away seemed wrong. But she had to get to safety. Whoever she was running from wasn't the enemy. Her father was. She'd save her fighting for him.

Branches scratched her skin. Rocks and roots did their best to trip her. Nora was standing from one such fall when Vin's voice reached her. *It is the army. They are in the forest. Some have wide eyes and vicious faces. Others are fearless, with blank eyes.*

Nora's heart dropped. Her father was using his Overseers. Thank the stone they weren't controlling all the king's people . . . but had her own people remembered to protect themselves?

"Shield fuel!" she gasped at Krey.

He pulled a bag of pulverized rock from his pocket. "Where's yours?"

"If I swallow it"—she pulled air into her lungs"—I can't talk to the dragons."

His brows drew together, but he didn't question her. With a

grimace, he shoved a small handful of pulverized rocks into his mouth.

Vin spoke to her again. *The soldiers are blind to your people until they get within swords' reach. The unicorns are clearly casting illusions. I do not know how the army became aware of our camp.*

Nora reached out to all three dragons. *Come to the north meeting area. Osmius, I'm sure my father is hidden under his dome and won't see you . . . but please fly in from the north just in case he's standing at the gate.* She gave them further instructions as she continued running.

At last, they arrived at their designated safe zone, a clearing far from both the road and the camp, hidden by thick trees. Three former militia members, Nora's messengers, stood outside their tents. They'd been staying in this place night and day, except when they flew on dragons to share messages between the various camps.

In less than two minutes, all three messengers were on dragons, flying toward the rebel camps to put out the call for reinforcements.

By the time the dragons were gone, Ovrun, Zeisha, Kebi, and Joli had also arrived. Nora huddled with her trusted leaders—her friends. "I need you all to eat shield fuel—except Zeisha." Her stomach tightened at the thought of her and Zeisha remaining exposed, but the two of them were her teams' only connection to dragons and the Well. They couldn't give that up.

Nora quickly shared what Osmius had told her.

"How did they know we were here?" Ovrun asked.

Krey replied, "Could be anything. Maybe Sarza's alive, or a traitor left our camp and told him everything. Or maybe the unicorns aren't as good at hiding us as we thought."

Nora turned to Zeisha. "Is there anything you can do to help?"

"I don't know. I need to listen." Zeisha moved across the clearing.

Joli watched her curiously. The skirmish with the king had shown her that something was different about Zeisha. But she never pried for details.

Nora turned back to the others. "Give me ideas. Good, bad, stupid, I don't care. We need a plan."

———

Zeisha sat, eyes shut, and dug her hands into the damp soil under the grass. She sensed the sleeping Well in the underground streams, bedrock, and, far beneath, magma. But something told her she wasn't meant to use the power in the ground.

She lifted her hands and reached out to the Well in the air, smiling as she sensed untapped magic all around her. Following a nudge in her heart, she opened her eyes and lifted her head. When she did, her mouth broadened into a smile of wonder.

At the edge of the trees, perhaps three mets away, stood a unicorn. Its slender snout, large eyes, and delicate, pointed ears reminded her of a cervida. But where cervidas were skittish and meek, this creature exuded awe-inspiring power, colored with a hint of viciousness. Its lustrous, silver coat stretched over strong muscles in its shoulders and legs. A bone-white horn—slender, sharp, and more threatening than any dagger—extended from its forehead. Zeisha got the feeling it was watching her through its pale-blue compound eyes.

Zeisha mulled over how odd it was that she could see the unicorn. It could certainly have hidden itself if it wished.

She became aware of a certain shimmer in the air around the creature. Maybe she could only see past the illusion because she was connected to the Well in the air. Could her power cancel out that of the unicorn's? Or was she seeing only the animal's magical essence, not its physical body?

To test whether the unicorn was purposefully showing itself, Zeisha disconnected from the Well. The unicorn disappeared, replaced by an image of the forest, complete with leaves ruffling in the breeze. Still smiling, Zeisha reached out to the Well in the air again. The unicorn popped back into existence.

A twist of discomfort invaded Zeisha's gut. Here she was, staring at a magical being who thought it was hidden. It felt like eavesdropping. She gazed in the unicorn's eyes and spoke quietly. "I want you to know I can see you."

The beautiful creature stiffened. Then its muscles rippled dangerously as it lowered its horn, pointing it at the young woman on the grass.

Zeisha remembered what Nora had told them recently—unicorns became violent if they felt threatened. And she'd broken through this beautiful creature's first defense: invisibility. Fear lit up her body, sending her an unmistakable command: *Move!* Another message, quieter yet just as strong, whispered, *Stay.*

Perhaps a year ago, she would've listened to her fear. But since becoming the Anya, Zeisha had learned to trust whispers in her heart over screams in her head. Despite the terror racing through her, she remained still.

The unicorn charged.

Zeisha sent out a wordless message—of apology and love and respect. The creature seemed to try to stop, turning its head to the side. But its momentum carried it forward. Its horn pierced Zeisha under her shoulder, penetrating several simmets before the unicorn halted. It backed away, red dripping from the tip of its white horn.

Zeisha fell backward with a loud cry. There was no pain, only a sense of heaviness where the horn had stabbed her. She was barely aware of the shouts and running footsteps of her friends as numbness spread up her shoulder. Across her chest. Down her side.

It had reached her chin when it occurred to her that her friends would want to know what had happened, that their grief would be greater if they couldn't explain it. Her lungs seemed constricted now, and her tongue felt too big for her mouth. But she managed one hoarse word: "Unicorn."

She gazed at the silver creature standing behind her friends, sent it a wave of forgiveness, and allowed her eyes to fall closed.

Kebi knelt over Zeisha, sobbing. Nora couldn't make out all the words, but she heard "please" and "love" over and over.

Joli pressed her coat against Zeisha's bleeding shoulder.

Ovrun ran off to fetch the blood lyster who was hiding in another clearing in the forest.

Krey sat by Zeisha, holding her hand, lips moving in what must be a prayer.

Nora knew she should cry or help or *something*, but her mind was full of the single word Zeisha had said.

Unicorn.

She faced the woods and spoke in the voice of command she'd learned from her father. "I know you can hear me! You wounded my friend. You probably killed her. I've heard unicorns are ethical creatures, but I can't believe that anymore." She stepped closer to the trees, scanning them, hoping to glimpse the beast. She saw nothing, no movement in her peripheral vision, no sunlight glancing off a poorly hidden horn. "You want ethics? Look at the person on the ground who's got your poison running through her body. She's the moral one. You're the monster! If I'm wrong about you . . . *PROVE IT.*"

Nora wasn't sure what she expected. An audible response? Miraculous healing? A reversal of time itself?

She waited. But the only sounds were her friends' words and cries, the clash of forces in the distance, and the grumble of a nearby bird. The only sights were the dim trees and the harsh, orange light of sunrise.

Nora shook her head, her shoulders drooping, and returned to the group.

"She still has a pulse," Krey said softly. "She's breathing, but it's very shallow."

Just then, Vin's voice reached Nora's mind. *Soldiers are attacking this location as well!* He sent her an overhead image of one of the smaller rebel camps by the river.

The moment Nora heard it, she knew her father had Sarza. How else would he have known multiple places to attack?

Helplessness pummeled her. She had no way to give instructions to the messengers on the dragons' backs. But Hatlin had chosen those riders because they were brave and strategically minded. He'd also put someone competent in charge of every camp. Hopefully the riders and commanders would send reinforcements not only to Deep Forest, but also to the other camps under attack.

As she considered what to do next, Osmius alerted her to a third camp invaded by the army.

Gild told her of a fourth.

Heart pounding with dread, Nora asked them to continue visiting all the camps, then to assist in the battles wherever they could, without getting themselves killed. When she was done, she gazed down at Zeisha again. She wanted to cry with Kebi or run after Ovrun to see if he'd found the healer yet.

But Zeisha would want her to think of the people who were fighting and dying for their cause. "Krey," Nora said.

He looked up. Tears ran down his cheeks. Nora would feel the same if it were Ovrun down there. She'd learned that you could still love someone you'd fallen out of love with. When Krey saw Nora's expression, he squeezed Kebi's shoulder and stood.

Nora took his hand and locked her eyes onto his. "People are dying. We need to end this thing. Now."

34

I have a fever, and my entire body feels like it got run over by a wagon. I keep expecting to expel my lungs with my next cough.

Ulmin insisted I stay at the palace. A doctor has the room next to mine, and while she's nice enough, she checks on me too often.

The prince is furious—not with me, but with the man who coughed on me at the ball. Beneath his anger, he's clearly terrified something will happen to me. His worries are baseless. The doctor assures me my symptoms are normal for this illness. I should recover within a week, just in time to handle all the rest of the wedding details.

But facts don't seem to penetrate the fog of Ulmin's fear.

-Letter from Ambrel Kaulder to Dani Kaulder
Dated Wolf 12, 180 PD

NORA HAD QUICKLY CONVINCED Krey that someone had to enter the stone dome and cut off the king's power. Such an action would strip him and his Overseers of their enhanced magic. Then Nora could take the crown and bring an end to the fighting.

After their agreement on those points, the discussion had deteriorated into a heated argument. Nora's face grew hot with anger as they argued over one important detail: who would sneak into the dome.

"Thousands of people didn't travel to the capital so you could get yourself killed in their name!" Krey spat.

Nora pulled apart her clenched teeth. "I'm not planning to get myself killed."

"Most people who get killed would say the same." Krey gripped her shoulders hard, passion and fear brightening his eyes. "Tell Vin to make the biggest hole he can in the side of that dome. Send our people in. See what they can do."

"They'd be fighting on two fronts, Krey! There are soldiers out here and more inside. And there are probably Overseers both places! I'd be sending them to their deaths."

"They're dying already, while we stand here arguing! They want to go to battle for you! Let them!"

Nora opened her mouth to answer, then realized the healer Ovrun had fetched was standing a met away. Her anger dissolved. "How's Zeisha?"

The healer spoke quickly. "I don't know. I did what I could, but it's magical poison. I don't have a way to remove it all. Her body will have to do the rest of the healing on its own."

"How likely is that?" Krey asked.

"It could go either way." He pointed to the thick trees on the west side of the clearing. "Ovrun's moving a tent into those trees. He'll carry her in there. Kebi said she'll care for Zeisha." He turned to Nora. "Your Highness, I need to get back to my station. There are injured people waiting for me."

Nora's eyes widened. "Yes—go. Thank you."

"Wait," Joli said. "I've bandaged plenty of wounds when our farm workers got sick. Can I help you?"

"That would be great," the healer said.

"Good luck," Joli told the group. She gave Ovrun a quick smile, then sprinted off with the blood lyster.

Krey was blinking hard, looking suddenly young and vulnerable. Nora pulled him into her arms. "I'm sorry."

He gripped her tightly. "Zeisha is strong." After a moment, he stepped back, wiping his eyes. "We don't have time for emotion right now."

"I know." She pulled in a quick breath. "Krey, something tells me I have to confront my father myself. I'd say it was God if I believed in him, but . . . I don't know how I know, I just do. I don't think his people will kill me."

"But he might," Krey said.

Her throat tightened. "I know."

"Damn it, Nora." Krey wiped his eyes again and spoke in a hoarse whisper. "I've lost enough people I love. I don't want it to happen again."

She froze. Yes, there was a battle raging in the forest nearby. Yes, she was determined to confront her father. To take the crown or die trying. Several life-altering events were vying for her attention.

But did Krey just admit he loves me?

She stepped closer. "That thing you just said? We're coming back to it later."

The corner of his mouth came up—the barest hint of a smirk. "Okay."

"I need to confront my father. So are you planning to keep arguing with me, or will you use that brilliant mind of yours to actually help me figure out how?"

His eyes shut briefly. When he opened them, they were full of steel. "I have an idea. You're not gonna like it."

In the last week, Sarza had immediately told her guard every single time she had a vision. She'd had several every day. Sleep deprivation, hunger, and stress had done the trick.

Most of the prophecies had seemed pointless. She'd seen a thief stealing an apple in Cellerin City. A storm over Deroga. Two guards falling asleep on their watches. The king had gotten more furious with her every time she gave him information he couldn't use.

Then yesterday, she'd had four visions, back to back. The first three had shown her where large groups of Nora's rebels were hiding. In the last vision, she'd seen the empty forest by the palace. Rebels suddenly appeared within the trees when the king's soldiers approached them. Sarza didn't know what to make of that.

Acid had eaten her stomach alive as she'd shared the visions with a guard, then with the king. She'd kept glancing through the bars, where Dani sat in the neighboring cell, staring straight ahead, her mind held captive by the king. If Sarza had held back one detail, she'd have had to watch Dani suffer. The king had often mused openly about torture options. Maybe he'd have his guards cut off Dani's fingers one by one, he'd said, or set her limbs on fire, or slice her tongue in two.

Dani was the closest thing to a loving mother Sarza had ever had, which was pretty sad, considering they barely knew each other. The king was well aware of Sarza's attachment to his sister-in-law. Dani was his key to controlling his personal seer.

An hour ago, however, everything had changed.

At dawn, Sarza had woken to a vision. It was a potential prophecy; she could choose how to respond to it. She hadn't spent more than a half second making her decision. She'd act. And she wouldn't tell her guard. Yes, Dani might get tortured. But Sarza's vision had told her there would be more suffering if she took the safe route.

She might not survive what was to come. She told herself it didn't matter. Death would be better than this damn dome, than mental slavery, than future madness. But some irrational part of her still yearned for the life she'd briefly had, surrounded by people who cared about her. She wanted that life again. It was a silly dream, but she couldn't let go of it.

The guard at the desk moved. Sarza stiffened as he walked to Dani's cell. He stood before the bars and grinned. "Stand up."

Dani obeyed, as Ulmin had instructed her to always do.

"Clasp your hands above your head and turn, like you're dancing." This guard treated Dani as a puppet when he got bored. He laughed as she did a slow pirouette. "There's army soldiers under this dome, you know. I want you to sing your thanks to them, loud and strong, like you're the soloist at a fancy concert. Go ahead, Dani, sing!" He gestured to the window, turning his back to Sarza.

It was time.

Dani drew in a deep breath. As the first note exited her mouth, Sarza reached through the bars and pulled the guard's gun from his holster.

The man spun to face her.

Sarza cocked the gun. "Unlock my cell."

"You know this won't work—" the guard sputtered.

Dani's strong alto voice singing "Thank you" nearly drowned out his words.

"Do it." Sarza aimed the gun at the center of his chest.

The guard unlocked the cell, muttering about how the king would kill him.

Sarza exited. "Get in there, and don't say another word unless you want your knees blown apart."

He stepped in the cell, and she locked it, then demanded he remove the knife from his pocket. He slid it under the bars to her, and she shoved it in her own pocket.

Sarza desperately wanted to release Dani, but doing so would ruin this plan and result in punishment for them both. She'd seen it in the prophecy.

No time to dwell on that. As Dani sang, Sarza instructed the guard to give her his uniform shirt. She put it on and tucked it in. It was huge, but it would do. As she slipped out the front door, Dani continued singing.

Electric lamps illuminated army soldiers all over the property. Sarza moved into the shadows. Her prophecy led her on a brisk walk to a tiny building on the west side of the palace property, behind the orsa stables. A large padlock held it closed. One earsplitting shot from her gun destroyed the lock.

She ran into the room and flipped the light switch, revealing a metal box, nearly as wide as the room and taller than Sarza. It was labeled "SOLAR BATTERIES." She circled around to the back of it and yanked out all the cables from four large batteries. The room went dark—along with the rest of the palace grounds, she hoped.

In the distance, people shouted. Sarza wanted to run, but her task wasn't over. She pulled out the gun she'd taken, aimed it at the back of the battery box, and shot one bullet after another. Every time, the gun flashed with eye-searing light and boomed with ear-destroying sound. Acrid smoke reached Sarza's nose. Through the crack between the destroyed door and its frame, she saw a flicker of fire-light. Her gun let out a hollow *click*. This was where her vision had ended.

The door swung open. Two men, one carrying a torch, ran into the little room.

Before Sarza could pull out the knife, someone grabbed her arms. "What do we have here?"

Sarza just smiled as he held her wrists with a grip as tight as shackles. She wasn't sure why she'd done this, and she didn't know if she'd survive the day or even the next few seconds, but she was certain of one thing.

Somehow, she'd just helped her friends.

Just as Krey had predicted, Nora hated his plan. But it was solid, or as solid as it could be with so many unknowns. He said a silent prayer of thanks that she'd agreed to it, despite the risk to both of them.

They watched as Vin approached and landed. Nora pulled the black-and-orange stone from her pocket and let Vin soak up its power. As the orange glow disappeared from Vin's body, she retrieved the stone.

She and Krey ran into the trees, stopping at Zeisha's tent, where Ovrun was updating Kebi on the plan. "We have to go," Nora said. "Take good care of her, Kebi."

"I will."

Nora, Ovrun, and Krey mounted Vin. Krey's heart thumped at a quick, hard rhythm, as if it could beat the uncertainty and fear from his chest.

When Vin rose above the buffer of trees, the sounds of fighting rose around them, louder than ever. Gunshots, cries of pain, and shouted commands melded into a terrible, violent song.

"Let's save our land!" Nora shouted as they left the battle behind.

Vin hadn't even gotten up to speed when he slowed and hovered over the trees east of the dome. He breathed yellow fire toward two patrolling soldiers, sending them scurrying away.

Then he drew in his wings and landed, facing the dome. As his passengers dropped to the ground, violent blue flames shot from his mouth. In seconds, he created a doorway in the magical stone. He didn't stop until he'd also blasted a hole in the fence inside the dome. That done, he lifted into the air.

Through the openings Vin had created, light from lampposts illuminated the palace garden. Several soldiers were already running toward the opening. Shots rang out.

Krey let out a low curse.

"Grab me!" Nora hissed.

Krey and Ovrun each took one of her arms.

"Don't shoot, I'm the princess!" Nora yelled. But shots and shouts drowned out her words. A bullet hit the edge of the hole in the dome.

"We can't go in there!" Ovrun said, pulling them away from the opening.

Suddenly, everything inside the dome went dark. The three of them froze. The gunshots halted.

"What happened?" Nora breathed.

"I don't know, but let's go in." Krey tugged at her arm.

They ran into the dark dome, Krey and Ovrun still holding Nora's arms.

The darkness under the dome was thick. High, narrow vents brought in a bit of sunlight, but almost none of it reached the ground.

Ignoring the continued shouts of soldiers, Krey navigated through trees and bushes. He held back a grunt when his shin hit a stone bench. Nora let out a soft gasp as she nearly fell. Krey and Ovrun kept her upright. They shifted their route frequently to stay away from soldiers.

Krey expected to feel relief when they reached the open space beyond the garden. Instead, his heart pounded harder. Hundreds of soldiers surrounded them. Dank, moist, dark air seemed to crawl along the skin of Krey's face and neck. An irrational fear swept through him—that the dome itself would fall and crush them all.

Then he saw moving lights in the distance—and as bad as the darkness was, lights were worse. *Don't come this way. Please.*

Nora pulled the two of them along. Krey bumped into someone. He kept going, his breaths coming even faster than before.

In his peripheral vision, he saw another light glimmer to life. Then another. They were flames, and they were multiplying. Getting closer. Before long, he spotted a soldier several mets away carrying a lit torch and several unlit ones. The man brought the cold end of one torch to the flaming end of another, lighting it and handing it to a soldier, barking orders as he did so.

Nora whispered something, maybe a curse.

"Just keep going," Krey breathed in her ear.

Nora pulled them to the left, where everything was still in shadows. But the flames continued to move and multiply. Soon, the whole area would be lit up.

"Run," Nora whispered.

They broke into a jog. "Heads down," Krey said.

Nora pulled them to the right to avoid a torch. Ovrun tripped, falling to his knees and bringing Nora down with him. They both leapt to their feet.

Suddenly, Krey became aware of whispers behind him. He resumed his jog, pulling Nora and Ovrun along.

But they weren't fast enough. Someone grabbed Krey's arm, yanking him away from Nora. A quick glance showed Krey that two other soldiers had Nora and Ovrun. They were shouting questions, mostly variations on, "Who the hell are you?"

Time for some acting.

Nora was first. "Oh, thank the stone! I'm the princess, and these men—"

Krey interrupted her. "Get your hands off me! We're bringing the princess to her father! Do you have any idea what I went through to find her?"

Ovrun shook off his captor and pulled Nora away from the person holding her. Flickering torchlight reflected off the gun Ovrun pressed into her side. "Everyone get back! The king told us to bring him the princess. You touch any of us, and I'll shoot her. Then what'll you tell the king?"

The hands holding Krey let go. Everyone stepped back, clearly unwilling to risk their princess's life. More soldiers gathered around, attracted by the raised voices.

Krey grabbed Nora's arm again. "Take us to the king!" he demanded.

A new voice, female and ringing with authority, joined the mix. "What's going on here?" Krey looked over to see a tall woman in army uniform, glaring at the other soldiers. When she'd gotten a quick rundown from the man who'd grabbed Krey, she turned to Ovrun.

"I'm a captain in the king's army. You'd dare threaten the princess's life?"

"All I'm saying is, I want to make it out of this alive, with the reward owed to me. If I drop this gun, someone'll shoot me and my friend and take the princess themselves. All you gotta do is lead us to the king. He sent us out months ago to find her. Trust me, he'll be glad to see us."

There was a pause. The woman stared at all three of them, then said, "The king's command was to bring his daughter to him if anyone found her. I'll lead the three of you to him. He can decide what to do about the threat you made."

She stepped forward, and Ovrun growled, "No closer."

Nora let out a convincing sob.

"Follow me," the officer said. "Eskel, Kadar, you guard their backs. Everyone else, get back to your stations. This could all be a distraction."

The other soldiers started to move, and Krey wanted to shout with triumph.

"Wait!" someone shouted.

Krey looked up. His stomach dropped. A middle-aged royal guard had arrived and was staring at Ovrun. Krey recognized the man from his time at the palace.

The officer stopped, holding up her hand to halt the rest of them. "What is it?"

"I recognize one of them. The big guy—Ovrun. He used to be a royal guard. He recently escaped."

The officer stiffened. "They said the king sent them out months ago to find the princess. He threatened to shoot her if we don't let them escort her to her father."

The guard let out a short laugh. "He's been in love with her since he met her, no way will he shoot her."

The officer spun around, pulling out a gun as she did so. "Don't move!" She aimed her gun at Ovrun. "Drop your weapon."

Ovrun did. Not that it mattered; he'd refused to load the gun, knowing he might have to point it at Nora. He and Krey were both carrying loaded guns too, but they were of no use in their pockets.

"Hands up," the guard said. "All of you."

They obeyed. Any fight might result in bullets. And bullets might catch Nora. As Krey held his hands up, he mourned the absence of his magic. What he wouldn't give to grab Nora and fly her into the darkness above. But taking down Ulmin was their goal, so all three of them were full of shield fuel.

Nora would have to confront her father on her own. Krey caught her gaze and gave her a small smile and a nod. "You got this."

"Step slowly toward me, Princess," the officer said. "No magic. We're not allowed to kill you, but we'll wound you if we must."

Nora took a small, slow step forward, then a second.

The officer turned to the soldiers around them and barked one more order:

"Kill the two men."

35

Other than a little cough and a touch of fatigue, I've recovered. Tomorrow, I'll return to Uncle Quin's.

Last night, I was still awake when my candle burned down to nothing. I was fighting my irrational fear of the dark when Ulmin came in. He couldn't sleep either. The queen has insisted he keep his distance while I'm sick, but tonight, he sat next to me in bed and dared to hold my hand. We talked, and when I started drifting off, he stayed where he was. Knowing he was next to me, I wasn't afraid.

Call me silly, but when Ulmin is with me, I feel like we can take on the world.

-Letter from Ambrel Kaulder to Dani Kaulder
Dated Wolf 16, 180 PD

"No!" Nora shouted.

No one seemed to hear her. All at once, panic entered every face except those of the blank-eyed soldiers. Heads swiveled. Guns aimed everywhere and nowhere.

A dozen versions of one question filled the dark space: "Where did they go?"

Nora spun around. The soldiers seemed to be looking through her. What the hell?

Something caught her eye, and when she shifted her gaze, she froze. Firelight glinted off the silver fur and blue, faceted eyes of a unicorn. It stood behind a soldier, its regal white horn piercing the air above his head.

It had come back to prove itself to her. Or maybe to seek redemption.

Nora didn't know how the unicorn had found them or why it had taken so long. For that matter, she had no idea why the unicorn's magic was even working on them. They'd all eaten shield fuel. Maybe it acted on the watchers, not those who were hidden.

Banishing the questions from her mind, she pulled in a shaky breath and gave the gorgeous creature a single nod. It blinked out of sight.

She turned to Krey and Ovrun. They were looking around, flummoxed. "Unicorn," she breathed. She didn't think the soldiers could hear her, but she wouldn't bet on it. "We're hidden. Let's go. Remember, they'll see you if you get too close."

She dashed toward a gap between two soldiers, hoping it was wide enough to preserve their invisibility. Krey and Ovrun followed. Half a second after Nora ran through it, a female soldier shouted, "I saw him, the one who used to be a guard! Then he disappeared!"

Nora turned her head, eyes wide. "Careful!" she hissed.

Keeping plenty of space between themselves and the soldiers filling the grounds, they sprinted to the chapel, where they halted, catching their breath.

As Nora had considered where her father might hole up, she'd kept coming back to this place. He'd want access to the stone that gave him power. In some twisted way, he might even expect God to protect his crown. One glance told her that her instinct had been right. Two dozen soldiers and royal guards stood at attention at the front of the chapel. Some held torches. Only one person merited such protection.

"How can we get in?" Nora murmured.

Krey did what he did best: strategizing. He kept an eye on the chapel, drawing in details with those sharp eyes of his. When they had a sound plan, they approached the chapel from the side, where the guards stood farther apart. The three of them weren't certain they could make it past without being seen, so Ovrun lifted his foot, then slammed it into the ground. *Thump.*

"What was that?" a woman asked.

"I'll check," her torch-wielding neighbor said.

Nora, Krey, and Ovrun slipped into the wide gap left by the soldier. Once behind the line of guards and troops, they pressed their bodies against the chapel's exterior wall and sidestepped around the corner and to the front door. Ovrun stood next to the door's hinges, while Krey and Nora waited on the other side.

Nora tried to slow her breathing but found it impossible. There was only about a met of space between her and the nearest soldier. If he turned, would he see her? Krey grasped her hand, rubbing his thumb along her index finger. Her breaths regulated themselves.

They'd only been there a couple of minutes when the officer who'd ordered Krey's and Ovrun's deaths ran up. Nora squeezed Krey's hand tight. Would she tell the king his daughter was somewhere on the palace grounds, invisible?

Eyes wide, the panting woman whispered with a male officer. Nora gritted her teeth as she watched their quiet, heated exchange. She couldn't hear a word of it.

After what might've been a minute or ten, the female officer nodded slowly, then turned and left. The man did nothing. Apparently they were too afraid of the king to tell him his daughter had infiltrated his magical fortress.

Her body still buzzing with tension, Nora gulped air into her lungs.

After perhaps a quarter-hour, the door swung open. As a soldier walked out, Ovrun shoved a knife into the space between the hinges and the frame.

The man who'd exited passed through the line of guards and soldiers, and the three invisible intruders entered the building.

"Hey, you didn't close the door!" someone said. "You wanna get us all fired?"

Ovrun retrieved his knife with a grin, just as someone pushed the door shut.

They walked through a dark hallway to the door that led into the main chapel area. Ever so slowly, Krey turned the knob. A little nudge, and it creaked open. They entered into a room lit by torches in wall sconces.

"Close that door! The captain must not have shut it all the way."

When Nora heard her father's gruff voice, an unexpected wave of grief rushed over her. With all her heart, she missed the man he'd been.

Not ready to look at him yet, she watched a guard cross to the door and close it. He returned to his post in front of the small stage. Another guard stood at the opposite edge of the stage. Both had blank eyes.

At last, Nora brought her eyes to the stage. Ulmin Abrios stood behind the pedestal that held the stone. The artifact was still covered with glass, but he was gazing at it with lustful worship. He looked even older than the last time she'd seen him, deep wrinkles forming a rippled map of hills and crevices across his face. His hair was shaggy and greasy, the sides matted. He reached into his pocket and retrieved what she knew must be animal brain matter, popping it in his mouth.

"Here we go," Nora whispered. She gave Krey and Ovrun a wobbly smile, then tiptoed to the stage and stepped onto it. She put a hand in her pants pocket, grabbing a handful of shield fuel, and nodded at Ovrun.

He charged across the small room, straight for the king. Thank the sky, Ulmin didn't flinch as Ovrun's loud footsteps reverberated through the space.

Ovrun was within two steps of the king when Ulmin's eyes widened and his hands came up. The unicorn's illusion had failed, as they'd known it would. Ovrun slammed into Ulmin, tackling him to the ground. The king freed one hand and shot a spear of stone at his attacker's back. It bounced off Ovrun's invisible shield.

Ulmin bucked and kicked and twisted, but Ovrun was far stronger. Nora pulled her hand from her pocket. Bits of milled rock dropped to the floor as she rushed to her writhing father.

As soon as he saw her, he pressed his mouth closed.

"Open his mouth!" Nora shouted at Ovrun as she fell to her knees by her father.

As Ovrun attempted to pry Ulmin's mouth open, the crack of gunshots filled the room. Nora glanced up to see both guards rushing onto the stage. The king had called for his slaves' help. Neither of them had guns out; the shots came from Krey's weapon.

Desperately, she tried to shove shield fuel in her father's mouth. He twisted away, lips tightly closed. The gunshots continued.

A pair of strong hands pulled Nora upright, pinning her arms to her sides. At the same time, Ovrun reached for the gun in his pocket. He wasn't fast enough. The second guard thrust a knife into Ovrun's side.

Nora screamed.

The gunshots halted. Krey must be out of ammunition. The room went silent except for Ovrun's low groan.

The guard who'd stabbed Ovrun frisked him and took his gun, before shoving him off the king. Ulmin stood and shouted at the guard holding Nora, "Restrain her, but don't hurt her!"

The arms around her tightened. She kicked, to no effect.

Ulmin turned to the other guard, whose ear had been grazed by a bullet. Despite the blood running down the man's neck, the creepy, placid expression on his face didn't change.

"Whoever was shooting, find them!" Ulmin shouted. "They'll be visible, as these two are. Go, quickly! Search the building!"

The man ran off.

Her father's words penetrated Nora's panic. He believed everyone had turned visible again. If he stepped away and could no longer see her, he'd rethink that supposition. She had no idea where the unicorn was or if it could hear her, but she sent out a telepathic message anyway. *Please keep me and Ovrun visible, but maintain Krey's illusion.* She paired the words with images, desperately hoping they made it to the creature's mind.

A quick glance showed her that Krey was now standing in front of the stage. She knew the look on his face. He was strategizing, considering every option, still determined to take down the king.

Ulmin stopped over Ovrun, who was moaning and squirming. Pure hatred twisted the king's face. "I trusted you, and you lied to me. You lied, you lied, you *lied!*" With each repetition of the accusation, he kicked Ovrun hard in the side.

"Stop!" Nora screamed.

Her father's furious eyes locked onto hers. He lifted his foot high, then stepped hard on Ovrun's hand, grinding it into the stage, eliciting a *POP* and an agonized groan. Seeing the horror on Nora's face, his expression shifted into a gleeful grin. "We'll let your boyfriend lie in his own blood for now."

He stalked toward his daughter, smile fading, until he was close enough for her to feel the heat of his breath. "Who was shooting in here?" His hand shot up to her neck.

He squeezed, letting in just enough air for her to choke out, "I don't know."

Letting go of her, he spat on the ground. "You took shield fuel." His voice lowered. "We're going to have a talk. Do you know what I told my officers today?"

"To bring me to you if they found me."

"That's right. They assumed I wanted you to remain safe." He looked down for a moment, and when he met her gaze again, genuine grief pulled his brows together and tugged down the corners of his mouth. "And I did. Because I won't let anyone kill you but me."

She squeezed her eyes shut against the cruelty of his words.

"Look at me," her father said.

She obeyed.

Tears streamed down his face. "I don't want you dead. But it's the only way to stop you from ruining our nation. And, sweetheart, I'll do it quickly. I won't make you suffer. You can die in my arms. With the one person who always loved you."

Nora swallowed bile. Her eyes swept the room, seeking Krey.

He wasn't there.

The loneliness she'd battled for months pummeled her heart. Sharai's words returned to her: *No one truly fights for others. We all fight for ourselves.*

But in her gut, she knew that was false. Krey wouldn't desert her. He'd fight for her with his life. He was somewhere nearby, waiting to act.

Or incapacitated.

Or dead.

The second guard, after all, had never come back. Maybe they'd met in the hallway. Maybe—

Her father interrupted her pointless train of thought. "You can't save your own life." His voice was flush with regret. "But if you answer my questions, I'll ensure Ovrun gets healed. He won't be free, but he'll be alive."

Sudden sobs shook her chest. She'd broken Ovrun's heart; now her only choices were to send him to prison or to his death? *I should've done this alone. Then he could've killed me, and the others would've found somewhere to live, free from the pain I've brought them. Now nothing will stop him from killing Ovrun, no matter what I say.*

"Calm down, sweetheart," her father said. "You can't answer my questions if you're crying." He gently took her face in his hands and brushed his thumbs across her wet cheeks. Disgust bubbled up in her, calming her weeping. His eyes turned cold. Greedy. "First question. Tell me about this invisibility magic."

Nora's father had imprisoned dragons. He'd do all he could to catch a unicorn if he knew the truth. She pressed her lips together and shook her head.

"Perhaps I should gouge out Ovrun's eyes," he said. "I didn't, after all, promise him a quick death." Gaze fixed on Nora, he took one step toward Ovrun, then another.

"Don't!" she screamed, "I'll tell you, I'll—"

Someone threw a gun across the stage, arresting Nora's words. It passed behind Ulmin and slammed into the stage's back wall. The king spun to look that direction, turning his back to Nora and to the stone.

The pillar toppled violently, smashing into Ulmin, sending him to the floor. The stone's case shattered. The pillar pinned down the king's legs. Stone and glass covered his chest and the floor.

Krey stood from where he'd been crouching behind the pillar. A wild grin filled his face. As Ulmin roared and grabbed one of the stone's pieces, Krey rushed to him and knelt in the glass by the king's head, pulling out a handful of shield fuel.

Suddenly, Nora's guard threw her to the floor. She looked up just in time to see the blank-faced man lunging at Krey. A knife gleamed in his right hand.

He thrust it into Krey's heart, burying it to the hilt.

Agony filled Nora's own heart, as if the knife had entered her chest. With strength she didn't know she had, she pushed herself up and kicked the guard's head. Her boot connected with his temple. He went down, unconscious.

Her father was still prone, the heavy pillar on his legs, his hands gripping the stone. Orange light covered his hands, arms, neck, and head.

Nora's gaze found Krey. His face and lips were pale, his eyes blinking slowly. Blood covered his shirt. She doubted he had more than minutes to live.

He gave her a weak smile and mouthed three words: *You got this.*

Somehow—she didn't know if it was due to magic or love or something else—Krey's strength penetrated into her pained heart. She knew what she had to do.

Turning to her father, she let her tears flow again. "Daddy, why?"

"Oh, sweetheart. Come here." He lifted one arm to her. "Let me hold you, honey." He released the stone. Orange light faded from his body as he began pushing himself up, stone and glass falling off his chest.

In one quick movement, Nora lifted her fist, opening it as it reached his mouth. The powdery shield fuel she'd pulled from her pocket fell through his gaping lips. A cry exited his mouth, but she slammed a hand on his chin, forcing his teeth closed.

Ulmin's eyes widened with panic. He fell back and grabbed her arm with both hands. His withered body was stronger than it should've been, but she was fueled by anger so intense, it roared through her limbs. He couldn't budge her, not a simmet. She held his mouth closed, watching his throat. He coughed. He squirmed.

He swallowed.

"Nora," he breathed. "No."

The shield fuel had a profound, immediate effect. Ulmin's fingers weakened, allowing Nora to yank her arm away. His skin paled, his cheeks sinking in. Tears flooded his eyes again. In a voice so weak as to be unrecognizable, he said, "I only wanted what was best."

But Nora had already shifted her attention back to Krey. That same incongruent smile remained on his pale lips. His breaths were quick and shallow. "Good job," he whispered, before his eyes rolled back into his head.

"Wake up! Krey, please!" She took his face into her hands, leaning in close. "I never got a chance to tell you, I lo—"

A voice behind Nora, warm and worried, interrupted her. "What happened here?"

In one violent motion, Nora spun around, a piece of glass digging into her knee as she moved. The guard who'd held her was kneeling behind her, conscious and in his right mind. Blood was clotting on his temple where she'd kicked him.

Deep inside, she knew this man wasn't responsible for what he'd done to Krey. She didn't care. "You killed him!" she screamed, aiming a punch at his bloody face.

He leaned back, evading her fist. Then he stood and ran away.

Numbness came over Nora, along with clarity. She pulled her sleeve over her hand and swept every bit of stone off her father's chest and away from his grasp. It might burn up his shield fuel if he touched it again.

He was clearly too weak to extricate himself from the pillar. Ignoring the soft words he directed toward her, Nora stepped over him. She knelt by Ovrun, who was pale, but conscious.

"I think I'm gonna be okay," Ovrun said. "Help Krey."

"He's dying." She shoved the words through her tight throat. "Or dead."

"Then say goodbye."

She moved to Krey and buried her face in his neck. He was still warm.

"Excuse me?" someone said.

Nora sat up with effort. Both guards had returned to the stage. The one who'd left to look for Krey was drinking something from a clay jug.

"My friend here's a blood lyster," the guard who'd stabbed Krey said. "Is it too late?"

Nora's tears returned. She couldn't answer.

The blood lyster knelt, wiping thick, yellow blood from his lips. "Let me try."

36

We heard the roads will be clear tomorrow! That means in a couple of days, I can give you this letter in person. We'll have less than a week to finish preparing for my wedding.

Queen Onna and Ulmin have spent the last week helping with arrangements. Ulmin is tireless. Yesterday, he helped workers assemble a dance floor. For a man who works with his mind more often than not, his body is remarkably strong.

-Letter from Ambrel Kaulder to Dani Kaulder
Dated Wolf 28, 180 PD

KREY'S EYES FLUTTERED OPEN. Nora was sitting beside him, holding his hand. But her attention was on Ovrun, who was next to her, fabric draped over his bare shoulders, talking softly. It felt like an orsa was sitting on Krey's chest, and for a moment, he didn't know why.

He looked down. His chest was bare, and a wound in the center was healing. Smeared, drying blood covered his skin.

It all came back—he'd been stabbed in the heart. He should be dead, but he couldn't imagine the afterlife would be this painful. Come to think of it, Ovrun had been stabbed too. He looked to be in decent shape. Someone must've healed them both.

"I thought the king kicked all the magic eaters out of the palace. Who healed me?" Krey croaked.

Nora turned to face him. Her face brightened with the prettiest smile he'd ever seen. "I look away for a few seconds, and that's when you decide to wake up?" She dropped a way-too-gentle kiss on his lips.

"It's my heart that got stabbed, not my mouth. You don't have to be so careful."

She laughed and gave him a moderately better kiss, before sitting up and wiping tears from her cheeks. "One of my father's two guards was a blood lyster," she told him. "Recently hired. My father must've thought it was the one type of magic that was more likely to help him than hurt him. The healer had to keep trying until his magic burned away your shield fuel. It got dicey, but here you are." She gave him another light kiss, then turned to Ovrun. "Uh, I suppose you should know . . . Krey and I are together now."

A low chuckle exited Ovrun's mouth. "I've suspected it since we were in Tirra. And I was sure when I heard the things you whispered to him while he got healed."

"Shut your mouth!" she cried.

With the hand Nora wasn't holding, Krey pushed himself up, groaning at the ache in his chest. "What sorts of things was she saying?"

Nora clapped a hand over Ovrun's mouth and glared at him. "Not a word. Agreed?"

Ovrun nodded, eyes sparkling.

"I'll get it out of one of you eventually." Krey took a moment to look around the stage. His and Ovrun's bloody shirts were sitting in a pile. The heavy pedestal he'd pushed over was standing again. Nearby was a pile of shattered glass. "Where's the stone?"

Nora pointed to a blanket-wrapped bundle in the corner. Her forehead wrinkled with worry. "We can't leave it there, but I don't know what to do with it."

Krey still thought they should hide it, but that wasn't his decision to make. "For now, we need to put it somewhere safe. After that . . . you'll figure it out."

"I hope so."

"Where's the healer? I'd like to say thank you."

Nora's large, brown eyes turned somber. "Once I told both guards that my father could no longer control them, they happily shackled him. I asked him to tell the army leaders he's stepping down. I made it clear his imprisonment will be a lot more enjoyable if he cooperates. He and the guards are in the emissary's office. I gave him twenty minutes to think about it." She glanced at a clock on the back wall. "I wish I hadn't given him so long. Every minute we wait, people are injured or dying. But the army may not follow me unless my father abdicates."

The door to the hallway opened, and the guard who'd stabbed Krey entered. "The king's made his decision."

Nora stood and turned. "What did he say?"

"He kept mumbling to himself—kept his eyes on the floor, and we couldn't understand anything he was saying. When we told him time was almost up, he finally looked at us and said, 'Nora can have my crown.'"

Nora drew in a sharp breath. "Did he tell you why?"

The guard gave her a sad smile. "He said, 'It's what Ambrel would want.'"

Nora's back was to Krey, but he saw her go still, her shoulders stiffening. He stood, drawing air through his teeth as his aching chest protested the movement. Nora turned toward him. He held both her hands, looking into her tear-filled eyes. "Your mother would be proud of you and your father right now." Still holding her hands, he lowered his head in a bow. "Your Majesty."

A small smile broke through her grief.

Nora gave her father two more bites of shield fuel. He grimaced as he ate it, but he didn't argue.

With her help, he stood. He was hunched over, barely taller than her now. Every line of his face and slump of his body spoke of his brokenness. She took one of his shackled arms and helped him shuffle out of the office.

Ovrun, Krey, and the guards waited in the hallway. Krey was wearing an undershirt one of the guards must've loaned him. Ovrun was still wrapped in a tablecloth, and Nora caught a glimpse of the blanket-wrapped stone he was carrying underneath. She'd instructed him to hide it somewhere safe as soon as he got the chance.

"Chin up, darling." The king's voice was as weak as his body. "Smile big."

Hearing his old mantra, she nearly burst into tears. The words reminded her of the days when she'd had him on a pedestal taller and more solid than the one in the chapel. She took his advice to raise her chin. But there was no way she could smile.

She'd hardly dared hope her father would abdicate. But as she listened to the scuff of his slow footsteps and felt his weight as he leaned on her, a realization slammed into her: somewhere along the way, Ulmin's physical strength had become inextricably linked to his magic. With shield fuel blocking all the magic in his body, he was terribly feeble.

Clearly, he'd been keeping himself perpetually influenced by the stone's power or his magical fuel or both. It might've been months or years since his body had been completely free of magic. And recently, he'd become undernourished and weak, aging far more quickly than

Nora would've thought possible. What had caused that? Was it his addiction to magic? Or had cruelty itself finally sunk its claws so deep into his heart, it was killing him?

Whatever the explanation, Ulmin Abrios had lost even the strength to hold onto his crown. That should make Nora happy—she'd finally taken him down. But pain gripped her chest and throat as the old man at her side gently patted her arm with a hand scarred by dragon fire.

By the stone, she missed her strong father.

A guard opened the door. Nora and her father exited.

Gasps and murmurs greeted the frail king. Nora fixed her gaze on a random soldier and commanded him to fetch the general.

"The battle is over!" General Etal cried from his position in front of Nora on Osmius's back. "We have made peace! Gather in the street!"

Nora listened to him call out the same words, over and over. Before long, combatants were streaming into the street south of Deep Forest. Osmius landed, and Nora and the general spoke with Hatlin and an army captain.

The battle, they learned, had been even at the start. The army was better armed, but the unicorns' illusions protected the inhabitants of Deep Forest. Some of the king's soldiers had defected, joining the rebels they'd already been secretly supporting. However, in the chaos of the dawn attack, some of Nora's people hadn't eaten their shield fuel. The fight turned in the army's favor as two Overseers brought some of the rebels onto their side, forcing them to attack their own comrades.

Then, at the same moment Nora's father swallowed shield fuel, the Overseers lost the power to control more than one or two people at a time. The tide had turned toward the rebels.

Throughout the battle, both sides had been hesitant to kill their fellow citizens, often injuring or capturing each other instead. Still, dozens had lost their lives. Nora scanned the faces of the army and her rebels, seeing horror and relief in their wide eyes.

Her actions were efficient and simple. By her request, Vin and Gild had already flown into the city with several soldiers from the palace. The soldiers would seek out the city's blood lysters, and the dragons would fly the healers to the four battlefields.

Next, she gave the Overseers shield fuel. After quietly assuring them she'd support them as they recovered from their dark addiction, she instructed a captain to bring them to the palace.

Nora and the general commanded the other combatants to hand in their firearms and return to their homes or wait for healing. They left it to Hatlin and a trusted army captain to enforce their commands.

Osmius took Nora and General Etal to the other camps the army had invaded to share the same messages. One battle had gotten particularly violent, and nausea filled Nora's gut when she heard about the hundreds who died there. Her nation had suffered grievous wounds today. Its healing would be as hard-fought as the battles had been.

By the time they finished, Nora was mentally and physically drained. She couldn't come close to anticipating all the tasks awaiting her at the palace. However, she'd told Krey that, before returning to the palace, she'd visit the clearing where they'd left Zeisha. She had to see how her friend was doing.

After dropping off the general in front of the palace, Osmius took Nora to the clearing.

As she watched him soar away, the tragedies of the day weighed down her heart like bags of wet sand. Dead Cellerinians. A fragile, broken father. And a friend who might not have survived the poison of a unicorn's horn. Heart pounding with hope and dread, she walked toward the trees where Zeisha's tent was hidden.

Before she reached it, Kebi stepped out of the trees. Zeisha was leaning on her arm.

A laugh burst from Nora as she ran up and drew Zeisha into a hug she hoped was gentle enough. "Are you okay?"

Zeisha's voice was quiet but steady. "I will be."

When Nora stepped back, her smile widened. Ovrun and Krey had emerged from the trees too. They were both wearing shirts they must've borrowed from palace staff. Krey walked up and took her hand, dropping a kiss on her cheek. "I thought you might want a few quiet minutes with friends before you go back to the palace. Joli is still helping the healer. But we got a couple of other people to walk with us over here. Deep breath, okay?"

She shot him a funny look as she inhaled deeply. Her exhale turned into a squeal when Sarza exited the trees. Then she saw the second person, and she fell apart.

"Dani!" There were only a few mets between them, but Nora's feet couldn't eat up the space quickly enough. Her aunt looked tired and thin, but by the sky, she was *here*, with open arms and a gentle smile. Her tight hug, full of acceptance and security, covered Nora in a warmth she didn't realize she'd been missing for the last nine months.

At last, Nora's crying calmed. Her friends gathered in a circle to discuss their next steps. Nora asked Dani to find Zeisha and Kebi a place to stay in the city until Zeisha recovered. She would've preferred for the two women to stay in the palace, but the stale air under the dome couldn't be good for Zeisha's recovery.

Ovrun offered to let them stay at his house instead. He insisted his mother loved hosting guests and that her cooking would have Zeisha back to full strength in no time. Zeisha and Kebi agreed.

Nora looked at Ovrun. "I'm going to make sure Joli and her parents have a comfortable place to stay while they rebuild." Seeing his relieved grin, she winked at him.

Sarza was shuffling from one foot to the other when Dani quietly turned to her. "I'm sure Nora would be willing to move a bed into my sitting room if you'd like to stay there."

Nora's eyes flitted between the two women. They'd clearly made some sort of connection. "That sounds perfect," Nora said, "if it's where you want to be."

"Thank you." Sarza's face softened in a genuine, joyful smile, an expression Nora hadn't seen on her before.

"Zeisha and Kebi, I'll send Osmius to escort you to the city," Nora said. "Ovrun, I'm sure he wouldn't mind carrying you too. I guess the rest of us should get back to the palace."

Sarza's smile faltered. "Just so you know, the batteries used for electricity are, uh . . . destroyed. Totally."

Nora let out a laugh. "Was that you?" When Sarza nodded, she said, "You saved our lives. Thank you. And I have a plan for bringing a whole lot more light to the place again." A few inquisitive looks came her way. She just smiled, took Krey's hand, and headed for the trees.

Somehow, Dani and Sarza had ended up way ahead of Nora and Krey as they walked through the woods. He certainly wasn't complaining. They probably wouldn't get many moments alone in the coming days.

His gaze drifted to her, taking in the thoughtfulness of her deep-brown eyes, the shoulders she'd squared against whatever was coming, the way her clothes clung to her curves. "Nora," he said, halting his steps.

She stopped too, turning to face him. "Yes?"

"I love you." The words flowed from his mouth, as refreshing and life giving as cool water. Saying it out loud felt amazing . . . until he took in Nora's wide eyes and the frown that twisted her mouth. Silence sat between them, thick and tense.

"Damn it, Krey!" she said at last.

He blinked, barely able to breathe. "Too soon?"

"No! It's just that I wanted to say it first. I was trying to decide what the best time was"—by now, she couldn't hold back a smile—"and you slid right in there and won the race."

Relief brought a giddy grin to his face. He released her hand and grabbed her waist, pulling her close. "What's the prize?"

Her lips brushed his as she spoke. "The prize is, you get to wait." She gave him the tiniest of kisses. "I'll say it back when I want to, and you'll have no idea when it's coming." Her lips moved up his jaw, dropping soft kisses along the way. Then they found his ear, and she whispered, "The other prize is, I might kiss you. A good kiss. But I haven't decided yet." She nibbled his earlobe, laughing when he shivered.

"Anything I can do to make it more likely?" he asked, his voice low.

Her mouth was still on his ear, doing things that heated him from the inside out. "I'm sure you could figure something out."

In a flash, his hands were on her face, guiding her to look at him, firm, but not forceful. She licked her lips and shot him a sinful smile, arching one brow.

He pressed his lips to hers. Part of him wanted to devour her, but instead, he took his time, exploring her mouth with his own, drinking her up like a dehydrated man at a spring. He let his hands run over her face, her back, her waist, her hips. His injured heart ached as it pounded against her chest, but he just held her tighter.

Panting, she broke the kiss and pulled back just far enough to look in his eyes. "Krey . . . by the sky, I love you."

He laughed, cupping her neck with his hand, her pulse racing against his thumb. "I thought you wanted to wait to say it."

"I've waited long enough. We both have, don't you think?"

He grinned, then gave her a soft kiss. Holding her in a tight hug, he murmured in her ear, "Want to stay in the forest? Live off the land, sleep in a tent, hide ourselves away for the next year or two or ten?"

She slipped her hand beneath the edge of his too-large shirt, rubbing his back, leaving tingling warmth everywhere she touched. "That's exactly what I want."

He gave her a lazy wink before taking her hand and leading her toward her palace.

THE STONE EATER: 11

Ulmin Abrios, former king of Cellerin, lay on his side on a soft bed, staring at the wall. Images floated through his mind.

Milled rocks swirling in a cup of water.

A dragon gliding on air currents.

Tiny, curved layers of a navy-blue substance, smooth on the fingers and the tongue.

He became aware of voices talking softly behind him. He let the words waft in and out of his mind, like the images had.

" . . . hasn't asked for it . . . ?"

" . . . doesn't seem to remember . . ."

" . . . haven't let anyone see him? . . . told anyone . . ."

"No, Your Majesty."

Those words struck Ulmin as important, and he flipped over in his bed. *Your Majesty.* Was that him? Was someone speaking to him?

The question dissolved as he squinted past a barrier made of bars. Warm sunlight shone through a window at the front of the little room, illuminating a young woman with glossy, black hair. His mouth curved into a smile. "Hello."

"Hello, Father."

Father. He liked the sound of that.

"Lunch is in an hour," she said softly. "Is there anything I can ask the chef to bring you?"

One of those images from a moment ago returned. Something navy blue, delicious and bitter and smooth. But he couldn't recall what it was, and the thought smeared into nothingness, like an ink-written letter caught in the rain. "No, ma'am." He gave the lovely girl another smile, before flipping over to face the wall again.

"I'll see you tomorrow," she said.

He thought perhaps he should respond, but then he forgot, because delightful pictures were flitting through his imagination again.

Rays of warmth reaching through the chapel's skylights.

The nudge of a caynin's nose against his hand.

Ambrel's eyelashes, heavy with sleepiness and love.

37

Dani, you're asleep next to me as I pen this. It feels silly to write you letters when we've been talking constantly since you arrived, but writing calms me. And what woman doesn't need some calming the day before her wedding?

I need to sleep, but I keep thinking of what my life was like three months ago, compared to what it's about to become. I can't stop wondering what tomorrow will be like. What tomorrow night will be like, when the festivities are over and it's only my husband and me.

I even wonder about these letters I've written you. Will you keep them, to remind yourself what a silly, lovesick girl I was?

-Letter from Ambrel Kaulder to Dani Kaulder
Dated Lalan 5, 180 PD

On the 201st anniversary of The Day, Nora woke to the light of a pink-and-orange sunrise streaming through her bedroom window. Thanks to Osmius, Vin, and Gild, who'd used stone-enhanced magic to burn away Ulmin's dome, the palace was a place of light again.

She dressed in a soft shirt and tailored pants she'd bought over a year ago. While she loved her fine clothes, she'd vowed to curb her spending on clothing. Her months away from the palace had revolutionized her views on many things, including how taxes should be spent.

On her second day as Queen of Cellerin, the royal bankers had shown her the balances in the monarchy's accounts. Due to her father's neglect of his nation's needs, she now had over a billion quins at her disposal. It sounded like a lot, yet she was quickly spending it—not on clothes, but on her people and land. The farms her father had burned were, even now, being rebuilt. The monarchy had sent payments to families of combatants who'd died—whichever side they'd been on. And the entire nation needed upgraded roads, irrigation, sewers, and electricity.

Nora couldn't handle even a fraction of such projects herself. She'd chosen ministers, consulted with them, and made decisions with their help. Today, however, would be different. Her schedule was empty but for one commitment.

Her coronation.

She was already the queen, but her people wanted to celebrate that fact. Hundreds of her supporters—those previously known as *rebels*—were once again camped around Cellerin City. Many of the residents of the capital were just as enthusiastic. They'd suffered under the army's occupation and were sorely in need of some fun.

It would be hours before it all began, and Nora was determined to enjoy her morning. She finished getting ready, then opened her window to air out the room. The bedrooms along this hallway needed renovating due to the fire, but that could wait.

Today, Nora would actually sit down for breakfast, instead of taking it to her office. Sarza and Dani were already in the kitchen, drinking coffee, while their new chef prepared breakfast. Nora hadn't had a choice but to replace Chef Pryn, the man who'd provided her father with his dark fuel.

She poured herself coffee, then sat across from Sarza and Dani. "Did you sleep well?"

"I did," Dani said with a wide smile. Every day, she looked more like herself, her face filling out again.

"And you, Sarza?"

Instead of answering Nora's question, Sarza said, "I need to tell you something." Her eyes flitted to Dani, who gave her an encouraging nod.

"What is it?" Nora asked.

"It's not that big of a deal, but I think you should know . . . since you might be depending on my prophecies. I would've said something earlier, but every time I see you, you're on your way to a meeting. Maybe we shouldn't talk about it on the day of your coronation though—"

"Sarza, it's okay. Just say it, whatever it is."

Sarza took a deep breath. "I finished that book you loaned me. I found out that seers go insane. All of them."

Nora's mouth dropped open. She knew little about seers; she hadn't even realized they still existed until she met Sarza. Part of her wanted to gather the girl into a hug, but she got the feeling that wasn't what she needed right now. "When will it happen?" she asked softly.

"Probably when I'm in my sixties or seventies. Maybe earlier."

Relief washed over Nora, and she almost said something like, *Oh, thank the stone, you still have decades.* Somehow she caught the words before they escaped. "Sarza, I'm sorry."

Sarza nodded, her jaw flexing as she clenched her teeth.

Nora continued, "You will always—*always*—have a home at this palace."

Sarza blinked rapidly. "A home?" Hope and disbelief were thick in her voice.

Not for the first time, Nora wondered just how dreadful the

seer's life had been before arriving in Deroga. "Always. In fact, I need to hire a royal tailor."

A hesitant half smile came over Sarza's lips, but she didn't respond.

Nora laughed. "I'm talking about you, Sarza. I'm asking you to be my tailor."

Sarza nodded, eyes wide. "I will."

As breakfast ended half an hour later, Hatlin entered and bowed. "Your Majesty."

Nora stood and grinned at the new Captain of the Palace Guard. "Hatlin! Want some breakfast?"

"I already ate. There's someone at the gate, asking to see you."

"No appointments this morning, remember? It's kind of a big day."

"I told her that, but she's insistent. I thought I should ask." His lips curled with disgust, like he'd eaten something rotten. "It's Sharai."

Nora sighed. After her father's abdication, a guard had informed her Sharai was being held in Dani's office. Nora had sent the traitor away without speaking to her. Sharai had been sending her notes ever since, trying to set up a meeting.

While Nora hated to put a damper on her day, she needed to get this over with. "I'll meet her in my office," she said. "You can escort her there. And I want you to stay for the meeting."

Hatlin nodded, but his scowl deepened. He'd never forgive Sharai for forsaking the princess who'd supported New Therro.

Nora crossed to him and took his arm. "Maybe she'll try to assassinate me, and you can break her neck."

That got a laugh out of him.

"Nora," Dani said, "can you come to my room later this morning? I have something to give you."

"Sure."

As she and Hatlin walked through the residence, Nora said, "I don't suppose you've heard back after our latest proposal?" Nora had been negotiating with New Therroan leaders ever since becoming queen. At first, they'd demanded immediate independence. She encouraged a gradual separation instead, which would allow the monarchy to invest into improvements in their province. The New Therroans had agreed to her general plan, but now they were negotiating a never-ending list of demands and details.

"Nothing yet," Hatlin said, "but we're close, Your Majesty."

Nora let out a quiet sigh. It had taken less than ten days for her to negotiate Cellerin's first-ever trade agreement with Deroga. If only the New Therroan leaders could be as agreeable as Eira and the other trogs.

Once they reached the palace's administrative wing, Hatlin left to fetch Sharai at the gate, while Nora continued to the office that had once belonged to her father.

To her credit, Sharai didn't grovel when she arrived. She performed a quick, businesslike bow. Nora stood behind her desk, not offering the other woman a seat. "What is it, Sharai?"

"Your Majesty, I've come to offer my support. We worked together well in the past, and I'd be honored to do the same now."

Nora kept her face impassive. "I learned a great deal from you, Sharai."

The woman nodded.

"I learned what loyalty isn't," Nora said. "I learned that a woman three times my age doesn't necessarily know a thing about relationships." She gave Sharai a long, impassive stare. "And right now, I'm learning the meaning of desperation."

"Your Majesty—"

Nora cut her off. "Thank you for all you taught me. However, I'm afraid I don't have the stomach for any more of your—what did you call it? *Support.*" She shifted her gaze to Hatlin, who was standing by the door, not attempting to hide his broad smile. "Escort her to the gate, please."

"With pleasure." Hatlin took the woman's arm and walked her to the door.

Just before they crossed the threshold, Nora said, "Oh, Sharai?" The woman turned. Iron entered Nora's voice. "Several of my advisors said the best place for you is in prison. If I hear even a whiff of you working against me, I'll agree with them." She nodded at Hatlin, who took Sharai away.

Nora sat on the edge of her big desk. "That was fun." Her smile disappeared when she thought of her next task, which would be far less enjoyable.

She exited the administrative building and took a deep breath of the crisp, clear air, waving at workers preparing for the coronation. It was a beautiful day, but she wished it were spring instead of fall. Perpetual darkness had killed much of the palace's plant life, and Nora yearned to step on soft grass instead of mushy dirt. Local plant lysters could've remedied that for her, but they were all helping at the farms the king had burned. With a portion of her nation's food supply on the line, Nora was more than willing to deal with dirty shoes.

Squaring her shoulders, she strode to the palace security office. Her father was in a cell, but she planned to move him soon to a vacant office her aides were converting into a bedroom. He'd still be guarded there, but it would feel less like a prison.

Ulmin had experienced two weeks of violent withdrawals. Once his cravings had abated, he'd spent a week talking to himself day and night, planning senseless escapes. After that, he'd calmed, reaching a state of contented, childlike confusion.

The other eight Overseers, who currently lived in the palace's employee dorms, were experiencing recoveries similar to Krey's. All their needs were met, including group sessions led by a woman who specialized in helping people who battled addiction. Krey often joined their meetings.

When Nora arrived in the security office, her father was hunched over the little desk they'd brought in for him, eating breakfast. He gave her a sweet smile. "Hello, Ambrel."

Nora's hands came to her mouth. She spun around so he wouldn't see her shuddering breaths. When she calmed and faced him again, he was focused on his plate, using the side of his fork to cut a piece of sausage.

He looked up and smiled again, this time showing no recognition. After swallowing, he said, "Good morning. I'm Ulmin."

Relieved, she tried to converse with him, getting mostly nods and gentle smiles in return. He finished his meal and went to bed, facing away from her. Feeling spent, Nora left the building.

Her energy returned a few minutes later when she reached her aunt's quarters. Dani answered her knock and beckoned her into the sitting room. "Sarza is taking a walk. It's just you and me. Have a seat. I made cookies yesterday."

Nora sat in a chair by the fireplace. Dani set a plate of cookies on the low table next to Nora. "I'll be right back."

As Nora moaned over a perfectly soft cookie, Dani scurried to her room. She returned with a beautiful box. The sides were a deep, glossy brown, and the top was inlaid with various shades of wood in a delightfully complex geometrical pattern.

Dani sat, holding the box, which was large enough to fill her lap. "When you were gone, I often woke at night. I can't tell you how many times I wished I'd given you this. I was afraid I wouldn't get the chance. Today seemed like the perfect day."

Nora's heart pounded. "What is it?"

"Letters your mother wrote me. They start when she first came to Cellerin City. They tell the story of your parents' courtship and marriage, and your birth and childhood."

Nora's chin quivered, tears springing to her eyes. Her mother's heart was in that box. It took everything in her not to grab it from Dani's lap.

"I waited," Dani said, "because there are personal details in here, things your mother probably never pictured her daughter reading. But in recent months, I've realized you need to see your father—and yourself—through your mother's eyes."

"Aunt Dani . . ." Nora couldn't get out another syllable.

"Don't read them today," Dani said as she transferred the box to

Nora's lap. "Once you start, you won't want to stop. And you'll probably cry the whole way through."

Nora sniffled and laughed. "What do you mean? I'm clearly handling this with aplomb."

Dani took her hand. "Tears are good, Nora. I've got a lot of them to catch up on." She skillfully changed the subject, helping her niece focus on the details of the day instead of the letters in her lap.

At last, Nora stood. "I'd like to spend some time with Krey before I get ready."

Dani wrapped her in an awkward hug, the wooden box between them. "Your mother would be happy to see you in love. I am too."

38

It's barely dawn. And I'm awake next to a broad-shouldered, sleeping man. His normally perfect hair is messy. His lips are begging me to kiss them. As tempting as it is, I'll give him the gift of sleep while I give myself, and you, the gift of a letter.

Many of my memories of yesterday have swirled together in a joyful blur, but some moments are bright and clear, embossed in my mind for eternity. I'll share one of them with you.

During the wedding, while the emissary droned on and on, I held Ulmin's hands and looked out at the crowd. You were crying (don't deny it), but Dad had you beat, his shoulders shaking with sobs as he watched me with the sweetest expression on his face. I met the gazes of friends, strangers, and the queen. Their obvious joy couldn't come close to matching mine.

I brought my attention back to Ulmin. His eyes were full of adoration. Then his forehead wrinkled a bit, and his face took on the expression he *wore when I was sick, a fearful look that begged,* Please don't ever leave me.

And I don't intend to. Because, Dani, if I did, I'm not sure he'd survive it.

-Letter from Ambrel Kaulder to Dani Kaulder
Dated Lalan 7, 180 PD

NORA WALKED across the hallway to Krey's guest room. When she'd invited him to stay there so she could have quick access to her top advisor, he'd balked. "No special treatment. I'll stay in the dorms." After the third time she sent an aide to fetch him in the middle of the night so he could help her solve a crisis, he'd finally relented.

He didn't respond to her knock. Maybe he was sleeping in.

Back in her quarters, she set the box on the desk in her sitting room. She opened her bedroom door to find Krey in her bed, propped on pillows, reading a book. Sunlight settled on his warm, brown skin, and a breeze from the open windows ruffled his dark hair.

Nora grinned. "You look good like that."

"What, reading?"

"No, lying in my bed." She sent an exaggerated eyebrow waggle his way.

He laughed and put his book down. "C'mere."

Nora sat on the bed, facing him. Krey must've seen the serious look in her eyes, because he straightened and asked, "What is it?"

"I made a decision about the stone." It was already in a new case —this one sealed on all sides, so no one could get to the powerful artifact without breaking the glass. But Nora had spent the last month agonizing over where to put it.

"I had to go back to basics," Nora continued. "From as early as I can remember, my parents taught me the Abrios family mandate: *Tell the story and protect the stone.* I've even heard that those instructions first came from the seer who tried to stop the apocalypse. I could protect the stone by hiding it, but it's radioactive. Someday, someone would find it, like they did two hundred years ago. Who knows what would happen then?"

"So you'll keep it here?"

"Yes, but I'm taking it out of the chapel. We'll build a new visitor center. I'm sick of the stone being tied up with religion. You say God is generous. I don't know if I'll ever be spiritual, but I know one thing for sure. I could never believe that a generous God killed most of the people on our planet in one day. I don't know what the stone is, but I can't keep telling my people it's connected to God." She waited, dying to know what he thought. At last, she grabbed both his hands. "Well? If you think I'm wrong, tell me!"

He gave her a soft smile. "Nothing you do will guarantee the stone isn't misused again. There's no perfect way to handle this. But your decision is wise. That has to be enough."

She hated the uncertainty in his voice, but she'd rather he be honest than tell her what she wanted to hear. After a deep breath, she continued, "Then there's the matter of telling the story. We've kept alive my ancestors' memories of The Day, but now we have a new story about the stone. One that only a few of us know."

"A dangerous story," Krey said.

"It is. And I won't share it with the world. But I will tell my children, when they're old enough. They need to know how the stone turned a strong man into a weak one." Nora swallowed, the image of her father's bowed back stark in her mind. "I won't hide the truth of the stone's power. But if any monarch takes advantage of it again, the rest of the Abrios family will have the right to take their crown away."

Krey tucked her hair behind her ear, then rested his hand on her cheek. "You make a good queen, Nora."

She laughed. "I have no idea what I'm doing."

"None of us do." He pulled her into a tight hug, then released her. "I brought you something."

"Can't we just stay in bed for the rest of the day?"

"Any other day, I'd jump at the chance." He got up. "I'll bring it to you."

He crossed to a chair at the side of her room and retrieved a flat wooden box, smaller and plainer than the one Dani had given her. Returning to the bed, he sat and placed the box on her lap. "Open it."

She pulled off the lid and gasped. Set atop glossy, blue fabric was her father's crown, a simple band of gold. A metalsmith had measured her weeks ago so he could adjust the crown. Then she'd forgotten all about it.

"When it came in, I asked Hatlin if I could bring it to you," Krey said. "He almost didn't let me."

She arched an eyebrow. "Well, you are a highly suspicious character."

He grinned. "Do you want to try it on?"

She lifted it. It was heavier than she'd expected, and its cool surface warmed quickly as she held it. Her breaths came faster, and an irrational fear shot into her.

Krey's warm hand found her knee. "What is it?"

"This crown . . . the things it meant to my father . . . what if I become like him?"

He gave her a soft smile. "If you want a fresh start, you could wear something else. What about that fancy crown you wore in Tirra the day we met?"

Nora swallowed hard, blinking. "It's not a crown," she whispered. "It's a headdress." That's what her father had always said. "I want to wear this one. I want to make it mean something different."

"I like that idea. Should I put it on you? Make sure it fits?"

She placed it back in the box. "It'll fit. It doesn't feel right to wear it until the ceremony." A mischievous smile took over her lips. "But I need to get dressed, and I'll want help with my buttons."

"Okay, I can go get one of the staff—"

She shoved him, and he fell backwards onto the bed, laughing. "Stay here," she said.

She walked into her closet and closed the door. Hanging from a hook next to the window was the dress Krey's Aunt Evie had made. For the last month, Osmius had traveled back and forth between Cellerin City and Tirra, carrying measurements, sketches, and messages. He'd grumbled that being a courier was beneath him, but when Nora had offered to find a local designer instead, he'd insisted on helping—just this once.

For a solid minute, all Nora did was stare at the glossy, Cellerin-ian-blue gown. It had capped sleeves and was fitted through the waist, flaring into a wide, floor-length skirt that made Nora desperate to dance. Sunlight glimmered on rhinestones that started at one shoulder and swooped down over the bodice in an ever-widening band, before scattering across the skirt.

Nora couldn't remember the last time she'd worn a dress. After slipping off her clothes, she pulled it from its hanger and turned it around, grinning in delight at the low back. Letting the dress puddle on the floor, she stepped into it and pulled it up, slipping her arms through the sleeves. Without the buttons fastened, her skin felt terri-bly, wonderfully exposed.

She walked to the door, then turned around, her back to her bedroom, before opening it.

Krey was already standing there. His hand trailed up her spine, from her hips to the base of her neck. "Wow."

"Wait'll you see the front."

"I'm not sure I need to. You've always looked great from the back."

She tried to slap him, but it was impossible with him behind her.

"And from the front!" he protested. "From any angle, really."

"Button me up, Krey."

His fingers felt electric as they brushed against her lower back, slowly fastening each button. When he was done, he ran both hands up her soft skin. "Turn around."

She did, the smooth, flowing fabric of the skirt swirling.

Krey blinked. Shook his head. Gaped. Licked his lips. And finally, spoke. "Damn, Nora."

"You like it?"

"You could say that." His hands came to her waist. He pulled her close and spoke into her ear, his voice warm and tantalizing. "I thought about proposing today."

She pulled back, eyes wide. "You did?"

"Yeah. But we've both been known to be . . . impulsive."

"Speak for yourself." She grinned. "I wasn't considering proposing to you until tomorrow."

He returned her smile. "We keep saying we need to act like adults and take things slow while we settle into our new lives. But, Nora . . ." He sighed, shaking his head. "You're making it hard to wait. I should probably tell you, unless you kick me out of this place, you're not getting rid of me. Ever." He watched her for a long moment. "Say something."

"Kiss me, you impulsive fool."

He let out a low laugh and gave her a kiss worth remembering. Then he stepped back and took her hands, his eyes tracking a lazy path down her body.

"Krey?" Nora said. He returned his gaze to hers. "We met a year ago today. We've been through more than most people go through in a decade. Along the way, you became the best friend I've ever had. I'm as sure about this as you are." She stepped close, sliding her hands up his chest and bringing them behind his neck, playing with the hair there. "I want you to ask me. Don't make me wait too long."

His mouth broadened in a slow grin. "How could I say no to a command from my queen?"

Nora stood back as Dani opened the gate in the fence outside the palace residence. Directly before them was the rear of a stage. Royal guards stood on either side, facing outward. "Ready?" Dani asked.

Nora had been acting as queen for weeks. Why was her heart beating hard enough to send the bodice of her dress fluttering?

"You *are* ready," Dani said.

Nora let out her breath. She was allowed to choose who crowned her. Several of her new ministers had lobbied for the privilege, and Nora had angered them all by choosing her aunt. Seeing Dani's encouraging smile, she couldn't regret the choice. They walked up a flight of wooden steps and emerged onto the stage.

Nora gasped. Thousands of supporters had crammed onto the palace grounds. They stood wherever they could fit—on the banks of the pond, in front of the stables, and extending all the way to the gate. Throughout the crowd, she knew, were some of her fiercest rebels, hired by Hatlin to protect her today.

Dani took Nora's hand and led her forward, then spoke to the people. The crowd hushed, though there was no way they could all hear her.

As her aunt spoke of the history of Anyari and Cellerin, Nora let her gaze wander over the people at the very front of the crowd.

First was Sarza, who gave Nora a hesitant smile when their gazes met.

Beside her stood Zeisha, holding hands with Kebi. Most of the color had returned to Zeisha's skin. They'd moved back to Deroga, but Nora had sent a dragon to pick them up this morning.

Eira was next to Kebi, sunlight reflecting off the elderly trog's long, white braid. She gave Nora a somber, respectful nod—the gesture of an ally. An equal.

Next was Ovrun, who flashed Nora an encouraging smile. Joli stood with him. Nora's eyes dropped to their clasped hands, and when she tried to hold back her huge grin, she failed miserably.

Ovrun had visited Nora and Krey at the palace a few times. The first time, he'd barely made it through the gate, flashbacks of his imprisonment turning him clammy and skittish. But he kept coming, determined to form new memories there. Each subsequent visit had proven less traumatic.

Once Joli's family farm was rebuilt, Ovrun would apprentice with them, learning what it took to administrate such a business. Before that, he'd undergo surgery on his hand to repair the damage Ulmin had done.

Finally, there was Krey. Nora had saved him for last, knowing that once she started staring at him, she wouldn't want to stop. By the sky, she loved him—his soft lips, his brilliant mind, his—

Focus, Nora. You're about to drool on your dress. She pulled her eyes from him, but her gaze immediately halted again. Aunt Min and Aunt Evie stood next to him, both beaming at Nora. She returned their smile, her eyes wide with confusion. She hadn't expected them to travel so far for a ceremony. When she looked at Krey again, he winked, then looked to the sky.

Taking the hint, Nora reached out to Osmius. *Did you carry more than a dress back from Tirra yesterday?*

Surprise, Your Majesty, he replied. *Krey did not know of it until today either. His aunts arranged it.*

Nora turned to Dani, just in time to hear the end of the blessedly short speech.

It's time, Dani mouthed.

Heart suddenly racing, Nora lowered herself into a kneeling position.

Dani stepped behind her, and the golden band settled on Nora's brow. It was a perfect fit.

Movement caught her eye, and she looked up. Three dragons— one deep purplish red; one golden, and one with scales of iridescent gray, circled overhead. The crowd gasped as the beasts blew great streams of yellow fire across the pale-orange afternoon sky.

A cheer went up, loud enough to hurt Nora's ears. She stood, held out her hands, and bowed to her people.

The rest of the day was a dream. They'd given out three hundred tickets for a grand, outdoor dinner and ball. During dinner, the sounds of raucous celebrations in the street drifted in through the gates. Nora wished she could join in.

After dinner, she fulfilled her duties by dancing with ministers and supporters, but as soon as she could, she sought out Krey. He held her close, eyes only on her, making her laugh when he skillfully swept her away from would-be interlopers.

Tomorrow, she'd make decisions about money and projects and people. She'd visit her father and remind herself to eat. She'd have meetings where she'd make half the people angry and the other half happy. Tomorrow, she'd act like a queen.

But tonight? Tonight, she'd revel in being a woman. Nothing more, nothing less.

Tomorrow, she'd rule.

Tonight, she'd dance.

EPILOGUE
TWO YEARS LATER

NORA HELD TIGHTLY to Krey's shoulders as they soared through the crisp autumn air. He made a sharp turn, and she grinned, relishing the thrill of flying on his back. They'd come to an agreement over a year ago: she'd fly with him at least once a month, and he'd ride on Osmius just as often. Gradually, both of them had conquered their fears.

Neither of them could afford to take today off. Nora had a list of top-priority items that would carry her into next year, and Krey had been working late each night preparing for the grand opening of Cellerin's first public library. But Nora had insisted that if they didn't get a break, their brains would cease functioning. Krey had been hesitant until she'd reminded him how much he loved enveloping her in his magic and flying with her. He'd quickly relented.

At last, they arrived on a flat shelf of rock on the face of Cellerin Mountain. Krey landed, and a huge, gray head emerged from a large cave.

Nora ran up to Osmius and held her arms out. He lowered his neck for her to hug it.

When she let go, she asked Osmius, "Ready to take us on a

flight?" Her brows rose, and she turned to Krey. "Osmius said he wants to show us something in his den."

Inside the cave, Osmius walked to a large bed of furs and used his claws to carefully remove one at a time, setting each to the side. *Come see,* he said.

Nora took Krey's hand and led him closer.

Osmius had uncovered something, but it was swathed in shadows from the cave itself and the furs still around it. He opened his mouth, revealing a ball of white flame that illuminated the space.

As Nora and Krey knelt on the furs, she gasped. Osmius had uncovered an egg. It was as large as her head and was covered in black scales in a basket-weave pattern. "Osmius," she breathed, "how?"

Taima laid it when you were in Deroga. She did not tell me of it until she was dying.

When Nora had repeated his words, Krey asked, "Why hasn't it hatched?"

A few moments later, Nora replied, "He says it doesn't usually take years, but . . ." She pressed her lips together, then swallowed and continued, her voice strained. "The baby can sense its parents' emotions. Excess sadness or anger will keep it inside its shell. That's why this one has waited."

All at once, the egg trembled. It was so slight, Nora thought she'd imagined it, until it happened again.

It senses my peace, Osmius said. *It shall hatch soon.*

Nora relayed the message to Krey, then turned to the dragon with a smile of awe. "Are we about to watch a dragon's birth?"

Osmius began covering the egg again and replied, *Not for weeks. Breaking an egg requires a great deal of strength and time.* Once Nora had passed that on to Krey, Osmius's voice entered her head again. *I shall be a father soon, Nora-human.*

She grinned and turned to Krey. "I don't know if you can see it in his face, but Osmius is enormously proud that he's becoming a father."

Krey chuckled and rubbed Nora's back. They exchanged a glance and a smile before he pulled her closer and looked up at Osmius. "We couldn't be happier for you. And . . ." His hand settled on Nora's abdomen, pressing her loose shirt against the slight roundness there. "You're not the only one."

Osmius lifted his face and breathed flames into the blackness above them. Nora had never seen such fire come from his mouth—glorious flares of pink, orange, yellow, and white that filled the cave with ebullient warmth.

Then he brought his head down, and Nora embraced his neck. When she let go, she was laughing. "Osmius says this is why he insisted we take our journey today. Soon, he'll have new responsibilities."

"So will we," Krey said with a smile. "Let's go."

Contentment washed over Nora as she and Krey soared through the air on Osmius's back. With their families expanding, she didn't know how often they'd get moments like this. She soaked up every sensation: Osmius's spicy, musky scent; the smoothness of his scales and the way the light reflected off their iridescent gray; the *crack* as he flapped his wings; the taste of the cool air.

Two and a half years ago, Osmius had promised that once she committed her life to someone, they could tour Cellerin's most spectacular scenery, including places where magic still lived. Krey had now been her husband for over a year, but responsibilities had made such a trip difficult to plan. Thank the sky Osmius had convinced her to do it today.

They soared over the Kamina Forest. The unicorns they'd seen on Nora's first tour were hidden, by trees or by magic. They continued to the nearby mountains and picnicked at the base of a majestic, hidden waterfall.

After viewing more wonders, they landed in the Therro Desert near a pond with incredibly clear, green water. "What's this?" Krey asked as they knelt by it.

A hundred times, Nora had been tempted to tell him about this place. She'd resisted, wanting him to experience it with no expectations. "Magical water. Drink some."

He raised a skeptical eyebrow but dipped out a handful and slurped it up.

Just as she'd done on her earlier visit, he jumped up and gleefully ran across the sand, spinning and taking great, bouncing jumps. Watching him, Nora laughed until her stomach hurt.

You looked just as foolish when you partook of the water, Nora-human, Osmius said.

I bet you did too. No wonder you wouldn't drink it in front of me.

Krey finally slowed, but he wasn't done. He knelt by Nora. Eyes full of mischievous life, he embraced her, then leaned back onto the sand, pulling her on top of him, kissing her like he hadn't seen her in months.

When his hands started wandering, she rolled off him, laughing. "We're not alone, Krey."

He gave her a feral grin, sat up, and began running again.

When Krey's magical energy abated, he sat by Nora. "That water is the greatest stuff ever. Can we have Zeisha do this to the pond at the palace?"

"You're a smart man, but that's a terrible idea."

Krey laughed.

They mounted Osmius again. The day had gotten cooler, so Krey draped himself over Nora to keep her warm. After a long, peaceful flight, they passed over Cellerin City, then continued toward the palace.

As they flew over the forested area where Nora's rebels had hidden two years before, she sent a message to Osmius. *Stop, please!*

He halted, hovering over the trees, his wings slowly beating the air. *What is it, Nora-human?*

Give me a minute. She thought she'd seen a flash of something metallic, though it may have been the setting sun reflecting off a stream. She squinted. *Can you drop closer to the trees? Above that little clearing to the left?*

He complied, and she drew in a sharp breath. Six silver unicorns stood in the clearing, all gazing up, their sharp, white horns pointed at her like arrows. For perhaps a minute, they stood unmoving. Then one of them dipped its head—more of a nod than a bow—before again raising its faceted blue eyes to her. It was the one who'd helped her; she was certain of it.

She took one of her hands off Osmius and reached out, as if she could bridge the gap between them. *Thank you,* she thought, hoping the creature understood.

All six unicorns disappeared.

Nora shook her head slowly. She was riding a dragon who spoke to her. The unicorn who'd saved her life had just revealed itself. And soon, she'd be back at her palace, taking on the burdens and joys of her country. By the stone . . . how had she gotten here?

She was still pondering that when Krey's hand found her leg, giving it a gentle squeeze.

With a smile, she reached back. He laced his fingers with hers. She closed her eyes, drew crisp air deep into her lungs, and lost herself in the warm magic of his touch.

———

THE END

———

Thank you for reading *The Stone Eater*! Reviews make a *huge* difference to authors and readers. Will you write a short review on Amazon? I can't tell you how much I'd appreciate it. (While you're there, click on my author page and Follow me!)

The Seer's Sister: Prequel to The Magic Eaters Trilogy tells the thrilling story of Anyari's past . . . and how two sisters tried to stop the apocalypse. Order it now.

I'd love to keep in touch and let you know when I have ebooks to give away! Join my Email Insiders at carolbethanderson.com.

If you loved this series and would like an opportunity to request early review copies of future books, join Carol Beth Anderson's Street Team on Facebook!

ACKNOWLEDGEMENTS

Well, here we are . . . The Magic Eaters Trilogy is complete! I'm thankful to all my readers, but I'd like to give extra thanks to those who helped me create the final book of this series.

My alpha readers are intrepid explorers, venturing into my rough draft to find whatever's golden in it . . . and to tell me how to make it better. Thank you from the bottom of my heart to these alpha readers: Becky Brickman, Kim Decker, Brenda Elliott, Brooke Hunger, Becki Norris, Nikki Tuggy, and DeDe Pollnow.

My beta readers for this book blew me away with their suggestions and their ability to find plot holes. My sincere thanks to all these readers: Eli Anderson, Eileen Curley Hammond, Kim Decker, Elizabeth, Robin Gonzales, Sarah Joy Green-Hart, Caroline Hannam, Lisa Henson of Capital Editing Services, Robin Higham, C.M. Irving, R. Mark Jones, Kathryn Lee, Tracy Magouirk, April Mcdermitt, Becki Norris (the best twin sister ever, my better half, she who completes me*), MarjorieS, Sarah Rothman, Adelyn Tackett, and Nikki Tuggy. This book is far better due to your advice.

*That's what I get for asking my twin sister how she wanted to be listed in the Acknowledgements.

Special thanks to sensitivity reader Louise Willingham, for her excellent feedback on scenes with Zeisha and Sarza. (Check out her novel, *Not Quite Out*.)

Big gratitude goes out to my ARC readers who found lingering typos before publication, and I'm giving an extra shout-out to Tracy Mercer, who won the typo-hunting contest.

It can be hard to come up with unique fantasy names! Many of the character and location names in *The Stone Eater* came from creative people besides me. Here are the contributors, with the names they suggested in parentheses: Ana Anderson (Zeisha, Lerenor, & Cerinus), Beth Harris (Cruine; Eksel, changed spelling to Eskel), Jamie Brown (Isle, changed spelling to Isla), Julie Simmons (Fayla, changed to Faylie), Kristina Adams (Kebi, Eira and Taima), Marie-Eve Mailhot (Evie), Melissa (Wallace, changed spelling to Wallis), Molly Norris (Kamina), Melissa Dials (Girro), Megan Koehnlein (Sarza), Julie Simmons (Phip), Elizabeth Belt (Osk), Heather (Pryn), Penny Brinker (Dera and Kadar), Janice Paiano (Lott), Shanna Johnson (Loryn), Bobbie Gladitsch (Kaulder), Patty Noonan (Varia), Emyth Brenn (Tiam), Lester Banks (Etal), Deborah Munro (Kadin), and Karen Heys (Quin, Reymi).

Mariah Sinclair (mariahsinclair.com and thecovervault.com), this cover is ah-ma-zing. Thank you!

Thank you to BMR Williams creating the map.

Thank you to all my Twitter friends who make me feel "un-alone" in this writing journey.

My thanks and my love go to God and my family.

Dear reader, thank you for giving your eyes and your heart to this series!

-Carol Beth Anderson
Leander, Texas
2021

ABOUT THE AUTHOR

Carol Beth Anderson is a native of Arizona and now lives in Leander, TX, outside Austin. She has a husband, two kids, a miniature schnauzer, and more fish than anyone knows what to do with. Besides writing, she loves baking sourdough bread, knitting, eating cookies-and-cream ice cream, and spending way too much time on Twitter. Beth is the author of the Sun-Blessed Trilogy, The Magic Eaters Trilogy, and *The Curio Cabinet: A Collection of Miniature Stories*.

Find Beth on Facebook, BookBub, and Goodreads, all under the name Carol Beth Anderson. She's also on Twitter and Instagram as @CBethAnderson.

Made in United States
Orlando, FL
29 November 2024

54663299R00275